The Scapegoat

The Scapegoat

OVID'S JOURNEY OUT OF EXILE

Michael V. Solomon

Published in the UK by Universe
an imprint of Unicorn Publishing Group, 2023
Charleston Studio
Meadow Business Centre
Lewes BN8 5RW

www.unicornpublishing.org

All rights reserved. Without limiting the rights under copyright reserved, no part of this publication may be reproduced, stored in or introduced into a retrieval system or transmitted in any form or by any means (electronic, mechanical photocopying, recording or otherwise) without the prior written permission of both the copyright owner and the above publisher of this book.

Copyright © Michael V. Solomon, 2023

A catalogue record for this book is available
from the British Library

5 4 3 2 1

ISBN 978-1-911397-43-4

Cover design by Unicorn
Typesetting Vivian Head

Printed and bound by Short Run Press, Exeter

To the memory of my mother,
and her almost hundred years of exile

Map of Ovid's Journey (Thomas Bohm)

Preface

The need to write this book began almost fifty years ago. In my teenage years I regularly visited my grandfather – an important political figure in Romania between the World Wars – in a forced labour camp in the eastern part of the Wallachian Plain where he had been banished, after many years of imprisonment. Just like Ovid, his punishment had come without even the semblance of a trial. During those summers I came to understand what exile is, what it means to be a scapegoat, and, most importantly, how freedom can take many different forms.

After university, for my first job I moved to Constanta, historically known as Tomis, the city where Ovid had been exiled. I began to research Ovid's relegation to the Black Sea, and – inspired by the parallels I saw between the poet and my grandfather, and even myself – I wrote a play about him. Sadly, the project was rejected by the local theatre. They told me precisely why: the subject could be seen as a criticism of the local Communist authorities. I had never wanted to leave Romania more, to exile myself.

Years later that wish came true, and with the liberty to travel came a new understanding of freedom – and of exile. Twenty-five years passed as I pursued my engineering career, but Ovid was never far from my mind. Eventually, I began to write about him again. This time I decided it would be a novel. I travelled to his birthplace, Sulmona in the Abruzzi

Mountains, to Rome, and finally back to Constanta, following in Ovid's footsteps.

Back in London, a multi-layered story about exile – and the ways out of it – waited to be written. The novel was soon published, in Romanian, by one of the most prestigious publishing houses in Bucharest – Humanitas.

Then, during the pandemic, I went through the book again, and with new insights, rewrote it for an anglophone audience – an audience who, following years of lockdowns and isolation, understand freedom and exile perhaps more than ever before.

Prologue

The Palatine Hill, Rome, September, AD 8

Ovid's attention, as he climbed the Palatine Hill towards Augustus' palace, latched on to the pigeons taking flight around him. It was a bad sign, and if he believed in auguries he should heed it, flee Rome and make for Sulmo without a moment's delay. His friends had warned him the moment they had heard of the Emperor's summons. This meeting, they had said, will end in disaster.

The pigeons descended earthward once more, coming to settle on the palace's fence, where they watched Ovid approach and pass though the Imperial Gateway. Two lictors stared at him with surly disregard as he neared. Either they did not recognise him or they did not care who he was.

'Publius Ovidius Naso. Here by order of Emperor Augustus.'

One of the lictors looked at Ovid with mounting contempt and then gestured for him to follow them inside the palace and through a sequence of labyrinthine corridors. They came to a stop in a large hall.

'Wait here', they said in unison – as if Ovid had a choice – before leaving him alone.

Ovid looked about him. The hall was filled with statues of old men, all now dead. Some of them he had met, and only two he had liked. One of the latter was Marcus Valerius Messalla

Corvinus, a staunch republican, his late patron and a good friend of the Emperor. Since his death last year, without his protection everything had changed for the worse for Ovid – his *Ars Amatoria* had been banned straight away, while the publishing of the *Metamorphoses* had been restricted. And now this meeting.

A soft-footed servant appeared. 'Caesar Augustus is waiting in the study,' he said.

Ovid's blood froze. *The study.* It was well known amongst the Roman elite that should the Emperor greet you there only trouble awaited. Few had ever seen it, and for those who had, not a single one would dare speak about it afterwards – with the exception of Corinna, the muse of his *Amores*, the woman whom he loved and abandoned to sex-obsessed Augustus to save his career. And who was now Ibis' wife.

Ovid followed the servant out of the hall and through a door into the dreaded space. There, in the middle of the room, a laurel tree – full grown and enormous – rose up from the floor and out through the opened ceiling, where its branches reached freely towards the sky. Ovid's breath quickened.

The Emperor's low voice sounded from behind the laurel tree. 'No greetings, Naso? Good. Spare them.'

Unsure how to reply, Ovid kept his mouth shut. Such was always the safest course of action around Augustus, who could misconstrue a single word with fatal consequences.

'Do you like my tree?'

Ovid took a few steps to his left, so he could see the Emperor reclining on a couch pressed up against a back wall. The most powerful man in Rome did not seem to be in a hurry.

'It's Apollo's love tree,' Augustus continued. 'Like my patron god, I enjoy love very much. Yet I have banned your books about love. Interesting, no?' He did not wait for a reply. 'Now tell me: do you know why you are here?'

'I am here,' Ovid said, keeping his voice meek, 'because you called.'

Augustus nodded, satisfied by the answer. 'Good. Then let us get this over with. I shall not ask you to betray any of your friends. They have already confessed more than I wanted to hear. I doubt you will have anything of interest to offer which might lessen your sentence.'

'My sentence?' Ovid spluttered before his voice caught in his throat. The burgeoning terror he had felt since disturbing those pigeons had been well founded. This was no meeting. This was a trial. *But what on earth for?*

'We shall keep this short. You have three options. The first is obvious. Kill yourself.'

'But Emperor, I do not know—'

'Since you do not believe in the afterlife,' Augustus interrupted, 'you have nothing to fear.'

'Please, I cannot understand—'

'It is a good option, I believe. Die and I shall ensure that, in Rome, your dignity and your books – with a few exceptions – will be saved. You will have a grand funeral. What do you say?'

'To suicide?' Ovid sighed with exasperation. 'Even were I to know the charges that are held against me – and I most assuredly do not – then I would still choose anything other than my own death.'

Augustus whistled through his teeth. 'I thought that might be the case. There is honour in this kind of death, but you have never been a man of honour. You are too vain for that. No matter. Perhaps you will prefer your second option.'

'Emperor, I must protest, I—'

'Exile. On some Greek island. You will lose everything but your life.' Augustus grinned. 'Even you must agree that suicide is preferable to *that*.'

Ovid felt dizzy. His poems were in danger. Death or exile – what choice was that? 'What if the jurors don't find me guilty?' he muttered.

'Jurors? What jurors? There will be no trial. You should know better than that.'

Ovid gasped for air. He considered imploring the Emperor further for answers, but held his tongue. Anything he might ask would only be ignored or interrupted. Instead, he waited for the third option. It was all that was left him.

'No thoughts, Naso? But you are normally so liberal with them.' The Emperor took a moment to gaze at the backs of his hands. 'All right. If you choose not to do the decent thing and kill yourself, and if you likewise choose not to settle on a Greek island, there is only one other alternative I can offer you.' Augustus paused. 'Relegation.'

'Relegation?' Ovid whispered.

'Relegation. No confiscations. But you will be spirited away from Rome with immediate effect. And you will never return.'

'Does that mean...' Ovid composed himself. 'Does that mean my poems will be safe? That they will not be banned from Rome's libraries?'

The Emperor took a moment to consider this. 'Yes. They shall remain. With the exception of the already outlawed *Ars Amatoria*, of course.'

'And this relegation. Where will it be?' Ovid could feel his hands begin to shake.

'To a place where you will be given the chance to change. At the ends of the earth. I have been there myself. I am not ashamed to admit that I liked it.'

'The ends of the earth?'

'Not far from the gateway to Hyperborea. By the Black Sea.'

Ovid felt as if he were suspended over a bottomless ravine, neither falling nor able to fly away. 'Pontus Euxinus', he whispered.

The Emperor breathed in deeply, as if absorbing pleasant memories. 'There is a port there, in front of the sacred island of Leuke, where Apollo has one of his finest temples. The priest there is a friend of mine. Truly, it is the best place on earth to experience transformations. And transform you must, Naso, for this... this...' – he waved his hand up and down Ovid's body with a dismissive snort – 'this is no acceptable way for any man to be.'

'But', Ovid protested weakly, 'it is outside of the Empire.'

'Isn't crossing boundaries one of your many talents?' Augustus rose from the couch and began to dust the leaves of the laurel tree with the sleeves of his tunic. As the foliage danced around him it caught the sun's rays, and Ovid felt as if a green-gold shower were falling from the ceiling.

For the first time since entering the study, he felt the sharp edge of rage. *There is no reasoning with him*, he thought. *The bastard thinks himself a god.* He cleared his throat. 'I demand to know what charges have been brought against me.'

Augustus pursed his lips. 'You are a nuisance, Naso.'

'And for this, for being a *nuisance*, I must be punished?'

'That is only one small aspect. Of course.'

'Then what is the rest of it? Why? Why? Why am I to be exiled?'

'Not exiled. Relegated.'

'It is banishment from Rome—'

'Or death', Augustus snapped. 'Now enough questions. Which is it to be? You have wasted too much of my time already. Shall I choose for you?'

Ovid stared into the eyes of his Emperor for as long as he dared. He could see, incontrovertibly, that there was nothing he could do to nudge Augustus away from the decision he had made. The man's resolve was firm. Ovid's choice was bleak, but simple – banishment or suicide. There was no other option. 'I choose the Black Sea', he said. 'To save my poems. From my understanding of relegation, it means they will be not be confiscated. They will continue to be published. You will not interdict them.'

Augustus became impatient. 'How many times do you need to hear the same answer? With the exception of *Ars Amatoria*, I will not ban them', he said. 'You know, without you, I truly believe that Rome will change for the better. Gods willing.' He turned his attention to the laurel tree. 'I shall have a branch of this tree dipped in gold for the temple on Leuke. You will give it to the high priest there, along with my regards.'

'How long do I have?' Ovid muttered, gazing down at the floor.

'If you haven't changed your mind and cut your veins by the end of the month, you will be escorted to Brindisum and placed on a boat for Tomis.'

So that was where he was to spend the rest of his life.

Tomis.

Ovid shuddered. Even the name sounded like a curse.

PART ONE

The Gate

Tomis, a port on the western coast of the Black Sea, six years later

Expecting the Unknown

The stone bench, too short to allow Ovid and his backgammon partner, the Aedile of Tomis, to recline in the customary manner, obliged both to stare at the board and only squint at each other. A bead of fresh sweat coursing down the Aedile's forehead indicated that he had cheated again. Dice games always brought out the worst strategies in this city magistrate, but now was not the time for a confrontation. Any accusation, no matter how well founded, would devolve into argument. Ovid knew he would need the Aedile's support as long as he were to remain in Tomis. Hopefully, that would not be for long. Rome's envoy, General Gaius Julius Vestalis, had arrived the day before and was due to pay him a visit. Finally, he hoped, the Emperor's pardon.

'Is there anything you will miss from Tomis?' the Aedile asked.

'The six years I lost.' Ovid threw the three dice from the leather cup, made his move, and then sat back, squeezing the armrest of the bench – the head of a stone lion. Thankfully the beast did not bite back.

All of a sudden a silence settled over the garden, smothering like imminent death. For three days the nerve-itching rhythms of clashing bronze pots had filled the air, and finally they had reached their conclusion. Outside Tomis's city walls, this year's Lemuria festival had ended. Ovid had avoided this particular celebration, as he had most of them since his arrival. Unlike the city's citizens, he took no pleasure in appeasing the lemures, those spectres of the restless dead that now, though somehow comforted, could wander freely for another year.

A gust of wind rustled along the wall from one forsythia shrub to another until it reached the lilac tree, which shivered warnings. The violet bells, hundreds of them, released their sweet spring fragrance, which would have filled Ovid with joy were it not tempered by the perpetual salty smell of rotten algae. He had never liked the sea, and this particular one – the Black – which began just two streets away from his house, he hated. He gazed over at the lilac tree, and smiled. He was not afraid of lemures. Indeed, he wished for their existence. It would give proof to the notion of afterlife, would mean that death was not death, that there was something waiting for them all beyond this earth. If there were any truth in such thoughts, it would at last free him from his fears of dying, but he knew there was not.

The sun disappeared behind a cloud, casting a shadow over the garden. A hedgehog appeared from beneath a shrub and began to nose around the stationary feet of Spiros, Ovid's only slave, who stood under the wooden portico.

The Aedile had taken his turn – if there was further trickery, it went unnoticed – and it was Ovid's go once more. He threw the dice with a generous flick of his arm, and when they tumbled to a standstill all sides showed six. The highest of the Vultures!

'Unbelievable. You know, the locals claim you are a magician', the Aedile said. 'Perhaps they are right.' He leaned back into the stone bench, conceding the game.

Rather than try to explain sheer luck, Ovid instead pointed towards the moss-covered statues which rested on a pedestal built into the garden wall. 'Blame my house gods.'

'Them?'

Ovid allowed a smile to creep across his lips. 'When I get pardoned, these you can have.'

'I'd rather have your slave.'

'He is not for sale.'

'Shall we bet on him?'

'No. You could get lucky.'

A loud banging echoed through the courtyard. It was the front door.

The general, thought Ovid. *Only Romans knock with their foot.*

The house came to life. It was the first time in a long while that he had seen his four lazy servants so animated, as they swarmed about each other in a clumsy pantomime. It was almost enough to make him laugh.

'I expect you will be leaving now', Ovid said to the Aedile.

'No. I must make my amends to the General.' The magistrate's tone was sincere. 'Last winter, when barbarians launched a large offensive across the frozen Danube, General Vestalis – who was chief centurion at the time – pushed them back and saved Scythia Minor and Tomis with it. Yet Tomis, as usual, failed to offer its gratitude.'

'Perhaps now is not the time for this… business.'

'Tomis *is* my business. Be generous. You will be out of here soon.'

Ovid nodded. The Aedile was right. Soon he would leave Tomis, and perhaps the magistrate might never have such an opportune time to speak to the General again. 'Fine', he said. 'But forgive me while I retire for a moment. I must prepare.' Turning on his heel, he made his way out of the garden towards his study.

As soon as Ovid was out of sight, Spiros approached the Aedile. 'I can't believe that you tried to bet on me. I told you I don't want to be anyone's slave. I want to be free. I don't want to stay in Tomis.'

The Aedile looked at Spiros with contempt. 'You want too many things. All at once. Help him to get dressed. And for once, don't be quick.'

Orange Powder for Everything

In the semi-obscurity of his study, Ovid marvelled at the rays that pierced the cracks in the window shutters and turned the dust particles into thousands of miniscule worms of light. They reminded him that miracles did exist, even if the afterlife did not.

A knot began to form in his stomach, restricting his breathing, as if he were being strangled from inside. He knew this discomfort, knew it well, and began to search for the only treatment that worked. The General would have to wait. There it was: the small leather pouch of orange powder, bitter and choking. Unlike the other mood-changing mixtures he had tried, this powder, provided by Antipater, the best doctor in Tomis, had never failed. Ovid thrust his tongue inside the container, and with the dexterity of a lizard flicked the concoction into his mouth. It did not take long for that familiar warmth to course through his body, and he breathed out contentedly. He had again escaped death. At least, for now.

Planting his feet firm and wide apart, his body straight and balanced, he imagined himself gripping the polished handrail of a racing chariot. He could feel the jolting racetrack beneath him, could hear the cries of the driver, see the obelisk of Apollo, there, directly before him. There could be no mistake. He was back in Rome. He had entered the Circus Maximus. Around him, the excited crowd cheered. Had they been waiting for him? The driver waved to the public, but Ovid kept his hands on the rails, his attention caught by the Palatine. Augustus had not yet finished building his huge white palace when Ovid had been relegated to the Black Sea, but now it appeared complete, resplendent in its opulence.

A voice – distinct, recognisable – drifted out from the crowd. 'The General is waiting.'

The wild cries and low hums of the Circus Maximus slowly began to vanish, fading away to reveal nothing but his study and, stood before him, Spiros. 'The General is waiting', he repeated.

Ovid nodded, allowing the hallucination to recede.

Spiros held out a folded garment, which lay draped across his arms like a fainted maiden. 'The toga with the purple border', he said. 'As you requested.'

'It had better be clean.' Ovid checked for pigeon excrement. 'And no moths.' He began to dress himself, surprised that, after so many years, the toga still fit him well.

Spiros held up a silver mirror.

'Take that away.' The last time Ovid had looked closely into that glass, the yellow spots he had seen on his face made him fear his liver was damaged. In Tomis no one polished mirrors.

Turning his back on Spiros, he was relieved to feel that his heart rate had subsided. Piece by piece, he rehearsed the protocol that accompanied a noble appearance – the gestures, the posture, the voice, the pace. The more he practised, the closer he felt to Rome.

'Open the door', he ordered, and stepped into the atrium.

The General was obscured from view by the supplicating Aedile. 'General, our association to honour god Augustus and goddess Roma begs for your protection. We would be delighted if you were to accept the patronage of our association.'

God Augustus, Ovid thought. *In my house?* He should have been disgusted by the idea, but instead he felt sympathy for the magistrate, and for all the provincials like him. Living so far out on the periphery of things, they had to work hard to attract attention.

The Aedile, spotting Ovid, held up his hand. 'Publius Ovidius, let me introduce General Gaius Julius Vestalis.'

The General, a lean young man already with grey hair, dressed in a plain woollen tunic, his military background betrayed only by his sandals, advanced and offered his hand. Ovid remained still. He let the man wait with his hand outstretched. In his house, only he decided with whom to shake hands.

The Aedile, always quick to understand a delicate situation, chose to intervene. 'Ovid, the General is the hero from Aegissos I told you about. It was he who last year saved Scythia Minor and, by extension, Tomis.'

Ovid smiled. 'Be welcome in my house, General', he said at last, holding out his hand so that their forearms met in a loud clap. Only now he realised how much he had missed this Roman handshake, and for a brief moment a sensation of camaraderie, of belonging, coursed through his veins. The orange powder had not suppressed every emotion.

'It is time for me to leave.' The Aedile backed away from the General and, as he made his exit, stopped beside Ovid and gently touched his shoulder. 'Thank you. I'll arrange you a quick passage out of Tomis, once you get the pardon.'

The Price of Freedom

As soon as the Aedile left, Spiros ceremoniously opened the double doors and invited the General inside. The stifling silence, which had filled the garden earlier, now moved into the house and took possession of the rooms.

Vestalis sauntered up to the set of small imperial statues which depicted Augustus, Livia and Tiberius, a strange gift Ovid had once received from his friend Cotta Maximus – the son of Messalla, his long-time patron who had passed away a few month before Ovid's exile – and which Spiros had displayed unsolicited on the house altar. 'Even from here', the General said with a half-smile, 'you're keeping an eye on them.'

And vice-versa, thought Ovid, but abstained from commenting. These pieces belonged in a box, and would remain in Tomis after he had left.

'That golden laurel branch. I have seen those only in the temples of Apollo.'

Ovid stared at the branch. What was it that he had been told to do with it? He shook his head, searching for the memory, but it would not come. All he knew was that taking it back to Rome would mean another affront to Augustus, and throwing it away would be an affront to Apollo. What an idiot Spiros was to display all these items, believing that they would impress a military man.

He hoped the conversation would turn soon to the matter of his pardon. Vestalis, however, seemed to be in no hurry.

He pointed at the mosaic walls with their dark and imposing mountains. 'This landscape is a good substitute for the real thing', he said, switching from Greek, Tomis's language, to an impeccable Latin.

'Perhaps. Although I've never quite felt that the pieces of the mosaic belong together', Ovid said. He turned to look at the General. 'Have you really recaptured the Danube Delta from the Scythians?'

'Sort of.'

'We were never told that it had been lost.'

'The first casualty of every war is truth. You must know it. It is not much different with art.' Vestalis looked again at the mosaic. 'Art really is a curious thing, isn't it? We see not only what is present but also what is absent.'

Ovid wondered how much this General truly knew of art and illusion. Yet, again, it was a conversation he did not want to have. It would only serve to delay the purpose of this visit. Pardon. Release. Freedom. Ovid pulled apart the heavy crimson curtain to the dining room. 'Can I invite you for lunch? It will be frugal, I'm afraid, but you are welcome to it.'

'Would you be offended if I stayed only for a drink?'

Offended, Ovid thought. *Hand me over the pardon and you can clear off immediately.* 'You'll like the wine', he said, tempering his thoughts. 'But I should warn you that the water here is miserable.'

The two men entered the dining room. On the low, square table surrounded by couches, two silver drinking goblets stood proud. In perfect order around them sat the best silverware, which Spiros had laid with care. A servant came forward to wash their feet, and what should have been a mere formality turned into a thorough cleanse, which Vestalis seemed to enjoy. *At least he can see that I've maintained standards*, Ovid thought as he watched the General sigh with pleasure. Spiros poured the wine and delivered it to the men's hands. They toasted Rome.

'Do you know,' Vestalis said, 'few believe you are still in Tomis. Fewer still believe you were ever here at all.'

Ovid leaned forward. He had thought that this rumour must have faded away by now. It had floated around Rome since his relegation. In his letters, his friend Greacinus joked about it. Cotta as well. What if this General was visiting him not to bring the pardon, but for some other reason? 'Have you come to check on me?' The wine gave him courage – or perhaps it was the orange powder.

'Most people think that you struck a deal with the Emperor. That he let you live wherever you chose if you just got out of his way.'

'Augustus doesn't make deals. For that matter, neither do I.'

Vestalis took a long and measured gulp of the wine. 'I read some of your latest poems about exile', he said.

'What did you think of them?'

'They deal with places that don't exist, where the snow hasn't melted for years and where the wine freezes into icicles. I wondered why. Why do this? Any of it?'

Ovid laid his cup down and looked Vestalis square in the eye, being sure to keep his voice level. 'What's your message, General?'

Vestalis placed his cup down beside Ovid's. 'How much do you admire Germanicus?' he said.

Admire? The truth of it was this – *not at all.* But that could not be said aloud about Rome's most successful General. After all, he was Livia's grandson, of imperial blood. 'General,' Ovid said, 'I've heard that you are a Celt. My knowledge of your kind is that you are direct and honest. So don't mince your words. Relay your message, whatever it is. And make it short, I beg of you. Have you brought my pardon?'

'No.'

The answer felt like a blow to the testicles. Ovid reached out to grab his cup and managed to lift it to his mouth. Once he had drained it, Vestalis picked up the jug and performed the refill. Ovid drank that down too. Sobriety was far from him, a dozen drinks back in a timeless past, and yet he knew the oblivion he craved would refuse to come close. Instead, he would need to balance through the torture of his scattered thoughts – the forgotten outcast suffering his slow death amongst these freezing winters and that horrible, ever-present sea. Life had failed him once more. Immortality was a hoax. Existence was meaningless.

'Publius Ovidius, I am here to bring you an offer. An offer to become the next imperial poet. To surpass Virgil even.' The General's voice had changed, grown deeper, more sonorous.

Ovid took more wine. 'Whose offer? Say only what is needed', he muttered, trying to hide his curiosity.

'Rome needs you.'

'Which Rome, General?'

Vestalis stood and, hand on his dagger, checked the room for eavesdropping servants. Once he was satisfied they were alone, he faced Ovid. 'The true Republic of Rome. Which must be freed from Augustus' tyranny.'

Ovid could not believe he had heard correctly. This was

conspiracy against the rule of law. Perhaps Augustus did not deserve to be defended, but Rome's peace surely did. It was not the first time that ambitious generals had tried to grab power. 'You're talking of civil war?'

'All the troops along the Danube and the Rhine are pushing for Germanicus to become Rome's next emperor. And he, in turn, wishes to become your future patron.'

'Which of my book does he like best? The *Metamorphoses* or my *Ars Amatoria*?'

'Neither. He wants you to start writing odes which will unite aristocrats and plebs, soldiers and civilians, young and old. Under Germanicus' banner. We are asking only for what you do best anyway. You should be proud that Germanicus has chosen you.'

Ovid stared at the General. He had delivered the proposal without hesitation, as if it were not high treason but sound logic. 'Do you really expect me to encourage this… this collective suicide?'

'Who else but you can make Rome dare to believe that young Germanicus can carve a new beginning? If you want to return to Rome in glory, this is your one chance.'

'I am no good at odes', Ovid said. 'You are too young to know, but I have always been the subtle, lonely rebel.'

'I disagree. Your only ode, the *Gigantomachia*, the battle of the gods, was an immensely popular success. That's why it was forbidden by Augustus.' The General produced a half-size scroll from his tunic and handed it to Ovid, who recognised the expensive blue-wax seal. It was the mark of the most influential protector in Rome alive, Paullus Fabius Maximus. 'Read it.'

Ovid opened the letter. It was brief, its message unfair.

Do the moral thing. Help Rome and pay your debts.
In friendship. M

For a moment, Ovid felt rage bubble inside him. Debts? The moral thing? How dared Maximus speak to him about helping Rome? What had Rome done for him? Maximus had been the one to assure Ovid that Rome would be so outraged by his relegation that obtaining his pardon would take but a few months – many years ago.

'What has Maximus to do with all this?'

'Senator Fabius Maximus is our most important supporter in the Senate', Vestalis said, retrieving the scroll and burning it with care over the oil lamp. Then – slowly, very slowly – he chewed and swallowed the remains of the letter, washing it all down with a healthy draught of wine. Instantly, his demeanour softened. His mission was complete.

'The old man will kill us all', Ovid whispered.

'This is your chance to become free.' Vestalis' voice was soft, calming. 'Isn't that what you want above all else?'

Ovid stared at the mountainous landscape on the wall. He would not engage in a debate about freedom with this military man. He picked up the bell from the table and shook it. Spiros appeared within seconds. 'Prepare the General's sandals. My guest is leaving.'

'I will be back in the early autumn.' Vestalis smiled. He looked tired now, older somehow. 'Be creative, poet.'

'Be successful, General.'

Spiros led Vestalis out of the room. By the time he returned, Ovid had passed out.

Keep Ovid Alive!

General Gaius Julius Vestalis dragged himself through the heat towards the main gate of Tomis. He damned the rule that forbade carriages inside the city walls during the daytime: it was the rule that was forcing him to walk. The intoxicating effects of Ovid's wine had not entirely worn off, and his thirst nagged at him. His two guards followed behind, the rhythmic clapping of their lead-soled sandals on the large, uneven stones driving him to distraction.

'Hurry up', he hissed at them.

'It's best we avoid the crowds returning from the festival, General', one of them replied nervously. 'They might invite us to join them for a drink.'

'Any news from Centurion Plautus?'

'He should be waiting for you in the garrison by now.'

The General allowed himself a sigh of relief as they came to the main gate. He climbed into the waiting carriage.

The driver set off at great speed, seemingly showing off his skills as he rushed the four horses along the uneven road. He began to shout back towards Vestalis: muddled explanations about the rags on the poles that marked the reed-covered huts they passed. 'That's where they sell the fresh oat brew. Delicious it is, and much cheaper than wine. I can stop if you want to fill up.'

'Shut up and drive', the General shouted back.

Soon they came to the camp's rampart. The horses slowed, and Vestalis could hear the agitated legionnaires they drew level with, each swearing in his own native language. Vestalis jumped from the carriage and marched down the main alley towards the praetorium – the officers' headquarters – his neck stiff, chin pushed out. The thick Tomis dust that had dogged his short journey was not allowed in here. Even the noise seemed to have been shut out.

Vestalis' lieutenant came forward to meet him. 'The troops are ready', he said. They were packed and set to start marching the next morning one hour before dawn, as was the custom.

'I have changed our plans', Vestalis said, pointing at the sun. 'There are another three hours before sunset. We will leave as soon as I meet Centurion Plautus.' He could taste the dying fumes of Ovid's wine on his own breath. 'And bring me a jug of water.'

'You'll want wine', the lieutenant said.

'Just do it!'

The lieutenant scuttled away, leaving Vestalis to enter the praetorium, which looked like a fort within the fort. The gate promptly opened, and guards escorted him to a building of red brick and a bright room with a shining mosaic. He let himself fall into the encrusted armchair, the only furniture present of any use.

The wait was short. Centurion Marcellus Plautus – the prefect of the auxiliary cohort, nicknamed the Commander – announced his arrival with the violent closure of the entrance door. Shaven, tanned and corpulent, he advanced in a rough soldierly manner towards the General. 'I hope you will at least deign to tell me why you came to Tomis with your troops.'

Vestalis fixed Plautus with a cool stare. 'I liked you better during the campaign', he said.

'During the campaign? When I openly distrusted you and you kept your distance?' Plautus sneered.

'You followed my orders. We won. That's all that counted.'

'Do you want to replace me? Is this why you are here?'

'The troops are needed in Thrace. I stopped here only to meet Publius Ovidius Naso.'

'The outlaw?'

'My personal friend.' Vestalis stretched out one leg, and then the other. 'Personal.'

The bald spot on Plautus' pate glittered as his snakelike face paled. He looked away. 'I hoped in all earnest that your visiting Ovid was a rumour.'

Vestalis sipped from the cup of water before him. 'Centurion Plautus, watch your tone. I may be younger, I may be less experienced, but I am now a general. And I want you to take care of Ovid.'

'I am an army man', Plautus said. 'The Aedile is in charge of him. I am here to serve Rome. I have little interest in civilians.'

'And what if no one gives a fuck about your interests?'

Plautus glanced at the closed door and lowered his voice. 'Under normal circumstances,' he growled, 'I would have killed you for that, General.'

Vestalis smiled, taking no pains to conceal his arrogance. 'But there is good reason why you did not. You know it and I know it. Now, follow what I am saying. I want Ovid to do well. Alive and writing.'

'I shall not babysit a poet.'

'Listen carefully. A friend of mine is looking for a first

centurion to his second legion. If you were not so stubborn, you would be perfect for the role.'

Uncertainty worried its way across the lines of Plautus' face. Uncertainty and, Vestalis could tell, temptation. 'Not one thing I was promised when coming here has materialised', Plautus said. 'If anything, I – and my men – have been forgotten.'

'Here is another promise for you. If anything happens to Ovid, I will hold you personally responsible.'

'But he is old and sick.'

'Perhaps. Or perhaps he simply needs to be sobered up. Buy him the best physician in town.' Vestalis slammed a leather bag on to the table between them. Coins. A multitude of them. Plautus looked from the General to the bag and then back to the General again. With the briefest of nods, he picked up the bag, weighing it in his hands.

'With this I can finally pay my men', Plautus said. 'As a sign of gratitude, you can have my tribune.'

The clasp of their right hands was more a seal than a farewell.

The Tribune entered the room soon after Plautus left it. He had red, bushy hair, a face that looked as if it never needed to be shaved, and a gaze so beyond reach it bordered on insolence. Such a look would have ended the military career of any of the General's own men.

Vestalis took out a silver coin and marked it with his dagger. 'You will send letters for me', he said. 'This will be your stamp. You need not sign the letters. Just mark each sheet with this.' He held the coin out.

The Tribune did not look at it. 'I am not an informer.' His voice was blunt, matter of fact.

'And nor do I expect you to be', Vestalis said, though he did not withdraw the coin, but held it there, between the two of them. 'What is your opinion of the Roman exile?'

'I know his name, but none of his poems.' The Tribune removed his gaze from the wall and looked into the General's eyes. Vestalis was pleased to see that there appeared to be no guile within them. The coin remained where it was. Vestalis knew its magnetic draw was beginning to work its way into the Tribune's blood, that soon it would grow irresistible.

'I'm giving you this chance because I trust Celts. As you know, I am a Celt too.'

The Tribune rolled his shoulders. 'Was it my pride that gave me away?'

'Your hair.'

Gently, the Tribune reached out his hand and took the coin. Then he stood straight, angled himself towards the door, and, louder than he should have, so that anyone listening outside might hear, said: 'I refuse to take your assignment, sir!'

Vestalis smiled again. 'Get out!' he shouted, matching the volume and tone of the Tribune.

The Tribune looked down at the coin in his hand. He passed his thumb over it twice, palmed it, flashed Vestalis a brief and complicit smile, and then strode towards the door.

Same Poison in Different Quantities

The new staircase trembled under Plautus' weight as he climbed to the first floor. This inn behind Apollo's temple had never entirely got rid of its dubious reputation, even after the city council had forced its greedy owner to refurbish. The man was a scoundrel, little more. Plautus could see him poking his head out of the door, perturbed by the arrival of a visitor at this late hour.

'The brothel is two streets away.' The innkeeper held his oil lamp out to identify the intruder.

Plautus decided to ignore the man. He was not worth his breath. Pushing past him, he made his way up the staircase. A door to his right cracked open and a short, bald-headed man peered out. 'Commander!' he said, bounding into the corridor when he recognised Plautus, his eyes twinkling. 'Has your gonorrhoea returned?'

Without a word, Plautus grabbed the man by the tunic, lifted him into the air and carried him back into the room to slam him roughly against the wall. 'What happened to the fucking Roman?' Plautus barked.

'Please, let me down,' the man said, raising his hands to protect his face. 'Please, Commander!'

Plautus dropped him to the ground, and his knees buckled under the sudden impact.

'Antipater? Are you injured?' The voice of the innkeeper

filtered through the closed door. He clearly did not have the temerity to open it and see for himself.

'He is still alive', Plautus shouted. 'Now leave us be.'

Footsteps sounded along the corridor, receding into silence.

Antipater gathered himself and rose to his feet. His legs shook and he found it a challenge to look Plautus in the eye. 'Which of my medicines didn't work? What do you want, Commander?'

'First, I'd like to know what the General and the old Roman wreck have in common.'

'How should I know? My friends are not his friends. You know this.'

'You fuck his slave. What did he tell you?'

'That he loves me.'

'I have no interest in that. What did the General talk to Ovid about?'

'Spiros was too afraid to eavesdrop.'

'This I can't imagine.' Plautus took two steps back. 'I have a task for you. I'd like you to keep Ovid alive.'

'Alive? I am afraid I cannot guarantee such a thing.'

'Why not?'

'Ovid is in his mid-fifties. At that age, he may die from a hundred and one causes, not least from the terrible Tomitan water. Men like Ovid drop dead every day. To pretend to you that I could keep him alive would be just that – a pretence.'

Plautus lowered his voice. 'You are the best physician in town.'

'I am the *only* physician in town. All the others are a bunch of false healers.'

Plautus pulled from his pocket one of the coins Vestalis had given him and placed it on the table.

Antipater's eyes grew wide. Rubbing the coin between his fingers, he examined it under the lamp. 'New', he muttered. 'Germanicus' head. Is he allowed to mint his own coins now?'

Plautus did not answer, but watched the physician, as, mesmerised, he gazed at the coin in his fingers.

'It's a lot a lot of money for a lost cause. And it is not enough to start building a proper temple for Asclepius, with incubation facilities and the likes', Antipater said softly, as if talking to himself.

Plautus grabbed the physician by the chin and spoke into his open mouth, spitting his syllables. 'If anything happens to Ovid,' he said, 'I will kill you.' He placed four more coins on the table.

Nothing more needed to be said. Plautus marched out of the room. Antipater slumped back against the wall, rubbing his face with one hand and cradling the coin with the other. The door creaked open and there on the threshold stood the innkeeper. Antipater nodded at him.

'You have many visitors today. Your lover is waiting for you downstairs. Shall I let him in?'

'No', Antipater said. 'Find me a carriage. I'm leaving Tomis.'

The innkeeper took a deep breath before answering. 'I can't.'

'You can't what?'

'I can't find you a carriage.'

Antipater threw the coin at the innkeeper's feet. 'You can do whatever I tell you to do.'

'I'm sorry.' The innkeeper stooped down, picked up the coin and laid it on the table. 'The Commander caught me on his way out.'

'And?'

'And he warned me not to help you flee Tomis. He was crystal clear. He has left two guards outside my inn to ensure that neither you nor I misunderstand him.'

Antipater kicked out at the table, missing by a few inches and almost falling over. 'Send Spiros up', he growled. 'I need to fuck him.'

Moments later, Spiros appeared. The innkeeper pinched the slave's bottom as he closed the door on the two men and left them to each other. Once they were alone, Antipater strode towards Spiros, but the slave held his hand out to stop him.

'Ovid is unwell', Spiros said. 'The General's visit confused him. He asked for you.'

'Unwell?' Antipater looked at the coin in his hand. 'Then I must help him.'

Spiros snorted. 'Are you mad? He is on the verge of death. Finally.'

'I cannot let him die.'

'You *are* mad. If you keep him alive now, what was the point of it all? Why have we bothered with any of it?'

'There has been a change of plan. Forget Ovid. Forget his death. I will attend to him, and then if we leave at dawn we can reach Callatis in a day or two and sail for Greece from there.'

'I don't want to be a fugitive slave. You know my contract as well as I do – as long as Ovid is alive I will never be a free man again. He must die.'

'You don't understand', Antipater snapped. 'If Ovid dies then that bloody Plautus will kill me.'

'Why would the Commander do that?'

'Never mind.'

'We should not even be having this conversation', Spiros

said, jabbing his finger into Antipater's chest. 'You said the orange powder would work. In weeks.'

'Usually it does. I don't know how he's lasted so long.'

'Then what can we do?'

Antipater felt suddenly exhausted. 'You still want Ovid dead?'

'I want my freedom.'

'And for this you are willing to risk my life?'

Spiros gazed down at the floor, and did not reply.

Antipater cursed the day he had fallen in love with such a base and selfish slave. 'Then we will make one final attempt', he said. 'And then you must help me escape. Before Plautus catches me.'

'How will it be done?' Spiros' smile was sly and hopeful.

'I shall change Ovid's treatment', Antipater said. 'Rosary peas. I have only a handful, but if done properly, it will serve. In a few days' time we shall leave Tomis together. You a free man. Me on the run.'

Spiros grabbed Antipater's hand and pulled him onto the bed. The doctor fell into his lover's embrace with a resigned grunt. As the bed began to creak to their rhythm, a banging sounded from below. It was the innkeeper, smacking on his ceiling with a broom. Infuriated – could he not get a moment's peace? – Antipater leaped from the bed and, naked, marched out into the hallway.

'Stop it!' he shouted. 'Or are you jealous now?'

The Unimaginable Life

When Ovid awoke the following morning, it was with an excruciating headache and a strange sense of disconnection. Had he really been denied pardon, and – stranger still – had he really been asked to commit high treason? For a few moments he allowed himself the luxury to imagine it had all been just a dream. Or nightmare. But as his familiar jittery headache slowly began to force its way back to the forefront of his consciousness, so too did reality. Before him, a singular task lay. To write an ode for Germanicus. It could bring freedom, or – more likely – it could bring death. Ovid stretched out his arms and legs. Was it worth the gamble?

Stuffing a stylus and some writing tablets into a leather bag, he slipped out of his house through the garden gate. He could not deny the thrill, the creeping sense of adventure that coupled this strange and dangerous enterprise before him, nor could he deny the illicit pleasure it brought with it. He felt alive, more so than he had for some time. The itches were gone. And perhaps, he reasoned, that alone made the lingering threat of death worth risking.

It was early, and most of the town were still asleep. The back streets were empty of people but not of household rubbish. Rubbish was everywhere in Tomis. Ovid stepped carefully through the detritus, thrown out by the citizens overnight, and now scattered and unrecognisable, fed on and sifted through by birds and rodents. Soon he approached the cliff, relieved to be free of these filthy streets, and navigated his way around the clusters of thistle bushes. The perpetual murmur of the sea, always a siren-song for Ovid, grew in volume as he neared.

Six feet from the edge of a cliff, he stopped. This was his favourite spot. Despite all his disdain for Tomis, this particular place had a beauty he could feel in his bones. Here, he often liked to imagine himself transformed into a huge and heavy bird, all ruffled grey plumage and an enviable wingspan, so large that even he was unsure whether he could take off. More than once he had become so immersed in the fantasy that he had almost run, almost jumped, just to see if he would actually take flight. But something deep inside stopped him each time. While his mind could allow him the thought of suicide, his body always refused.

Ovid lowered himself to the grass, assumed a position which, under the right circumstances, had proven to bring him inspiration – head bowed over his knees, like a foetus – and allowed his mind to wander.

... my muse... where is my muse?... is she gone or just unwilling to help?... perhaps confused by the dimensions of the ode's subject... perhaps confused by the absurdity of it all... could this be a sign?... the sign that it's finally time for me to give up elegy, to switch to the epic style, to allow the drama... to take solace in it, to find safety there... for there will be little safety in this ode... can I even finish it before spies inform Augustus about it?... surely there is only one way this can all end... murder... a murder even Livia would salute...

Ovid lifted his head. A gust of wind assailed him with the strong and salty stench of rotten seaweed. He felt the pressure of nascent memories as they jostled for space against the walls of his mind. They were there, somewhere within that smell, tied to Livia, to Augustus' wife…

The Gulf of Naples! Baiae! It all surged back to him in one great, rolling tide. That day – how long ago? Twenty years? Could it really be? – with his wife, Fabia, in the villa of her cousin, Senator Paullus Fabius Maximus. Back then he had not known Maximus so well – he was not the friend he would later become – and Ovid remembered the trepidation and reserved respect he would harbour around his wife's cousin in those days. After all, one did not treat lightly the most trusted adviser of the Emperor Augustus.

The evening had been calm, peaceful even. Maximus lit candles while his wife, Marcia, wearing her hollowness with customary grace, played the harp, and the sea splashed some hundred feet below the terrace. The sunset, Maximus said, called for a poem – would Ovid read from his *Ars Amatoria*? The lady, he added, would enjoy it especially.

Ovid followed the trajectory of Maximus' pointed finger, and was surprised to see on the terrace a woman leaning over the enormous white marble balustrade. He had not noticed her before. Draped in an extravagant beige cape, she was trying to arrange with her pink-gloved hand a rebellious strand of hair that kept falling forward from her covered bun. She had her back to them all, and Ovid could not be sure if she was even listening. Yet when he began to recite, she immediately uncovered one ear and turned slightly in his direction. Her cape slipped, displaying, for a brief moment, a naked shoulder. Was it, Ovid wondered, an invitation?

Hoping to draw her out yet further, he lowered his voice,

and she turned a little more. He sensed he had her undivided attention, though he still could not see her face. Coming to the end of his poem, he chose another, this one licentious, the type he usually recited for good friends only. And this time, as he reached the conclusion, she clapped her hands, and turned to face him.

Ovid forgot to breathe, forgot to close his mouth, forgot even to blink. Those hands of hers, which continued to clap as she sauntered towards him, those pink-gloved hands could change the life of any man in the Empire, be it for better or for worse. He was being applauded by the most powerful woman in Rome. The Empress. Livia herself.

'That was good', she said. '*You're* good. Now, make me laugh.' The command was crisp, devoid of hesitation. Livia got what she wanted when she wanted.

Ovid gazed at her. There was something about her stare which devoured him, something love-hungry and, without doubt, irresistible.

'Why don't you tell Livia Augusta about the metamorphosis of the hunter Actaeon?' said Fabia, and added: 'As you intend to write it.'

For a moment, Ovid paused. Was he really about to tell her this story, this kernel of an idea he had barely worked out yet? It seemed foolhardy from Fabia to choose this when he had numerous finely crafted pieces at his disposal. But Fabia wanted this particular story and he could not, would not, disappoint her.

'As we all know,' Ovid said, 'Actaeon accidentally saw the goddess Diana bathing, and for this she transformed him into a stag. However, this was not to punish him, but to get him ready for love. Diana was filled with lust for Actaeon and, shortly afterwards, changed herself into a deer. But then came tragedy for poor Actaeon, whose own hounds, not recognising their master, ripped him apart. What seemed an accident was not. Jealous Apollo, who had always longed to have sex with his twin sister, but feared Zeus' anger, had altered the hounds' sense of smell.' Ovid looked at the Empress. 'Do you think it is far-fetched?'

Livia burst into laughter. 'That is what you will write? My husband will not like it. He may even want to punish you for laughing at his patron god. But I will not let him. For now you are safe.'

Later, after the poem had been made public, the Empress's predictions had proved true. Augustus did not like the rewritten story of Actaeon at all. He did not demand Ovid's punishment, but he did make his displeasure known. Twisting subjects and writing about everyday titillation to achieve fame was unworthy. In his opinion, minor poets should take example from Virgil and Horace, for there was glory in following their footsteps. Not in this kind of base and immoral perversion.

Once they became true friends, Maximus often liked to remind Ovid of that evening on his terrace – and always with a sly smile. 'Livia, not me, is the reason that you remain invulnerable. She likes you and your poems hot.'

Ovid let the memory wash over him as he gazed out at the Black Sea. Through the years of his banishment in Tomis he had thought of Livia, wondered whether it might be by her hand that his pardon would be granted, by her grace that his return to Rome would be allowed. Of course it had not happened, but Ovid had long suspected that, though she had never brought him back, it was likely that her influence all along had kept him alive.

He thought once more of Vestalis' offer, of the ode to Germanicus. To write it would be to shake off Livia's protective arm for good – Germanicus may well have been her grandson, but everyone in Rome knew that it was her son, Tiberius, whom she was grooming to be the future emperor. Ovid had never been averse to risk, had often taken it gladly, but displeasing Livia could, he knew, be the last mistake of his life.

Perhaps he should have taken Augustus' advice all those years ago, perhaps he should have denied his character and instead dedicated himself to the emulation of Virgil. After all, wasn't Virgil just another opportunist at heart? Wasn't Rome's official legend, the *Aeneid*, no more than a commission, a monumental delusion? But no, Ovid had spurned the imperial advice and instead chosen to tease the Old Man, to mock his rules and to scorn Rome's elite. That was easier than writing an ode, subversive or not.

Ovid pushed his hand deep into the leather bag, searching not for the stylus but for the receptacle containing the new medicine Antipater had given him. Finding it lodged beneath a writing tablet, he pulled it out and held it up to the light. He did not know why the physician had replaced the trusted orange powder with this new concoction, but he hoped it would be just as effective.

Nowhere are People What They Seem to be

Ovid could feel the creeping sickness inside him. Alien and unnerving, it was like nothing he had experienced before. Nevertheless, he had his suspicions – suspicions he desperately hoped were little more than the wanderings of a distrustful mind. Today, he told himself, spurred on by the sharp sense of doom growing within, the safest place to be in Tomis was not by the cliff but in the city library.

Housed in a private mansion – the former residence of a wealthy Greek who had deluded himself into settling in Tomis and then left after ten years when the erratic weather became too much to bear – the city library was, without question, an odd space. The various scrolls kept there ranged in subject matter from natural history to questionable philosophy to forbidden magic, the private passion of that old Greek merchant. There was no poetry. Augustus would have loved it. Ovid did not.

He did, however, like the Librarian, an amiable soul who spoke Latin, played dice fairly, and was the best – and perhaps the only – educated man in Tomis. Not too long ago, the Librarian had refused the chance to become a city magistrate, and for this decision Ovid had liked him all the more. They met regularly to trade paper, papyri, octopus ink, wax and writing tablets, and when Ovid needed his poems copied he knew the Librarian would always give him a good price. There was little in this world of which he did not have at least a fledgling knowledge, and Ovid hoped he might be able to identify the new medicine Antipater had given him.

'Poet!' The Librarian laughed as Ovid entered, his enormous body shaking with pleasure. 'What are we looking up today?'

Ovid walked towards him, paying attention to his steps. His sickness was evolving into pain, and he felt unsteady on his feet. 'I feel like I have been poisoned', he said. 'Do they grow hemlock here?'

'It's most probably something else. But you're in luck', the Librarian said. 'Somebody who knows everything there is to know about healing and poisons is in town.' He turned towards a beggar who skulked among the alcoves. 'Hey, Scorillo! Hemlock. Do they sell it in Tomis?'

The beggar came forward into the light. Ovid observed him warily: this stranger looked part Greek cynic philosopher and part Roman drifter. In one hand was a stretched papyrus scroll. He raised the other and gave a feeble wave. 'If you had taken even water hemlock' – Scorillo's voice was faint, croaky – 'you would be dead by now.'

Though Ovid had never met this man before, he could not help but feel a sense of relief, of hope, at his words.

'You know,' the Librarian said, 'if you're worried about yourself, you shouldn't be. Commander Plautus was given the order to take special care of you.'

'Order? By whom?'

'By General Vestalis.'

'Vestalis ordered Plautus to take care of me?'

'Yes, and in turn Commander Plautus ordered Antipater to look after you.'

'But how do you know this?'

The Librarian smiled. 'The good doctor's landlord, the innkeeper, is a friend. He likes to confide in me. Sometimes more than I care for.' The Librarian shook his head, reached into a bag below the table, and produced a coin. 'Commander Plautus paid Antipater with one of these. It's brand new. A sesterce minted in Vindobona. Are you aware of the city?'

Ovid nodded. A sharp stabbing pain wrenched down his side and stole his words. He understood better Vestalis' determination. 'What other news do you have?'

The Librarian lowered his voice. 'A ship from Thessalonica has brought another Roman envoy to town.'

The pain was worsening. Ovid felt as if all the air were escaping his body. He could not care less about envoys. The only thing he wanted now was to breathe freely.

'... he looks too young to be a politician,' the Librarian continued, 'and too old to be innocent...'

Unable to contain himself any longer, Ovid let out a long and low moan. His chest, constricted enough already, seemed to be tightening yet further with every passing second.

'Ovid?' the Librarian said, placing the coin in his pocket and coming around the table to his side. 'Are you all right?'

'I don't...' Ovid gasped. 'I don't feel well.'

The Librarian placed his warm hand on Ovid's shoulder. Its weight gave little reassurance.

Ovid could feel the panic rising inside him. 'I swallowed them,' he hissed. 'What was I thinking? I swallowed them!' He jammed three fingers down his throat, but no vomit would come. '*I swallowed them.* If they enter my heart I shall die!'

'You swallowed what?'

'The peas Antipater gave me.'

Scorillo had come forward to join them both, lowering himself so that he could look into Ovid's darting eyes.

'A hundred needles are stinging my arms!' Ovid cried. He suddenly remembered the physician he had met all those years ago in Sicily, a specialist who had described to him the symptoms of a heart attack. The clearest warning bell, he had said, was a series of pains in the upper left arm, and Ovid had those in abundance. What was it the physician had said next? *Once the numbness freezes the legs, hopes of survival plummet.*

'Bring some water', Scorillo said, his Greek well enunciated.

The Librarian hurried away to fetch some, and when he returned upended the jug into Ovid's mouth, who spasmed as he gulped it down.

'I need a physician', he said, panting.

Scorillo took Ovid's swaying head in his hands and cupped his palms over his cheeks. 'You need to breathe', he said. 'Breathe.'

'He is suffocating!' the Librarian protested.

'Shut up! And bring my bag and a cup of water. Rush', Scorillo shouted, as he grabbed Ovid's head and placed a leather scroll holder between Ovid's teeth. The Librarian returned with the bag, and the two of them managed to pour a muddy liquid through Ovid's almost-clenched jaws.

How much time passed before Ovid realised that he was still alive he could not tell, but at some point he tasted the sweat from Scorillo's palms as it coursed down his cheeks and on to his lips. It was disgusting, yet somehow it helped to settle his frantic mind. That and the breathing. He took the warm and salty air in through his nose and expelled it from his mouth. It was working. The pain began to recede; his heart rate slowed.

'Was it...' Ovid took another deep breath. 'Was it a heart attack?'

'No.' Scorillo removed his hands from Ovid's face and wiped his palms on his tunic. 'Far from it. But you *are* very ill. If you care for your well-being you should attend tomorrow's festival of the Targelia and rid yourself of your secrets. Some of us are as ill as the secrets we hold.'

'I know what will make me feel better', Ovid said. 'Some wine.'

Scorillo shook his head. 'The wine might be part of your illness. You need to stop serving Dionysus. He uses fear to rule your life. Fear and instant gratification.'

Ovid stared at Scorillo. Serving Dionysus? He had never served any god. Fortuna in his youth, maybe. 'Will I be torn apart by his bacchantes like Orpheus?' Ovid gave a weak laugh. 'Is that what you are saying?'

'Yes.'

'Why haven't I ever written like Orpheus?'

'You haven't been in hell. Yet.'

'I've been in Tomis. That is hell enough.' Ovid turned to the Librarian. 'Who is this man?'

'Scorillo?' The Librarian seemed to think about the answer. 'A Dacian. A Pythagorean. A healer.'

'A Pythagorean?' Ovid said. 'I should have known.'

Scapegoat by Choice

The dawn of the Targelia festival broke to find Ovid hunched over his table, scribbling names and wishes onto tiny papyrus scrolls. When each was complete, he screwed it into a ball and threw it into the cast-iron oven beside him. The room had begun to fill with a pungent and robust smell, and Ovid could not help but wonder if it came from the secrets themselves. Still reluctant to participate in the festival, he had begrudgingly accepted that perhaps Scorillo had been right, that it was important to explore his secrets, and the act of doing so had proved more appealing that he had anticipated.

He reached for a new scroll and began to write across it. *May my enemy Ibis and all who wish my destruction die.*

It was childish, he knew, and if it were ever to be read by unwanted eyes it would harm him. Ovid wondered if perhaps the festival of Targelia was just one enormous ruse, invented by clever but unskilled spies to discover the innermost thoughts of idiots. He would not put such base trickery past the people of Tomis. They were more than capable of it. Were their secrets even worth knowing?

In Sulmo, where he had grown up, there had been a similar ritual. Purification messages were written on a sheet of pewter and consigned to the fountain inside Hercules' temple. Ovid remembered how his father had obliged his entire household to follow the tradition. The foolish man. Like many of the boys his age, Ovid had ignored the priests' warnings of curses and stolen the messages from the temple to read in dark corners. By and large they were bland, devoid of imagination, self-serving and petty, and it was from that time that Ovid learned two things: that people were cautious with even the most inconsequential of secrets; and that curses held no power.

His own father's messages had been amongst the most dull, never ranging further than wishes for good health, or money. *I have always disliked my father*, Ovid wrote on a new scroll. He read the words back and then spoke them out loud. There was a catharsis to the act, for this was precisely the type of sentence one could not utter in public. To do so risked being disinherited, at best.

'I have always disliked my father', he said aloud, revelling in the liberty of it. Self-centred and provincial, his father had pushed him to leave home and join the military, and when Ovid had refused, threatened to disinherit him. Fortunately he had died before managing to do so. Ovid knew that his dislike – no, *hatred* – of any power-obsessed man, including Augustus, had begun with his father.

A loud banging on the door made him freeze. These were secrets he did not wish to share. Perhaps this festival allowed a necessary purge, after all.

He stood and answered the door. The Librarian waited outside. 'It's time to go', he said.

'One minute.' Leaving the door open, Ovid hurried back into the room to gather his things.

The Librarian peered inside. 'How many curse scrolls have you written?'

'Four', Ovid said, stuffing them into his pocket. 'But I'm not finished yet. A few remain.'

He bent over the desk and, with a trembling hand, scribbled: *I wish Augustus' death.*

Even to think it was dangerous. He knew what would happen if, by accident or on purpose, somebody read those words. Immediate execution. No trial, no discussion. It was, after all, treason.

'Are you now ready?' asked the Librarian from the doorway.

'Not yet.' Ovid hovered over the sixth scroll, unsure of exactly what it was he wanted to write. *The death of Augustus,* he thought. *Is that really what I want? His heir Tiberius would never pardon me. We know each other too well.* He kept his gaze focused on the papyrus, and allowed himself a miniscule smile. *Germanicus would pardon me,* he thought, *if I wrote him his ode...*

On the sixth scroll Ovid wrote the single word *Tiberius*, and then marked the last two scrolls to distinguish them from his other, more innocuous wishes. They even deserved a separate pocket of his tunic.

The Librarian greeted him with a kind pat on the shoulder as they walked out into the streets together. 'Shall we exchange scrolls?' he asked.

Ovid's hands instinctively moved to shield his pockets.

'I will take that as a no', the Librarian laughed. 'Though I should tell you that sharing your secrets with someone can set you free.'

'I prefer to be alive.'

The Librarian laughed again, and led the way through the crowd – which was beginning to clog the streets – as they neared the forum. Finally they reached the wooden altar in the middle of the square and stared up at the bowels of sacrificed goats that hung on display for all to see.

'There is nothing to be read in these deformed organs.' The voice came from the crowd. Ovid turned. He did not recognise the man.

'They gave the animals too much wine', said another.

'Everyone who drinks a lot', the Librarian replied, 'has bowels as useless as these.'

'At least they didn't bleat', a third bystander said, before pushing himself away.

'*Demeter! Ceres!*' The voice of the priest rang out above them all.

Ovid stretched his neck to watch the mass begin.

'*Gaia! Cybele! Isis!*'

As the people chanted the myriad names for Mother Earth, the drums began to sound from behind Apollo's temple, growing louder with each beat. Women holding smoking bowls passed through the crowd, spreading the smell of burning herbs. The drumming settled into a monotonous rhythm, and with it dancers poured forth, stamping the ground and then leaping high above the pavement. A chorus of flutes began to drift over the beating and thudding. Despite all his years in Tomis, this was the first time Ovid had experienced this collective madness first hand, and he understood now how contagious it was.

'Chant your wishes out!' the Librarian shouted from beside him. 'They boil within you! Get rid of them!' He began to bellow unintelligible phrases into the air.

Ovid did not follow the Librarian's advice, but those around him did.

'My uncle should pay his debts!'

'My neighbour should cut down the tree hanging over my fence!'

'My husband should give up that whore!'

The circle of floating dancers opened up to reveal an enormous creature – a colourful reed scarecrow, its body dressed with skins and necklaces – propped up on long black and white poles. The scapegoat.

'Tomis deserves a human scapegoat, not a lifeless puppet!'

'Don't vote for this city council next year!'

'Where do our taxes go, if they cannot afford a real scapegoat?'

'There is someone inside there. Just look closer, if you dare.'

A doubter speared the scarecrow with a stick. Ovid heard a gasp. When the doubter tried to remove the stick, he couldn't. One of the dancers broke it and the convoy moved on.

The dancers began to carry the straw figure through the crowd, trailing two goats – one black, one white – behind it. People beat at the scarecrow as it passed, punching at limbs and kicking at genitals.

'Be off with you!'

'May the divine life keep its perpetual vigour, untainted by the weakness of age!'

'Jump, goat, jump as high as the crop will grow!'

The chaos was overwhelming, and Ovid – recollecting himself for a moment – was surprised to realise that his fear had vanished. In fact, all he wanted to do was dance or, better yet, float. Was he under some sort of spell? Did spells even exist?

'Push your curse-scrolls into the scapegoat', the Librarian said as it approached them. 'Get rid of them.'

Ovid looked closer at the scarecrow. Already its garments had begun to tear apart and the wooden structure was showing through the ripped clothes. There was a man in there, jerking and twisting from time to time as he bore the blows of the crowd.

'Stuff in your scrolls!' the Librarian ordered.

The pressing masses from behind pushed Ovid against the cortege and, on impulse alone, he copied those around him and shoved first the four innocuous papyri into the straw puppet and then, after a moment's hesitation, the two bearing the names of the Emperor and his adoptive son.

Bright laughter rang out from inside the scapegoat, laughter Ovid recognised. Curious, he leaned in to take a quick glimpse, but the Librarian pulled him back.

'Don't get too close', he said. 'You will be torn apart.'

'By whom? Who is it?' Ovid said. 'Do I know him?'

The Librarian nodded. 'Scorillo is inside the scapegoat.'

'But why? Don't they kill scapegoats here?'

'They will not kill him. He is too clever for that.'

'Still, why bother?'

'Because those who play the scapegoat not only purify a place, but themselves too.' The Librarian turned away.

A sudden jabbing in his back caused Ovid to whip around. A towering figure confronted him, and for a moment the whole world seemed to collapse. It was Augustus.

'You can't be...' Ovid whispered.

Augustus grinned. 'Life can go very wrong', he said.

Confused and flailing, Ovid lurched back from the ghastly apparition, stumbling into the scapegoat and sending scrolls everywhere. He watched in horror as those around him bent down to pick them up and hand them over to Augustus, who took each one calmly, his eyes never leaving Ovid.

'This isn't possible...' Ovid refused to believe what he was seeing.

'No?' Clutching the scrolls in his hands, Augustus advanced on Ovid who, with a mounting terror, watched the crowd part around them both.

This is a trick of my mind, Ovid thought, *an illusion, a fake*. The real Augustus, even if he were travel to the island of Leuke, would never deign to immerse himself in such a lowly gathering as this. Someone, or something, was tricking him. But for what purpose, he could not fathom.

'I missed you, Naso,' Augustus said, his breath hot and raw on Ovid's face. 'Rome is rather dull without you. Nobody has ever dared tease me like you used to.'

Ovid searched for how to reply. Should he play along with this charade, or try to expose its deceit?

'I've been worried about you,' Augustus continued. 'I've read the poems you've written in exile. They started well, but then the wit began to fade. Are you quite well?'

Fine, Ovid thought. *I shall play along. Perhaps I shall find some answers, whether they are true or not*. 'Why haven't you pardoned me yet?'

'Have you delivered my golden branch, as I asked you?'

Ovid shook his head. Lying had never been an option. 'No. I have had more pressing matters to consider. For example, I still cannot figure out which one poem caused my exile all those years ago.' Ovid held his breath. The real Augustus would have exploded in rage at such impertinence.

'Which *one* poem? That would be like trying to determine

which pebble transforms a pile into a heap. Do not disregard the law of small changes. Enough will always add up to a noticeable transformation. And is that not one of your beloved themes? Noticeable transformations? Metamorphoses? It is certainly one of mine. After all, this is how one builds a lasting empire. Changes and transformations.'

Ovid smiled knowingly. He was talking with a ghost. 'In that case, you should be pleased by the latest revisions to the *Metamorphoses*. The latest changes and transformations.'

'I have read them. Partially. They are still a collection of philosophically unsophisticated and ethically repulsive fragments.' Even though this was not Augustus, his arrogance had been replicated impeccably. 'They are works of deceit, little more. Worthless illusions.'

Ovid could feel real rage building inside of him, which was absurd, because who felt anger at an imaginary conversation, which surely this was? 'My poems neither induce nor remove illusion. They are not paintings, they are mirrors.'

'You might be right. Selling lying mirrors as works of art is what revolts me.'

'And you have come all the way from Rome to tell me that?'

Augustus laughed and began to check through the scrolls. He reached one with a mark on it, and his laughter stopped. He thrust the papyrus towards Ovid. 'You have never failed to disappoint me. Is wanting my death your innermost secret? I knew you did not want freedom. Nor to give up drink. Hopefully you don't intend to commit high treason by helping Germanicus.' He snorted. 'You are nothing but a petty poet in search of immortality.'

There was no point in holding back against this misplaced

apparition. 'I despise you, Augustus!' Ovid cried. 'I shall finish writing the *Gigantomachia*. I do not care that you opposed it years ago. Rome will learn how our gods need a cunning mortal hero to save them.'

'Me?'

'The hero will never be you.'

Augustus reached inside his tunic to produce a laurel branch. He waved it up towards the sky and then dropped it.

The branch lay between them and Ovid, barely questioning why, bent down to pick it up.

'Poet! Don't touch it!' The voice brought Ovid back to his senses. He looked up. The cortege had stopped in front of them, and Scorillo leaned out of the scarecrow.

Before Ovid could ask how Scorillo knew about the laurel branch, the mob – unhappy with the planned stop – forced Scorillo back inside the scarecrow and the cortege moved on.

Letting himself be swept along by the crowd, Ovid drifted away from the square, in front of the main gate, along the city wall and then down to the cliffs, where an enormous bonfire sent plumes of black smoke into the sky. His mind felt emptied, drained, and he struggled to focus. The conversation with the apparition – or whatever it was – had left him queasy and unsure of things.

'They shall come!' The booming voice of the high priest ripped him from his reverie. Ovid watched as the straw scarecrow, now abused almost beyond recognition, was carried towards the pyre.

The Librarian appeared from the crowd.

'Where did you go?' Ovid said.

'I could ask the same of you.'

They looked up towards the scapegoat.

The high priest began to chant. In his hand he held a fresh laurel branch. Laurel trees did not grow in Tomis, that much Ovid knew. Reaching into his pocket, he found the tiny scroll that had infuriated Augustus. *Had the illusion been real? But how?*

'Tear the pharmakos apart!' someone screamed.

'Are they going to kill Scorillo?' Ovid said.

The Librarian did not answer.

'Don't feel sorry for scapegoats!' another man shouted into Ovid's face.

'They need to burn!' cried yet another.

The carriers lifted the scarecrow and readied themselves to push it into the pyre. Scorillo chose that moment to slip down from the straw figure and run away. The crowd booed as he hurried off.

'Don't let him run away!'

'What a farce!'

'No wonder the evils will return!'

'If we can't find someone to carry our wrongs into the underworld, we are doomed!'

'Why are they letting him go?'

The high priest, appeasing the disgruntled crowd, threw seeds into the flames and prayed loudly. 'The crops will grow, demons of all sorts will leave us, our women will be fertile, our land safe.' He gave a signal to one of the carriers, who released the two goats. The crowd, baying for the blood they felt was due, drove the goats towards the cliff. The first, maddened by the swarming people, jumped to its death unchallenged. The second, resisting the efforts of its pushers, tried to escape, but to no avail. It was caught, picked up, swung by its legs and let fly over the edge of the cliff.

Ovid watched the spectacle with indifference, too exhausted from the events of the day to feel anything for the goats, or for the mob who had gleefully killed them, and were now milling about and congratulating each other on another successful Targelia. With only enough strength remaining to carry him home, Ovid was about to turn around and make his way back when he felt a hand on his shoulder. It was Plautus.

'What a surprise to find our esteemed poet at such a barbaric event.'

'Barbaric?' Ovid shrugged. 'I have seen worse. As, I imagine, have you.'

Plautus laughed. 'You were spotted by my wife and her sister.' He pointed towards two women, well dressed and elegant, and as a result rather outstanding amongst the general citizenry of Tomis. 'They have implored me to invite you to dinner.'

Ovid did not answer. Plautus, sweetening the offer, began to describe the many succulent courses he would prepare, but Ovid was not listening. Instead, his attention was fixed upon the young man who stood alongside the two women. Ovid would have recognised him anywhere, for he had known him since he was a boy. It was Lucius. Corinna's son. He could only be here for Ovid. Not as the emissary of a pardon, but as the harbinger of death.

Escape from Reality

The Greeks had never been able to agree whether this mood-shifting sea they called Pontus Euxinus was black or blessed. The Romans chose to see it as unfriendly, an opinion which Ovid shared, though today it remained calm and sedate, dribbling between the mussel-covered rocks some twenty feet below.

He thought back to the Targelia festival, to those two maddened goats, one pushed over the cliff, the other jumping freely. *And which goat*, thought Ovid, *am I? Will I ever be willing to jump, or do I need the push?* Drifting like the seas below, his mind meandered away from the goats and to his hallucination of Augustus. The Emperor's message, even delivered from an incorporeal state, was pretty much clear. Ovid was and would remain an outcast. What else was there to do but jump?

The hysterical cries of the seagulls overhead rattled Ovid's nerves. He took two steps towards the lip of the cliff and leaned over. Down on the rocks, more gulls tore at a corpse with their blood-covered beaks. Ovid imagined himself down there, those beaks piercing his own skin, stripping away his appearance and leaving only his inner being on display for all to see.

Appearances, appearances. He was eighteen when a philosopher had warned him that those who searched for the truth beyond appearances often became stuck within their quests forever. If Ovid were to succeed at life, he did not have to delve beneath appearances, but only accept that he would never truly know himself. Ovid had complied at first – and the philosopher had been right, success had come to him – but once he had all he wanted, he of course wanted more. He looked for the philosopher and discovered the Pythagoreans – or maybe they discovered him? He began to use transformation stories as a means to search for both immortality as a poet and some existence beyond perception. There was some irony in the fact that in Rome he had never found what he was looking for, and that it was in Tomis that he had begun to glimpse it. Perhaps Scythia Minor, as Augustus had suggested all those years ago, really was a blessed place. Perhaps it was here and only here that one could migrate, with full consciousness, into the Other World.

Ovid peered back over the cliff. On the rocks there were no birds, no body, no blood. He didn't jump. Maybe he never would. The sea crept over the pebbles and washed away what had perhaps never been there. Ovid sighed, thought of Augustus again. He could not stop thinking about him. The Emperor, or the illusion of the Emperor, permeated his every thought. What was it that, in a fit of rage, he had screamed at the apparition during the festival? 'I despise you, Augustus! I shall finish writing the *Gigantomachia*.' A gutless threat, or a determined promise? Ovid could not deny that the time certainly seemed ripe to return to his *Gigantomachia*, the battle of the gods, the most daring subject he had ever imagined. Of course, the outcome – the triumph of the Olympians – could not be changed, but he could perhaps depict Jupiter and his despicable gang struggling for their very existence, with all their moments of fear and uncertainty. It would enchant the public and, even better, would infuriate the Emperor, especially if he made it clear that the hero of that war had actually been Hercules, the shepherd god, and patron of Ovid's native Sulmo.

He had left the *Gigantomachia* unfinished many years ago, back in Rome. He remembered how even Messalla had seen the danger of the poem, threatening the end of his patronage and, worse, their friendship, should Ovid pursue his idea. Yet now, here in Tomis, he had nobody but himself to decide what he should and should not write. Indeed, there were those who *wanted* him to complete it. Vestalis. Germanicus.

Casting the *Gigantomachia* would prove no challenge, and even with the most subtle of tellings his public would understand his allusions. Augustus as Jupiter was self-evident. And no one better fit the role of Mother Earth than the Emperor's wife, Livia. If Ovid ever wanted to enjoy Rome's society again, Tiberius would need to be Hercules: the official heir as the hero. And Germanicus? That youngster had always been spoiled, surrounded by sycophants, and surely had no meaningful part to play in the politics of the epic or of real life. But Germanicus was his customer. Without him he would never return to Rome – alive. Perhaps he could be the high priest, the passive saviour of the Olympians.

Ovid stared again down the cliff. He had the opportunity to write his first substantial work since his exile, but if he jumped it would never come to be. He tried to imagine how Rome (which had always, in his imagination, taken the form of a she-wolf) would devour his book. And Augustus would devour him. The repercussions were clear: death. And yet, with not a small measure of delight, Ovid realised that he did not care so much – that, in fact, he felt defiant. He had not felt so strong in years.

'Master!'

Ovid turned to see Spiros approaching from some hundred feet away.

'These men are looking for you.' On either side of Spiros, as close as if they were manhandling him along, were the two young Romans: Lucius and his companion. Even from this distance Ovid could see how tightly Lucius gripped Spiros' shoulder, and he did not like it. The three men waded through the knee-high brambles and ankle-deep mud holes. Spiros' tunic was ripped, and his face betrayed his terror. Ovid looked over the cliff edge and down at the drop. He remembered the two goats once more. Jumping was no longer an option.

The three men drew near. 'Master', Spiros said, panting.

Ovid forced a nod and, with some effort, stiffened his back. He knew he looked old and tired, and his tunic was dirty, but he did not care. 'Spiros, thank you for bringing them to me', he said. 'Now go home and prepare food. The Romans will be joining us for dinner.' It was the best way to get rid of his slave. Ovid did not want him to witness what was going to happen. Spiros, grateful to be granted release, turned on his heel and fled.

'Dinner?' Lucius smirked. 'With you? I cannot imagine anything I would rather do less.'

'Let us speak without pretence', Ovid said once he was sure Spiros was out of earshot. 'Why are you here?'

'To see you die.' The young man spoke calmly and then pointed at Ovid's clothes. 'But before that, I have enjoyed observing the deplorable state you are now in. Publius Ovidius, the elegant and always perfectly groomed darling of the most exquisite parlours, dirty like a pig! What a pity only I get to savour such a sight.'

Ever since leaving Rome, Ovid had feared this visit. Sooner or later, Ibis would send a killer. That it would be Lucius, he had not expected. A chattering and whooping distracted his thoughts. He looked over his shoulder.

'Roman! Roman!'

A bunch of young children were making their way across the wasteland towards him, waving their hands. Witnesses. He felt a semblance of relief at their proximity. 'Then I am glad', he said to Lucius, 'that you have found your pleasure here in Tomis. One must take it where one can find it.'

'The real pleasure will be in watching you jump off this cliff.'

'And why would I do that?'

'The order is from Augustus. You are to commit suicide.'

'I see. So you *have* spoken to him. I presume you have proof of this order?'

'Words are proof enough, especially for an exile.'

Ovid looked hard at the young man. Corinna was everywhere within him, from the set of his eyebrows to the melody in his voice, that presence which was at once pleasant and lethal. 'I am sorry,' Ovid said, 'but I have all the reason on this earth not to trust anyone linked to Ibis.' He took a step forwards, feeling emboldened by the group of children, whom he could hear were growing ever closer.

Lucius placed his hand on his dagger. 'Suicide is the Emperor's preference', he said. 'But he has allowed us other options.'

Ovid knew he only had to delay these two men for a few

moments longer, and then the children would be upon them. 'I wonder,' he said, 'did your mother ever tell you the truth?'

The young man's eyes flashed darkly and his jaw tightened. He kept his hand on his dagger. 'The truth?' he hissed.

'About your real father?'

'What do you know about my father?'

Had Ovid even wanted to answer the question, it would have been too late. With a sudden urgency, the children surrounded them and, sensing the hostility in the air, began to shout and declaim.

'Help!'

'They want to murder Ovid!'

'Help!'

'Romans go home!'

'Romans go home!'

'Romans go home!'

The children knew how to make themselves heard.

Lucius removed his hand from his dagger and smiled at them. The children quietened but did not move away. Leaning in close, Lucius placed his lips beside Ovid's ear. 'By tomorrow morning,' he whispered, 'I expect you to have killed yourself. I shall not delay my departure. Your corpse is to accompany me to Rome.'

If there were more children around, this world would be a better place, thought Ovid as the two Romans walked away along the cliff.

Learning to Let Go

Darkness hung over Tomis like an enormous web waiting to be torn apart by the dawn. Ovid opened the door of his study, feeling the cool air wash over his face. He was too exhausted to sleep. Only these nighttime hours remained to him. Once the sun began to rise over the Black Sea, Lucius could be upon him at any moment.

If he could wish for anything – aside from some miracle of safety – Ovid would wish that he had written something of value during his time here in Tomis. In Rome, it had been as if some mysterious energy had chosen to inhabit him, to flow through him and transform itself into words by the movements of his busy hand. Yet here, in this godforsaken city at the ends of the earth, nothing of worth had come to him.

All those years wasted. What had it all been for? Perhaps the only thing he had learned from his exile was that crossing boundaries was a tiresome passion – and here he was, on the eve of crossing the greatest boundary of all. Into the Other World that now seemed more real than ever. Would it be frightening? Or spectacular? And could it, if such a thing were physically possible, ever be captured in verse? He had laboured long over other frontiers – the borders separating art from nature, savagery from civilisation, ignorance from culture – and these were, in part, why his *Metamorphoses* had been so successful – but how could any of that compare to what he faced now, in this quiet Tomitan night, with but one dawn left to him?

It was time to dress. He needed something appropriate for the occasion. Spiros entered the study. It was clear from the shadows around his eyes that he had found little sleep either. 'What are you going to do?' he asked his master.

'Dress up in the ceremonial toga, I think.'

'That's not what I mean, and you know it.' Spiros' voice cracked as he spoke. 'They're going to kill you.'

'Since when can you read the future?' Ovid looked at Spiros. 'Actually, send the toga with the purple border back to Rome. I will wear a plain white linen tunic. It is all I need.'

'Do you know, I thought being your slave would be a shortcut to everything I wanted', Spiros said as he began to retreat from the room. 'Money. Rome. Freedom from my provincial existence. What a terrible mistake that was.'

Ovid spoke to him softly. 'It could have paid off.'

'How was I to know you would be the first man in my life who did not want to love me?'

'That would not have solved the matter.' Ovid could have explained, but felt no inclination. Perhaps one day Spiros would read his *Ars Amatoria* and finally learn the difference between whores and courtesans, between lust and love, and learn too that none of them should or could rely solely on sex. 'Bring my breakfast', he said instead. 'A glass of lukewarm water.' *Like in the good old days in Rome*, he thought, and watched Spiros' back as he left through the doorway. Despite the slave's obstinacy and general reticence to do anything required of him, he had been good company during this tortuous exile.

With only a few hours left to him, there was one final act Ovid could perform, one final gift to give. He took down a scroll and began to write across it.

When Spiros returned, he handed Ovid the cup and, in exchange, Ovid passed him the scroll. 'Here is your freedom. It comes with two conditions,' he said. 'First, all payments from myself and my house will stop with immediate effect. You shall have no claim on any further remuneration from this moment onwards. Second, you shall not in any way use or bear my name. That latter clause is in our agreement anyhow, as far as I remember.'

'Master…' Spiros' eyes flitted back and forth between the scroll and Ovid, and small cries of joy rose from his throat. Ovid wondered if the sexual act also drew these kinds of noises out of him, and felt pleased that he had never sullied their relationship by trying to find out. 'Thank you!' seemed to be all Spiros was capable of saying, and he repeated it again and again, grabbing Ovid's hand and kissing it. 'Thank you! Oh, thank you!'

'You will hate me sooner than you think. When you realise that you are poor, homeless and six years older.'

'I will never be a slave again!'

Ovid took the scroll from Spiros and laid it down on the table. He wrote out the final line, reading aloud as he did so. 'I, Publius Ovidius Naso, set my slave Spiros free before the agreed time. Spiros waives all his financial claims.' He held out the pen. 'Sign.'

Spiros wrote his name and then, in another rush of excitement, kissed Ovid's hand once more.

'Now pack your stuff and get out of my house.'

'But what about you?'

Ovid smiled. 'Your days of worrying about me are over. You are a free man now. And so am I. Go.'

With one final kiss of his hand, Spiros grabbed the scroll from the table and sprinted out of the door.

The sun had begun to rise. It was time. All that was left to do was choose the place of his death. Had his end come in Rome, he would have awaited his murderers in a bath, a decision to lessen the potential mess of blood stains. But Tomis did not deserve his consideration, and so he would choose the setting most appropriate for a poet – the library. He imagined himself spreadeagled on the floor, blood flowing from his stab wounds, his right hand holding a scroll, a single finger pointing at a word or phrase, the obscure reasoning behind which would drive historians crazy for years to come. *What had the poet wanted to tell us in his last moments? What was he trying to say when they so ruthlessly slew him?* Ovid smiled to himself. To leave behind an unsolvable puzzle would be good sport.

He took one brief and final turn around the garden, hoping he might see the hedgehog of which he had grown so fond, but the little creature remained in its hiding place. *It knows better*, Ovid thought. As he made his way back into the house, the caretaker came running towards him.

'Spiros has deserted you! The traitor fled!'

Ovid looked at this man and realised he had never before heard him speak. To him, the caretaker had always been something of a nonentity, a characterless workhorse, but as he looked at him now Ovid could see the clear intelligence that shone from his face.

What else have I missed?

'What's your name?'

'Argyris,' said the caretaker.

'It was not desertion, Argyris. I gave him his freedom.'

'A good move from your side, master, a good move indeed.' Argyris spoke in excited barks. 'That slave attracted death.'

'It was not a plan, as such,' Ovid murmured. 'More impulse.' And, as one of his final acts, it had given him a not insubstantial amount of pleasure. To bestow freedom. There was no more he could offer. After all, he could not take it with him. 'Come with me.'

As instructed, Argyris followed Ovid through the house to his study. Here and there, he babbled a few words to himself, not Greek nor Latin, but the primitive Gaetic which was popular out here on the coast of the Black Sea. Ovid had never tried to learn it, but had nonetheless absorbed the language by virtue of being surrounded by it for so many years. Therefore he understood Argyris' mutterings – those that he could hear, anyway. Something about kindness and secrets, about the right thing to do.

In the study, Ovid took down another scroll and scratched some new words on to it. Then, standing up, he handed the papyrus to Argyris. 'Here is my last will,' he said. 'Take it. You will see that after my death my household in Tomis will become yours.'

'But, master—'

Ovid held up his hand to silence him. 'No discussion. It will be yours and yours alone to do with as you will. I ask only that you give my scrolls to the Librarian, that you destroy all my wax tablets, and that you take the hedgehog with you, wherever it is you shall go.'

Like Spiros, Argyris' cheeks had grown wet with tears. Unlike Spiros, he did not kiss Ovid's hand or flee the study, but stood firm before him. His mouth opened and closed as he wrestled with his decision, and then he lifted his chin, met Ovid's gaze, and spoke clearly in Greek. 'There is a secret way out of the city', he said. 'It does not lead through either of the gates.'

'How do you know about it?'

'Hidden in the middle of the grove of trees on the wasteland, near the cliffs, is a well. Only a few know of its existence. I should not be telling you this, but...'

Ovid reached out his hand and laid it on the caretaker's shoulder. 'You are a good man, Argyris', he said.

The caretaker wiped his eyes. 'Yes', he said. 'Yes, I am. I will show you. Come with me.'

'I am too old for that.'

'Maybe, but on the back roads there are many gods to protect you.'

Ovid might have been sceptical of the existence of the gods, but these small ones not even he could ignore, if he wanted to stay alive.

Fortune or Abundance

The back streets were empty and so was the wasteland. Argyris, hesitant to go any further, pointed out the grove of trees. 'I must return to the house', he said. 'You will find the well in there.'

'Thank you.' Ovid took the caretaker's proffered hand and then watched as he turned on his heel and hurried away. The lure of the well was strong, but escape had never been in his constitution. He would not, he resolved, flee Tomis. He hadn't always made the wisest decisions, but he minded being regarded as a coward. A coward relinquishes his trustworthiness, and without credibility the transformation stories Ovid had written about, far fetched as they were, would have become little more than a laughing stock. Not what he had intended them to be: an affront to the powerful – gods and humans alike. No. Cowardice was not an option for him, nor for his legacy. He would stay in Tomis. And he would meet his executioner with his head held high.

Ovid waited until Argyris was out of sight and then began walking in the other direction, away from the trees and along the coast road.

Before long, he reached the lighthouse at the end of the Decumanus, the major road that linked the tip of the Tomitan promontory with the main gate. The lighthouse keeper, spotting him from a window, leaned out over the balustrade and hissed his name. 'Ovid! Avoid the forum!'

Ovid did not reply, but waved his hand in gratitude. *So Tomis knows I am hunted*, he thought. It remained in his interests to attract as little attention as possible. Coming from the Decumanus, he spotted a man briskly walking in his direction and, heeding his own advice, lowered his head and hunched into his tunic. But it did not deter the man approaching, for he quickened his steps and was upon Ovid before he had a chance to call out to the lighthouse keeper.

'What are you doing here? Are you mad?'

Ovid raised his head, relief coursing through him as he recognised the Librarian.

'I am on my way to the library', Ovid said, choosing not to add – *to be murdered there.*

'Don't be a fool.' The Librarian grabbed at Ovid's arms. 'Let us go to the temple of Fortuna. We will ask the goddess for protection. We both need it.'

Ovid didn't question why the Librarian needed the goddess's help too. He doubted Fortuna would care much for his plight – at home in Sulmo, she was not so much the goddess of good and bad luck as the goddess of abundance – but it was worth the attempt. What else was he going to do while he waited for his end?

Together they continued along the road, rounding a corner and making their way towards the temple. It had been a bold move from the Tomitans some centuries ago to entrust their city to Fortuna when Hyperborean Apollo and Dionysus reigned as the two revered gods of the Thracian shores. The daring statement had paid off. Out of all the Greek ports that dotted the western Black Sea, the Romans had felt safest in Tomis's harbour.

Though it was still early in the morning, the temple was not empty. Shadowy figures wrapped in capes squatted here and there, praying to the statues.

'Here', the Librarian said, pulling Ovid towards the statue of Fortuna that stood in one of the temple's darker recesses. 'Let us pray together.' He knelt, and Ovid, though he had not prayed for some time, followed suit. As he lowered his head he felt the Librarian's hand on his shoulder. 'Flee Tomis.'

Ovid looked beside him at the Librarian, who kept his head bowed and his eyes closed.

'You need to get out of the city', the Librarian said. 'You need to move on.'

'You can't force me' Ovid replied.

'And I can't leave you behind.'

Leave me behind, Ovid thought. Was everybody but he planning on fleeing Tomis? Was that why the Librarian had come to find him? He imagined the two of them – an unlikely duo – crossing Thracia in pursuit of Greece, imagined the tremendous levels of patience he would need to endure the Librarian's litanies about what it meant to live a good life. How on earth would they ever expect to cover so much ground unaided? How on earth would they expect to reach safety without tearing each other's throats out? It was unthinkable. *Leave me behind?* Ovid felt himself sneer. He would make the choice easy for the Librarian. He would leave *him* behind. Without another word, Ovid marched from the temple, alone. The best place to be murdered was still the public bath.

To Test Eternity

On the southern side of the promontory, built over two blocks, a new brick edifice – surrounded by shops hidden under lively painted wooden porticos – separated the Tomitan forum from the harbour. Inside were the new baths. Ovid strolled towards the gate, feeling a strange kind of inner peace. The sun was already high in the sky, and it was a miracle he had survived so much of the day.

'How can I help you?' The man who staffed the entrance was unfriendly and kept his gaze on the ground.

'Call Beatus.' Ovid intended to speak to the bathing master in person.

The man loped off into the building. Before long, the door opened onto a bright and sunny courtyard. In the middle stood a tall fountain which did not yet function. No fountains in Tomis would work until the new aqueduct was finished. Beatus, a strong and imposing Scythian, appeared around the fountain and greeted Ovid with his customary brevity. 'We are closed.'

'Under this new management you deal with exceptions all the time.'

Beatus sighed. 'Follow me.'

Ovid trailed him through the courtyard and into an over-large corridor, where flickering oil lamps rested in head-high trays and turned the shadows on the stone floor purple. *What a perfect place to meet my killer*, he thought as they entered the apodyterium, the barrel-vaulted dressing room. The walls were covered in amateur sketches of crude figures coupling, the positions laughably implausible.

Beatus began to undress him. Ovid had never been comfortable with the touch of another man, but he acquiesced. What did it matter any more? What did any of it matter? Beatus handed him a towel to wrap around his waist while he went to fetch a clean scraper and an oil flask from the clothing compartment. 'This is from Africa, cypress-scented.' He indicated that Ovid should smell it.

'I'm more interested in the scraper. How sharp is it?' Ovid said. *Sharp enough to cut my veins without pain?*

'I sharpened it myself', Beatus said, and with fine, long movements began to stroke the instrument down Ovid's back. It felt dangerous, but it had a soothing kind of hypnotism to it, and it was only when a clap at his right ear wrenched him out of his reverie that Ovid realised he had begun to drift off.

He opened his eyes. A skinny youngster with darker skin glared at him.

'This will be your personal trainer today, Publius Ovidius', Beatus said, and then turned to the bath slave. 'Be warned. He doesn't fancy boys.'

The slave grinned – knowingly, it seemed. 'In that case,' he said, 'I have something perfect for him. Please, sir, follow me.' He led Ovid through the building and towards the gymnasium. Even before they reached it, Ovid could hear the giggles and the excited laughter of women echoing along the high-ceilinged passageway. The noise grew louder as they approached the inner court. A group of Thracian whores played ball. Ovid had never seen any of them in Tomis before. They were all, he could not help but notice, in their prime.

'Which one do you want?' the boy asked.

Ovid ignored the question. 'When did they come?' Usually, whenever a new lot of prostitutes arrived in town he was informed.

The boy shrugged. 'These particular ones won't be here long. The ship that arrived the other day will take them away soon enough. I guess to Rome.'

In one form or other, Ovid thought, *whether it be as ashes or as an embalmed corpse, I will make the trip along with them.* For a moment, he wondered where he would be buried. He wrestled his worries into submission. *Carpe diem.* Enjoy the moment. There were, after all, only a few moments left to him. Involuntarily he touched his penis, and was surprised and a little pleased to find it erect. He rearranged his towel to hide it, but when the ball came his way and he tried to impress the women by catching it, the towel fell from his waist.

'Wow', exclaimed one of the women.

'Join us, old man!' shouted another, staring lasciviously at Ovid's genitals.

'Let's make the old man happy', suggested a third.

'Go!' the boy whispered. 'They never ask twice!'

The idea was a tempting one, but the notion that he might be murdered while having sex killed his desire. A noble exit for a man in his twenties, perhaps, but for one as old as Ovid, it would be little more than humiliating. He threw the ball back with unexpected skill and then pulled the towel up to cover himself once more. When the women realised he would not join them, their disappointment seemed genuine.

'You should have gone to them', the boy admonished him. 'It's not worth being so shy these days.'

'I can assure you', Ovid replied, 'that timidity is not the problem.'

The boy shook his head as if he could not fathom this old man, and then led him into the tepidarium, the sweat room. It was pleasantly warm, and, best of all, empty. Beatus awaited them both. The boy raised his shoulders to signal his lack of comprehension as they approached, and Beatus grinned. 'So the whores did not tempt you?' he said, gesturing for Ovid to lie down on the stone table. 'How very noble. And unexpected.'

Ovid closed his eyes as Beatus massaged his back, feeling his sweat and fear mingle with the oil as it was kneaded into his skin.

'You are tense, Publius Ovidius', Beatus said when he had finished. 'I recommend the caldarium next. It is nicely hot in there.'

Slowly getting to his feet, Ovid walked across the room. Beatus opened the door of the caldarium and gently pushed him against a wave of steam. Blinded by the fog, he stumbled forward, the disconnected threads of light around him augmenting the rising sensation that he was entering some kind of suffocating underworld.

The door closed behind him, and Ovid heard a cough. Who else was here? Could it be them? His killers? Was that why Beatus had pushed him inside? Did he know? Did they all know? He should have stayed with the whores. His first instinct was to run back to the door, but he doubted he would make it even that far. He tried to gaze into the viscous fog, hoping that he would at least see the face of Lucius before blade pierced flesh.

'Sit down!'

Ovid knew that voice. It was Plautus. He moved towards it, eventually making out the form of the Commander on a wet stone bench, gathering a heap of towels to make room. *Perhaps*, Ovid thought, *Lucius has outsourced the killing. Perhaps my death will be at Plautus' hand. Time will tell.* He sat beside the Commander.

'Rumour has it you are leaving Tomis', Plautus said, with a touch of irony in his voice.

Ovid was about to answer when the sound of a man clearing his throat came from the other side of the room. 'Who else is here?' he asked.

'Ursus. My bodyguard. I keep him always as close as possible to me. Even in the baths.'

Would Plautus be his murderer? Plautus had always been stupid but never deceptive. 'What are you doing here?' he said.

'Waiting for you to come.'

'Here I am. What next?'

'Next, we return to your house. And I shall double the guards.'

This made no sense to Ovid. 'Am I to be your prisoner?'

'"Prisoner" is a strong word', Plautus replied. 'Let's just say this. I'll not allow those two Romans to take you out of Tomis. I don't care if they have brought you your pardon. You are to stay here.'

Ovid turned to face the centurion. 'But Commander', he said. 'They are not here to pardon me. Do you not know?'

'Know what?'

'They are here to kill me.'

'Oh.' Plautus considered this statement for a few moments.

'So your life hangs in the balance. And you have chosen to come *here*?'

Ovid smiled. 'This seems as fine a place as any to die.'

'Perhaps you are right.' Plautus sniffed. 'Then let me wait with you. You can tell me a poem.' After a short pause, he added: 'Please.'

The 'please' was more surprising than the request itself, and it compelled Ovid to oblige. He began with one of his shorter poems, but, warming to the recital, followed it with something longer, one of his favourites. *Not a bad way to end my life*, he thought. He was about midway through another when he was cut short by the caldarium door opening with a crash. Two torches, all that could be seen through the vapours, entered the room, projecting ethereal shadows across the ceiling.

Ovid recalled how, some thirty years ago, he had asked one of his Pythagorean teachers how man should best deal with the moment of death. The advice had been simple – *wilfully interrupt all thoughts.*

As a draught through the open doorway stirred the vapours into a whirling vortex, Ovid closed his eyes and allowed himself to be pulled into a state of stupefaction, somewhere between presence and absence, between being and non-being, between eternity and a single moment. Here should have been lasting nothingness. Yet nothingness was precisely that, and therefore impossible to cling to. It evaded him as quickly as it had appeared.

Ovid opened his eyes. The intruders were advancing on him. What a pity he had come to his senses before being killed. Nevertheless, he discovered that although the only thing that had terrified him in his whole life – the moment of death –

was at hand, he was not scared. Finally, he understood that there was nothing to be scared of. If death was a passage to somewhere else, he needed only to be patient and he would find out where; and if death was a passage to nowhere, then what did it matter? How can one fear nowhere?

One of the attackers was close enough now for Ovid to make out his visage through the mist. It was Lucius, here to fulfil his promise. The Roman raised both his torch and his sword to shoulder-height and, with a manic leer, leapt forward.

Plautus' heavy push threw Ovid sideways across the slippery stone bench and onto the floor. The Commander grabbed the heap of towels and pushed it towards Lucius, who, unable to stop his momentum, plunged the sword deep into the towels with his whole weight. With astonishing speed, Plautus twisted the towels, causing the sword to drop to the floor, and then pushed forward with all his might, sending Lucius cascading backwards across the caldarium. Deftly picking the sword from the floor, the Commander charged after the Roman, and with both hands brought the blade down into his chest. His aim was sure: Lucius was dead in an instant.

'Ursus!' Plautus shouted. 'Do not let the other escape.'

'I did not, sir', came the bodyguard's voice from the gloom. 'He is dead.'

Plautus lifted one of the lamps from the walls and held it first above his victim, and then above Ursus. 'Our Roman visitors', he said.

Beatus appeared in the room, followed by a horde of slaves, who slipped across the blood-muddied floor as they stared at the carnage.

'You deserve to be killed too for letting them in!' Plautus

shouted. Beatus bowed his head meekly, took Ovid by the elbow, and helped him to his feet before gently guiding him to the pool room. Plautus followed.

Ovid slipped into the silver, glinting water, so innocent and clear, devoid of any trace of what had just happened in the caldarium. 'Wash yourself', he said to Plautus. 'Wash away the evil the aggressors carried.'

The Commander obeyed, ducking himself under the water and scrubbing at his skin. 'So it seems you were right, after all, poet', he said as streaks of red soaked into the water around him. 'They were not here to pardon you.'

A Veil of Justice

The tense atmosphere inside the City Hall made itself known the moment Plautus passed the city guard. The members of the city council, as agitated as bees in smoke, chattered and squabbled amongst themselves. No one wanted to be here for this extraordinary meeting, but each man understood its necessity – the killing of two Romans would not remain without consequence, and even if vengeance did not come from Rome, then, at the very least, the governor of Macedonia would call into question the reputation of their city. This had to be avoided at all costs. It had taken generations for Tomis to demonstrate that it could govern itself as efficiently as its neighbouring cities, and while it had not been easy to renounce dictatorship and adopt instead the Greek model of collective decisions, it was clear to all now that democracy worked and that they needed to do everything within their power to keep it that way.

'Are we going to begin?' Plautus asked, his voice booming out over all others. 'I need to be in the garrison.'

A hush settled across the hall as the Aedile, nodding, rose to his feet. 'Fellow citizens. The founders of Tomis, the Milethians, laid a solid foundation for our city. The last time it was in peril, the protection of our gods and of the Roman troops under General Vestalis saved us. It remains our duty to honour both, gods and Romans alike.' He turned his attention towards Plautus. 'Commander! I formally request you to describe to the council what happened in the bathing establishment yesterday.'

'Two men stormed into the baths and were killed', Plautus said. 'Simple as that.'

'There is nothing I resent more than having to take a matter on trust alone', a councillor said as those around him mumbled in agreement.

'Then don't', Plautus replied, shrugging his shoulders.

'Was Ovid there at the time of the incident?' the Aedile asked.

Plautus nodded.

The butcher, always eager to have his say, leaped in before the Aedile could continue. 'We need to be both dutiful and just. The power of the people and the power of the law are paramount—'

'Citizens!' the ironmonger interrupted. There was general relief that the butcher had been quietened, and general frustration that the ironmonger – who was just as vain and idiotic – was about to begin. 'I can only repeat what I have been saying for years. Publius Ovidius Naso must leave our city! We cannot accept the fury of Rome that will come our way when they learn an exile has murdered an official messenger.'

'Our business as city council is to do justice', the blacksmith said, his voice strong and clear. He was used to getting his way. 'And for this we need the truth.'

'That is why I have asked Centurion Plautus to join our meeting today', the Aedile said.

An elderly landowner, who usually made his journey into the city only in wintertime when life on his estate was too dangerous, addressed the council. 'I agree with the Aedile, even if he is a newcomer here. However, as we all know quite well, there is no such thing as one single truth, and we should not waste our time hunting for that here. Above all else, we must follow the law. It is in the best interest of our city. And it is authority, not truth, that makes the law.'

'But if we don't intend to find and punish killers, then what sort of community will we become?' the blacksmith said. 'Ovid should be punished!'

'Could any of you imagine Ovid possessing the skill and the power to handle a sword, let alone to kill anyone?' The Librarian had to raise his voice to be heard from the back of the room. Few had seen him enter.

'It would not be the first time', the butcher said, 'that Tomis has condemned an innocent man. Unfortunate, yes, but to save the city, justified.'

'We need a scapegoat', the landowner said.

'Tomis has never fared well with scapegoats', the Librarian cut in.

'There is nothing wrong with scapegoats.' The ironmonger added a lilt to his voice, hoping for a laugh from the assembly. He did not get one.

'As long as they themselves agree to the role', said the Aedile without humour.

'There is not one person present who believes that an old poet could murder two young men', the Librarian said.

'One rather important fact has not yet been considered.' The new speaker of the council, a farmer, had a meek and timid voice, and those on the other side of the hall shouted at him to speak up. 'Witnesses reported that the strangers entered the bathing establishment fully dressed with unsheathed swords. Maybe it was self-defence.'

The gathered councillors erupted into murmurs. If this were true, the strangers broke the law. And trespassers could be killed. Suddenly, a way out of the crisis was in sight.

'As a free citizen of Tomis and member of its council, I ask for a public vote', the ironmonger said. 'If we don't punish Publius Ovidius Naso, we must at least get rid of him. He has brought only trouble to our fair city.'

'Is this request in the name of justice?' the Librarian asked.

The Archon, the chief magistrate, who had thus far listened but not taken part in the discussion, stepped up to the podium. 'The request for a vote is fair', he said solemnly.

'If we vote Ovid out,' Plautus interjected, 'we oppose the Emperor's wish for him to be exiled here. It was Augustus himself who commanded that Ovid be sent to Tomis, and it is he alone who can call him back to Rome.'

'Who said we have to send him back to Rome?' the ironmonger said. 'Out of the city is enough.'

'We shall ask advice from the governor of Macedonia.' The Aedile looked about him for support, but the clients of the ironmonger had become vociferous and drowned him out with their shouts.

'Banish Ovid!'

'Exile the exile!'

'We want Ovid out of Tomis!'

'As does he!' the Librarian shouted. The assembly quietened. It was rare to hear the Librarian raise his voice. 'For him, we are a pain at the end of the world.'

'And what are we for you, Librarian?' the Archon asked.

The Librarian smiled without warmth. 'Tomis is the most wonderful city in the world. That is the only answer you will ever get out of me. Regardless, we should consider that what we think of as home, Ovid thinks of as an abominable place to live.'

The Archon thought for a moment. 'So I suppose', he said, 'that to banish Ovid from our city would not be a punishment for him.'

'Far from it', the Librarian replied, pleased that he had finally been listened to. 'It would be a blessing.'

'I see.' The Archon nodded. 'I see. That will not do.' He looked out over the assembly and addressed them as one. 'The request for a vote has been taken back.'

The hall filled with voices as the gathered councillors sought to reconcile what seemed to have happened – in short, nothing at all. Ovid would not be held accountable for the murder of the two Romans. The ironmonger attempted to make his dissent heard, but his laments were soon overpowered by those around him. It was time to turn to more urgent matters, such as the new taxes for slave traders using their port, which needed to be resolved before they could all return to their homes.

Seeing the matter was now closed, Plautus and the Librarian quietly made their way out of the hall. Taking sides hadn't been easy, but it had been much easier easier than remaining neutral.

Family Support

Plautus crossed the threshold of his doorway to find his wife, Dokia, her sister, Cynthia, and his servants gathered in the hall, waiting for him. No words were said, but the looks on their faces were enough to tell him of their relief that he had returned, that he had returned alive.

'That Ovid', Plautus said, sinking into his armchair, 'has brought me nothing but bad luck.'

Dokia raised her arms, palms upwards, and the servants recognised the signal to clear the room. Cynthia remained, unable to take her eyes off Plautus. 'Wine?' she asked him softly.

'We are fine, thank you, sister.' Dokia spoke for her husband. 'The one thing we need right now is to be left alone.'

Lowering her head in submission, Cynthia disappeared off into the darker recesses of the house.

'Have some mulsum', Dokia said once her sister had gone, reaching for the wine and honey that she knew had a calming effect on her husband, and handing it to him. As he gulped at the concoction, she dried the sweat from his forehead. 'So it went well', she said.

'Hardly.'

'You are back from the city council. For me, that means it went well.'

'Until the governor of Macedonia makes his decision. The

man is notoriously difficult to predict. Especially when it comes to how to deal with Rome.'

Dokia sighed wistfully. 'How I would love to leave Tomis. For Alexandria. Or Libya. Anywhere really, anywhere out of here.'

'What are you missing? I thought you felt at home here.'

Dokia stopped daubing his forehead and stood in silence for a moment. Plautus knew she was weighing up her answer carefully. 'When my people married me to you,' she finally said, 'I was promised things. I have never forgotten them.' She paused. 'Nor have I given them up.'

Had anyone else been present, Plautus would have admonished his wife for saying such things, but here in this room, alone with her, he felt only sympathy.

Dokia went on. 'At that time, you were the most resourceful officer on the Upper Danube. Our marriage sealed a peace attempt between the Romans and the Dacians, one of many. My people were given the chance to bet big. If the new province, Moesia Inferior, had been founded as planned by the governor of Macedonia, you would have been its military commander by now. And your wife, a Dacian princess...' Her voice trailed off. She refilled his cup of mulsum. 'Husband, it is not you by whom I feel betrayed. We share the same fate. We were both promised something, and we were both denied those promises. In my case, it was by my uncle, the king of the Dacians. For you, it was by that young Roman general at the Upper Danube.'

'Germanicus.' Even the name made Plautus wince.

'Germanicus', Dokia echoed. 'I never liked him. As each day passes, I resent him more. Do you know, I feel revenged a little by you killing those Romans.'

Plautus gazed up at his wife. Despite the passing of the years, her cheekbones had remained high and her skin young – the kind of woman the Greeks, no doubt, would have called a Hyperborean beauty. 'I must admit,' he said, 'I have taken some solace in the idea.'

'That Celt general, Vestalis, should be delighted with you. You have done what he asked.'

'My task is not complete yet.' Plautus spat on the floor in disgust. '*Task*,' he said. 'I am being treated like a jail-keeper. Right now my fortunes have not sunk *that* low.'

Dokia laughed aloud, and Plautus suspected that his wife might be a little intoxicated. 'A jail-keeper! You are the guardian of the key.' She composed herself. 'You must continue to keep Ovid safe. For both our sakes. Let me help you.'

'How?'

She smiled. 'I have my ways. I am more than one of those women who love nothing but perfumes and make-up.'

'I thought you liked them. Then what do you love?'

'You, my husband, of course. And our son. He too must leave this dreary city. The education he gets in Tomis does not prepare him for life.'

'He does well in school.'

'Everyone does well here.' Dokia sneered. 'But the boy has no ambition. He is up on the wasteland all the time, playing that stupid game all the children so love. *Romans and Barbarians*. His mind is only on how to become a military man. And do you really want him joining the army?' She laid a hand on her husband's chest and slowly began to work it beneath his tunic.

Plautus wasted no time in pulling his wife into the bedroom.

It had been a while since she had last allowed him inside her, and they clawed at each other with noisy exuberance. Cynthia, ear pressed against the wall of their room, bore it painfully, and, unable to resist, began to masturbate.

You Will Die Many Times

Tomis's forum was a joyous place. The bright sky made the colours sing and the people loud. Drunken sailors tumbled from the three merchant ships and swaggered across the streets, infusing the city with so much life that even Ovid could not resist the pulsating spectacle, provincial though it was. He wondered if, should he board one of the ships, it would take him as far as Greece. He had never had the courage to ask a captain to get him out of Tomis. *Perhaps I fear freedom*, he thought. He looked around him, picking out faces within the crowd. He knew who he was looking for: the Emperor Augustus coming to challenge him for the death of Lucius. His presence bordered on impossible, but ever since the Targelia Ovid had kept an eye out for that famous face.

A market woman, known for offering opinions no one asked for, caught hold of his left hand. He tried to pull himself free, but her grip was surprisingly strong, with all of her weight behind it. She opened his palm, folded it, and then began to chant, displaying her missing front teeth. Her breath slowed, and when she repeated her melodious murmur for the third time Ovid began to recognise the incantation. It was protective. She was guarding herself against what she had seen in his palm.

Intrigued by her chants, two of the woman's market neighbours peered over. Without asking, one reached out and unfolded Ovid's palm once more. She gasped and dropped his hand, that the other woman took up and held. 'That deserves double pay', she said.

'Old man.' The soothsayer stopped her incantations. 'Why are you scared to find out who you are?'

'Fine. Who am I?' Ovid said, handing her a coin. 'Here is silver. Much more than your usual copper. So skip the introductory riddles and tell me the truth.'

'There is so much truth. What truth do you want to know?'

'Am I going to become immortal?' This was the only thing of interest.

She began to laugh. 'There are many people in your life that you need badly.'

'I told you I didn't want riddles.'

'You told me you wanted truth. This is truth.'

'All right, but for the money I've given you, you can at least name them. Which people do I need?'

She tilted her head back and began to chant once more. 'Hear, sky, hear…'

Ovid lost patience. 'This is useless. Give me my coin back.'

The soothsayer looked back at him once more. 'There is a man in your life who needs you as much as you need him. A man who does not know fear. You must get hold of him.'

Vestalis, Ovid thought. *It has to be. That man has no concept whatsoever of fear.*

The soothsayer shook her head as if she had read his mind, and then began to crane her neck back again. Before she could launch into further incantations, Ovid interrupted her with a question.

'Will I ever be able to write anything major?'

'Your mind is clogged.' She paused and gazed deep into his eyes. 'You are approaching a turning point in your life.'

Everyone in Tomis knows that, Ovid thought. 'Will I die?'

'Many times. You will die many times.'

One of the other market women, who had been listening to the entire conversation, butted in. 'Tell him that the grove of trees will save his life and then let him go. He is a nuisance.'

'Mind your own business! He is scared of darkness', the soothsayer shouted, hitting her acquaintance with her sandals.

'The grove of trees?' Ovid said. Hadn't his housekeeper Argyris mentioned a grove of trees? Within them was the well down which he had suggested Ovid flee Tomis.

'I can't see him wanting to escape his misery', the other woman said. 'He doesn't know how to deal with youngsters. And if the children don't accept him, he can't do anything about it.'

'Sod off!' The sandals went on the attack once more.

'What is she talking about?' Ovid said, exasperated.

Batting away the other two women, the soothsayer took hold of both of Ovid's hands. 'You go home now', she said, her tone morphing from commanding to caring. 'She is waiting for you.'

'She? Who?' Ovid stood. What a waste of time this was. No one was waiting for him at home, no one except Argyris. He pulled himself away from the soothsayer and her two neighbours.

Walking back through the marketplace, a high-pitched voice caught his attention. He had heard it before. 'Be saluted, Roman! Three ladies would like to talk to you.'

Ovid stared down at the skinny figure before him. It was the boy from the baths. 'Ladies?'

'You will remember them, sir. We saw them together.' He was talking, Ovid realised, about those Thracian whores he had seen playing ball. There had been twelve of them. Why did three now want to speak with him?

'What is all this about?' Ovid asked.

'They want to be fucked by a true Roman. It might not make sense to you, but for them, coming from these barbarian lands, it is an accomplishment. It will be worth your while, I am sure.'

'Go!' came a voice from behind Ovid. He turned. It was the soothsayer. 'Go!' she repeated. 'Do not miss this chance!'

Somewhat overwhelmed by the instructions and imperatives, Ovid allowed the boy to take him by the hand and lead him through the streets to a narrow alleyway where few people passed. Three women waited for him there.

They were beautiful. Their hair – the colour, the shape of their buns – betrayed the signature style of Tomis's best-regarded hairdresser, and the daring folds of their robes revealed their individual nuances in subtle but arresting ways. Ovid's eyes settled on the one in the middle. It was she who had invited him to join their game in the gymnasium, she who had thrown the ball. She took a step forward.

'Sadly, we must leave this city soon,' she purred. 'Before we do, we would love to say goodbye to a hero.'

The boy grabbed excitedly at Ovid's elbow. 'Don't miss this occasion, sir!'

The prostitute giggled at his words and, as she did so, the sun came out. She took another step forward. The dappled white played across her face, turning her skin an almost translucent white, even whiter than Corinna's. Ovid stopped himself. He did not like the comparison. He pushed Corinna from his mind and focused on the woman before him. As she neared, he caught the scent of her cheap perfume. *She deserves a better fragrance*, he thought.

'So', the prostitute said. 'Will you permit us?'

'Permit you?' Ovid croaked, his throat dry.

'To say goodbye to you. In our own way.'

Lust coursed through him, so sharp it was painful. He wanted this woman. She spoke for all three. But where could he take them, where could he have them all to himself in this tiny, cramped city? The cubicles of the brothel were overrun with hungry ants and sometimes cockroaches, and he did not wish to repeat the shameful past experiences he had endured there. The two or three inns were out of the question too, unless he wanted to perform to spectators. Perhaps the locals would not be able to see through the thin walls, but they would certainly be able to listen to the party in all its detail, and this they would share for years to come with anyone willing to buy them a drink.

'Come,' he said, 'let me show you my house.'

He led the way through the forum, hoping that no one would accost him, hoping that he could make it home with these three wonders as quickly as possible. Lately he had become fearful of venereal diseases and had taken a long hiatus from having sex with prostitutes, but all that was suddenly of no consequence to him whatsoever. He was overcome with desire, and he liked it.

Along the way he passed the ointment shop, and stopped. It was just about to close for the afternoon break. He strode inside before the door could shut.

'The best you have!' he ordered.

Freedom in Lust

As Ovid arranged the girls into a perfect tableau, he allowed himself to take his time. He had always agreed with the sentiments of the Greek sculptors: that total nudity was less inviting than suggestive dressing. He wrapped a stola over the buttocks of the most voluptuous of the three women, who wriggled as though she liked it and made sure one heavy, superb breast plopped against his busy hand.

'He's not got it up yet!' She laughed in a way Ovid found both vile and vulgar. All three women looked at his flat tunic. This was taking too long and they were growing bored.

'Perhaps he was a hairdresser as well as a poet,' Ovid's favourite said, 'and doesn't do anything with women. Just takes men up the arse. It would explain the other day in the thermae.'

'Oh no', said the most voluptuous. 'What a stupid idea we had. He's just a clapped-out senile type. It'll take hours.'

'Don't worry', Ovid said. 'You will be paid all you are due. Now, you, raise your left arm… yes, like that, but higher…'

The prostitutes did not mind lassitude, their second natural state, but they did mind boredom. Perhaps he should try and hurry things along a little. He did not want them to become vicious. That would ruin the tableau.

Ovid turned two of them against each other so their breasts touched, then squashed them together.

'Ah, that's what he wants. Why didn't he say?' The two automatically began to kiss and touch each other, which Ovid put an immediate stop to.

'No,' he said. 'Stay still.'

'No? No?' There was that laugh again. Vile and vulgar. 'Perhaps he's just some sort of frustrated festival designer. All he wants is to stage tableaux.'

'Perhaps he's gay.'

'Perhaps? I'm sure of it. Look down there. Nothing at all. Not even a twitch.'

They were losing interest, he could tell. They sagged inwardly and continued to grumble to each other about his impotence. He did not bother to answer them, but instead opened the third girl's legs and dabbed the expensive oil over her genitals. She wriggled and gasped, pretending to enjoy it.

The other two, still pressed against one another, started to complain. They wanted wine or drugs or, better yet, both. They also wanted money to hold and music to keep them entertained. Most preferable of all, they wanted young and erect boys.

'He hasn't got a stalk on for us.'

'What can you expect? He's little more than someone's weak grandfather. They get soft at his age.'

'Only hard when it's feeding time.'

'Is that right, old man? Do you only rise for breakfast?' Whether to taunt him or to test the veracity of the theory, the voluptuous girl squeezed a nipple into his mouth. 'Like a big baby...' She reached a hand down and began to toy with his penis.

'How old is he?'

'I'd say seventy.'

'Judging by this saggy thing, he's even older. You should feel it!'

'Get used to it, girls, this is what is waiting for us in Rome. Clapped-out old ruins.'

Trying to maintain at least a semblance of his dignity, Ovid removed the prostitute's hand from his penis and folded his tunic over himself. 'I am fifty-six', he said, keeping his voice as calm and steady as possible.

'Let's not be so mean', his favourite commanded. 'Taunts and jibes excite only cruel men, and this poet is nothing of the sort.'

'That is true', another said. 'And if we do not get to work soon we will be here all night and will miss the taverns.'

Ovid suspected this was the real reason behind his favourite's encouragement. He did not reply and let them fall into what sounded like a well-rehearsed dialogue of arousal, one which would have sent wild even the feeblest of men. He remained quiet, and the conversation descended yet further into realms of filth he had barely thought possible, as they offered him every practice they knew.

They talked on, and he continued with his arrangements. He was almost there. The two pressed against each other had their hands exactly where he wanted them to be. All that remained was to bend the third forward so that her buttocks and genitals were on display, and then to direct her to pull aside each cheek. She did so and he dabbed on the oils, making her vagina glisten. This was it. The perfect tableau for lust. It could be no more inviting.

He stood back to look at the arrangement he had produced. It was glorious.

‘I see the poet is ready’, his favourite said, her gaze fixed on his erection.

He took a step forward, ready to plunge in, and stopped. A frozen wave washed through him, shrivelling his penis and leaving him numb. This was not perfect. He knew perfect, he knew it well, and this was far from it. ‘No’, he murmured, and then, louder: ‘No. No.’

‘For mercy’s sake, what is wrong now?’ the voluptuous one cried.

‘You are not Corinna’, Ovid said.

And then he turned and walked from the room. His *Art of Love* had served him for nothing.

Ships from the South

An Egyptian beauty with forty rowers, three masts and two decks arrived in the port. Since it brought with it the autumn preserves, it piqued the interest of all and did not need to wait on Tomis's quay to be unloaded. Even the laziest of the stevedores gave up their endless dice games and queued up to be hired, hoping to stuff their pockets with the precious herbs and rare seeds stored in the amphorae on board – amphorae which could be broken and made to look like an accident with ease.

To the side of the line of hopeful workers, Argyris the caretaker was deep in conversation with the ship's captain.

'Are you sure you want to stay in Tomis another winter?' the captain asked, handing over two expensive-looking leather cylinders.

Argyris shrugged at the question. He was more interested in the cylinders. 'How much do you want for these?'

The captain named his price.

'That, if you do not mind me saying so, is outrageous', the caretaker replied.

'Perhaps', the captain said. 'But it is known in every port east of Byzantium that in Tomis there is an Aedile who pays whatever one may ask for a letter addressed to his exiled Roman.'

Argyris rubbed his unshaven face. '*His* exiled Roman,

eh?' he said. 'How interesting. I also happen to take care of a Roman. Out of curiosity, would you take me and my Roman with you to Greece?'

The captain's eyes darkened. 'If your Roman and the Aedile's are one and the same, then it is too dangerous.' He handed Argyris the scroll. 'You can pay me later.'

Facing Fears

It was the flickering of the lamp that softly pulled Ovid into consciousness. How long his eyes had been open for, he had no idea, but that haze that blurs the boundary between sleep and waking had seemed to hold him for an eternity, and remnants of the dreamworld he had finally been wrested from still danced across his mind.

Ovid rubbed at his eyes and stared about him. The house was still. Too still. The women had left, but how long ago? An hour? A day? Maybe two? Argyris must have dealt with them. He produced only a hoarse rasp, audible to no one but himself. His tongue was dry and heavy in his mouth. His head pounded.

With great labour, Ovid pulled himself to his feet and shuffled to the nearest table, where, amongst the detritus, a single silver jug stood. He grabbed at it and feebly upended it into his mouth. A few drops of wine reached the back of his throat. It tasted awful. He needed more. Better yet, he needed the orange powder.

The curtain-door felt heavier than usual as he pulled it aside and stumbled into the atrium. There, the torn cushions and scattered wool were no competition for the enormous stain of red wine on the wall. Above it, he could make out a dent in the plaster where the jug had smashed, and below, on the floor, the ceramic shards glistening in the red puddle.

'Argyris!' Ovid called, clearing his throat to reveal a semblance of voice. 'Where are you?'

The answering silence reminded him of the truth: only the caretaker and the cook had remained. He needed to take on more servants. He should begin to rebuild his home. First, he would require cleaners. This devastation was too much to bear. Gods, how many nights had they rampaged to create such a mess? Only the altar was spared.

Ovid made his way through the atrium to the kitchen area to wash. Normally he would only clean himself in the dark and greasy room outside the kitchen during the long Tomitan winters, when the weather did not permit him to visit the public bath and he was forced to perform his ablutions here, close to the kitchen furnace – but, for now, it would serve. He needed to wash himself, and he had little inclination to step out into the busy streets.

As he poured water over his head – gasping when it splashed down his back – he heard a wail, followed by another, and then yet another. He dried himself off and looked into the kitchen to see Argyris, bowed over the supine body of a man in the far corner. 'Corrales,' he moaned. 'Oh, Corrales. What have they done to you?'

Ovid approached and, when the caretaker saw him, he lifted the dead man's head, displaying it to his master.

'My cook!' Ovid gasped. Corrales' face was frozen in a rictus of pain and fear, clear evidence that his passing had been protracted and terrible. His eyes bulged from their sockets and his tongue, swollen like an erect penis, poked out from the bloodied vomit that filled the cave of his mouth.

'Who killed you?' Argyris cried. 'Who poisoned you,

Corrales?' He hugged his friend's body, only to squeeze a stream of vomit from the dead man's throat that splashed across the floor. 'You were always too gluttonous, man. You could never abstain from tasting stuff that was not meant for you.'

Shocked, Ovid took two steps back. His head reeled and he felt his heart rate soar. 'What do you mean?' he asked.

'Look', Argyris shouted as the glow of a flame lit the curves of a small receptacle that appeared to have been tossed into the corner. 'The amphora.'

Ovid bent down to pick it up, then brought it to his nose and took a deep breath. It was the new wine that Spiros had offered him the other day: he would recognise that scent anywhere. Even the smell of it was beginning to make him sick. Did this mean that Antipater wanted to kill him? On whose order? Lucius would never have come at him with such a womanly tool of murder. Lucius had wanted to run Ovid through with his sword, had wanted to see his end, feel it, up close and certain. This was surely not his handiwork. But then who else was to blame? Spiros maybe? Or could it have been those three women, one or even all of them? The caretaker leapt to his feet and swatted the amphora from his hands. It crashed to the floor, spilling the remains of his medicine across the tiles.

'Poison', Argyris said, staring at Ovid. 'My friend has always been a very curious man. He paid for his curiosity with his life. And saved yours.'

'I... I...' Ovid stumbled backwards, fighting for words, fighting to make sense of any of it. How lucky he had been not to be killed by the substance he thought would better his life. Did this apply to the orange powder as well?

Ovid took a deep breath and gathered himself. Now he needed to deal with the corpse of his cook, the poor man. 'He will receive the attention all members of my household expect', he said. 'Go and fetch help, then move his body to the dining table in the atrium. I need a new table anyhow.'

The caretaker ran from the room, reappearing ten minutes later with two stevedores. Together, the three men gently lifted the cook's rigid body and carried it into the atrium, where they laid it upon the table and then took a few steps back.

'Let us say a prayer for him', Ovid said. 'Who was his favourite god?'

'Asklepius', Argyris replied.

Ovid recited the only prayer he knew, mentioning Asklepius whenever a god's name was required. He kept his voice low and took care not overdramatise the words. When he had finished he bowed his head, took one last look at the tortured face of his cook, and then walked out of the atrium and to his study.

Argyris followed him. Once the door was closed behind them, he held out a leather cylinder.

'What's that?' Ovid asked.

'A letter to you from Rome', the caretaker said, and then added: 'Uncensored.'

'Why', Ovid said, 'has it found itself with you and not me?' He looked carefully at Argyris. Was this man a spy? Perhaps he was being suspicious, but what man would not be given the events of the past week?

'The Aedile pays twenty-five dinars per letter.'

'What letter?'

'Any letter addressed to you coming from Rome.'

'Bastard.' Ovid nodded. 'Then perhaps a better question for

me to ask is why you have brought it to me and not to him?'

'Because you deserve better.'

Ovid took the leather cylinder from the caretaker, popped open the lid and pulled out the scroll. His eyes fogged as he recognised his wife's handwriting.

Fabia's messages were always short and unsophisticated, and this one was no different, its sentences succinct and to the point. Augustus was terminally ill. His end was visibly near. Tiberius would become the next emperor of Rome. The city was transforming, and all within it dreaded the metamorphosis.

And then, at the very end of the letter, came one sentence that Ovid could not tear his eyes from. He read it once, and then again, and then over and over until the syntax bore into his very soul. Fabius Maximus had committed suicide. His dear friend. His confidant. His patron. Gone. The death of his friends was a fact of life Ovid was always unwilling to accept, until he was forced to. There was no doubt that Maximus' death was related to Augustus' anger in one way or another. Perhaps the Emperor had found out about the conspiracy of Germanicus' generals – whom Maximus supported. Whatever had happened, Maximus was now gone, while he, Ovid, lived.

Innocence and Energy

The light changed from dark blue to violet and, one by one, the ironmonger's cocks began to crow, heralding the dawn. Ovid had not slept. Too many deaths, and all at once. All night, his head had raged with the angry sorrow of grief as he mourned the loss of Fabius Maximus. Midway through the night, resigning himself to the fact that this particular bout of insomnia was incurable, he had risen from his bed, dressed warmly, eaten a hunk of dry bread, and then stepped out into the darkness.

His wanders had brought him to the cliff. He considered sitting on the edge, but doubted the soil would hold him. And so instead he stood and watched as the sky lightened and the sun rose. His hands trembled at his sides. His wet eyes blinked at the calm sea.

A chatter of voices brought him to his senses, and, looking to his left, he saw the same group of children who had surrounded him and Lucius when that forbidding dagger had hung between them. It was no exaggeration to say that they had saved his life. He smiled and waved at them, and, interpreting it as an invitation, they ran towards him calling his name. Amongst the boys were one or two girls, who looked as swarthy and fearless as their male friends. The lankiest reached Ovid's side first.

'Tell us how you managed to kill the Roman,' she demanded with a piercing look.

'Tomorrow is his funeral', one of the smaller boys said.

'My father promised to take me along', shouted another.

'Mine too.'

'We have never seen a dead Roman before.'

'We never saw a living Roman before you came along', the lanky girl said.

By now they had encircled Ovid. He liked children – as long as they were not his – and smiled as their queries and assertions overlapped each other.

'Are all Romans as courageous as you?'

'Do you even know fear?'

Ovid laughed. 'That I know well.'

'Do you know what *I* hate?' the lanky girl said, and the others shushed, eager to find out. She was a dominant figure in this little band, and Ovid admired her for it. 'I hate school. Especially rhetoric. Romans might need to learn it, but we Greeks learn from our mothers how to twist words.'

Accord rippled through the group. Eloquence was not for them.

'Don't be so sure', Ovid chided. 'There is a misery that comes with the inability to express yourself.' He repeated the sentence in Greek in case he had not been understood, and then regretted being so didactic when he was met with silence. He changed the subject. 'But what about athletics? All children love that. Doesn't it make school worth it?'

The lanky girl blinked her thick lashes. 'His father', she said, pointing at one of the smaller boys, 'refused to approve a pay rise for the teachers this year, so they've stopped bothering with athletics. They only do the minimum.'

'It was the city council's decision!' the small boy squawked.

'And your father is the Archon this year!' He pushed his tongue out at the girl, and when the rest laughed at her, Ovid was pleased to see that she laughed too. He felt a swell of optimism from these children, and was grateful for it. They helped take his mind off Maximus.

'What year are we in?' Ovid asked.

There was a stir or surprise. Why was he asking them this?

'Come on. What year are we in?'

'The first year after', said one of the boys.

'After what?' Ovid asked.

'After the last Olympiad.'

'And how many Olympiads have there been?'

Silence. Realising the question had been too difficult, Ovid answered for them.

'There have been one hundred and ninety-seven, including last year's. But do you know this next question? Who was the victor in the stadium race?'

A hand shot up, and all faces turned in eager suspense towards a fat boy with scruffy hair. 'Demostenes?' he said.

The lanky girl erupted into giggles. 'He's a famous trumpeter!' she shouted, and all laughed, including the fat boy. 'My father wants me to play trumpet like him, but I don't', she continued.

'Ask us more questions!' another girl said, overcoming her shyness.

'Okay.' Ovid pretended to think while he scratched his head. 'How long is a stadium?'

'Much too long', the fat boy said, but nobody laughed, and, overcome with awkwardness, he stared at the ground.

'I won't give you the answer so easily. I'm going to show you how long a stadium is. Try and keep up with me and count my steps and let's see who gets it right.'

Enlivened by the game, the children followed Ovid with their eyes glued to his feet as he stomped forward, away from the cliff edge.

'One hundred and sixty paces!' the lanky girl shouted when he came to a stop and drew a line in the dust with his sandal.

'Correct', he announced, and the children applauded while she beamed. 'Do you see this line? The first to run from here to the cliff and back again will win a wreath. Are you ready? Go!'

As one, the children sped off, running at full pelt towards the cliff, kicking up dust behind them that settled in Ovid's mouth and made him cough. He did not mind so much. Spending time with these children, absorbing their innocence and energy, was a tonic. Two boys ran side by side, their cheeks puffing as they gathered all their reserves to outrun each other. Ovid was not surprised when the taller of the two crossed the line first.

'My mother said I am no good at running.' The boy who had come in second place was furious with himself.

'How can you say that when you almost won?' Ovid consoled him. 'That did not look like defeat to me.'

'Good. Because I do not fear defeat.'

'Are you trying to convince me or yourself?' Ovid twisted a wreath from the branch of a nearby shrub and bestowed it upon the winner. All the other children had returned by now and those who were not jealous clapped their friend.

'Let's run one more time!'

'Yeeeah!'

Before he could stop them, the children were tearing off

once more, back towards the cliffs. The winner charged after them, his wreath flying off his head. He did not stop to pick it up. Perhaps he had not even noticed. It made Ovid laugh out loud. In the past he might have wished he had a similar capacity to live in the moment. Now, he was simply grateful to live.

Farewell to a Son

The funeral of Lucius took place on a fresh and blustery day. Ovid did not know how many people would attend, but he expected a sizeable number – appearances made in the name of curiosity rather than mourning. The chief magistrate had been surprised when Ovid volunteered to take on all the costs and, to assuage his guilt as much as possible, even contributed towards the building of the aqueduct.

With the day still young, he clicked his way across the large paving stones of the Decumanus towards the promontory, and two crossings before the temple of Fortune he entered the quarter of the wealthy. He had been offered a house there and he had refused. It was not that he didn't want to live side by side with the local elite, but simply that he believed a pardon more likely if he kept his dwellings humble. The extravagant house earmarked for him had been given shortly afterwards to a wealthy newcomer: the present Aedile. Now it served as the interim resting place for the young Roman's body. In front of the house was displayed the funerary wreath, and two lictors – the Aedile's bodyguards – stood by the entrance. The door, framed by an Ionic portico, was open, and Ovid crossed the threshold without hesitation.

A long hallway filled with the scent of melted wax and burning incense led into the belly of the house, and at its end a gold-plated statue of Augustus stood proudly in an alcove.

Ovid did not look at it as he walked through the adjacent double doors and entered a large room, empty save for the corpse, lying on its back, surrounded by flowers and candles. Ovid pulled one of the many chairs lined up along the walls close to the young man who had come all the way from Rome to murder him, and to find his own death.

He stared down at the lifeless face, so serene and peaceful – lovable, even – beneath the wax veil that had been draped over the body. It reminded Ovid of the only other time he had been allowed to watch this boy, many years ago, back when Corinna had accepted, not spurned, his help. There she was, embedded deep in her son's face: his eyes her eyes, his mouth her mouth. He could see her now so clearly, the way she cried, the way she smiled. Overcome with a yearning to touch that face, Ovid bent over the body, close enough to embrace it, and brushed one light finger across the sleek cheek. A rush of memories surged through him at the contact, and he gave himself over to them.

There was Corinna, in a light green gown, dancing her way towards him. He could see her perfectly, those dark eyes so alive, the joy that trembled within her at the announcement she was desperate to make. 'I am pregnant!' The words had not been spoken but laughed, tinkling with delight.

'Is it mine?' Ovid had asked her. He had regretted the question ever since.

Corinna had not answered him. She had merely smiled. A smile which could have meant anything.

'It can't be *his*!' Ovid had shouted – meaning, of course, Augustus.

Again, Corinna had not answered, had kept the mystery

of her child's father to herself, not just for the pregnancy but beyond, after Lucius had been born and then into his childhood. Only once did she make any allusion to it in Ovid's presence, when the boy was one year old, and in a jealous outburst she had icily told Ovid: 'I am nothing more than a courtesan for you and Augustus. But the senator you call Ibis does not treat me with such disdain. He has married me and recognised my son as his. *He* is the father.'

He might as well have been, for all efforts Ovid had made to win the boy's friendship had been in vain – the child had treated him with as much hostility as had Ibis, if not more.

Another memory began to haunt him. From before Corinna's pregnancy. In Fabius Maximus' villa outside Rome he had read from his not yet published verses of the *Remedia Amoris*. The hall had been full of friends, foes and spies, none of whom was there to hear about love – rather, to learn how far Ovid had dared to tease Augustus, and how subtly he had cared to code his attacks on the moral rules of Rome. He had stood at the podium, preparing his scrolls, when the Empress Livia, Marcia – Maximus' wife and Livia's confidante – and other well-known ladies had taken their places in the front row directly before him. The distinct scent of a perfume made him shiver, and he did not need to raise his eyes to know that amongst Livia's retinue was Corinna, to whom he had dedicated his poems. Ovid became nervous. The Empress had never done anything devoid of purpose. Not in public, at least. By including a courtesan in her entourage, she wanted to shock. To provoke.

'Naso!' Livia called out loud enough for all the audience to hear. 'Let us all see what your ideal woman looks like. Maybe we will finally comprehend what you mean by love.'

'Augusta,' Ovid had replied, 'these poems are primarily addressed to men. They also should be taught how to love, and how to behave with their beloved woman.' He remembered how he had launched into his recital, and how quickly he had captivated his audience: controlling their feelings, toying with their emotions, and above all rousing their entire beings – body and mind – at will. If he had played the lute they would have followed him like the beasts had followed Orpheus into the Other World – and back again. His message had been clear: Rome was changing, and men must change too. Of course he had to mention Apollo, Augustus' patron, but everyone understood that Rome's transformation was thanks to Eros.

Sadly he had not been able to reach the end of his recitation. Unimpressed, a page had tiptoed over to Livia's side, bowed, and whispered something into her ear. The Empress stood and waved at Ovid to stop. 'Give them to me', she said, pointing at the scrolls. 'All of them.'

'But they are unfinished', Ovid protested.

'You need to learn to let go, poet', Livia warned.

Ovid stood stock-still, perplexed. *Let go of what?* He was about to voice his confusion when the page, who had retreated to the doorway, announced the arrival of the Emperor.

'Augustus!' the page called out.

Ovid felt sure he heard Livia mutter: 'Idiot.'

Followed by a dozen friends, the Emperor stormed into the hall, stopping at the podium beside Ovid. 'I have been told this is the place where the art of love is celebrated.' His voice dripped with contempt. 'But where is the music? Where are the dancers?'

Livia stood. 'Dear husband, Publius Ovidius has just

finished his recital from his *Remedia Amoris*. Would you excuse my friends and me, please?'

Augustus did not answer his wife. Instead, he cast his eyes across her entourage, studying each individual in turn with his predatory gaze. He settled on Corinna. 'You I don't know', he said.

Instead of looking helpless or confused, Corinna held the Emperor's stare with assured confidence.

'Dear husband.' Livia's voice was honey-sweet and sticky. 'This is Corinna, to whom Ovid has addressed his poems. It was I who invited her. I hoped our matrons might see that our poet's art of love exists for all the women of Rome.'

Augustus smiled at Corinna, and Ovid was dismayed to see how she smiled back. She was enjoying the attention. She was feeding off it.

'Publius Ovidius', the Emperor said, still looking at Corinna. 'Teach us the way of love.'

Ovid glanced at Maximus, and then struck an uncharacteristically modest tone. 'I force no one to learn from my wit. I am merely the channel through which the muses send to this world their knowledge about love. Just like Apollo does when he heals.' His voice had begun to tremble, but it remained loud enough for the audience to hear, and to pale in response. Apollo was Augustus' protector, and the Emperor was supposed to know how the god communicated. Ovid, it seemed, was calling that into question. It was a dangerous assertion to make. Blasphemous, even. Members of the audience might have gasped had they not feared reprisal.

That was the afternoon when Ovid's relationship with Augustus changed for the worse forever. But he became Rome's darling. From then on, whenever he lacked a decent subject for a quick success he would write ambiguous verses about the conflict between art and nature, between restrained pleasure and sophisticated lust. The conflict between Apollo and Dionysus he did not even need to address. His poems aired Rome's frustration with Augustus, who, driven by raw power and earthly pleasure, contradicted all that he preached. His audience saw in their poet's rhetoric that the Emperor had chosen in Apollo the wrong patron, and that now he was stuck with him.

It was also the afternoon when Corinna had flirted with Augustus, displaying her skills, her body, her love of naughtiness, giving the Emperor what he yearned for – her youth – in front of everybody.

You need to learn to let go, poet, Livia had told him. Now, stood here, leaning over the dead body of Lucius laid out upon the bier, those same words echoed around his mind. Perhaps he still needed to let go, to let go of it all, his hope for a pardon, his hope for freedom, for a return to Rome, his hope for anything. Let go. Let it all go.

Behind him, a door quietly opened. He turned to find the Aedile approaching.

'Nobody knows how you escaped death, Naso,' he said, 'but that you did. You are as lucky in life as you are at backgammon. I can only repeat myself. You must be what Tomitans have suspected you of being from the very beginning. A magician.'

Ovid sensed a note of levity in the Aedile's voice, but he would not smile in response. He was grieving, after all. He did not tell the Aedile that, back in Sulmo, people along the valley regarded his family as magicians. 'Would you have preferred to see me in this dead man's place?' he said instead.

The Aedile stopped beside the body and took a long and thoughtful look at it before answering. 'As magistrate of Tomis,' he eventually said, 'my answer is *yes*. This Roman, the son of a senator, could perhaps have changed the somewhat gloomy perception of our city – the same gloomy perception which you have so masterfully perpetuated in your poetry. For we have grown tired of that perception, you know. So very tired. How nice it would be for Rome to think of us as something other than a shabby and derelict garrison town filled with illiterates and camp-followers.'

'I am a poet, not a chronicler,' Ovid said, taking care not to raise his voice. 'Though I do not expect you to understand the difference.'

The Aedile laughed. 'I must suspend my disbelief enough to read your poems. Do not make me suspend it yet further.'

Ovid was growing tired of the conversation. He changed the subject. 'Where did you get such skilled embalmers?' he asked, nodding down at the serene face of Lucius.

'Why, would you like to book them for yourself? They accept advance payments.'

A small boy, not unfamiliar, entered the room.

'My son,' the Aedile said, introducing the child. 'Jason.'

Jason whistled a tuneless greeting through his teeth. 'Hello, Sir Bird.'

'Sir what?' Ovid said.

'We call you Sir Bird because we could never be sure whether or not you would jump from the cliff. Now we know you wouldn't. Maybe we should start calling you Sir Stadium.' He turned to his father. 'He made us race each other.'

Ovid recognised him at last – the skinny boy who had

squawked at the lanky girl up on the cliff after she accused his father of denying the teachers their pay rise. So this was who she had been talking about.

'Behave yourself', the Aedile snapped, and his son scurried from the room. He turned back to Ovid, produced a ring from his pocket, and, with sudden deference, said: 'One of the embalmers gave me this. It is his. I wonder if I should send it together with the ashes to Rome.'

'Why ask me?'

'You knew him, didn't you? You knew him well?'

Ovid sighed. To agree would do no harm. 'Yes', he said. 'Better than any of us would have liked.' He wanted to say more, that this dead man was his only true opponent for Corinna's love that had ever existed, but he stopped himself. Such an admission would reap no favours.

The Aedile handed Ovid the ring. 'Let me give you some advice', he said, the deference still present in his voice, accompanied by a glimmer of kindness. 'Start packing. With or without a pardon, you must go. In Tomis people are superstitious. And victims are loved as little as aggressors.'

Ovid nodded. Victims, aggressors; Tomis, Rome; pardon, execution – what was the difference between any of them? Without another word, he performed a short farewell bow, and found his way out of the house unescorted.

Wine, the Reliable Friend

When the invitation came for dinner at Plautus' house Ovid accepted with a mixture of trepidation and relief – the former at the prospect of dull company; the latter at the knowledge that there would, at least, be good wine.

The Commander's dwelling represented more than simple wealth. It was a real domus, one in which the authority of the paterfamilias was omnipresent, even in his absence. Along the atrium walls busts of familiar yet unknown men – Greek copies of famous faces, Ovid realised – gave the place the heavy atmosphere of the newly rich.

Dokia, the lady of the house, appeared by his side, laughing softly. 'Isn't our fake ancestor gallery impressive?'

Self-deprecating humour deserved to be rewarded. Ovid smiled as he turned to face her, ready to reply with something suitably witty but inoffensive, when a wave of her stifling perfume cut him short. Her large, round brown eyes spotted his hesitation and seemed to interpret his silence correctly, for she excused herself, and when she returned moments later she had changed the scent. He found himself somewhat in awe of her perceptiveness. Not only could she organise a Roman home, but she also knew how to read men: two qualities which served any woman well in life.

'This is an interesting piece', Ovid said, pointing at a simple statue sculpted from clay, the likes of which he had not seen before.

'It is from my birthplace, and is not one of my husband's favourites. I am Gaete, from the mountains north of the Danube. Dacian. Uneducated Romans call my kind barbarians, but our kingdom is as old as Rome, if not older. And our language resembles primitive Latin, as you might have learned by now.'

Ovid enjoyed listening to her talk. She had a silky tone to her voice which was alluring. He began to wonder how her curled hair would feel on his chest, tried to guess the size of her breasts and the width of their areolae.

'Dokia!' Plautus strode into the room. 'Please do not bore our guest.'

'He is not bored.' She smiled with a self-confidence Ovid coveted.

'He is only being polite.' Plautus' reply was practised. 'Can't you see that?'

'Not at all', Ovid said. 'I have been learning about the Gaete. A fascinating people. Tell me' – he turned to face Dokia – 'is it right that the Gaete believe themselves to be immortal?'

The Commander let out a loud groan, but the delight on Dokia's face was enough to tell Ovid that he had chosen the right side in this particular marital dispute.

'Doesn't everyone?' she said. 'Romans, Greeks, the Gaete – whether we admit it or not, we all like to think of ourselves as immortal.'

'Immortality guarantees a future', Ovid said. 'That is why we obsess over the idea so much.'

'Indeed, but I have always been more interested in the past than the future', Dokia said.

'So tell me about the past.'

'Another interminable history lesson', Plautus muttered.

His wife ignored him. 'The Gaete originally came from the far north. That is why we are so hardy. After our displacement, we followed the constellation of the Great Bear. It took us south, where we settled in the Carpathian Mountains.'

'Around the new Hyperborean pole?' Ovid realised he was keen to impress her with his own knowledge.

'We call the sacred mountain Kogaion,' Dokia said, 'or simply Om.'

'There is only one way I can get through this,' Plautus said, his voice loaded with cynicism. 'And that is wine.'

Ovid looked at the Commander, remembering the energy his father used to waste on other ignorant Roman officers stationed around Sulmo. Time and time again he had attempted to explain to them their proud Paeligni history, and not once had a single one of them been interested. Romans, no matter their birth, cared only about Rome, and Plautus was no different. Nevertheless, he had the wine, and if there was one thing Ovid wanted more than to trace the soft curves of Dokia's body with his fingers it was that. Plautus thrust a cup into his hand, and with the action his wife fell silent. She seemed to understand that Ovid's affection for her had just been overridden.

'So,' Plautus said, 'who was the Roman?'

'I wonder myself who he really was,' Ovid replied.

'Do you know at least why he came after you?'

Ovid emptied his cup in one long draught and then held it out to be refilled. 'Oedipus,' he muttered.

'What's that?'

'You know the legend. Boys secretly desire to kill their fathers.' Immediately he regretted his words. One cup of wine and he had already said too much.

'I hope you're wrong', Dokia said. 'My son would never harbour such terrible thoughts.'

'Him I cannot speak for', Ovid said.

'I should like you to meet him.' Dokia turned to the servant who held the jug of wine. She took it from him and instructed him to find her boy. As he left the room she topped up Ovid's cup, but not, he noticed, her husband's. Ovid drank some more. It was good wine. He could feel it melt down his throat, feel it warm him from the heart outwards. He should be careful what he said next. Probably it would be slurred.

The servant reappeared, followed by the boy, and, at his side, Dokia's sister, Cynthia, who – stiff and contained – greeted him with a half-smile.

'My husband would never ask you any favour', Dokia said, 'but our son needs help. Would you teach him rhetoric over the summer? I am worried about his education.' Her voice, caressing and insistent, plied him with unspoken compliments, while her eyes, half-open, watched for his answer.

Ovid took another gulp of wine while he formulated his reply, choosing his words carefully so as not to stumble over them when they came, but by the time he was ready to give his answer the boy had taken offence. 'I don't want you either!' he shouted at Ovid before running out of the room.

'I will go after him', Cynthia said. Ovid watched her leave, admiring her non-challenging tranquillity.

Dokia laughed once Cynthia had departed the room. 'You like her', she said.

'Her gaze reminds me of my grandmother', Ovid replied. What he did not say was that his grandmother had been the only person who had never disappointed him.

An Offer One Can Only Refuse

The next morning, face up on his bed, Ovid felt his body cast in lead. The sensation was familiar, and he knew he could keep the anxiety at bay so long as he remained immobile. Aches pulsated from his head down his neck and along his back, bringing with them a flood of shame. He had been drunk. Again.

He lifted his head an inch. A small amphora had been thoughtfully placed within reach, and he grasped greedily at it. The effort of remembering needed to be supported by more wine.

'Light', Ovid croaked. 'Bring more light.'

No one appeared, and as the shame morphed into anger on the tide of fresh wine, he pulled himself from his bed. His feet were swollen in the unlashed sandals, and vapours of sweat emerged through the collar of his tunic. He peered at the water clock – one of the many useless presents he had received over the years from well-intentioned friends – to see that it showed noon. That meant nothing. It always gave the same reading.

Argyris entered the room with a bucket of steaming water.

'I called for light,' Ovid snapped, 'not a bath.'

The caretaker placed the bucket on the floor. 'You have unannounced visitors, sir.'

'What? Now? Throw them out!'

'I will get you a fresh tunic.'

'Get me something for my headache instead. And then tell my visitors to go away.'

Argyris stuck out his nose. 'She does not mind waiting. There is time for a wash.' He left the room, and, grumbling, Ovid began to clean himself. When the caretaker reappeared with a tunic, he begrudgingly put it on before following him out into the atrium.

There, in the middle of the room, stood Dokia. 'Please excuse the invasion', she said.

Ovid approached her, noticing the Egyptian lavender she wore. A vast improvement on her previous scent.

'You left rather abruptly last night', she continued.

'I was...' – he did not want to say *drunk* – '... tired.'

'So we thought we would pay you a visit now.'

'We?'

Cynthia appeared from behind a curtain-door, dragging alongside her a ten-year-old boy. Ovid recognised him but was not entirely sure why. Hadn't Dokia asked him something last night? Something related to this boy?

'My son, Carp', Dokia said. 'He was quite taken by you last night.'

'No, I wasn't', Carp sulked, staring at the floor.

Now Ovid remembered. Dokia had requested that he tutor this boy, that he teach him the fundaments of rhetoric. 'Then what brings you to my house, young rebel?'

'Rebel? Him?' Dokia smirked. 'I wish.'

Carp looked at her with open disdain. 'My mother brought me here', he said.

'No,' Cynthia corrected him, 'your bad marks at school brought you here.'

'My husband and I are so grateful that you agreed to tutor him', Dokia said.

So he *had* assented to her request? Ovid could not remember. But that did not mean it had not happened. Far from it. Wine made him agreeable, and then it made him forget all about it. 'I've never taught anybody anything', he said.

'Nonsense. We learn from your poems every day.'

The flattery was blatant, but it was also working. Ovid let his gaze travel briefly down to Dokia's jutting breasts. He was powerfully attracted to this woman, and if she wanted to stroke his ego then he would not stop her.

'Let me sweeten the deal', she continued. 'You may also keep my sister. She runs a household well. Something I suspect you are in need of.'

I would rather keep you, Ovid thought as she teasingly rearranged the folds of her robe. 'I suppose', he said, 'that we can try.'

Dokia flashed a brilliant smile and held out her hand – an accord and a farewell combined in one gesture. Ovid took it, and then watched as Argyris led her from the room, leaving Cynthia and Carp standing side by side as if awaiting instruction. The latter took a step forward and adopted a proud stance. 'You don't want me as a pupil', he said.

'Carp!' Cynthia admonished.

'It's true! Look at him! He's just doing what my mother tells him. Like everyone.'

'That's not true. I'm here for you, aren't I?' Cynthia protested.

Carp looked at his aunt with pity. 'You're only here because Mother doesn't want you in the house anymore.'

'Perhaps the first thing I should teach you', Ovid said, 'is politeness.'

Carp blushed, but maintained his stance. 'I'm going outside to play,' he said. 'I'll come back later. You can tell my parents we had our first lesson, if you like. I don't care. Sir Bird.' Before Ovid could protest, he fled the room.

'A wilful boy,' Ovid said as he watched Cynthia begin to walk around the room, running her hand along walls and over furniture. 'But he'll come round, I'm sure.'

'Don't blame him,' Cynthia said, a dreaminess to her voice. 'This is a strange house for him. He does not feel comfortable.'

'So I must teach him *and* make him comfortable?'

Cynthia smiled – a beguiling smile, laced with a soft but uneasy charm – and then left the room. Only Argyris remained.

'Was that what I was woken for?' Ovid said. 'One command and two desertions?'

'Give the boy time,' the caretaker replied. 'He will come around.'

'Time. That is one thing I have plenty of in this godforsaken town.' He picked up his cup, downed what wine remained inside, and then refilled it from a nearby jug which Argyris had artfully placed while Dokia flirted him into submission. 'Time and wine. What else of worth is there in Tomis?'

The caretaker excused himself. Ovid could not blame him. There was no fun to be had in watching an old man grow drunk. Perhaps one day he should relieve Argyris of his duties, and make of him instead a drinking companion. No, that would never do. The caretaker would surely get a taste for it, and all work would soon fall by the wayside. There was only room enough for one old soak in this house.

Ovid finished his cup and moved back to the jug, now half-full. When his days began in this fashion they tended to follow just one direction: a slow and ambling route towards oblivion. It did not bother him. Better that than the terrible anxiety and fear that the wine kept at bay. He poured another cup and was about to make his way to the kitchen for more when a skein of smoke drifted into the atrium and caught his attention. He looked out the door to the garden. There, from the narrow windows of the servants' quarters on the first floor, the thin white smoke belched out into the open air.

Seized by panic, Ovid rushed out of the atrium and towards the source of the smoke. His thoughts went straight to Carp – the ungrateful little toad had set his house on fire! As he climbed the stairs, the smoke became stifling, the odours of incense and burning rubbish turning his stomach. He plunged through the thin linen curtains which separated each cubicle from the next, his head swimming with exertion and asphyxiation. Finally he found it: the fire, burning in the middle of the room; and Cynthia, her eyes red from the smoke, crumbling incense over the flames.

'What are you doing?' Ovid cried.

'Join me', she said, holding out her hand.

He tore down the curtain-door and began to beat at the flames.

'No!' Cynthia protested. 'You will put it out.'

'What do you think I am trying to do?' He had killed the fire at its edges, but its heart still burned with a fierce intensity.

'But the spells must be fumigated.'

'Stop this nonsense!'

'I would never let Carp in a house soaked by spells.'

Ovid ran into the corridor, returning with a jug of water,

which he threw over the fire. White choking vapours filled the room.

Cynthia let out a thin moan.

Ovid wheeled on her, red-faced and panting. 'Get out of my house', he hissed. But she did not move, and it was he who left the room first.

Out in the garden, Argyris and Carp watched. Ovid stormed towards them. Another man stood behind Carp. Ovid recognised him immediately – it was Scorillo, the beggar from the library, the scapegoat from the Targelia festival.

'Now what is *he* doing here?' Ovid cried, holding his hands up to his head and massaging his temples. Who else was due to arrive? Plautus? The Aedile? Augustus himself?

'Dokia sent him here', Argyris said, and pointed at the travelling bag Scorillo carried. 'With that.'

'So I am to house three people? Why not four, five, a dozen? Why not a whole family?'

'Scorillo *is* family.' Cynthia had appeared behind him, her clothes bedraggled and reeking of smoke. 'He is my and Dokia's elder brother. And he has brought my belongings. You want me to keep your household, don't you?'

Ovid felt the world around him begin to spin. It was all too much, this sudden influx of visitors, all of whom seemed to be related and all of whom seemed to want to live in his house and demand his time and energy and slowly kill him like the parasites they were. He could cope with it all no longer. He had had enough. 'Get out', he said. 'All of you. The boy. The aunt. The elder brother. You are not welcome here.'

Scorillo held up his hands. 'Do not be so hasty, old man', he said. 'I will go. That will suffice. But let her stay. Please.' He pointed at Cynthia. 'If you want to change, she stays.' He smiled at Ovid, and suddenly Ovid could see the resemblance between him and Dokia, between them all. 'And change you must', he said, before striding out of the garden.

Provincial Politics

Spiros, who had changed his hairstyle and the way he dressed since Ovid set him free, wiped at the pristine bronze statue in the Aedile's office with the sleeve of his tunic. 'I wonder if Augustus resembles this object.'

The Aedile did not reply, but stared into Spiros' eyes.

'What?'

'You shaved today. I like that.'

Spiros ran his hand over his smooth chin. 'I didn't do it for you.'

The Aedile laughed. 'Of course you didn't. Everything you do is for you and you alone. As you are so often at pains to remind me. But I have no spirit for this particular discussion today. I am more concerned with Plautus' plans.'

'What plans?'

'That is precisely my question. What are his plans? First, he orders Antipater to keep Ovid alive. Now, he allows his demanding wife to dispose of her sister in Ovid's house. Why do they want Ovid to tutor their imbecile son?'

'I don't have the answers. I am a free citizen without the money to embark on the next boat to Greece.'

'Then what do I pay you for?' Spittle flew from the Aedile's mouth.

'You pay to fuck me. Everything else is a bonus.'

'And what a bonus it is.' The Aedile turned to look out of the window. 'Something is going on with that Scorillo fellow too. I don't trust him.'

'I hear he is Plautus' wife's brother.'

'Yes, I hear the same. That does not concern me so much. What worries me is how close he is to the Librarian. I am sure they are plotting something.'

Spiros shrugged. 'Why don't you ask them?'

'You are superbly useless.' The Aedile began to run his hand through his lover's hair.

Spiros placed his own hand over the Aedile's. 'This is all dirt', he said gently. 'You are better off staying out of it.'

'You are, of course, probably right. But I want what I want.'

'And what is that?'

'I need to know what is happening in my city. With Ovid, with Plautus, with Scorillo, the Librarian, Antipater – with all of them. You get back into Ovid's house where you can spy on him and I will help you get a passage on a ship to Greece.'

Spiros smiled, for he wanted that more than anything. 'Return? As what? Nobody wants me there.'

'Build up a story. It must be convincing. And heart-breaking.'

Recasting the Battle of the Gods

Cynthia had immersed herself in a fury of cleaning and was creating such a commotion as she scoured the house that Ovid knew if he was to get any writing done it would have to be elsewhere. Gathering his belongings and not bothering to say farewell to his new… what even was she? Maid? Servant? Ward?… he made his way to the library.

The windows were shuttered and the entrance barred from the outside, but the library boy let Ovid in through the back door, explaining that the Librarian was away at his country villa.

'I retreat here and he retreats there', Ovid muttered. 'I know who is the luckier.'

He made his way down the hall toward his favourite spot – an alcove that basked in sunlight for most of the morning – only to find it occupied by Scorillo. 'You', he said, 'seem to be everywhere these days.'

Scorillo smiled. 'This alcove is conducive to work.'

'I know. It is my favourite. You have intruded.'

'Is this not a public place?' Scorillo looked around himself with exaggerated swings of his head.

'As far as I know scapegoats are banned from public places.'

'This custom doesn't apply in Tomis.'

'No wonder the city is sick.'

'Tomis has only itself to blame for that.' Scorillo stood,

stretching his arms behind his back so that audible pops and cracks sounded from his spine. 'I would like to thank you for keeping my sister.'

'I had little choice in the matter.'

'And yet you have not kicked her out.'

'I doubt she would concord even if I did. She is in my house now. Cleaning. Making a mess as she does so.'

'She is making improvements, in her own way. You will feel better for her presence in the end.'

'Do you know what would make me feel better? Orange powder. I ran out of it. Can you provide some?'

'No. That particular powder from the good doctor Antipater is poison. What you need is far simpler.' Scorillo picked up the lute which lay beside his feet on the floor and began to pluck a gentle melody, a simple looping tune which rose and rose in an irresistible crescendo until it filled the room. 'You see?' he said once the tune reached its conclusion. 'Your heart rate has dropped, hasn't it? And your anxiety levels with it. This is the power of music.'

Despite himself, Ovid was impressed. 'You play well', he admitted. 'I cannot deny that it has a soothing effect.'

'Music has far more power than Antipater's drugs. So too does poetry. Your words soothe others, much like music.' Scorillo began to gather his things from the desk. 'I presume that is why you are here? To write? Then do not let me get in your way. You have important work to do.' Without a further word, he departed from the alcove and disappeared.

The library boy hovered at Ovid's elbow. 'Bring more light', he instructed the child, who sped off down the hallway, returning with a single candle that he placed on the desk. Ovid sighed. It would not be enough. The sun had set and darkness was beginning to fill the library. But even a thousand oil lamps would fail to light the way to the poem he needed to write: the ode that would shake Rome.

He began to scribble verses, but none seemed to make sense. The more he tried to squeeze Germanicus into the role of the larger-than-life hero, the more he had to accept how natural it felt for Augustus, and not Germanicus, to fit that image, to play Hercules. His whole life, Ovid had looked for wit and double meanings to mask his messages, but now, when he wanted to write something unambiguous, plain, straightforward, even dull, the kind that Virgil, that power-pleaser, might write – when he wanted to write something like that, he could not. And yet he must, for it was how he would pay the price for his pardon.

Perhaps it was the *Gigantomachia* itself that was the problem, perhaps it was not fit for purpose. Long ago, Augustus himself had warned Ovid that he should not stir up the Roman gods, but should let them live in peace; the *Gigantomachia* was a Greek matter, and he should mind his own business, if he had any. Likewise, his then powerful patron Messalla had threatened the end of their friendship if Ovid embarked on the subject. Ovid had taken it all to heart and abandoned the *Gigantomachia*, turning his attention to the *Metamorphoses* instead. This was a couple of years before his banishment. But now that General Vestalis had asked him to write this ode for Germanicus, wasn't it the perfect time to revive the *Gigantomachia*?

He studied the outline. It was straightforward, and he could keep it consistent with all the Greek authors. The Titans would be defeated, but the Olympian gods, though victorious, would change, transformed by the moments of fear and uncertainty they had suffered in the fray. Yes, Ovid thought, the story itself was simple, and presented no problem. Perhaps, instead, the difficulties lay within the characters themselves. The players.

The more he thought about it, the more clear to him it was that Germanicus in the role of Hercules, the saviour, was unimaginable. Maybe, as an alternative, he could be Jupiter? And Augustus cast as Mother Earth was an intriguing prospect: he could rebel against the very laws he had enforced as emperor. As for Tiberius, he would be perfect in the role of the losing Giant. But Hercules? If not Germanicus and if not Augustus, then who in all of Rome could be the hero…

The inspiration came to him in a flash of delighted realisation. Of course. There was a perfect candidate for Hercules. Livia. She was the real hero of Rome: she had saved the Roman aristocracy by marrying Augustus, she knew how to fight any battle, and, above all, she knew how to force a victory. Added to that, she was far more spiritual than anyone in Rome suspected. And far more cynical too. Just like Hercules, the patron of Ovid's Sulmo.

Ovid stared at the candle. *Livia as Hercules*. Did he dare write such a satire?

When Darkness Falls

Ovid fancied that he could smell the sulphur as soon as he turned the corner of the street. Once he reached the entrance to his house, he knew he was not mistaken: the corridor reeked of the stuff. He had hoped Cynthia would content herself with removing dirt and spells with water and fire only, and prepared himself to confront her, when he remembered his grandmother's words – no evil, no matter how big or small, could resist sulphur.

He could not deny that Cynthia's efforts had managed to bring the mosaic floor of the corridor to a pitch of shine and importance he had not seen for some time. The atrium, too, was unrecognisable with its rearranged objects and lack of clutter. Cynthia had even washed out the wine stains from the frescoes – without, unfortunately, destroying the paintings.

Yet something was missing. For a moment, he could not discern what – and then it came to him. The three silver statues of the imperial family were no longer there.

Cynthia appeared in the atrium, simply turned out in her dark red tunic and absence of jewellery – not even the inexpensive bracelets women often wore at home.

'The statues…' he said.

'Are gone. We don't believe in living gods, do we?'

'Do not let Augustus hear you say that.' Ovid looked about him. 'This place is transformed.'

'There is better. Come.'

He followed her towards his bedroom. The years of dirt and hidden jumble had been accosted with an evident relish, and when he saw the pile of rubbish stacked up in one corner of the room he understood just how filthy it must have been. Shrivelled wineskins, dirty pots, beakers, amphorae, and, worst of all, a profusion of empty bags coated in the residue of orange powder. 'It has been six years of exile', Ovid said, hoping to explain it away with one sentence.

'I thought you were a poet', she said, picking up one of the bags and holding it at arm's length from her face. 'Not a drug addict.'

Ovid gave her what he hoped was a fierce look. 'Are you here to clean my house or my life?'

'I can do both.'

'Don't.'

With her free hand, she picked up a dead wineskin. 'You can't be very creative once you've swallowed these. No wonder you feel unwell all the time.'

'You are not my wife, and I do not need to be nagged. There shall be no more disturbances in my house. I need a certain disorder.' How right he was, he surmised, to have only male servants. Men were lazy and sloppy and sometimes dangerous too, but they seldom sniffed around or gave their opinions where they were not wanted.

She waved both objects at him. 'You are either blind on purpose or you genuinely do not understand. I am not nagging – you can do what you like. This is about *me*, not you. I will not live in a house where the whole town gossips about the master, and about the true cause of his ill health.'

'Which is?'

'These!' she shouted. 'These! The two gods you rely upon!' She threw away the wineskin and the sachet.

He needed to regain control, and he needed to do so calmly and firmly. 'I merely want my dinner. Is it ready?'

'It is.'

She led the way into the triclinium. As he followed, he watched the dip and rise of her crow-black hair, tied back in a bun and fixed with a wooden pin. He could not help but wonder what it would look like, let down and cascading over her loose breasts, and his breathing quickened as he imagined all the hours of hot activity he could spend with this woman. Such thoughts were the province of young men, and he was surprised by the sudden vividness of them – which only made the excitement yet more intense. He prayed she would not turn around, for if she did she would doubtless notice the erection thrusting to free itself from his clothing. He would need to deal with that soon, in the privacy of his own room.

They reached the dining room. If Cynthia noticed his state of arousal she said nothing, but merely led him to his chair. He sat down, marvelling at how much he wanted this woman. Gods, how he wanted her. But there was a problem. He had never slept with his personnel, and he was too old to start now.

'Since I have never employed you as my servant,' he said, 'you are not my servant.' A spoken contract, or a spoken lack of contract. Whichever it was, saying it aloud confirmed it.

'Good. Because I have never been anyone's servant.'

There was an intimacy to her voice which, had it come from any other woman, he would have dreaded. He could almost hear the mocking laughter of his father, telling him not to play with fire and to visit the brothel if he needed a woman. Yet here he was, feeling somehow secure in the presence of Cynthia and realising that he would not like to feel otherwise. 'Join me for dinner', he said.

'I need to change.'

Don't, he wanted to yell. *Just undress!*

She left the room, and, blind with lust, Ovid grabbed at his penis which – too long waiting, bursting for release – tumbled him into a deep shaking spasm. He groaned with pleasure, knowing that perhaps she might hear him, but unable to stop himself.

When Cynthia returned, it was clear her change of attire had not been designed to seduce, challenge or persuade. Nevertheless, she was worth all his attention. She wore a thin golden necklace and a palla of blue linen, as elegant as the arrangement of her hair and the serenity she radiated. She carried a silver tablet and placed it before him.

'Watch out. It's hot. The cook warmed it up more than once.' The neckline of her palla unfolded and her breasts, half-wrapped in a soft linen band, were suddenly there, right in front of his eyes. She let him look as much as he liked. 'Though the taste may have suffered', she said.

Finally she stood straight, left the room once more, and returned with her own plate, which she took to her chair at the far end of the table.

'I like your perfume', Ovid said. 'Is it the same as the one your sister uses?'

'Indeed. It was mine first, but she liked it so much that I gave it to her. Well, after she disinvited me, I took it back. Doesn't it suit me better, though?'

The provocation in the question was abundant, and Ovid knew that to enter into that particular conversation would be like stepping into a beehive – without protection. He would not go there. He started to eat.

'Is it true that you are Rome's ultimate expert on love?' Cynthia asked.

'Only when it comes to giving advice.'

'And what advice would you give to me?'

'I have no advice for you', he said timidly. 'I doubt you need it.'

Cynthia smiled at that. 'How is Rome?' she said.

'Different. Very different. If anything, it defies imagination.'

'Do you miss it?'

'Constantly. I dream of the day I may return.'

'And in these dreams… who is on your arm as you make your grand entrance?'

Ovid looked at her and saw, from the raised eyebrow and half-smile, that she was teasing him. He laughed, long and loud, and she did too.

'A beautiful woman', he said. 'The most beautiful.'

It was the kind of dinner he used to long for. The food, which really did not matter, was spicy enough for euphemism and allusion and light enough for fun and levity. They shared an open-ended intimacy, one whose outcome was desirable but not foreseeable. The servants were absent.

'Haven't you missed music in your house here?' Cynthia asked as she cleaned the table and placed, according to tradition, some fruits on the house altar.

'Why? Can you play?'

She did not answer but instead picked up the lyre propped

against the wall and began to pluck. Her unbitten fingernails played the strings with surprising dexterity. Where did barbarians learn such skills, Ovid wondered, remembering Scorillo playing the flute in the library. The music brought a peace to the evening which, though in stark contrast to the arousal with which he had begun it, seemed now to be a fitting conclusion. The first lamp began to die out, and Ovid considered asking for it to be refilled – but to do that would shatter this harmony, and he had no inclination for such. Instead, he closed his eyes, and allowed the music and the darkness to absorb him. He had not felt so calm for a long time.

But it did not last. Shouts and curses began to sound from the entrance, and then echoed down the corridor towards the dining room. Cynthia abruptly stopped playing and Ovid rose to his feet just as the door crashed open. Argyris appeared, carrying an inert body which he dropped to the floor.

'They wanted to rape him.' His words were ragged, punctuated by deep and panting breaths. 'I could not allow it.'

Ovid looked at the body on the floor, the eyes swollen, the tunic ripped. 'Spiros!' he said. 'Get him to his room. Now.'

The caretaker did as he was told. Ovid turned around to apologise to Cynthia, but in the turmoil of the disturbance she had vanished.

Age Meets Youth

Ovid cradled the dream-catcher in his hands. In reality it was little more than a clay pot filled with horse hair, a gift from his wife which he had brought to Tomis out of a sense of duty rather than belief. He had never trusted dreams for the same reason that he had never trusted oracles: interpretations were subjective, easy to manipulate, and he had no patience for all the various sorts of translators.

Still, if the dream-catcher did work, he hoped it had caught those he had suffered through last night: a confusing array of images and soundscapes which ran the whole gamut of sensuality, from the glorious sex of Cynthia to the brutal rape of Spiros. He felt as if he had barely slept.

Argyris stepped lightly into the room. 'Good morning,' he said. 'You have visitors I don't know how to deal with.'

'Visitors? At this hour?' Ovid rubbed at his eyes.

'It is not as early as you might imagine,' the caretaker replied.

'How is Spiros?'

'Sleeping.'

'And Cynthia? Is she still here?'

'As far as I am aware. I have not seen her, but I have no sign that she has left us.'

'Good.' Ovid stood and stretched. A burst of high-pitched shouts drifted into the room, coming from close by, as if a school class had moved into the house. 'Children?' he asked.

Argyris nodded. 'Children.'

Donning a clean tunic, Ovid padded down the corridors to find them in the entry hall: the young crowd from the cliff edge. He was beginning to recognise them now. Plautus' son, Carp. The Aedile's boy, Jason. And their leader, the lanky girl one head taller than the rest. 'Good morning, sir!' they chorused.

'And good morning to you.' Ovid smiled. 'To what do I owe the honour of this visit?'

'We were worried that you were angry with us', the lanky girl said.

'Angry? Why would I be—'

'I'm sorry for the other day', Jason interrupted. 'For calling you Sir Bird.'

'I found it funny', said Ovid.

'We missed you at the funeral', somebody said.

'Our parents told us the council wants you out of Tomis.'

'But we don't.'

The young voices came thick and fast, overlapping and drowning out one another. Ovid raised his hands before him. 'Easy,' he said, 'not so fast. Let an old man keep up with you.'

The children giggled. Some pulled haggard faces and said '*Old maaaan*' in the deepest voices they could muster. Ovid found himself chuckling at their impressions of him. He liked these children.

'Bring some water and some pieces of honeycomb', he instructed Argyris, who hurried off to fetch the treats.

'Are you going to come to our grove?' the lanky girl asked.

'If you invite me.'

'We do!' four of the children called out together, like some mischievous choir.

'Where do you write your poems?' Jason asked.

'Sometimes in my head. Other times on wax tablets. Here, let me show you.'

Ovid pulled open the study door and the stream of children flowed through. He watched Carp, who, though more restrained than the rest, shared their enthusiasm.

'If my cubicle was this messy my mother would kill me!' one of the smaller boys shouted, as the youths careered around the room, picking up and examining even the most inconsequential pieces of detritus. To them it was all new, all novel.

The lanky girl had remained by Ovid's side. 'What language do you write in?'

'Latin.'

'Do you write in Greek as well?'

'Yes. Sometimes.'

Jason, more interested in their conversation than in the myriad objects strewn about the room, came over to join them. 'Have you ever tried to write in the Gaetic language?' he asked.

'I have tried. It is not easy.'

'Can you read us one?'

'Not a Gaetic poem. They're not good enough. But maybe I can read you one of my poems about the Emperor Augustus.'

'Why would you write poems about him?' Carp asked.

'Should I not?'

'I think that when you write a poem for someone it is like praising them. Even if it is a little cruel it is still an honour. So why write poems for a man who punished you?'

Ovid looked at Carp. 'You make a compelling argument. But, for a poet, it is a fact of life. One writes poems for one's emperor. And Augustus is my emperor. He is yours as well.'

'My father says we are free people. Like our forefathers', said the lanky girl.

'Really?'

'Yes', Carp said, joining their little circle. 'That is true. You were exiled from Rome, weren't you? Well, no one can exile us from Tomis.' He paused for a moment, and then added: 'I think.'

'If you were exiled from Tomis,' Jason said, 'where would you like it to be?'

'Greece', Carp replied.

'I asked Ovid!'

'But I *am* exiled', Ovid said. 'Right here.'

'No, but...' Jason grew flustered as he tried to explain himself. 'I mean... I mean if you *could* have chosen, where would you have gone?'

'If I could have chosen, I would have chosen to be deported home.'

'A Roman cannot be exiled in Rome', Jason replied, then added cautiously: 'Can he?'

'It wouldn't be exile', the lanky girl said. 'It'd be more like being grounded.'

'That's how my father punishes me', Carp admitted.

'Rome was not really my home', Ovid said. 'The place where I was born, where the estate of my family is, where graves of my ancestors are, is some two hundred miles eastward from Rome, in the Paeligna Valley, surrounded by the Abruzzi Mountains. The city is called Sulmo.'

'What you described resembles the place my mother comes from', said Carp.

The children began competing in descriptions of places their parents spoke about. Suddenly the incessant chatter that had filled the room hushed, and Ovid turned to locate the cause. Cynthia had entered. She spied Ovid and began to make her slow way towards him.

'Wow', the lanky girl whispered. 'She's *beautiful*.'

'Yes', Ovid agreed. 'Yes, she is. Her sister even more so.'

Carp gave him a disapproving look. Cynthia reached their little group and, before greeting Ovid, made sure to smile sweetly at each of the children who, in turn, blushed or giggled or simply smiled back. 'I am thinking about going to the market', she said to Ovid. 'Would you like me to get anything for you?'

'Perhaps we need some things, but I have not had the chance to decide. As you can see', Ovid swept his hand across the room, 'we have guests.'

'Oh, we can leave, if you like', the lanky girl piped up. 'We only came to apologise.' She hollered a few words and, as if by magic, the rest of the children assembled beside her.

Cynthia was impressed. 'A fine level of command', she muttered, and the lanky girl swelled with pride.

'Goodbye, Ovid!' the children sang.

'For you, I shall be Sir Bird', Ovid said.

'Goodbye, Sir Bird!' the children sang.

'Goodbye, Mrs Ovid!' said one or two of the cheekier ones.

And then, in a whirl of chatter and thudding feet, they were gone.

'I had no idea you were so paternal', Cynthia said once they were alone.

'There is much about me you do not know', Ovid replied.

How a Princess Loves

Once Ovid had drawn up his list of requirements from the market, Cynthia set off alone. The soothsayer spied her out when she was choosing vegetables and sidled up next to her. 'You don't want these peppers', she said, swatting them out of Cynthia's hands. 'What you want is one of my freshly picked herbs.' She opened her palm to reveal a small pile of crushed leaves. 'This one works against love. Perfect for you.'

'Why so?'

'Because in your case love means trouble.'

Cynthia ignored the herbs and picked up a single olive from those spread across the table in front of her, testing it for firmness. 'Why should I believe you?' she said. 'You weren't even able to bewitch my sister into keeping me in her household.'

The soothsayer panted like a dog. 'You didn't need me for that. You could have done it yourself. You know how.'

'My charms didn't work.'

'You've forgotten. Shame on you.'

'I don't need these herbs. But I do want some medicine.'

'What kind?' The soothsayer smiled, honey in her voice once more.

'A medicine to help him write.'

'Writing will do him no favours. For him, there are only two ways to get out of Tomis: by magic or by pain. But magic he despises. And pain he fears.'

'I don't want him out of here. I want him writing.'

The soothsayer opened her greasy bag, took out two black jars and raised them to chest height. 'One silver coin', she said. 'Each.'

'What are they?' Cynthia peered inside the jars, trying to discern their contents.

'Serpent fat. The best medicine against lust.'

'How will that help?'

'Lust is a dangerous illusion. It distracts old men.' She stared at Cynthia. 'And it shakes young women.'

'I couldn't care less about him', Cynthia snapped.

The soothsayer laughed. 'If you haven't made love to him already, you will. He will make you rich and maybe pregnant. But you should not follow him. And you should not keep the child.'

'Two silver coins.'

'Yes, two', the soothsayer said. 'You will need both jars.'

'Then give me those herbs as well. Two coins for all of them.'

The soothsayer nodded, agreeing to the conditions. 'A wise idea', she said, handing the two jars to Cynthia and then pouring the herbs into her outstretched palm. 'Protection against both lust and love. A wise idea indeed.'

A Spiritual Sisyphus

The forum, its stale air wrought by rough cries, was covered by a stifling copper haze, behind which patches of cloud changed the intensity of daylight. Ovid, on the way to the library, walked past his preferred tavern. Two men stood outside, clutching cups of wine and rocking back and forth on their feet.

'Ovid!' one of them cried. 'Where have you been? We have missed your stories!'

'Is it true that the murdered Roman was your son who came to bring you home and that you killed him by mistake?'

'Or did you kill him because he refused to take you back?'

Ovid ignored the questions and continued walking. Any answer would have fallen on drunk ears, and was therefore pointless. At the library he let himself in through the back entrance. A soft and lilting melody drifted down the halls, and, compelled by it, he went to find Scorillo. There – seated once more in Ovid's favourite spot, the sunlit alcove – was the healer, playing a flute.

'Is the Librarian back?' Ovid asked.

'No. He asked me to take care of the place.'

'That should not be too difficult, considering I am the only customer.'

'Very funny.' Scorillo placed the instrument on the table beside him. 'But here you do not need to test your wit. Instead, state your business.'

Ovid felt the urge for honesty. This healer, he realised, had that effect on him. 'I need to write', he admitted. 'I need to write something I have never written before. And I can't. There is nobody who can help.'

'Do you want help?'

'I think I do.'

'Just write about sex. As long as men rule the world, women will make sure that sex is in short supply, so there will always be an audience for poems about it. It has served you well so far, why not continue?'

Ovid shook his head. 'I need to write an ode. Even a tragedy would do, probably.'

'Tragedy is dead. We live in an age of reason. That is what guides our life, none of that fate nonsense.'

'I am a crusty old man, too lazy for any new ideas.'

'Me too', Scorillo said, and reached for the flute once more.

The flowing notes, seemingly devoid of intervals, pinched senses Ovid was not aware he had. He felt powerless, and he liked it. Was Scorillo some kind of charmer? Mesmerising and hypnotising with his flute? Barely realising what he was doing, Ovid began to ramble with a strange and revealing spontaneity, confessing things he would never have admitted even under the heaviest inebriation – about his native Sulmo and his father; about his fear of dying; about his obsession to be remembered after death; about his third marriage, to Fabia... Where was it all coming from? And where was it all going?

Scorillo resolved the melody and took the flute from his lips. It was clear he had been listening to every word. 'After everything you told me, I can help you', he said.

'How?' Ovid's voice broke on the word, exhausted by all that had come before it.

'I will guide you to change. And hopefully the new "you" will be able to write the ode.'

'What's wrong with me?'

'You suffer from the illness of self.'

'Never heard of it.'

'Self-centredness. Self-pity. Self-absorption. Self-delusion. These feelings must be familiar to you.'

'Perhaps. Even so, what can be done about it?'

Scorillo fingered the tip of the flute. 'First, you need to cleanse your body and then your mind. Do not worry about the soul right now. Instead, think only of relearning how to live.'

'What if I don't change?'

'Then you are not going to write as you aspire to.'

'And die forgotten in Tomis?'

Scorillo shrugged. 'Consider yourself lucky that you can choose anything related to your death. Most men cannot.'

'These are not the words of a healer.'

'I am not just a healer. I am also...' Scorillo paused. 'I am also a priest. A struggling priest, but a priest nonetheless.'

'Funny. I always imagined that you would hate the gods.'

'The Roman gods, yes. My protector is Zamolxis, the god of Gaete.'

Ovid allowed himself to swell with knowledge. No matter what he had lost over the years, he had never lost that. 'I know of this god Zamolxis. I saved him for the second part of the *Metamorphoses*', he said.

Scorillo nodded. 'Augustus is a great admirer of Zamolxis.'

‘That doesn’t make sense. Zamolxis was revered by the Pythagoreans. And Augustus hates the Pythagoreans.’

‘It doesn’t make sense to you. But we have digressed’, Scorillo said, standing. ‘Do you want my help?’

Ovid nodded.

‘Good.’ Scorillo blew out the candle on the table. ‘I’ll take care of you.’

The Soldier, the Poet and the Children

Ovid's days began to fall into the same routine – a routine that left no space for writing. Not for years had this much time passed without him putting pen to paper, even to write a letter, and yet he found he did not miss it. Training the children on the wasteland had become a passion. Each morning, very early, he walked alone up to the cliff edge and waited for the children to arrive. He wished somebody had taken the time to do the same for him when he was a child in Sulmo. His life might have turned out rather differently had he been encouraged to attempt athletic training, and perhaps to compete properly, facing losses and victories in the ancient Greek competitive spirit.

One morning he arrived there to find not the children waiting for him, but Plautus. 'Are you avoiding me, poet?'

Ovid kept his eyes fixed on the Commander's. 'I thought you were campaigning.'

'I wanted you to teach Carp rhetoric, not… whatever this is.'

'Learning to compete and to be polite is the best education a boy can receive at his age. I assume you learned the former, but never the latter. Carp misses both.'

'Carp should not want to become a soldier.'

Plautus' assertion caught Ovid off guard. A father who did not want his son to follow in his footsteps? The notion was alien. 'But how else to pull him out of this provincial mud?'

'The limits of their language are the limits of their understanding. As a poet, I thought you would have agreed.'

Ovid stared at the military man in disbelief. 'Where has all this wisdom come from? Did you capture some philosophers in Scythia?'

'Irony.' The Commander smiled. 'Your last defence.'

'I suppose you want me to teach your son that too.'

'Yes!' Plautus shouted, his patience wearing thin. 'That is exactly what I want! That is exactly why I came to you. Gods, conversation with you is maddening.'

'And will be with Carp, if nobody teaches him to be polite.'

'Enough.' The Commander cut him short. 'I can see we are getting nowhere. General Vestalis asks if you are busy writing the ode you agreed upon.'

'Tell him I am not.'

'I can see that, so why not?'

'Tell him it looks bad to be unsuccessful at writing verses', Ovid said. 'But it looks worse to be dead.'

'At least your fear of death is normal.'

'The rest of me is not?'

Plautus took a step forward and lowered his voice menacingly. 'No, poet', he said. 'No, it is not. Which is precisely why I have yet something else to say to you. Do not touch Cynthia.'

'I have never fucked servants.'

In a flash, Plautus wrapped his hands around Ovid's throat. 'Servant?' he hissed. '*Servant?*' The Commander squeezed. As Ovid fought for breath, he noticed with an odd sense of detachment that, instead of fear, it was excitement and curiosity that seemed to mark this unfamiliar experience. Who was it who had said that fights were not about the enjoyment of violence but the sensation of arousal? Strangled by Plautus, he became aware of his penis enlarging. He thought longingly of the three whores.

Slowly Plautus began to loosen his grip, and Ovid gasped for air. 'She is not your servant. Do not debase her with such a word.'

'You,' Ovid wheezed, 'should read my *Ars Amatoria*.'

'Why so?'

'For a valuable lesson.' Ovid rubbed at his neck. 'Never juggle sisters.'

He wondered if perhaps Plautus might lunge for him again, but both men were interrupted by the sight of Carp, who came running towards them, his knees bleeding from falls.

'Look at him,' the Commander whispered. 'Running around and tripping over like an idiot. You call that training for life?'

'This is what boys do when free.' Ovid smiled and raised his arms to greet Carp as he approached. He would continue to train these children, no matter what Plautus threatened. He could not disappoint his young friends just because he wished to stay out of trouble.

And isn't that curious, he thought. *Somewhere along the way, I must have changed. When on earth did that happen?*

Another Messenger of Death

The market day was nearing its end. The vendors had packed most of their goods away and were preparing to go home when hysterical shouts brought the forum back to life.

'Look!'

'Death!'

'Someone important!'

Approaching the harbour of Tomis was a war galley. It glided across the water, propelled by three banks of oars. In full display for all to see was the coat of arms of the governor of Macedonia, and, more prominently, a huge black wreath.

'Who has died this time?'

'A governor, I wager.'

'Murdered. It must be.'

The crowd assembled on the pier. Word was sent to the Aedile, who came out in his litter immediately, and waited to one side a few steps away from the pier.

Once the ship was held fast, a huge man, virtually a giant, sped up the shaky ladder and jumped across to the platform before anyone could offer him help. He slowly arranged his tunic and scratched his back, making apparent his considerable size, and then looked about himself without hurry. 'So this is Tomis.' His voice was deep, resounding, and the crowd cooed with admiration.

The Aedile opened the door of his litter, patted his oiled hair, greeted the onlookers with the thin smile so favoured by politicians, and marched towards the newcomer. The crowd, undecided over which protagonist would give more entertainment, waggled their necks to and fro like fowl, eager not to miss a single thing.

Four men climbed off the boat and joined the giant, standing either side of him. The Aedile greeted each in turn and then, with a certain reluctance, said: 'So. Who has died?'

'I have instructions from the governor of Macedonia to deliver the news to at least a dozen city councillors at the same time', the giant replied, his tone official and perfunctory.

The Aedile nodded. 'I will send word ahead for the magistrates to gather.' He looked at his litter. It was far too small for the messenger, let alone for his four friends. 'Come, let us walk to the town hall together. It will give the magistrates time to convene.'

The crowd parted as the Aedile led the five men down into the town. One boy looked like he might reach out and touch the giant, but a cold stare quickly changed his mind.

'Commander Plautus will join us also', the Aedile said.

'Plautus?' The giant grimaced. 'I thought he was supposed to be campaigning this time of the year?' He exchanged a look, but no words, with one of his companions. 'Haven't our Thracian allies been granted the honour to protect the region?'

'They might have been, but they do not', the Aedile replied.

'Maybe Tomis is not meant to become capital of the Black Sea's western shore.' The giant paused, and then muttered

Plautus' name, turning it over in his mouth. 'What is his garrison good for? Perhaps I must have words.'

'And how about Ovid? Does he remain here?' the Aedile asked.

'Of course. Where else would he go?'

'We have been expecting repercussions from the senator whose son was killed', the Aedile said.

'There are more important things to worry about right now.' The giant's face looked preoccupied, as if chasing away unwanted thoughts.

Unwanted Help

Ovid opened the garden door to find, beneath the forsythia shrub, the hedgehog, laid out upon a small pile of orange powder. It looked dead. He crouched over the creature. Its needles were as sharp as always, but the hedgehog did not recoil when he touched the cold tip of its nose. His eyes filled with tears. The message – whoever had sent it, either the caretaker or Cynthia – was clear. The orange powder was poison.

Two trails of ants were competing to reach the hedgehog's corpse. Ovid chased them away with his finger, misdirecting them off along different trails. To drown them would have been easier, but he could not bear to let them die too.

Behind him, pebbles crunched under his feet. He stood and turned to see Scorillo. 'Servants and low-class guests, if unobserved, are always rummaging around', Ovid said.

Scorillo laughed. 'No wonder you can't write. I'm surprised you haven't committed suicide yet.'

'It's not a reason to kill my hedgehog.'

'Love saved your life, poet. Someone intended to get rid of you. And you, instead of dying, fell in love with this poison.'

Ovid thought of his dead cook, who had drunk the wine mixed with rosary peas. He shook his head. 'The treatment has been dependable, effective and at hand.'

'You must give it up.'

'What am I supposed to use instead?'

'A prayer', Scorillo answered.

To his surprise, the mention of praying did not send Ovid into a spiral of terror. Instead, his mind fixed on the sound of the sea nearby, as its waves pulled up and down the beach in a never-ending dance. 'State your method', he said.

'Let us start by getting on our knees and praying to the gods.' Scorillo knelt right there, on the pebbles of the garden.

Only slaves and the powerless do that, Ovid thought, remaining on his feet. 'I don't know how to pray. Nor to whom.'

'Just start a dialogue.'

'With whom?'

'At first, with yourself. The rest comes later. You need only to pray a lot. Quantity matters. It keeps your thoughts, if not streamlined, then at least from meandering too much.'

The stench of rotten seaweed found its way into the garden, caught on the same breeze that played with the shrubs, amused them, teased them, flattered their flowers. And, along with the stench, the sound of approaching footsteps.

'What are you doing here?' Cynthia screamed, her pitch unearthly. 'Get out! Get out and never show up here again. Never! Never!'

Scorillo remained on his knees in the pebbles. 'Hello, sister', he said, nonplussed.

'Leave Ovid alone with your bullshit. Zamolxis doesn't exist, and if he does exist, he doesn't care.' Cynthia spat on the ground. 'It was because of him and his priests that I had to give up my children and my country. It was he who accepted my husband's sacrifice. I despise him!'

Scorillo stood up. 'Yes', he murmured. 'You are quite right.

I do know. But does Ovid?' And with that he left the garden, not pausing to look back.

Cynthia turned to face Ovid. 'I am sorry that you had to witness that,' she said.

'You had a husband?' Ovid said. 'You have children? What happened to your family?'

He watched, as in the space of a single moment the anger on Cynthia's face transformed into grief. She fell back against the door frame and he moved towards her. She held out her arms, needing to be nurtured, to be healed.

'It was outside the four-year ritual.' Her words came slowly, aimed at the hard ground. 'The Dacians needed to convince Zamolxis to keep the Romans south of the Danube. They looked for a messenger to send to Zamolxis with our wishes and needs, and my husband, the bravest of all Dacians, put his name in the ballot box. His honour was always above our love. I begged my father to save him, to remove his name from the sacrifice list. That is not an unusual procedure, especially in wartime. My father asked his brother, the king, but the request must have angered him, for when it was deferred to the warriors' council it seems that he had personally named my husband to be sacrificed. And do you know what? My husband, the idiot, even thanked me for helping bring about the decision. He threw himself on the fourteen spears gladly. He died right away. Everyone thanked Zamolxis for his benevolence. I told them that if they continued to kill their best sons, the Romans would conquer us without a fight. The king took pity on me then and I was not killed on the grave of my husband. I wish the pity had come earlier, and he had spared my husband.'

'Did the Dacians defeat the Romans?'

'We did', Cynthia said, and Ovid noticed that the flash of pride in her voice faded as quickly as it had appeared. 'But our king, the idiot, sealed the peace with the Romans by marrying his other niece, my sister Dokia, to the second officer in command. Plautus.'

'I see', Ovid said, wondering how widely known all this was. Had he been the only one ignorant in all of Tomis? Or had Plautus kept the acquisition of his wife a secret from everyone? 'What happened to you?'

'I was incensed. And so I began to speak out. I told whoever would listen the kinds of truths only widows and madmen dare say aloud. A year later they took my children away, declaring me mad. I believe they would have killed me, but the priest of the oracle, a childhood friend, took my side and I was spared. My father was ashamed, deeply ashamed. He chased me away, told me never to set foot in my home again.'

'You were exiled…'

'Yes.' Cynthia nodded. 'It is not a fate reserved only for poets.'

'And so you came here.'

'I wanted to go to Rome and start a new life there. As a prostitute. But before I boarded the ship my sister convinced me to think it over.' She stood. 'So there you are. My story. You know it. And I have made myself vulnerable.'

'Perhaps if I made my own confession, it would make you feel better.'

'My vulnerability for yours?' For the first time that day, Cynthia smiled. 'Yes. I think you are right. I think that would make me feel better. Please. Go on.'

Driven by an unfamiliar compulsion, Ovid told her about General Vestalis, about the ode, about Germanicus, opening like a mussel powerless against the sea. 'But how can I write such an ode?' he said. 'How can I?'

'Use magic', Cynthia replied. 'The one thing that the powerful fear and the market women do not. They can help you master the words, the right words. They can do things of which you have never dreamed.'

'Such as?'

'Such as enabling your mind to enter an ethereal harmony, one produced by none other than the vibration of the celestial spheres themselves.'

Cynthia was beginning to sound like a boring Pythagorean. 'What if I am too old for such a journey?'

'There is only one way to find out.'

Perhaps she is right, Ovid thought. *Give the market women money. What have I to lose?* He got to his feet, and, holding out his hands for Cynthia to take, helped her rise. He was about to ask her to accompany him to the market, to introduce him to the women, when he was cut short by the *slap-slap-slap* of feet running over tiles. Spiros appeared in the garden, his chest heaving, his eyes manic.

'You again?' Ovid asked.

'Master.' Spiros caught his breath. 'There is a ship. It will take us to Greece, should we so choose. But we have to be on board by midnight. One hundred dinars and only one bag per person.'

'Greece?' Cynthia clutched at his arm. 'You are going to Greece?'

Ovid ignored her. 'Who else knows about the ship?'

'Probably everyone. It sails directly to Thessalonica. It is no secret.'

'But you will be a fugitive!' Cynthia cried. 'No, Ovid, no, you cannot, it would not be—'

'Augustus is dead! Tiberius has taken over.' Spiros' shout rang across the garden. It seemed to silence the whole world.

Augustus, dead? Incredible as the news was, it was not impossible. *Everybody dies at some point.* The thought of his own death produced the usual knot in Ovid's stomach. Yet the name of Augustus' successor, Tiberius, turned the familiar discomfort into panic. It meant that the plot of Germanicus' generals would never materialise, and, even worse, that some insiders would start talking to bolster their careers. If Ovid were named as a co-conspirator, no matter what he had or had not agreed to do for Vestalis, it would mark his end. And not just banishment this time. Certain death. Tiberius would see to it, and he would see to it rapidly.

'Where is the news from?'

'A ship from Macedonia arrived today. The city council is debating on the matter as we speak.'

Ovid gazed at Spiros. 'And you would help me escape?'

'Yes,' Spiros panted. 'If you do not, your safety in Tomis cannot be guaranteed.'

Ovid pointed down at the inert hedgehog, the orange powder beside it. 'I don't believe you,' he said. 'You brought this poison into my home. You sought my death. Why would you now seek my survival?'

Spiros pressed his palms together and supplicated before his former master. 'All I ever wanted,' he said softly, 'was to be a free man. I thought your death would grant me that. I was wrong. I needed only your words, which you gave me without demand.'

'You are telling me that you have changed?'

Spiros nodded. 'You might say I have endured my own metamorphosis.'

'So I freed you from slavery, and you are now in my debt?' Ovid allowed himself a wry smile. 'That's absurd.'

Spiros smiled back. 'Absurd, perhaps. True, yes. You gave me my life back. Now let me help you save yours. Get ready to leave this place. Now. The captain is willing to take us. This is your chance, master!'

Gaetic Poetry

A solar eclipse had been predicted. It would mark the midpoint of these funereal festivities held in honour of Augustus. But it never came. The sign, or lack of it, was deeply inauspicious, and what had been thus far an ordered and respectful ceremony soon began to devolve towards a chaos no one wanted. The sea was agitated, and the high priest of Apollo from the island of Leuke was late, which prompted the Archon to kill the goat himself. It was a messy affair, completed inexpertly. Eventually he retrieved an organ in one piece – the liver – and held it aloft to the packed forum. The sacrificial smoke wound in lazy curls, leaving only uncertainty as to whether or not Tomis, and Augustus himself, had accepted the offering.

The Archon climbed down from the altar and sat with his fellow dignitaries, who faced the fractious crowd and maintained an uncomfortable silence. Among them were the giant, his four guards, and, of course, the Aedile.

'I have seen little honour for Augustus yet', the giant sighed. 'But perhaps things will be improved by the athletic competition. I assume there will be one?'

'Of course', the Archon said, and then leaned in close to the Aedile. 'A competition? When were you going to tell me we needed a competition?'

'I had hoped we might get away without one', the Aedile

whispered back. 'Few of the children here are inclined to take part in such a thing.'

'How do you know?'

'My son Jason tells me. He and his friends have no sympathy for Augustus.'

The Archon was amazed. 'No sympathy? What on earth do you mean?'

'Because of his ill treatment of Ovid. They will not honour anyone, emperor or not, who has wronged their teacher.'

'Keep that to yourself, for the gods' sake', the Archon hissed, looking back nervously at the giant, who appeared not to have heard.

'You were the one who asked me.'

'So.' The giant stood up and flexed his portentous chest. 'The athletics. It will be soon, I hope?'

'It seems we are having some problems mustering our competitors', the Archon said, preferring to stay seated than to stand beside the giant.

'Problems?' The giant snorted. 'This whole ceremony has been beset by *problems*. If you cannot manage situations such as these adequately, perhaps you should reconsider your application for the next term as leader of Tomis.'

'But...' The Archon raised his hands, supplicating. 'But I have invested so much in this city, so much time, so much energy, so much of my own money.'

'Consider your investment a bet. And consider your bet lost.' The giant did not speak loudly, but the resonance of his voice carried his words across the forum. The crowd stilled, perplexed, as he ordered his guards to close around him. There was danger in the air, threat, and the public gathered in the forum could not decide whether it would make for good sport or for a theatre of horror.

The giant, seemingly sensing that all focus was on him, turned to face the crowd. 'Perhaps I have expected too much,' he said, 'too much from what is little more than an inconsequential and provincial town.' He paused for heckles, shouts, boos, but none came. That he had cowed the entirety of Tomis appeared to please him. 'But do we not have someone of true worth and fame amongst us? Someone who can turn this farce of a ceremony around and offer Augustus the honour and dignity he deserves? Where is Ovid?'

Out in the crowd, anonymous until now, Ovid was dismayed to see those heads around him bow like sunflowers in the evening. The giant spotted him in a moment.

'Ah,' he said. 'There is our noble poet.'

Spying a way to deflect the ill-will that had been building towards him, the Archon jumped to his feet and pointed at Ovid. 'Tomitans and friends!' he cried. 'Publius Ovidius Naso, our esteemed co-citizen, is the only one among us who met the divine Augustus in person. How wonderful, how apt it would be, to hear him read, here, now, in honour of our dear, departed Emperor.'

A smattering of applause ascended from the crowd. Ovid decided to believe it denoted acclaim.

'It is too much for us to expect that the noble poet has any scrolls with him from which to read,' the giant said, a smile playing about his lips. 'But that should present no problem to one as vaunted as he. Ovid, come up here. Recite – if not from your memory, then from your imagination.'

The challenge was as evident as it was inescapable. Those

around Ovid looked away, refusing to meet his eye, and a clear pathway formed as those in front parted to let him through. As if sleepwalking, Ovid climbed the steps to the narrow wooden platform in front of the improvised altar. The silence was immense, exactly the kind he usually craved when taking to a stage, though this time he would have given anything to be drowned out, to be ignored, to be booed off.

Clearing his throat, he wiped sweat from his forehead and, in Latin, began. 'Divine Augustus, you taught us honour.'

Before him, two or three of the men turned to each other, puzzled. They had not understood, could not speak Latin. He took a breath. What was the point of saying anything if it remained incomprehensible? The giant and his guards would prefer their Latin, of course, but why should he favour them over Tomis? Why should he favour anyone – Tomitan, Roman, Greek, Dacian? No, he would speak the language of the people. He would speak Gaetic. Whether they liked what he had to say or not, they would at least understand it. Of that he was adamant.

'Divine Augustus, from wherever you are now, protect us please. For what use is your death if it does not show us the path towards the gods?'

The crowd, grateful for his switch to Gaetic, remained silent, following his words with wide-eyed eagerness. He became eloquent under their collective gaze, loquacious and comfortable, and began to tell them the story of Augustus and Livia, and of how their partnership – he did not use the word 'love' – changed Rome forever. His audience, perceiving his words to be a poem, absorbed them as if they were ultimate truths. Behind him, he felt the approving presence of the giant and his guards, and the swelling relief of the Archon and the Aedile.

Ovid was only glad the children were not there to hear him. They would have seen through the false sycophancy of his words in an instant. And they would have thought him little more than a shameful boot-licker.

Banished from Exile

The pale light of the oil lamp, which he had instructed should burn all night, seemed so calm and in such stark contrast to the crashing and cracking that filled his head and reverberated inside his chest. Augustus was dead. Augustus was dead. Still, he could not reconcile himself to the truth of the simple statement. Augustus was dead. Could it really be?

A deafening banging on the gate interrupted his insistent thoughts. *So they have got to me before I could flee*, he thought. In truth, he had been expecting it. He almost felt relief that it – that *they* – had finally come. Spiros' plan to escape on the ship to Greece had sounded too good to be true the moment he heard it. He should have known that he would never see midnight, the hour of their proposed departure. Tiberius' ascension to emperor was Ovid's death knell. If the new ruler did not want him dead immediately, he would soon, and there were countless men who would surmise that, and take actions into their own hands. What better way to find favour with the new Emperor?

Ovid got out of bed and began to dress. He needed to look good. Outside his room, he heard the familiar footsteps of Argyris making his way down the corridor, towards the entrance. Cynthia came to him, gabbling instructions at breakneck speed, imploring him to do things he would not have attempted even in his youth – to climb roofs, to jump from wall to wall, to sprint across neighbouring gardens. To escape. He told her to light the candles.

'But you need to flee the house, to get away.'

'You don't know that. They, whoever they are, may be bringing good news.'

A splintering crash. They had kicked the gate down. Shouts, calls, hollers filled the night air.

'Go, Ovid', Cynthia pleaded. 'They do not bring good news. You know this.'

Ovid nodded. 'I know', he said. 'I know. They are going to kill me.' It did not seem real. Perhaps it was not, perhaps it was all some dream or hallucination, perhaps he was still down there, wrapped comfortably in the sheets of his bed. He tested reality with a joke. 'Was my Gaetic poem really so bad?'

Cynthia did not laugh. *So it wasn't a dream*, he concluded. In dreams, his humour always landed well.

Plautus' first centurion, the Squarehead, burst into the bedroom, followed by a huddle of legionaries. The oil lamp flickered and went out, surely a bad sign. 'Publius Ovidius Naso', the Squarehead said, throwing two travel bags down to slide across the floor and come to a rest at his feet. 'One is for clothes, the other for wax tablets. That is all.'

They were not going to kill him in his house. That was a relief.

'You have ten minutes. By its end, we leave, whether you are packed or not.'

'Amend your manners, officer. I shall follow you when I am ready.' Unlike the time he had been taken from his villa by Augustus' guards, tonight he would not be dominated.

'You are a brute', Cynthia spat at the Squarehead. 'I shall get Plautus to tame you.'

The name of his commander caused the Squarehead to take a step backwards, his eyes betraying the dilemma that every predator must face sooner or later – whether to save his own skin by giving up his prey. 'Commander Plautus has departed for Macedonia', he said tentatively, and then, stepping forward once more: 'Ten minutes.' He left the bedroom, ordering his soldiers to follow.

'Why is this happening?' Cynthia said. 'Augustus is dead. Why can't they leave you alone now?'

'Tiberius', Ovid said, refusing to elaborate. He would let the name of the new Emperor pass his lips but once and then never more.

'There must be something we can do.'

He took Cynthia's hands in his own. 'There is something you can do', he said. 'I don't want my ashes sent to Rome. Please. Instead, send them to Sulmo, in the Abruzzi Mountains. My homeland.'

Cynthia reached beneath her cape and pulled out a terracotta figure, which she pressed into Ovid's hand. 'Take this and you'll come back alive.'

Perhaps I don't want to come back to Tomis, he thought, but chose not to say. He did not want to disappoint her yet further.

The Squarehead reappeared in the bedroom. 'Time's up.'

'It has not yet been ten minutes!' Cynthia protested.

'No matter. We are leaving.'

Ovid thought Cynthia might shriek profanities at the centurion, but instead she did something which embarrassed even these world-weary soldiers. Leaning in, she kissed Ovid on the lips, kissed him so passionately and for such a long time that the Squarehead looked away. At that moment, with her lips still locked on his, she pushed a small pouch into Ovid's palm. She broke off the kiss and hugged him, whispering into his ear: 'I saved some of your orange powder. For emergencies. Use it instead of a dagger. It will kill you less painfully.' She squeezed his fingers around the pouch.

The Squarehead ordered the soldiers to take the travel bags, packed or not, and then indicated for Ovid to follow him outside.

'Wait!' Ovid shouted. 'I shall not fail my duty because of you and your men.' He grabbed a parchment, unrolled it, and wrote in large letters: *Everything I own in Tomis is Cynthia's. Publius Ovidius Naso.*

He placed the parchment on the table, took one final look at Cynthia, and then allowed the soldiers to lead him out. *There is no pattern to this horror*, he thought as he was marched from his house. *I have lived a hundred deaths, and this one is yet different again*. The garden that he knew so well, the bush in which the hedgehog had lived, it all now seemed so small. He wished he had more time. It was the only important thing. Time. And his was nearing its conclusion.

The litter carried him fast, slipping through the back streets with a slyness that made him queasy. It was all so quiet, all so hidden. What a way for a man to die. He would have felt insulted if he had not grown so numb from it all.

The litter stopped. Ovid was ordered out. To his surprise, they were already far from Tomis. Perhaps he could run away, plead, bribe. But he knew each action would be as futile as the other. He breathed deep, trying to muster some form of dignity with which to meet his end. 'At least tell me,' he said to the nearest soldier, 'who is behind this.'

The soldier smirked. 'You will find out soon enough.'

Hands grabbed him from behind, dragging him across the sharp stones and into a covered wagon. It smelled of death and urine. Somewhere inside, from one of the dark corners, came the perceptible sound of a man's breath. In, out. In, out. So this was he. His murderer.

'Who are you?' Ovid said. 'For god's sake, let me know. Just let me know. It is all I ask. Who are you?'

'It is me.' The wagon, more wooden cage than army vehicle, lurched forward. Light filtered in, illuminating the smiling face of Spiros. 'It is me, master.'

PART TWO

Okeanos, the Great River of the North

The Lower Danube, late autumn, AD 14

At the Border of the Known World

Ovid had slept and woken and slept and woken several times. When the wagon came to an abrupt stop he was lurched back into full consciousness. The choking smell of stale urine, some of it his own, seized his stomach and he heaved out a mixture of semi-digested vegetables and meat.

Outside, he could hear the driver swearing at the mules, and nothing else. There was only a stillness, one which, after the incessant rattling and shaking of the journey, seemed almost otherworldly. The wagon started up again, as abruptly as it had stopped, and Ovid was thrown on to the floor. He did not bother to get up. Instead, he lay where he was, amongst the stink and the noise, somehow detached from it all, able to observe himself. How odd that, down here in the grime and filth of this wagon floor, the future did not seem to count and the past was all but forgotten. He was simply present. Was this what it took for the mind to free itself from the constraints of the body, this degraded physical state? Was this how one could achieve a new consciousness, where one could find the very essence of being human?

'Let me wash your face.' It was Spiros, his voice ripping through Ovid's reverie, bringing him back to the aches and pains of his old body – the exhausted arms; the swollen feet; the dry mouth. 'You will feel better, master.'

Without waiting for a reply, Spiros began to pour water over Ovid's head, turning the mud of the floor to marsh.

'Stop it!' Ovid shouted, pulling himself to his feet and swatting the bucket from Spiros' hand. 'Stop it now!' He fell back on to the narrow bench with a heavy thump.

'I feel useless', Spiros moaned.

'And what exactly do you want?' Ovid stopped. He should not be so cruel. After all, ever since Ovid had granted his former slave freedom, Spiros had become – paradoxically – devoted to him. The fact that he was here by his side as they ventured into the unknown was a blessing, not a curse.

'I want to do something', Spiros said, looking at his own feet in dismay. 'Something to help.'

'Then tell me this: what are we doing here? Why are we on this wagon? Am I to be killed? And are you too?'

'Do you not think I have asked them the same questions?' Spiros pointed to the colourful bruises that peppered his face. 'I know that it was Plautus' men who took us out of Tomis, and I know that they are brutes. They are led by a young tribune, though he has little power amongst them.'

'Maybe you should have tried to fuck them.'

'Them? Oh, they are far too tight for me.'

Ovid smiled despite himself. He had meant to cut Spiros to the quick with his little barb, but the riposte, delivered with faux superiority, was undeniably funny. He had to admit it. The wagon stopped once more and, quieter now, he asked: 'They beat you?'

Spiros nodded, presenting one cheek and then the other so that Ovid might see the full extent of his bruised but smooth face, which might never have known a razor. Instinctively, Ovid passed his palm over his beard, feeling the rough, greasy brush.

'I will shave you as soon as we find civilisation', Spiros said.

'Will we find civilisation?'

'I have been assured of it.'

'So you know where we are going?'

Spiros nodded. 'Some place where a ship shall await us.'

Ovid eyed him warily. 'How can you be so sure of this?'

'My beating was the cost of the information.'

'Well?' Ovid crossed the wagon to sit beside his former slave. 'Go on, man. Tell me. Where are we going?'

Spiros opened his mouth to speak, and then clamped it shut again as a flap from the wagon's cover was lifted from the outside. Daylight streamed in, followed closely by a young man: Plautus' tribune. 'Publius Ovidius.' His Latin accent, though foreign, was pleasant. 'You can get out and stretch your limbs now.'

Before Ovid was on his feet, Spiros was already outside the wagon, leaping through the aperture and then poking his grinning head back inside. 'You must see this view, master. It is stunning.' Spiros reached out his hands, helping Ovid towards the opening. Ovid stumbled outside.

The majesty of the view surpassed anything his imagination might have prepared him for: a greatness beyond comprehension, filled with an overwhelming space and distance of such power that the very sight crushed all thought. It was a river. A huge river. His gaze moved over islands covered by willows, over yellow-brown fields of reed floating in patches on the water, and towards the thick line of green-grey mist that shrouded the opposite bank. He straightened his back, his chest swelling with joy. At his feet stretched the great river of the north.

In their myths, the old Greeks had called it Okeanos. The new Greeks preferred the name Istros, while the people of the region – the Gaete, Thracians and Celts – referred to it as the Danube. The Romans, latecomers as always, Latinised it into Danubius. So many names assured confusion, but all denoted one thing: this tremendous river, which surrounded the Greek world. The Argonauts had claimed to have sailed it upstream to retrieve and bring back to Greece the Golden Fleece. Even Hercules himself – Ovid's grandmother's hero-god – was said to have herded cattle on one of the river's islands. And then, of course, beyond it, beyond this legendary Okeanos, further to the north, lay the mysterious country of the Hyperboreans, the forefathers of humankind, the only people Augustus had ever admired.

The Tribune pointed towards the top of the neighbouring hill, where a huge grey fort, non-Roman by the looks of it, sat stoically. 'Axiopolis', he said with barely veiled wonder.

'Axiopolis?' Ovid snorted. It was where rumours claimed Augustus to have met – long before Livia, even before his first wife Claudia, stepdaughter of Mark Anthony – the Hyperborean princess whom he had wanted to marry, much to his family's dismay. 'Axiopolis doesn't exist. Every Roman knows that.'

The Tribune turned to face him. 'Romans are ignorant. Most, anyway. Just accept that you are at the border of the Roman world.'

Whether it was the legendary Axiopolis or not, a real town existed beyond the fort. Ovid was led to an inn and given a yellow-painted cubicle. To his relief, he did not have to share with anyone. After the degradation of the wagon, the cubicle seemed to him luxurious, with its large straw mattress untarnished by stains of blood, urine or intercourse.

A curtain hanging over the cubicle's entrance constituted the door, and it was not long before Spiros appeared through it.

'We are free to wander about the inn's yard as we please. But I have been told that we should not go outside unless escorted.'

'Why?'

'People here have a monetary value. Strangers are kidnapped and sold. Slaves are in high demand.'

'Nobody would ever dare trade a Roman citizen.'

'If I were you, master, I would not test that hypothesis.'

'No matter', Ovid grumbled. 'After that wagon ride, I feel too ill to go anywhere. Even the thought of a meal at a tavern turns my stomach.'

'Is there anything I can do to help?'

'Yes. Leave me be. I need some time alone to recuperate. I will call for you when I am feeling a little more myself.'

Bowing and nodding, Spiros retreated from the cubicle through the curtain, and Ovid was alone once more. He lay down on the straw mattress and gazed at the spider web in the corner of the window. What were spiders like here at the edge of the world? Was their bite lethal to an old man? Should he kill the creature? Even the idea was exhausting. He pulled out the sachet Cynthia had pressed into his hand back in Tomis and, after a long hesitation, sniffed the orange powder. It surprised him that, even though he knew it was poison, the familiar feelings of comfort and pleasure were not spoiled.

A servant came through the curtain. 'Your bath is ready, sir.'

Ovid raised his head. 'My bath?'

'It has been requested for you. Please, come with me.'

He followed the servant out into the corridor where a steaming bathtub was indeed waiting for him. Climbing in, the hot water sent sharp trills of sensation up and down his skin, momentarily taking his breath away.

'Would you prefer the horn or the silver strigil, sir?'

'Silver', Ovid gasped, and then closed his eyes as the servant scraped away the dust of all those miles of travel. He was skilled at his job, dispatching the layers of dirt smoothly and with ease. After having been transported like an animal, Ovid wallowed in the relief of feeling something close to human again.

The Okeanos came back to him, that first sight of it in all its magnificence, all its splendour. Had he known the world to be capable of such beauty he would have chased it from the second he learned to run. He glided down towards the river, the dreaded wagon behind him, his feet floating just above the grass. The water was the most beautiful he had ever seen, but he knew better than to enter it, for to do so would sweep him far away, not just to the edge of the known world, but perhaps over it. Instead, he followed the riverbank, tracing its curves and undulations, pushing onwards, always onwards, until – there before him – a low, perfectly rounded hill. And in the hill, a tunnel. And at the entrance to the tunnel, a woman.

'More warm water, sir?' The servant balanced a steaming jug on the edge of the bath, and Ovid waved for him to pour the whole thing in. He pushed his limbs out as far as the tub would allow, arching his back and feeling his neck pop and crack. The water was glorious – soft and intimate. Eyes still closed, he heard the servant quietly steal away, leaving him alone.

He imagined the entrance to the tunnel once more. The woman beckoned him towards her, and as he neared unwrapped the orange scarf from around her body and let it flutter in his direction. He followed her. They turned the first corner into a cave and, picking up a staff from the ground, the woman began to knock it rhythmically against the walls, as if signalling their presence to the very centre of the Earth.

They continued on, he behind, she in front, always knocking the staff. Something about her – the hair, perhaps? the curves? – reminded him of Livia. He thought lovingly of her insatiable desire to command the future, regardless of Augustus' inclinations. She had been a secret priestess of the Mother Goddess, divining single-handedly, seeking out the truth that remained unobtainable for others. He missed her. He wondered where she was now. In mourning for the dead Emperor, no doubt, and perhaps in fear too.

In the perfect darkness of the cave, Ovid felt breath upon his neck. Gently he was helped into a garment, the air moving around him as the clothes were lifted with a rustle. He heard a forced scratch of stone on stone, someone igniting a fire perhaps, so that the darkness might soon be over, as in the ceremonies of Isis.

Light filled the room. The woman, head uncovered but face turned, walked towards a stone block busy with an assortment of objects. Her hands chose a silver bowl and she plunged her face into its contents. Then, straightening her back, she turned and opened her eyes wide. She was not Livia. Livia he would have recognised. No, this was the Hyperborean high priestess of Apollo, the Pythia: the medium through which the god of healing chose to express himself. Ovid could see that she knew everything about him. Her look mirrored his fears, his dependence on hope, his infatuations, his self-centredness, his obsession not to die. He knew he was allowed to ask a question, but only one. He could not decide which. Why couldn't she read his mind and save him the effort?

The Pythia flicked the tip of her finger at a bronze bowl, then placed twelve beads of salt on a small silver tray, lit the candle underneath, and waited. A thin yellow sulphurous smoke gently tickled his nostrils. It was the sign that she would speak her prophecy.

'Your next self will be free.'

Next self? Bullshit. The message was neither ambiguous nor obscure, but closer to meaningless. The sort of generic nonsense the market women of Tomis would come up with in the hope of securing a coin. Despairing that he might have lost his chance, he asked the first question that came to his mind. 'Will I ever return to Rome?'

She must have felt tricked, for her mask began to fall, followed by the white skin that slipped from her face and disintegrated into dust. 'Know yourself first', she said, and then her mouth too was gone. She raised what once had been her right hand, now only bone and knuckle, and held up three skeletal fingers.

The cold water of the bathtub woke him, chasing away the last glimpses of his dream. Disoriented and confused, he leaped out of the bath and fled to his room, where he sat on his bed, arms wrapped around his legs and chin resting on his knees, as he had so often in childhood. He repeated the Pythia's prediction to himself. 'Know yourself first.' It was a bland sentiment, superficial even, daubed on the walls of every Apollonian temple and barely given the time of day by serious philosophers.

'Know yourself first.' He snorted, filled with scorn at himself. He was Ovid, one of the greatest Roman poets to have lived. He should have known better than to put his faith in the illogic of dreams.

The Crossroads

Ovid slept better that night than he had in years, and when the day began to come alive he wished for just a few extra hours to sleep yet more. He rubbed at his eyes as steps sounded along the corridor outside his cubicle. He knew even before his former slave pushed aside the curtain-door and entered the room that it would be Spiros.

'I told you it would happen, and I was right! They have just struck a deal.'

'What on earth are you talking about?'

'We have been sold. Just as I predicted. It's what they brought us here for.'

'Nonsense.' Ovid climbed out of the bed.

'This is no lie, master.'

Ovid looked at Spiros for some time, seeing that, indeed, there was no hint of trickery in his eyes. 'It is true?'

'As I say. We have been sold.'

Ovid scratched his beard. 'How much am I worth nowadays?'

The sum Spiros named was not unreasonable.

'And you?'

'That's for both of us.'

'Do you know who the buyer is?'

'Someone who wants to listen to your poetry for the rest of his life and to fuck me for the rest of my youth.' Spiros produced a wineskin from a bag and pulled out the stopper. 'Have some. It will ease the change from a free man to a slave. Trust me. I drank much when you bought me in Corinth.'

'I need water, not wine', Ovid said, though he felt unconvinced by the sentence. Would he truly have the courage to face his fate sober? He pictured Oedipus' father, approaching the crossroads. To his own surprise, Ovid wished Scorillo was here.

Spiros opened the window's shutters. 'Listen', he said. 'They're out there now.'

Disagreeable voices drifted up from the yard below.

'What if they recognise him?' said one.

'He will be drunk and drugged', said another. 'Nobody will know who he is.'

'Will such be enough?'

'More than enough. Consider. He has lived in Tomis for years and hardly anybody recognised him there. Now he is older, greyer. I assure you, it will not be a problem.'

'And his slave? He is certainly well known in Tomis.'

'Him they can have for free.'

Ovid leaned back from the window, the reality of it hitting him. 'Those bastards', he muttered. 'They really have sold me.'

'Us', Spiros corrected.

'It will not happen. I will not let it happen. They will not take me.' Barefoot, Ovid marched out of the cubicle and down the corridor to the alcove with its barrel of fresh water. He plunged his hands in up to the elbows, splashing his face until his blood raced and the walls were soaked. 'My tunic!' he ordered.

Spiros brought it to him, along with the single travel bag he had succeeded in packing in Tomis before the Squarehead had spirited him away. He dressed and then reached into the bag, which was too heavy to run with, pulling out the unwritten wax tablets, a stylus and some coins, and placing them all inside a smaller linen sachet.

'Are you coming?' he asked.

'I think I might take my chances here', Spiros said.

'Are you sure?' Ovid watched his former slave. He was a good mixture of intelligence, perfidy and spite. He would fit in well in Rome. If they took him there.

Lacking the time for a proper farewell, Ovid clasped Spiros' hand once and then fled from the inn. Outside, the courtyard teemed with legionaries busily hurrying around the wagons: loading, unloading, swearing and joking. He kept close to the far wall, hoping that they would not see him as he sidled out, delighted when not one did. The gatekeeper at the back entrance was happy to receive a silver coin instead of the usual copper one, and with that Ovid was free. Out in the open, the sky turned from pink to primrose, and as he took the narrow track up the hill he was surprised to find that his body was no longer the numb sack of exhaustion he had grown so used to over recent years, but was instead as light and willing as it had been in boyhood. The breeze was fresh as he ascended, hoping to find a vantage point from which to check the best way to reach the Danube. Once there, at the great river's edge, he would be sure to find a ship to sail him upstream, and from there to Vindobona, Germanicus' headquarters.

The hill reached its peak. The view from up here was even more grandiose than it had been before. He was indeed in Axiopolis. At the base of the hill he could see the most famous crossroads in Scythia Minor that linked Greece via Tomis with the North, and, along the river Danube, Germany with Scythia. As Ovid gazed upon it all, the rush of excitement that surged through his veins seemed to light his soul on fire – so much so that at first he barely noticed the hand that laid itself upon his shoulder.

'You should not have left the inn unescorted.'

Ovid whipped around to face the Tribune. 'You again?'

'I must admit – I am impressed you made it this far', said the young man.

The rush was still there, coursing around his body. He gave in to it. 'Why don't you just kill me?' Ovid shouted, allowing the anger to clench his fists and narrow his eyes.

'Because I haven't been ordered to do so. There are surprisingly many things you do not understand', the Tribune replied, maintaining his calm.

'How dare you?' Ovid yelled. 'How dare you, you little prick? I don't care if you're my appointed murderer or not. You're not my judge. You know nothing about me. So do not deign to presume what I do and do not understand.'

The Tribune stared at Ovid with his washed-out blue eyes. 'Oh, I know about you, poet. I know you want to be free, but can't. I know that the Danube – once meaningless for you – is now a possible escape route, but I also know that you are afraid to cross borders into the unknown. And here is what I know above all: you are a slave to your own delusions.'

'Creep back into the cunt of your mother!' Ovid shocked himself with the violence of his own words. When had he learned to swear like a barbarian stevedore?

The Tribune was shocked too. But only for a moment. Within seconds, the shock passed and was replaced by visible anger. 'Normally, I would have killed you for that', he said. 'But you are under my protection. I shall send my men to fetch you, miserable man.'

Before Ovid could reply, the Tribune turned and walked away down the hill.

Two Obols

Alone once more, Ovid wasted no time and made his way straight to the river. The piers were deserted. Gulls hovered undisturbed above the platforms, screeching their laments over the absence of a morning fish market. Between the boats dragged up on to the pebble beach, men repaired their nets and swore.

Ovid walked from one boat to the other, the merciless north wind wrenching tears from his eyes. They were mere fishing vessels; there was no ship to grant him passage upstream. If he could find his way to freedom, he might as well just throw himself into the river, and let himself be taken by the current to one of the many murderous whirlpools, passing-points into another world.

'Who else is for the other shore?'

Ovid looked about him to identify who was calling. When he did, he darted across the pebble beach, waving his hands in the air. 'Me.'

An apparition with a red tunic and conical hat repeated the call. 'Who else is for the other shore?'

'I am coming! Wait!'

The man looked like Charon himself, the grimy ferryman who rowed the dead across the River Styx to the Underworld. Maybe, Ovid thought, it was really he, Charon, and in front of him were in fact Stygian shores. Was it too much a stretch of the imagination to suppose that the Danube was not only Okeanos' but also Lethe's stream? And what a wonder it would all be if true. If he could not escape this place, the next best alternative to immortality was to enter the Underworld alive. He would experience the same as Hercules, Prometheus, Orpheus and Aeneas when they were ferried across the Styx. It was the place his rival, Virgil, had reached only in his fantasies – and Augustus never.

'Be quick! Hurry! You are holding us back.'

Ovid climbed aboard. 'How much?' He had only a few coins with him.

'My price never changes,' the boatman said. 'Since time immemorial, it has always been one obol. How many are you?'

What a bizarre question, Ovid thought. 'How many can one be?'

'That depends,' the ferryman said.

The four hopeless and shivering passengers who waited in the boat stared at Ovid, imploring him to shut up and pay the fare. Ovid handed over the obol.

'Now we must wait for a sixth passenger,' the boatman said, pushing the coin deep into his pocket

'What if none shows up?' Ovid asked.

'Someone always does.'

'Here.' Ovid produced a second obol. *Perhaps I am two, after all*, he thought. *An exile and a poet*. 'Take it. Then we can move on.'

The faces of the four passengers lightened with relief.

'What do you carry in your bag?' the boatman asked, refusing the second coin.

'Four wax tablets.'

The boatman hesitated but did not reply. As he readied his oars, Ovid's attention was caught by a familiar voice hollering from afar. He turned to look back up the shore. It took him some time to accept that the clumsy movements of the boy running towards him were not an illusion. Ovid jumped from the boat.

'Nobody does this to me', the ferryman shouted.

Ovid held out his arms. Carp ran into them and embraced him with all the warmth and devotion of which only a child is capable.

'Dear Carp!' Ovid said. 'What on earth are you doing here?'

'Publius Ovidius!' Carp struggled to catch his breath. 'I am so glad that I caught you.'

'But how…' Ovid was at a loss. Had this boy followed him all the way from Tomis?

'That's the boy who arrived last night with the Roman soldiers', one of the passengers explained to the boatman.

'A strange lot', another passenger said.

'Very weird.'

'And naïve to believe that a ship would pick Roman soldiers up from here.'

'It has never happened before.'

As much as Ovid wished to follow the conversation, he could not take his focus from the boy. 'Why you are here?'

Before Carp could answer, the boatman knocked three times on the deck. 'Stranger,' he said, 'we are departing now.'

Step into the boat or be left behind.', the boatman called.

Ovid took Carp's hand and ushered him toward the ferry, but the boatman stopped him. 'Today he cannot come.'

Ovid looked at the river, at the boatman, at Carp, and then at the boatman again. 'I paid for two.'

The boatman shook his head. 'Today, this boat is for adults only.'

'What's so special about today?' Ovid asked.

'Get in.'

Preparing for Samhain, to Celebrate the Dead

Carp, running, crossed the packed tavern, trampling over the squeaking planks and stumbling twice as he fought his way between the legs of the drunken customers, who eyed him with curiosity more than discontent.

'Boys should not be allowed to enter pubs,' someone called out. 'Especially a fucking port tavern!'

'What's so wrong with my place?' the publican – who had never been hard of hearing when it concerned his business – shouted back.

Laughter filled the room, and as Carp sprinted up the staircase and out of sight, the drinkers returned to their cups of mulsum – that honeyed, watered wine so adept at curing morning jitters – and bowls of copadia, the trusted pork stew.

Carp reached the top of the staircase and turned the corner to the sleeping quarters, launching himself through the curtain-door and into the cubicle. 'Ovid left on a boat without me!' he wailed.

Scorillo did not move, keeping one eye in place against the largest crack in the window shutter. 'No. He can't have. Tonight, no boat crosses the river.'

'Don't you understand that I saw him sailing away? I don't want to go anywhere without him.' Carp became furious. 'I want to be with Ovid. If I cannot, I would rather return to Tomis.'

Scorillo turned away from the window to face the boy, who was angrily stuffing his clothes into a worn-out sack, sending up plumes of dust to glitter in the beams of light that pierced the shutters. 'You are stirring up the universe with your excitement.'

'You said that Ovid would be happy to see me.'

'I said no such thing. You told me you wished to follow your tutor, your mother insisted that you visit our family. I merely agreed to take you along.'

'But why agree if you knew Ovid would only reject me?'

'He definitely didn't. I saw how hard he tried to get you accepted on the boat.' Scorillo looked down at the boy. Carp's face was damp with sweat, his hair tousled, his expression defiant. 'Perhaps Dokia was right and a visit to our family in the Dacian mountains would do you some good. You need educating.'

'I don't care. I want to go home.'

Scorillo shrugged. 'I shall not force you. Your father's soldiers can.'

'Why would they do that?'

'Because they have orders to escort Ovid upstream to meet a Roman general.'

'General Vestalis?'

'I guess so.'

'Well, Ovid escaped them.' Slinging the bag over his shoulder, Carp marched from the room, back down through the inn and out into the courtyard. Scorillo followed close behind him.

'Where are you going?' The Squarehead blocked their exit.

'Home', Carp said.

'The boy wishes to return to Tomis.' Scorillo positioned himself between Carp and the Squarehead.

'Wishful thinking', the soldier said. 'We are to escort you until we pass the Iron Gates. Commander Plautus' order.'

'What's going on here?' The Tribune, accompanied by his legionaries, tramped into the courtyard.

'Carp,' Scorillo said, 'go inside.'

'Do not tell him what to do', the Squarehead said. 'The boy is my responsibility.'

'That is not what his mother told me', Scorillo said.

'No. It is what his father told *me*.'

'Is this so?' The Tribune stepped forward. 'You seem to have forgotten your protocol, centurion', he said. 'You launch into an argument with the boy's uncle without even thinking of saluting me.'

The Squarehead, taken aback a moment, soon composed himself. 'Ave Caesar', he said, stretching out his right arm.

'Better', the Tribune said. 'Now, to the matter at hand. Publius Ovidius Naso has just defected across the river.'

'You messed up the plan, Tribune. You were supposed to deliver Ovid to Vindobona. But do not worry. I'll get him back.' The Squarehead turned towards his legionaries. 'Men, prepare a boat.'

'You will do no such thing', the Tribune said.

'And why not?'

'Roman soldiers crossing the river will provoke the Dacians. I cannot allow you to do so without Commander Plautus' written order.'

'I can get Ovid back,' Scorillo said. 'I need no one's permission to cross the river. And I will provoke no one.'

The Squarehead considered the proposal, nodding slowly. 'Perhaps this is our best option,' he said.

'Two questions.' The Tribune looked Scorillo up and down. 'Why would you do that? And why should we trust you?'

'To answer your first question, I would do it for my nephew here, who has developed something of a soft spot for our famed poet.' Scorillo laid a hand gently on Carp's head. 'And to answer your second, you cannot trust me. But that is your problem, not mine.'

'Do you really think you can find him, uncle?'

'It is unlikely he has made it to the mainland. I suspect the boat he boarded has stopped at one of the river's islands. Tonight everyone here celebrates Samhain.'

'What is Samhain?'

'The Celtic festival of the dead, the beginning of winter,' the Tribune said.

One of the legionaries spoke up. 'This night, only the dead are supposed to travel across the Danubius.'

'Now I understand why the boatman said the ride was for adults only,' Carp said.

'Was Ovid trying to abduct you?' the Squarehead asked.

Carp shook his head. 'I wish.'

The Squarehead turned to Scorillo. 'You are willing to cross?'

'Yes. But I will need a boat and four rowers. It will be best if they, like me, are also not superstitious.'

The Squarehead produced a bag with clinking coins and faced the crowd that gathered around them. 'You heard what this man needs. Who wants to earn some money today?'

As the willing prospects clamoured around the centurion, each shouting their credentials, Scorillo took the opportunity to bend down low and whisper into Carp's ear. 'Make your way down to the river now. Do it quietly and make sure no one sees. Wait for me where you last saw Ovid.'

'Are you really going to bring him back?' the boy said.

'Yes. Then the three of us will make our way to Dacia. Together. And free from all these soldiers.'

Carp gave a wide and toothy grin, before scurrying off into the jostling crowd.

The Crossing

High on the hill above the river, now peaceful, Axiopolis was still in sight, the bright and contrasting colours of its landscapes blending into homogeneity. Ovid gazed at the town from the ferry, as the boatman steered them through the currents with practised ease.

'Has anyone ever jumped overboard?' Ovid asked.

'Not once. They know the uselessness of such an action. I would drag their soaked and chilled body back into the boat and then charge them for the dry blanket.'

'Let me rephrase the question. Has anyone ever fallen overboard?' The skiff was shaky and sat low in the water. Ovid could imagine that on rougher days the adverse waves might topple the odd man here or there.

'Of course. But I still charged them for the blankets.' The boatman looked away from Ovid and over the river. 'If you are haunted by fears or doubts, keep them to yourself until we have landed. The passage is safe. I guarantee it.'

Ovid wanted to ask how anyone could feel safe on the border between the worlds. Even the Argonauts, that unmatched selection of heroes, had needed Orpheus, the fiddler, on board their ship. As a Thracian, Orpheus had local knowledge of the Danube, or perhaps the river had understood the magic of his songs. But here on this little ferry? Was the boatman really so adept? Ovid looked at him. He had taken his hands from the oars and was peeling an onion. Its sweet vapours, blown by the breeze, were working their effect on the passengers, who wiped their eyes as if they were a group of professional mourners.

'What are you looking at?' the boatman snapped.

'At you,' Ovid replied. 'Unlike the rest of us, your eyes do not water.'

'Why should they? I do not feel sorry for anyone.'

What more proof did he need that he was indeed crossing the Styx, thought Ovid. 'You know,' he said, 'from the moment I met you I thought of Charon. Perhaps you really are him.'

The boatman grunted. 'Charon,' he said, rolling the word around his mouth in a way that suggested the comparison did not displease him. 'My name is far more ordinary. I am Angus.'

'Angus is the best there is,' one of the passengers said, holding out a wineskin to Ovid. The sour smell teased a point somewhere behind his tongue, which flooded his mouth with saliva, but he resisted the temptation to drink. That, he knew, was thanks to Cynthia. He fingered the bag of orange powder in his pocket. Scorillo would not have been pleased.

Angus threw the onion into the water and grabbed the oars as a whirlpool suddenly appeared beside the skiff. Ovid gazed into it. Was it truly, as people said, an entry to the Underworld? He felt a compulsion to leap into its vortex. The gamble, he reasoned, was perhaps worth it. Even if the Underworld did not exist, the swirling power of the water would crush the life from him in an instant, and all his doubts would be over. He moved to the side of the boat, edging closer to the water, staring deep into the abyss.

'Sit down!' Angus yelled. Swinging his oar across the skiff, he knocked Ovid on to his backside.

‘That was unnecessary.’

The oars smacked into the river’s swells again and again, and the whirlpool gradually began to fade from sight. The tip of the boat dipped and rose with a hypnotic rhythm, and Ovid fancied he could hear intermittent high-pitched tones coming from the surface of the water – no doubt, the nymphs of the river. Their song, if that was indeed what it was, made no sense to him. How could travellers have been attracted by such dissonances? Perhaps it was not music after all, but quite the opposite: the deadly call of sirens. He crawled back to the edge of the boat to hear better.

‘He’s doing it again’, one of the passengers shouted, grabbing Ovid by the tunic.

‘Leave him be’, Angus replied. ‘I think that this time he needs to throw up.’

Throw up? Ovid scoffed at the thought as he leaned over the river. But then, to his surprise, he vomited into the water.

The violence of the evacuation brought him back to his senses. He scrabbled into the centre of the boat and looked around him, a little surprised to understand that his fellow passengers were just as real as he was.

‘You’re not the first to struggle with the crossing’, the boatman said, and Ovid could hear the warmth in his voice. ‘But it looks like you’ve come out the other side of it now. Good. You can enjoy the rest of the journey.’

Soon the sun emerged from behind the rainclouds, sharpening the dull, milky light and bringing the shore into sight. The passengers, emboldened by the change in weather, began to speak and laugh loudly – at all the wrong things. But the mood was contagious and Ovid soon found himself joining in. It became one of those moments that are so rare in life, and so very dangerous in Rome, when everything – life, career, politics, death, and even the Emperor himself – becomes the subject of jokes.

Over the reed thicket before them, crows wheeled, black and powerful, bleating their famed messages.

'Yes, yes,' Angus called up to them, 'we are coming.' At the sound of his voice, the crows changed their pitch, stressing different tones. What had at first sounded like a sign of welcome now seemed closer to the death cry of a slaughtered animal. What were they singing of? A kill? A sacrifice? Like the music on the river, it seemed to Ovid that there was a code beneath the everyday reality of things, a code which he could not discern.

Four wax tablets, he thought, *will not be enough to capture this world.*

It took the boatman two strong pushes to enter the thicket, and the ferry found its way between the floating islands of half-dried cane. The mottled greens and light browns of the water revealed their proximity to the mud below the surface too late, and the boat became stuck fast. One by one, the passengers were forced to step out into the cold knee-deep water.

'Why have you come this way?' one asked. 'Normally you enter the harbour.'

'Today the harbour is closed', Angus replied. 'They prepare for Samhain.'

'Samhain? We want to go home.' The passenger laughed without mirth. 'We are not Celts.'

'Tonight,' the boatman said, 'we all are.'

Resigning themselves to the reality of things, the passengers tramped through the mud in single file. One produced a flute – much longer and less polished than the instrument Scorillo had played – and the music, light and magical, picked out currents already in the air as they found and followed a meandering path up to the bank.

'Why is he doing this?' Ovid asked.

'To lure out snakes.'

'A snake!' The man in front of Ovid broke the line in terror. 'Kill it!'

Ovid saw its tail as it swam away from them. 'It's harmless', he said. 'A friendly water snake.'

'How do you know? Are you a healer?'

Ovid chose not to answer, and perhaps that was a mistake, for rather than halting any further questions, his silence only seemed to attract them.

'Who are you, anyway?'

'Where are you from?'

'Where are you going?'

Ovid dismissed them all with a disdainful sweep of his eyes, a gesture he had mastered long ago. 'I am too old for so many questions', he said, pleased that this seemed to put an end to them, pleased yet further that the snake was saved.

Angus took the lead. The melody he chanted, more sombre and haunting than the flute song, echoed off the surface of the water. It somehow made Ovid feel safe. A young willow marked the shore. 'At last', one of the passengers said as he climbed up on to dry land. 'Even pigs do not get dirtier than this.'

'Appearances don't count here', the boatman chided.

'Are we not to be fetched by a wagon at least?'

'No wagons on the day of the festival. Maybe tomorrow, but today, no.'

'I will never cross the river with you again', the passenger said.

'On odd days, you will, for I am the only one who does not mind them.' Angus struck out into the field and away from the river. 'You are welcome to walk with me to the harbour. Tomorrow you might find a boat to get you to the other shore. Or you can make your own way elsewhere. Choose what you like. I do not care.'

'Are we not on the far shore?' Ovid asked.

'No. This is only an island.'

As the passengers dithered at the water's edge, Ovid set out after the boatman. He had nowhere else to go.

An Outpost of Hyperborea

They had reached a row of briars that hid a narrow coastal road, when a wagon pulled by two oxen came trundling along towards them.

'You lied', one of the passengers said to Angus. 'You told us there would be no wagons today.'

The boatman shrugged his shoulders and said nothing.

'Driver!' The passenger moved into the middle of the road and raised his hands above his head. 'Stop!'

The driver pulled up alongside them. He was of an indefinable age, his one distinguishing feature the enormous hooked nose that protruded from his face, so large Ovid felt the need to touch his own, which people said was also rather large.

'Welcome to the land of the Hyperboreans!' he announced with mocking laughter. 'You are welcome to celebrate with us.'

There followed a heated argument, the dialogue rapid and controversial. The four passengers were not there to celebrate anything. They wanted to go home. Ovid tried to follow along as best as he could, but he was not well versed enough in the Gaetic dialect to understand much of it. Memories of his first few months in Tomis came to him, when he had doubted that he would ever understand the locals, for their language, the Gaetic that resembled a primitive Latin, was too full of elusive words with ever-shifting meanings.

The argument came to an end. The four passengers cursed as they refused to climb on to the wagon and prepared to walk away.

'If I were you,' Angus said, turning to Ovid, 'I would follow them.'

'Don't scare him away!' The driver laughed, revealing his long front teeth by pulling back his upper lip, as a horse does when urinating. Then he plugged his nostrils, as people in Sulmo did when chasing away demons.

'Haven't I earned the right to have some fun?' Ovid said.

'Certainly, you have', Angus replied. 'But it will be a long night with an unpredictable outcome.' He removed his conical hat and red tunic, laying them down on the floor of the wagon, and suddenly he no longer looked like the ferryman who rowed the dead across the River Styx to the Underworld. No, he merely looked like any other tired old fisherman, the kind who would share his worries with no one, not even his wife. He had visibly deflated. Perhaps being on land was the cause.

The oxen pulled the wagon back into motion and the jolt thrust Ovid between two sacks of dried herbs. It was not uncomfortable, and he closed his eyes and listened to the driver and Angus talk.

'Business has been sluggish.'

'It will pick up again.'

'Perhaps, but I do not want to start carrying salt and slaves. Then I would be in another business altogether.'

'At least you would not complain it was sluggish. The demons of the salt crystals would change you quicker than anything else. Transporting slaves might transform you too, for they are likewise surrounded by demons – the demons of their lost freedom.'

'Why do you want this man?' Angus asked.

Ovid understood that they were talking about him.

'Because tonight he will purify us and himself at the same time', the driver replied.

The wagon arrived in an empty and dusty marketplace surrounded by solid mud-brick houses, windowless wooden warehouses, ill-maintained barracks, and cheap dormitories. The driver watched Ovid and Angus as they climbed down on to the ground. 'Look at that', he said, pointing to a two-storey-high wooden arch, tall enough to be a gallows. Around it, men rhythmically drove poles into the ground with heavy hammers, their pounding enough to wake the gods. Women organised themselves around three steaming copper cauldrons, preparing a brew that smelled so odd Ovid half-expected to see human limbs emerge from it.

The centre of the precinct was marked by a pyre – a huge hexagonal pyramid with a vaulted entrance. Ovid, hypnotised by the view, tried to understand why it felt so sinister. In a panic of memory, his mind reeled back through the many scenes of collapsing pyres he had witnessed in his life, settling especially on those that had trapped people inside and burned them alive, indifferent to their desperate efforts to escape. The last of this sort had been in Tomis.

He would, he decided, steer clear of the pyre.

The Making of a Scapegoat

For the first time in his life, Ovid realised, he was outside the borders of the Empire, outside Rome's jurisdiction. Did that mean he was no longer an exile? Or, rather, did it make him an outlaw?

In his hands was a wax tablet. He gazed down at it, feeling helpless. What possible sentence could he commit to the wax that would go on to live for eternity? Agitated, he scribbled marks like those of a dying spider. *Life, if given a chance, will defeat death.* He considered scratching the sentence away. Such banality.

These tablets – shiny, black, neutral, and limited – were a pity to waste on drafts. Drafts embodied his untidiness, they revealed either too much or too little. Drafts were always about imperfection. Their very nature demanded it.

He looked again at the line he had written – *Life, if given a chance, will defeat death* – and then held it up against the backdrop of the lazy river, the changing light of the advancing night bringing with it a damp, cold mist. His words did this place no justice, no justice whatsoever. What was it that Orpheus had done differently while he was here?

'Hello there! You must be hungry.'

Ovid looked up, startled, at the high-pitched voice. To his side stood a middle-aged, well-proportioned woman, offering him a hot loaf of bread, two red apples and an unhindered look at her dangling bosoms. He wondered if they would harden when caressed. For such a sight, even in the twilight, he always had an appetite.

'These are not to be eaten', she said.

Did she mean her breasts? Ovid hoped not.

Some distance away, the driver and Angus the boatman watched the scene attentively.

'He doesn't qualify as a scapegoat', Angus commented. 'Scribes don't do good messengers.'

'Why are you so protective?' The driver did not bother to hide his irritation.

'He was my customer. When, on the southern shore, they find out I ferry people to be slaughtered, I'll lose my business. And so will you.'

'That is not my concern', the driver said. 'My duty is my concern. And I shall finally deliver to this community the scapegoat they are waiting for.'

He walked towards Ovid, and at his approach the woman scarpered.

'You are invited to celebrate the smoke', the driver said. 'Are you familiar with smoke rituals?'

Ovid nodded. They were foul-smelling and choking affairs and not his favourite. 'Do you also perform an incubation?' he asked, hoping to show off his knowledge.

'Only for the guest of honour.' The driver smiled. 'I can convince the council to name you as this Samhain's guest of honour. Would you like that?'

Ovid nodded again, hoping to conceal the prickles of pleasure that darted along his spine: his importance had been recognised even outside Rome's borders.

‘Come with me then’, the driver said.

They walked away from the river and to a shed, its chimney already smoking. Wolf furs hung over the entrance, some with their menacing heads still attached, and the driver pulled them aside to reveal seated men, hard to distinguish through the dense vapours, who reacted nervously to the interruption. ‘You again?’ one of them shouted.

‘I have two presents’, the driver said, pushing Ovid forward. ‘For the gods to speak, we need a scapegoat.’

The driver held up a leather bag, and one of the men grabbed it. Ovid could see from his dress that he was a priest of sorts. He forced the bag open and plunged his nose into it, for a moment resembling the dreaded Minotaur, half-bull half-man. The driver then took out a necklace of black and white dried fruits, held it aloft for all in the shed to see, and wrapped it like a serpent around Ovid’s neck.

‘Figs?’ Ovid whispered, smelling the necklace. ‘Real figs?’

‘Sacred figs from Greece’, the driver said. ‘That land to which we have exported our gods.’

The priest’s powerful voice filtered through the smoke. ‘Why do you think this stranger is the man?’

‘None of your predictions has ever materialised’, the driver said. ‘And we are fed up with our stinking lives. Prepare him, and you will see that he will save us.’

‘What’s his name?’

‘Do not bother with details. Just get it right this time.’ The driver barked his commands and then turned and left the shed.

There was space for no more than six steps through the darkness over bodies that did not protest. When Ovid’s stretched-out hands bumped into the reed wall, he let himself down to the ground. Slowly, images and figures began to resolve themselves through the smoke. He realised that there was an inner circle clustered around the hearth. One of them stared at him. It was the same priest who had grabbed for the driver's leather bag so greedily.

'Where are you from?'

'Tomis', Ovid replied. 'On the Black Sea.'

'I know where Tomis is. You smell neither Greek nor merchant.'

'I am a poet. A Latin poet.'

'An unusual trade.'

That needed to be put right straight away. 'An art, not a trade.'

'It seems to me that poetry is the trade of making things up.' The priest took a deep breath, as if hoping to fill his lungs with the smoke. 'Not many of your colleagues have ever crossed the river. Except, of course, the most famous of you all: Orpheus.'

'And he seemed not to like it here', Ovid replied, unafraid, 'for he returned to Thracia.'

'By that time he was a drunkard and an effeminate. I hope you are neither.'

'*Be quiet!*' The command came from the other side of the hearth, from an individual Ovid could not make out. Then, as if in answer, the sound of stricken chords.

Orpheus' lyre, Ovid thought.

'You are right', the priest conceded. 'We need not find out who our guest really is. Now is the time to pray that the smoke will help us accept the unspoken as a blessing, not a harm.'

From the hearth a thin, scintillating column of white smoke rose upwards, as if trying to escape the shed. Part of it found its way through the chimney, but the rest, as if raging from being denied freedom, filled the room with the itching smell of burned herbs. Ovid felt the sweat spring out across his face and raised his hands to wipe it away.

'Don't touch your face! It brings bad luck,' his neighbour warned, and Ovid's hands fell back to his sides.

A whining began, resonating around the shed until it became a drone and then a chant, huffed into the smoke by the gathered men. Ovid recognised some of the words.

Abalon, Abalon, Appolon, Appolon, Leto, Letona, Jo, Jon…

The priest rose to his feet and began to circle the hearth. 'We can't tell the people that this year ahead will be worse than the last one.'

'Agree. We shouldn't predict misfortune.'

'*We* were never mistaken. *They* interpreted us wrongly. The truth is embedded in error.'

The voices came thick and fast through the smoke, and Ovid could not tell who was talking and who remained quiet. As they debated, he pushed his hand through the reed wall behind him, creating a hole through which he could breathe fresh air. He had attended incubation rituals like this in the past, and he had always cheated, never brave enough to submit himself fully to the choking fumes and embrace intoxication.

'Give the stranger the potion!'

'Should we not prepare him first?'

'There is not enough time.'

'But what about the down-going…'

'What about the up-coming…'

'What about the fair-birth…'

'Hear me! There is not enough time!'

Two pairs of hands grabbed Ovid from behind and held him under the armpits, while thumbs pressed on his jaws until his mouth opened. A minty liquid flooded down his throat. *This*, Ovid thought, not fighting back, *is how it must feel to be raped by the gods.*

He was released. Slowly, both worlds – the inner and the outer – began to change. He knew not to resist, and to hope only for a pleasant experience. The men, mere shadows now, moved their lips, but no sound reached him. They were voiceless singers somewhere between a choir of ghosts and a mime show. He closed his eyes. The fumes, no longer thick and choking, numbed his senses as he felt an all-encompassing stiffness work its way along his body. Powerless, immobile, he was briefly surprised to discover that, beneath it all, was a profound sense of adventure.

Ibis, the Bird

The brilliant flash of white light blinded Ovid, and it was through touch that he recognised the dented mask of Janus that hung on the front gate of the house that could only be his. So he was back. In Tomis. Eyes clearing, he grabbed on to the bronze ring of the knocker, swaying from side to side as if he had just arrived home from the tavern, drunk as a pig.

One gentle push and the gate opened. All these years, and he had never been able to teach his servants, Spiros included, how to lock it properly.

The corridor was gloomy. Suspended from the visitor's hanger, he could just discern the outline of his old toga, the one with the thin purple border, the mark of his knighthood. It was his most symbolic garment. To wear it would be to change identities, to become the one he did not want to be: the stiff, pedantic, self-important, dull Ovid whom only Augustus had ever liked. He felt no joy in the idea of donning the toga, but something inside told him that if he wanted to continue his journey, he would need to do so. He opened his tunic and, unbidden, his raw self hatched from his chest like a misshapen bird, like a rodent with wings. Before it could fly away he managed to wrap it in the old toga. Then he slammed the gate with as much force as he could muster to warn all in the house of his return.

He moved through the rooms. No piece of furniture was

missing, nor had any been added. The atrium was deserted, the horrible frescoes were still there. The door to his bedroom was closed, as it should be. The silver statues of two domestic lares, that useless present of his wife Fabia, stood polished atop the house altar. *They don't belong in my house in Tomis*, he thought, but removing them now was a waste of time.

An unnatural green-blue light filtering through the open garden doors marked the only difference in his otherwise unchanged house. He drifted towards it. Stretched wall to wall, high above the garden, was a huge, diaphanous spider web, its skeins breathing, sighing and gasping. Cynthia met him beneath it, radiating expectation. She looked as attractive as she had ever been. Much more appealing than her sister. But as she neared he saw what it was about her that was missing – her undulating movements left no shadow.

'Welcome', she said, her gleaming eyes working their way down his toga, coming to rest at the hillock produced by his embarrassingly stiff penis. Gently she placed one hand over it, and his passion poured from him with unprecedented abandon. They conjoined in the longest and most visceral love-making he had ever experienced, a naturally flowing mixture of well-worn postures and new inventions, the kind only mature lovers can conjure.

Spent, Cynthia left him to fall back on to the bed while she rose and approached the window. With no care for her nudity, she opened the shutters, letting in the world. The breeze stirred the dust in the room. Satisfied, Cynthia settled back down next to Ovid and caressed his hair.

'What happened to me? How have I come to return?' Ovid murmured.

'Did they give you a potion?'

'Yes.'

'If you could remember its aftertaste,' she said, 'I could tell your journey.'

'It was only smoke.'

'Have they forced you to sit on seven mid-sized stones? They might have called that a snake assembly site.'

'No.'

'Have they pushed three beans in your mouth?'

'I can't remember.'

'They must have given you the choking potion with the bittersweet aftertaste. Perhaps you felt your throat swelling, your windpipes blocked, and yet, instead of a dread-inspiring death, you became more alive than ever. Your mind split from your body. Is that the truth of it, my love?'

'Who knows?' Ovid muttered. He gazed at Cynthia. 'Was this what it was for? So that I could be together with you?'

Cynthia shook her head. 'There is more. But for it you must leave this house.'

'To go where?'

'The wasteland.'

'To find the children?'

'To find Icarus.'

'Icarus!' Ovid spat the name. 'What could that failure possibly teach me?'

'Go and find out.'

He was on his feet, no longer in the house, but somewhere in the city, lost. It was not the Tomis he knew. Streets led to alleys and alleys led to dead ends and with every step he could feel the physical transformation taking place beneath his toga.

He would not look. He would merely keep trying, pushing on and on until he found his way to the wasteland.

Finally, the familiar cluster of trees. Then, the poles that marked the starting line of the running track. He was here.

At the edge of the cliff, someone waited. Icarus? He hurried towards him, and as he passed a thorn bush his toga caught upon it, tearing apart. It fell to the ground in tatters, revealing the huge, stinking grey seagull he had become. Ovid the seagull stopped, gazing down at his feathers. Was this true metamorphosis? He was a bird, but he thought like a man. And yet the seagull he was inside was not *it* but *I*.

The man at the cliff edge had all the traits of the Icarus he knew from classical Greek vases: the long and beardless face, the high eyebrows, the aquiline nose. However, on closer inspection, he looked more like the son of Ovid's Tomitan neighbour, the unbearable blacksmith. Had another father sent his son to deal with him? Ovid pictured the blacksmith and Daedalus, side by side.

'Glad you came', Icarus said. 'I can teach you to fly.'

Ovid had no desire for such. 'Will you also teach me how to fall from the sky?'

Icarus stared at the plumage that poked awkwardly around Ovid. 'Perhaps you do not need my tutelage, after all.'

'From your mistake, I have learned to avoid the merciless sun.'

'The melting wax was not the real cause of my disaster.' Icarus dealt his words out with care. 'I wanted to see the sun's real face. Instead, I saw only the deadly mask he hides behind. My flight transformed my father more than me. I was set free by the crash, while he had to carry on.'

'Then I must rewrite', Ovid said, more to himself than to Icarus. Daedalus' story in his *Metamorphoses* needed to include this, the notion that flying was a transformation in itself. There was definitely something in that, perhaps the beginnings of a proof that the Earth was exclusively human, that the gods were only there to mess things up.

While he contemplated, Icarus stepped behind Ovid and, with one forceful push, thrust him over the edge of the cliff. Before Ovid could shout at his aggressor, his wings opened and his world was turned around: sea a new ceiling; sky a new earth. He felt the weight of the wings on his back, the pain of the vice-like grip that clutched at his head, and saw that the waves above had been set in motion by forces that did not make sense. Reason overrode instinct, and with it he plunged upwards into the sea.

Within the cold water – a world neither dark nor shapeless, but fluid and the brightest of blues – the grip on his head tightened, and he felt each individual finger as it pressed into his skull. A hand, not his, pulled backwards, and Ovid's head was wrenched from the water. He gasped for air before being plunged back in again, and then, moments later, the hand pulled him out once more.

Ovid flapped himself on to his back, choking and wheezing. Above him loomed his personal enemy, Ibis, his hands red and dripping wet.

'Not even in my nightmares can I get rid of you!' Ovid screamed.

'You should let that hate go', Ibis said. 'You have me to thank for everything.'

'What twisted logic is this?'

'*I* made you the poet you are. If *I* had not taken your Corinna away, you would have written nothing more than those cheap and sentimental love poems of which you were once so fond. *I* asked Augustus not to kill you but send you to Tomis. You owed me everything and as gratitude you killed my son.'

'No!' Ovid refused to accept it. This bastard had done everything he could to make him feel unwelcome and unwanted in Rome. He had challenged him without mercy, both in public and in private, lambasting him as little more than an imposter. And so Ovid had proved himself to Rome. He had written the *Metamorphoses*. With every story that had dripped from his stylus, he had felt purged, renewed, accepted. But to think he should thank Ibis for spurring him on? Preposterous. 'You were always conceited', he said.

Ibis launched forward, grabbed Ovid by the head again, and plunged him face first back into the water. 'I should have killed you a long time ago!' he yelled as Ovid fought beneath him. 'Nothing but a self-centred provincial. I am here to put an end to you.'

As much as he tried, Ovid could not free his head from Ibis' grip. *Down*, he thought. *If I cannot go up, I must go down. It is the only way.* Flailing with his wet wings, he pushed himself deeper into the water until he was fully submerged and swimming, swimming towards the dark abyss. Ibis was behind him, giving chase, he could sense it. He would catch him soon, smash his head against the seagrass-covered rocks. There was only one thing to do. In one deft motion, Ovid pivoted, turned, and bit down on his pursuer.

Two spongy, blood-filled bulbs glided into his mouth. He tore at Ibis' scrotum with his teeth. The water around them turned sticky and warm, but Ibis had hold of his head once more. The grip was too powerful, he could not escape it, Ibis would soon twist his skull off. Ovid opened his mouth to shout, spitting out the testicles. '*Help!*' he screamed. The water began to fill his throat. '*Help! Please help me! I cannot do this alone!*'

The Island Council

The driver crossed the empty market square and came to a stop at the house of the local council. Before entering, he rehearsed aloud some introductory phrases, and then knocked three times. The door swung open.

'Come in and enlighten us', the group elder said. 'Did the stranger accept the role of scapegoat?'

'I chose not to ask him', the driver replied.

'Does he yet wear the necklace?'

'I placed it upon him with my own hands.'

'Good', the group elder said. 'Good.'

The breadmaker, she who had offered food to Ovid by the river, spoke up. 'I do not trust him. He preferred to ogle my breasts rather than eat my bread.'

'We do it too. And yet you trust us', said one councillor.

'But I would never hand over all my worries to you.'

'More importantly,' Angus, the boatman, said, 'what if he is innocent?'

The driver laughed. 'Who among us is that?'

'I've seen his groomed hands, I've seen the thin feet protruding from his sandals', Angus replied. 'The man has never worked a day in his life. He is useless for carrying anything to the gods, let alone our shortcomings. The gods will not listen to him.'

'As they don't listen to us', the driver said.

'We need a proper vehicle to carry away our flaws', the breadmaker said. 'Not him.' She looked to the group elder.

'When bonfires on the other shore send us their light,' he replied, 'the gods will send us the answer. They have always done so, when asked.'

'They do not tend to be precise.'

'Nevertheless.' The group elder held out his hands, palms forward, indicating that the matter was closed. 'We shall not let this opportunity go.'

The driver looked around at his compatriots. 'I am about to give up', he said. 'Are we really ready?'

The group elder let out a long and loud breath. 'Yes', he said. 'Yes, we are.'

A sharp banging sounded at the door. It was the watch, who had run all the way from his station at the pier. 'A boat from the other shore approaches our island. What shall I do?'

All eyes turned to the group elder. 'Turn him back', he said.

'On Samhain?'

The breadmaker removed from her bag a pendulum, a rusted key on a length of leather string, and let it swing over the table. Seemingly of its own accord, it began to describe wider and wider circles. She smiled, and, keeping the pendulum aloft, looked over it towards the group elder. 'As you said, the gods will send us the answer. And here it is. Our real scapegoat has arrived.' She pinched the key between thumb and forefinger and returned it to her bag.

The group elder smiled. 'The newcomer will be our scapegoat.' He pointed to the driver. 'Go and welcome him. Ensure he is well-fed, half-drunk and hallucinating by the time we are ready to sacrifice.'

'And what about the one who calls himself a poet?' The driver did not seem pleased either with the assignment or with the call.

The group elder stood, crossed the room and opened the door. 'This is not a year to have two scapegoats', he said, before stepping out into the fresh air.

The Eleusian Smoke

Scorillo stepped out of the boat, knelt down in the mud, prayed, and then walked up the mild slope to the road towards the entrance of the village. It did not take him long to reach the marketplace. He supposed it was as good a place as any to start looking for Ovid. The driver, followed by another man, stopped him just when he was about to ask one of the women preparing the festivities.

'Who are you?' asked the driver. 'State your business.'

Scorillo had rehearsed his reason for crossing the river over and over in the boat. It flowed from him like water. 'I have come to retrieve a lost madman.'

'A madman, you say?'

'He believes himself to be a Roman and a poet. He also claims sometimes that he is mastering the art of transformation. Does that not sound mad to you? He has been taken by one of your boatmen. So he must be here somewhere.'

The driver measured Scorillo head to toe. 'I do not believe I can help you. In this village, Romans do not get lost, and transformations are rarely required. Why don't you return before it becomes too late for that?'

A faint breeze drifted through the marketplace, bringing with it the smell of smoke coming from the building where Ovid was held prisoner. Scorillo sniffed at the air, then cupped his palms and held them up to his face. 'Isn't that a waste?' he said.

The driver eyed him with suspicion. 'Isn't what a waste?'

'To start preparing a madman as scapegoat.'

The driver smiled. 'How can you tell?'

'By the smell of the smoke. I always knew the Lower Danube was abundant in herbs, but I never knew kykeon grew here. How interesting.' He took another deep breath. 'Yes', he said. 'Definitely kykeon. The smoke of the Eleusian mysteries. Who would not recognise it?'

'Me', the driver snarled. 'So, whoever you may be, you should leave here. Now. Consider yourself unwelcome.'

Scorillo took a step back. 'Tell me, who is it here who has mastered the blend so perfectly? I have a business for him.'

'What kind of business?'

'I am prepared to buy the madman out. You will not find me wanting for money.'

'What else do you have to offer?'

The driver's words trailed off as Scorillo struck up a tune, its melody simple yet haunting. It looped, repeating itself every fourth bar with a hypnotic cyclicism. The driver reached forward and plucked the flute from Scorillo's lips.

'Fine!' he panted.

Scorillo handed him a bag with coins.

'Follow me', the driver said.

With his head low and shoulders hunched, the driver led Scorillo through the streets to the shed, pulling aside the curtain and pushing Scorillo inside. A chorus of angry voices reacted to the sudden intrusion.

'Get out. Do not disturb us', the priest snapped.

'The council thinks that he is the right scapegoat', the driver said, nudging Scorillo deeper into the shed. 'Take care of him.'

He lowered the curtains and strode away.

'It's too late now', the priest protested.

Passed from hand to hand, Scorillo kept quiet as he was guided through the smoke. He tried to make out faces, outlines, but all was a hazy blur, just limbs pressed up against him, guiding him roughly towards a dark corner, where he was swatted to the ground like a dying fly. Beside him came a voice he recognised. Ovid's. Over and over, it repeated the same words.

'... help... please help me... I cannot do this alone...'

The Sacred Shed

Ovid opened his eyes wide. The palm that caressed his face was smooth and dry. The fact that its fingers did not crawl into his eyes was reassuring.

'Who are you?' he bleated.

'It is me. Scorillo. I came to get you out.'

'Scorillo?' The voice fit the name, but how on earth had that man arrived here, in this smoky shed beset by his nightmares?

'Did they give you a potion? Or is it only the smoke?'

Ovid could begin to discern him now, those familiar features, that face of Cynthia's brother. 'It really is you?'

'Of course it's me. Now answer me. Did they give you a potion?'

'Yes.'

'And had it a rusty aftertaste?'

'Yes.'

'Have you met any of the characters from your *Metamorphoses*?'

'Yes!' Ovid said. 'Yes! I have seen them! But...' His voice became wary. 'How did you know?'

'I too have visited Eleusis in the past.'

'I fear for myself, Scorillo. I fear greatly. What is wrong with me?'

'Right now, everything.'

'What can I do? What can I do?'

'Follow me. Away from here. Now. Carp needs you', Scorillo said.

'Carp...' For a moment, Ovid could not recall from where he knew the name.

'Yes. Carp. The boy from Tomis does you good...'

Tomis, Ovid thought. *The boy. Commander Plautus' son. Of course, of course.*

'With luck, you may be able to change your fate.'

Ovid sniffed. 'What difference is there between luck and fate?'

Scorillo looked about him. All eyes in the shed were on the two of them, studying intently, drinking in every word that flowed between them. 'Do not be a fool, Ovid', he hissed. 'Come with me now.'

'It is, I fear, impossible.' There was no hope in the poet's voice, only self-pity, resignation.

Scorillo puffed. 'Tomorrow you'll be dead. They kill the scapegoat here.'

'They can't kill me. I am the eternal scapegoat. My life repeats itself again and again. I have grown to it.'

'The scapegoat...' the priest murmured, and those around him repeated the words, chanting them over and over until they seemed to become suspended, visible, in the smoke.

'Carp needs you. You must change to learn. Or learn to change.'

'You are right, of course, Scorillo', Ovid said. 'In fact, if I could go back to Rome, doubtless I would do everything again exactly the same. But do not worry yourself about it. There is a kind of immortality in repetition. The only immortality I will ever find.'

‘Fine’, Scorillo said. He rose to his feet and snatched the cup from the priest’s hands. Without further explanation, he plunged it into the bowl with the potion, then held the cup out for Ovid. After a short hesitation, Ovid took the cup and drank quietly.

The priest looked at the roof of the shed with gratitude, oblivious to Scorillo who – softly, slowly – began to edge closer to the fire.

Fire Follows Water

'Fire! Get out! Get out now! Fire! Fire! We shall all burn like rats!'

The shouts wrenched Ovid from the depths of his stupor. He was surrounded by flames.

Scorillo was on him. Hustling him to his feet, he ripped the fig necklace from his neck and tossed it at the priest who, stumbling from side to side, yelled: 'This is the end of the world! I saw it!'

'We all did', Scorillo said, kicking down one of the disintegrating walls and hauling Ovid out into the fresh air. 'Are you here?' he shouted, shaking Ovid by the shoulders. 'Are you present?'

'Yes!' Ovid spluttered, holding tight to his bag with the wax tablets.

'Forget the tablets. We must flee. Now. The boat awaits us at the pier. We have a mission. A large boat is waiting for us. For Vindobona.'

A mission? A large boat? Vindobona? The words sounded alien to Ovid's ears. He gazed about him at the carnage. The shed burned with ferocity, the wind twisting its flames to flow like lava. People danced and shouted about the square, proclaiming the fire to be a sign from the gods, favourable and generous. Ovid heard one of the locals yell into the sky: 'Apollo is pleased with our gift! The scapegoats have carried the message.'

Scorillo pulled Ovid close. 'The scapegoats,' he hissed. 'That is us. They think we are dead. If they recognise us we will soon be roasted on the real pyre.' Grabbing the poet by his tunic, Scorillo marched him towards the road that led to the pier.

The driver blocked their way, his feet planted firmly.

'Mark my words,' Scorillo said, 'if you do not let me pass, this time you will see only my blade.'

The driver held out two small leather bags. 'I am not here to stop you. I am here to help you.'

'Why would you help us?' Scorillo fingered the dagger at his side.

'Because I love my people. Stupid as they are, they are still my people. And they think that finally their lives will change. It is for the best if they continue to believe you are dead. You must get away from here.'

'I agree. If you would but move.'

'First, take these bags. They are my gifts for you. One bag contains poppy seeds. But be careful with your quantities. Too little is a waste, too much will carry you dangerously far away. The other bag contains the herbs of the smoke. Now run for your lives!'

Giving Ovid a mighty push, Scorillo took both bags and followed him along the road, away from the town.

'Easy!' Ovid said as they stumbled through the darkness, the receding light of the fire behind them. 'Do you think we are on the wrong shore of the Danube?'

Scorillo, edging ahead, shouted back over his shoulder. 'There is no right or wrong shore. It is time for a real journey, Publius Ovidius!'

'Crossing the river to arrive here was enough of a journey

for me.' Ovid's voice had grown sulky, but he kept pace with the healer in front of him. 'I am finished with journeys.'

'Nonsense. You who have written the *Metamorphoses* must know the difference between a crossing and a journey. Death is a crossing. Life is a journey. Which do you crave, poet?'

Ovid did not need to answer; Scorillo understood him well enough. 'You said there is a large boat waiting for us?'

'Oh, yes,' Scorillo said, and he laughed. 'The *Argos*.'

The Argos

The little craft sped across the river. As the clouds began to lighten around them, Ovid saw it, silhouetted against the land: a wide and worn-looking ship, moored beside the same pebble beach he had escaped from. *How long ago was that? Hours? Days? Weeks?* He was not sure. Time had become fluid in Hyperborea, and who even knew if the minutes that had elapsed there contained the same duration as those that had passed on this side of the river?

Their small boat nestled up alongside the *Argos*' stern.

'Climb aboard', Scorillo said. 'And wait there.'

'Are you not coming too?'

'I will join you soon. But first I must fetch Carp.' Scorillo leaped out of the boat and splashed to the shore.

Helped by the oarsman, Ovid climbed the rigging of the *Argos* to find himself on an empty deck. Under normal circumstances he would have explored the contours and borders of his new home, but his head whirled with words, and he did not want to waste them. He sat down in the centre of the deck, pulled out a wax tablet and a stylus, and began to write.

Journeys filled his scrawled phrases. It was a worthy theme, one that had made Homer immortal. The story of the magical journey of the Argonauts, from heroes to gods, was as ingrained in his culture as the very language in which it was told. Fifty men, hand-picked, for years on a quest, struggling through the waters of the world and returning by the great river of the north, the Okeanos, arriving home with the trophy of true wisdom. Or was it divine knowledge they discovered?

His train of thought was interrupted by a voice that came from somewhere just above his shoulder, and that recited Orpheus' hymn, 'To Musaeus'. '*Learn, o muses, from my sacred song... What rites most fit to sacrifice belong...*'

Ovid turned to look at the young man who, freshly shaven and smiling at him without a hint of malice, bore little resemblance to the Tribune he knew. 'You seem changed', Ovid said.

'I could say the same about you.'

'I have good reason for that.'

'As do I', the Tribune said. 'Whenever I come close to the flowing Mother Goddess, I feel reborn.'

'Why do you recite Orpheus?'

The Tribune continued to smile. 'You shall see why in the coming days.'

'*Master*!'

Ovid knew the voice well. Before he could turn to greet it, Spiros had sprinted across the deck and fallen to his knees at Ovid's feet.

'I have prayed for your safety every moment that we have been apart! Where have you been?'

'Get up, man', Ovid said, not without kindness, as he helped Spiros to his feet. 'It is good to see you too.'

'You are well? You are healthy? Safe?' The words tumbled from his former slave's lips without constraint.

'Perhaps', Ovid said. 'I will tell you later. When I know myself.'

Splashing sounded from below, and the three men looked over the side to see a boat filled with soldiers – commanding their movements, the Squarehead.

'Is this arrival good or bad news?' Ovid whispered to the Tribune, but he gave no reply.

One by one, the men popped up on to the deck. The Squarehead came last.

'It is fair to say that I did not expect to see you again', Ovid proclaimed with as much joviality as he could muster.

'Oh, but I did, poet', the Squarehead growled.

'What are your plans for me?'

'Plans? Soldiers do not make plans. We merely follow orders. Perhaps I should ask you what *your* plans are. It would be good to pre-empt them, for it seems that wherever you go trouble appears.'

Ovid smiled sadly. 'Back in Sulmo, my brother used to say the same thing. But that was a long time ago. He died young.'

'Mine was killed while trying to escape', the Squarehead said.

I have never heard him speak so tenderly, Ovid thought. 'Escape from what?'

'From my protection.' The Squarehead was the only one who laughed.

A gust of wind blasted the men from the side, sending Ovid reeling across the deck. The Squarehead leaped after him, grabbing his coat and pulling him into his arms just before he toppled into the water. The wind died as abruptly as it had arrived, and the centurion released Ovid.

'These tricky winds along the Danube are unpredictable', he said. 'As am I.'

The Celtic Hercules

Heating up the struggling shades of the sky, the blue light of the morning began to spill like oil over the Danube. The wind was favourable but it counted for little: the mast of the *Argos* was broken. Instead, twenty unskilled oarsmen drafted from the Squarehead's soldiers pushed the vessel upstream with surprising steadiness.

The hills of the southern shore loomed ever closer, a sign that their passage through this web of arms and tributaries flowing around scattered islands was coming to an end, and that the Danube would soon become one single majestic river again. Far down the river, Ovid could just make out the garrison of Durostorum, headquarters of a Roman legion.

At the tip of the prow, the Tribune and the Squarehead stood side by side. Ovid realised that, somehow, he was growing to like both men. He admired the Squarehead's ability to deal with life head-on, matter of fact; and the young Tribune had a hidden sensitivity which, under other circumstances, he would have attempted to cultivate.

Off to the leeward side, Scorillo played his flute. The tune was puerile and irritating, but nobody told him to shut up: they could not bear to see the look on the face of Carp, who danced around Scorillo's legs, beaming at each note. Ovid crossed the deck towards both, ruffling Carp's hair and wondering at the deep and silent affection he had developed for this boy. He looked at him for a moment more, and then dragged his feet into the tent. For a long time he lay on the mattress and stared with open eyes into the sheepskins above him, thinking back to his reunion with Carp.

'Why didn't you take me along?' was one of the first questions the boy had asked.

'It was the boatman who didn't. Though, in hindsight I agree with him. Some journeys are meant not to be taken by children.' Ovid had spoken softly – Carp had clearly been hurt by his absence, and he had not wanted to exacerbate the pain.

'Bollocks. There was one more free place in the boat. I saw it.'

'You should be glad you did not join me. That island was no place for you.'

'But how can I learn from you if I am not by your side?'

'Why would you even want to be by my side?'

'To share what you have.'

'What do I have?'

'A vision. You want to be free and so do I.' And Carp had launched himself into Ovid's arms for a hug. Then, just as abruptly, he had pulled himself out again.

'I am sorry', Ovid had admitted, but Carp had not replied. It seemed he had said all he needed, for ever since he had returned to his playful, childish ways, charming rather than annoying the men on the ship.

As the days passed, time slowed, and the ship became a stultifying platform of inescapable monotony. The soldiers, when it was not their turn to row, kept to themselves, gambling away whatever meagre possessions they owned on increasingly ludicrous propositions. On the deck, a tent had been erected for the old man and the young boy – Ovid and Carp, both of whom needed protecting from the merciless sun – and before long it became the meeting point for them, Scorillo, Spiros, the Tribune and the Squarehead. Sometimes Scorillo would play his flute, at others Ovid would recite his poetry, and when things were particularly quiet Carp would sulk and pester his tutor, but never asked again why he had not taken him across the Danube all those many days ago. By and large, the men whiled away their hours inside the tent with two tools: stories and trivial philosophy, neither of which held any particular interest for Ovid.

Scorillo had a particular fondness for philosophy, trying time and again to inculcate the Pythagorean way of life into them all, Ovid especially. He wove it into each of his monologues, sometimes with a considered subtlety, but often with none at all.

'Nomads, they called themselves Celts, used to settle along these very stretches of river', he remarked one morning after their breakfast. 'They would follow the salmon, moving upstream as the fish did. It was a compulsion, perpetually swapping one life for another.'

'I prefer the settled life', Ovid said.

'You could learn a lot from those nomads. Their lives were defined by movement, by change. You would not have seen them revisiting painful situations or picking at old wounds. They gave no credence to such garbage.'

'My past is not garbage', Ovid said, riled.

'But it is rife with misery. Only change can help you break that pattern.'

'I don't want to change! I want to write!' Ovid knew the

outburst made him sound like a pimpled adolescent, but that did not stop it from being the truth.

'A cup of wine is what you need, master', Spiros said, before turning to Scorillo and wagging his finger. 'I know him better than you ever will.'

'Wine is the last thing he needs.'

'I no longer partake in it, Spiros', Ovid said.

'You see.' There was a glint in Scorillo's eye. 'You *are* capable of change.'

Through the tarpaulin of the tent they heard the Tribune approaching. Scorillo opened the flap and invited him to sit. 'You should tell Ovid about the Celtic Hercules', he said. 'About Oghma.'

'The *Celtic* Hercules?'

The Tribune nodded. 'We all have our different Hercules, but without understanding the link between him, Orpheus and the Hyperborean Apollo, no one truly understands the hero-god, or his twelve labours.'

'No one, I suppose, but you Celts.'

'Precisely.' The Tribune smiled. 'Our Hercules, Oghma, was also the god of poetry and eloquence. People feared him for his force, but followed him for his wisdom.'

Spiros looked like he was about to object, but the Tribune silenced him with a hand movement, the kind that dismissed the possibility of any different opinion.

'We Celts see Hercules as the father of our forefather, Celtus. He seeded in us his unpredictable anger, but also his force and his honeyed tongue. Not many miles upstream from here, in the middle of the Danube, is the island of Erythia. It was here that the Hyperborean King Geryon kept his sacred cattle, and here that Hercules came to steal them. But to steal a herd one must be patient, clever, and very lucky.'

'Greeks are all of these things,' Spiros interjected, hoping for a laugh that did not come.

'King Geryon introduced Hercules to one of his daughters,' the Tribune continued. 'History has forgotten her name, but not the fact that she took his wits away.'

Ovid thought of how differently he knew the legend. His grandmother in Sulmo would not have recognised this Hercules.

'The princess took him to a blessed valley, just north of the strait of the Danube on the Hyperborean shore. Hot springs gushing from the womb of Mother Earth had turned the spot into a lush and heavenly paradise, surrounded by impenetrable mountains. Hercules was welcomed by the people there, and he in turn taught them the craft of living well.'

'That was Prometheus,' Spiros said, whose interruption was greeted again with little more than an awkward silence.

'For us,' the Tribune explained, 'Prometheus is a lesser hero. He was a thief, and we despise thieves.'

'Was not Hercules a thief when stealing the cattle?' Ovid asked.

'That is not a word I would use to describe him. But allow me to continue with the story. Hercules and the princess had many children, the oldest son being Telephus, who would go on to become king of the Lower Danube. We, the lowland Celts, honour Telephus as our forefather.'

'Yes,' Ovid said, 'I know of Telephus.'

'But Hercules' marriage to Telephus' mother would not last. Soon the passion disappeared, their union faltered, and

Hercules remembered the task he had set out to actualise. Returning to Erythia, he succeeded in stealing King Geryon's cattle and then began his return home, for which he chose to cross the mountains into Italy. And it was there, in the High Alps, that the daughter of another Celtic king fell in love with Hercules. Her name was Celtine. She knew that to keep Hercules she would need to hide the herd so that he could not leave until he found it. She tucked them away in the depths of the mountains, far from any civilisation, and then set about working her charms on Hercules. It was a success. Celtine gave him two sons: Celtus and Latinus.'

'Latinus?' Spiros said. 'I believe I can see where this story is heading.'

'Celtus stayed with his mother, while Latinus helped his father find the cattle. Together they moved the flock through Italy from north to south. Somewhere along the way, father and son drifted apart. Hercules moved on to complete his labours, while Latinus built up a kingdom, the kingdom of the Latins.'

'I suppose that makes sense', Ovid said. 'My ancestors in Sulmo knew only that Hercules and his cattle came from the north. Your version of events would be quite the revelation to them.'

'What happened to Hercules next?' Carp asked.

'In whose version?' the Tribune said. 'Mine or your tutor's?'

Carp pointed at Ovid, and the men laughed at his transparent loyalty.

'Well,' Ovid said, 'instead of heading south and at some point sailing towards Greece, Hercules crossed the mountains westwards and reached a place with seven hills and a swampy river. There he stopped again because two twins saved by a she-wolf needed help. To build up Rome.'

'That account sounds even more far-fetched than my Dacian stories', Scorillo said. 'But less so than Virgil's *Aeneid*.'

Ovid became alert. The name Virgil never left him indifferent.

'Why don't you write this combined Hercules' story down?' the Tribune asked.

'It's more suspenseful than any metamorphosis', Spiros said.

'I agree it is compelling', Ovid said, while thinking how to combine it with the *Gigantomachia*, which stubbornly refused to be caught in words. 'But, as yet, too flimsy. It needs more details.'

'They can be found', the Tribune said.

'Where?'

'In the Herculaneum, Hercules' temple on the other side of the Danube, a few miles from the Iron Gates', Scorillo said.

'At another important crossroads', the Tribune added.

'Surely you do not want to cross that river again, master?'

'He will', the Tribune said. 'For history's sake.'

Spiros grew frantic at the thought. 'How many times will you have to play Orpheus? When will you learn that getting Eurydice out of the Underworld is impossible?'

'Calm yourself, Spiros', Ovid said, laying his hand on his former slave's arm. 'Your comparison holds no weight. Orpheus was an idiot. His failure to rescue his wife was hardly laudable, and nor was his dying like a decadent drunkard, torn apart by bacchantes during a wild orgy. He could have run away, if he hadn't been plastered.'

'And that', said Scorillo, standing up and stretching out his legs, 'is exactly why I am so pleased you have given up drinking.' He pulled the flute from his pocket and struck up a tune as he left the tent, Carp – unable to resist the pull of the music – scurrying after him.

'There is another version of that story', Spiros said miserably. 'Eurydice did not want to be rescued.'

Ovid, tired from all the talking, sat back and closed his eyes. Of course, all myths had a thousand different versions, the myriad twisted interpretations that transformed like dialects as they travelled across the lands. Would he really need to cross Okeanos yet again to find on the other shore the story of how Hercules helped the Olympians? Why should the Roman public want to know about this arguably absurd story, especially now that Augustus' death had perhaps rendered it meaningless?

The Power of Denial

Ovid opened his eyes. All had left the tent, all except Scorillo and Carp, who had returned while he rested. 'Have you accepted the situation you are in yet?' Scorillo asked.

'What situation is that?'

'One of transformation.'

Carp said, 'He looks the same to me.'

'We are all being transformed', Scorillo said, 'whether we like it or not. But those of us who accept it can reap the benefits. Those who deny it cannot.'

'And yet', Ovid replied, 'I feel no change. I feel the same, if perhaps older.'

'Look at yourself!' Scorillo said. 'Look at where you are! Aboard a ship sailing the mighty Danube! Okeanos! You have been to Hyperborea, to Axiopolis. You have delved deep into your dreams, and your nightmares. You have escaped death on the island in the Danube. You are not the same as you were when driven out of Tomis. Can't you admit this?'

Ovid looked at Carp. 'If I have changed,' he said, 'it was this fellow and his friends who helped me the most.'

'Yes!' Scorillo called out. 'Yes! Now you are beginning to see! We are all of us here, with you, for a reason. We all have our part to play in your transformation, and in one another's. This is the essence of it! Carp will help you win your struggle, as you in turn will help him win his!'

'What struggle does this boy have,' Ovid said, 'other than which sport to favour?'

'Carp has the greatest struggle of all of us. To become king of Dacia. And if he is to become our king,' Scorillo's voice was steady once more, 'he must learn how to master his feelings. The only person he trusts to teach him anything is you. His beloved tutor. He must see you fight and win against your feelings, he must see you overcome, see you deal with them, so that he can learn by example. Do you see? This is why I help you. Now you know everything.'

Ovid stared at the healer, open-mouthed. *The boy a future king? Could it truly be?* 'But…' he stuttered. 'But… how? How is this to come to pass? And how am I to help him if I cannot change?'

'You *do* change. You change every time you write. I have seen it, we all have.'

'It is true, master', Carp said. 'I have witnessed it myself. When you are lost in your writing, it is as if you become someone entirely other.'

Ovid thought about it. 'I suppose…' he said. 'I suppose that… that when I write, when I am deep in the flow of words, much is different. My body warms up. My thoughts come easily. I find myself in a world I neither hate nor fear. Where past and future are present.'

'This is peace of mind!' Scorillo shouted, jumping up and down with such abandon that he almost broke a plank. 'You've got it! I knew you'd get it!' He squeezed Ovid in his arms.

'And that is it?' Ovid said, bewildered. 'That is what you have been trying to teach me?'

'What?' Scorillo beamed. 'What have I been trying to teach you? Say it!'

'That in a world of stillness, I cease to exist. And I am not afraid of my new state.'

Scorillo's feet became so light that he danced his way around the deck three whole times.

The Surprise

'How long until the Iron Gates?' the Tribune asked. At the mention of the famed place, Ovid – who stood just within earshot – inched closer to listen.

'Soon', the skipper said. 'But with this low water, I am afraid they may be beyond the limits of our navigation.'

'The ship is strong and we are all brave enough to make it. We must reach Erythia.'

Erythia, Ovid thought. The sacred island of Hercules' tenth labour, which he had never believed to have existed. In his grandmother's version of the legend, Erythia was where the hero-god convinced some of Geryon's demons to serve him. Those that stayed behind were said to remain there still, guarding the secrets of the king's magic powers. Meeting them would change anyone's life.

Without alerting the Tribune to his presence, Ovid tiptoed away across the deck, searching for Scorillo, hoping to inform him of the Tribune's plans. Yet he could find him nowhere. He must be below deck, perhaps accompanied by Carp and Spiros. But the stairs were blocked and Ovid could not go down. So instead he moved to the rail and waited, watching the dizzying river as it sped past. It was a hypnotic sight, like a million azure snakes rising up the side of the boat, ready to transform themselves back into the living people they had once been: a metamorphosis that brought him anxiety rather than comfort. This tumult was the call of the Iron Gates, he knew, and it would only intensify the closer they got. Though he had never been here before, he had heard the stories. Men experienced strange states in this part of the world.

The Squarehead appeared at his side. 'Can I have a word with you?'

'What choice do I have?'

'None. So now listen. Just before the Iron Gates we'll get off the ship and bypass the gorge by road. On the other side of that mountain' – he pointed off into the distance – 'is a small garrison. But we will not get there. Instead, we will dress you as a veteran and escort you to a port in the Adriatic Sea. If asked, we'll say that your superior, Commander Plautus from Tomis, in gratitude for your long years of service, has granted you a visit to your birthplace: Rome. I'll put you on a boat to Italy, and once there you will be able to find your own way.'

This was a trap. This could only be a trap. Or maybe Plautus was acting on Vestalis' order? Ovid considered the options. Why did he care what the Squarehead's motivations were, so long as he was finally shipped back to Italy? He felt himself weaken, first gradually, then rapidly. Did he not want to go home?

'Let me ask you this', Ovid said. 'Where will Carp go? To the Dacians?'

'No. He'll come with us. You'll take care of him. You'll find him a school in Rome.'

'But won't the Tribune object?'

'He may not live long enough to find out.' The Squarehead marched across to the Tribune, who was still deep in conversation with the skipper. Ovid followed a few steps behind so that he might hear.

'This river is too rough, the water too low', the Squarehead barked. 'We need to cross the mountain by foot.'

'Embolden yourself, centurion', the Tribune replied. 'We shall be fine.'

'Fine? We shall be smashed to smithereens!'

'I suggest', the Tribune said, 'that you do what you did in Tomis. That is, be less visible.'

'If you want to kill Ovid in the rapids, that is your business, but you are not going to endanger the boy. We are on two different missions, don't you remember?'

'I don't want to kill Ovid.'

'In all fairness, I don't think that you know what you want. To me it seems that either the orders you've received were not clear enough for you, or you have a problem with them.'

'The orders I follow are not your concern.' The Tribune looked back out towards the river. 'Tomorrow morning we continue by ship.'

Slipping Away

A plank was lowered from the deck to the pier. The Tribune and his guards crossed it first, to be swamped by the bored women – unadorned with lipstick or fancy garments – who had appeared from the forest to assess the new arrivals.

'This is our chance', the Squarehead hissed to Ovid. 'Quick, follow me. We will slip away while they are distracted.'

Grabbing hold of Carp's small hand, Ovid crossed the plank behind the Squarehead and they dashed into the forest, convening moments later with Scorillo, Spiros and three legionaries.

'Wait here', the Squarehead commanded. 'I will secure us transport.'

He disappeared off into the trees.

'Are you sure this is a good idea, master?' Spiros asked. 'I find the centurion a difficult man to trust.'

Ovid looked across at Scorillo. 'What do you think? Do you trust the Squarehead?'

Scorillo allowed himself a brief chuckle. 'Of course not. But he worries me less than the Tribune. I say we should go. Stick with him while he proves useful.'

Within minutes, the Squarehead returned. 'Quickly', he said, ushering them through the forest towards a concealed roadway, where a cart and two mules waited. 'This will serve.'

'How did you persuade someone to lend you this?' Spiros asked.

'Who said I persuaded?' The Squarehead looked darkly at the former slave, who could not hold his gaze. 'Poet, you get in first.'

Ovid did as he was told, clambering up into the front of the cart. Carp came next. Scorillo and Spiros were ordered to walk alongside the Squarehead and his legionaries. Spiros objected.

'Hey!' Carp shouted as Spiros climbed in, turning around to face him. 'Get out of here!'

Spiros, soft-voiced, said: 'You don't know how tender I can be, especially with young boys.'

'You turn my stomach.' Carp pushed Spiros, and despite the weakness of his youth succeeded in toppling the man to the ground.

Spiros pulled himself to his feet and, enraged, shouted: 'Why have they sent a boy like you with people like us?'

'Hush!' the Squarehead said. 'Keep your voice down.'

Spiros ignored him. 'I'm sick of having to deal with the silly predilections of a child.'

'I said hush!'

'This is no place for—'

The Squarehead's fist cracked into Spiros' jaw. He drew his arm back to strike again, when Scorillo sprung forward, grabbed Spiros and flung him away. 'Do not hurt him! If his blood flows here it will curse us all!' Scorillo shouted.

'Do you deign to command me?' the Squarehead growled.

'Leave him be!' Scorillo snapped back. 'It will ruin us all.'

Two legionaries pushed Spiros inside the cart and dropped him on the wooden floor.

'I gave you no such order!' barked the Squarehead.

'Orders be damned', Scorillo retorted. 'It was the right thing to do.'

Face red and shoulders heaving, the Squarehead removed his gladius from its sheath. 'No one commands me here but the gods.'

'Put your sword away, centurion.' Scorillo flexed his arms.

The Squarehead flung himself at Scorillo, who jumped backwards and landed deftly on his feet, withdrawing his dagger. The Squarehead leaped down after him, and Scorillo darted forward, dagger outstretched, but the centurion avoided the blow and hit back with the pommel of his sword. The men faced each other, crouching low, breath heavy.

'Stop this!' Ovid yelled, rising to his feet. 'Stop this now!'

For the briefest moment, the Squarehead looked up at him. It was enough for Scorillo to lunge forward and sink his dagger into the centurion's chest.

For Ovid, it was as if the light around him changed. Spots of decay grew like mushrooms in his peripheral vision. He climbed down from the cart and rushed to the fallen centurion. It was not too late to meet his blinking eyes.

'Idiot', the Squarehead said. 'Why did you intervene? Don't you want to return home?' He let out a deep, guttural rattle.

'I was trying to stop you both. I'm sorry.' Ovid held the man's head in his hands.

The centurion's face turned a deep red, blood flowed from his nose, and then his stare froze. He was dead.

Ovid lowered the lifeless head to the wet earth, stood up, and looked about him. Along the road, the Tribune, followed by his guards, had arrived on the scene. He examined the body of the Squarehead, shook his head and tutted. 'Should have worn his breastplate.'

The Iron Gates

The death of the Squarehead wrought a change in the Tribune. It was as if, without his usual challenger, he could act with more consideration and less impetuousness. When the impending storm failed to move in their direction and the waters of the Danube failed to rise, he surprised everyone by declaring that the Squarehead's idea to bypass the Iron Gates and travel by wagon over the mountain was, in fact, a sound one.

More carts and mules were summoned, the Squarehead's soldiers and the Tribune's guards were accommodated, and the caravan set off up the mountain. Scorillo played the flute as they travelled – to Ovid it sounded like a lament, or an elegy – and the miles passed slowly. Carp fell asleep, his head in Ovid's lap, while Spiros, recovering, scratched nervously at his skin as if he had been bitten. Ovid tried to doze to the rocking of the cart, but unconsciousness would not come. He was coming to realise that in Tomis he had been almost happy with his despair – he had lived his days out, drinking his wine and taking his powder, numbing himself against the non-existence his life had become. Change, on the other hand, was frightening. The Squarehead's proposal to flee over the mountains to the Adriatic Sea had been so strange that it almost seemed to have originated from his imagination. Why should Plautus want him to return to Rome? And take his boy along with him?

The Tribune raised his arm and the caravan stopped. He helped Ovid off his cart and insisted he follow. Together, they walked the footpath through a dry thicket until they arrived at a glade where some narrow stone stairs led down to a rock protruding from the face of the mountain like a terrace. Deep down, many hundreds of feet below, the river boiled and thundered into a huge crack in the mountain. The gate to the world beyond.

The Tribune breathed deeply and closed his eyes. *Is he enjoying the moment*, Ovid thought, *or praying?*

'I brought you here', the Tribune said, opening his eyes once more, 'to witness Hercules' major work: the liberation of the Thetis, the sea, and the creation of the Danube. It is one of the few places where the past is ever-present, and where the present renews itself continually.'

'It is breathtaking', Ovid murmured.

'I believe our stories of Hercules concur when it comes to this place', the Tribune said.

'Tell me yours and I shall let you know if my grandmother would agree.'

The Tribune smiled. 'It was the Titans, those Hyperborean heroes, who decided that their relatives from Mount Olympus were too abusive, sex-obsessed and humourless to rule the world. And so Zeus and his allies hired a young hero to perform every task necessary for achieving immortality. They sent him to the north to create a border with the Hyperboreans. Hercules split a mountain and freed from the sea our Mother Goddess, the Danube – or, as the Greeks would call her, Okeanos.'

'Yes,' Ovid conceded, 'this all sounds familiar to me.'

'But it is here that our stories might diverge. You see, the history of this river is the history of the Celts. Once the sea began to flow, many moved to the mountains upstream, some going as far as the Alps and probably even beyond. The ones who stubbornly stayed along the valley of the river, my people, believed that they would be rewarded for their loyalty. But they were not. And so they became obsessed with those others, the ones who had done better than them.'

'The same story could be told about those who were left behind in Sulmo,' Ovid said. 'They too resented their brothers who had moved to Rome.'

'These people of whom you speak,' the Tribune said. 'Could they have left Sulmo if they had wanted to?'

Ovid shrugged. 'I don't know. As you are no doubt aware, I am no good at making up legends.'

'My people could not have left even had they desired it. Mother Danube would not let them.'

The Tribune, silent now, stared down at the tumultuous river below, and for a few moments Ovid fancied he might hurl himself into it. But then he righted himself, raised one arm, and pointed towards a thin column of white smoke that drifted upwards from between two mountains on the far side of the Danube. 'Do you see that vapour?'

Ovid nodded.

'That is the Herculaneum, Hercules' temple, with its famous ceiling showing the constellation of the Great Bear. In its library you will find all the books you need to write about these places. And you will write about them as nobody else can.'

Whether or not the Tribune had chosen to pique Ovid's

interest, he had picked precisely the right words. 'Do you really believe all this?' Ovid asked.

'It is the only thing that makes sense to me.' The Tribune's eyes grew distant. 'No place on earth has been more systematically wronged than the Lower Danube. The Greeks dismissed it as pre-mythical, and the gods and heroes who originated here – Dionysus and Orpheus and such like – were branded as unpredictable drunkards. As for the Romans, they have never cared about history. It matters little to them that Hercules and his Hyperborean wife were their real ancestors, that Latin is a Hyperborean language, that Aeneas' ancestors and all Trojans came from the north.'

Ovid could barely contain his excitement at the truths which were spilling from the Tribune's lips. This, this was where his story lay. This was what needed to be told. 'What about the Gaete and the Dacians?' he asked, eager for specifics. 'Aren't they also direct descendants of the Hyperboreans?'

'They are, but when they adopted the teachings of Pythagoras through Zamolxis they built a kingdom, found gold in the Carpathian Mountains, and settled down. They didn't need to travel.'

'And all this is to be found in the books of the Herculaneum?'

The Tribune nodded without hesitation. 'Much more.'

What a story! He could take it directly to Rome, this elaborate confusion about crossing borders. It would destroy all of Rome's old claims that borders belonged to the army and to the barbarians and should therefore be avoided, and it would reward his public with that singular pleasure that can be derived from insight, when long-held beliefs are turned upside down and all are given a fresh, new, equal start.

He had his story, and with it his purpose. On the far shore, the mountains promised a journey to a place that perhaps had never existed, one in which poets were gods and gods were the servants of mankind. But even to experience this, he would not cross the river again.

Reunion

The caravan reached the port on the Danube shortly before dusk. The innkeeper at the derelict-looking tavern offered them free stay if they bought food and drink. Working women were not allowed upstairs. Ovid, Scorillo and Carp moved in.

In Tomis, Ovid would never have imagined that lying all by himself in a proper bed would count as a luxury. First Axiopolis, then this nondescript port on the Moesian Limes. His breathing slowed the moment he closed his eyes, and it was not long before sleep – and its concomitant dreams – engulfed him.

The strigil that scraped along his back told him where he was: at the baths. The touch of the man who worked on him was gentle, considerate, and Ovid relaxed beneath his hands, his lips touching the warm and wet marble surface on which he lay. The touch was refreshing and sensual. He had once been told that some sculptors felt the urge to have sex with their statues. Perhaps this was what that felt like.

The cleaning stopped. Helped to his feet, he was guided through an opening to an adjacent room, where bright blue light played through the windows in the ceiling. Colourful statues peopled the room, models of physical excellence against whom Ovid did not wish to compare himself. This was no longer the baths, but a library. It occurred to him that it was the same library the Tribune had mentioned to him high above the Iron Gates, in the Herculaneum on the northern shore of the Danube. How he had arrived here he could not recall.

Carefully, he descended rose marble stairs towards one of the statues: Augustus as a young general, finger pointing upwards. It was one of the many copies of Livia's favourite. The penis was enormous. Feeling like a naughty schoolboy, Ovid reached out to touch it, and then recoiled when the pointing finger folded into the rest of the fist and the arm began to move down to the side of the torso. Ovid backstepped across the room. The statue followed.

'Come,' it said, the voice vivid and too real not to be Augustus', 'you are surely not surprised.'

Ovid looked about him for a door to flee through, but the room had sealed itself off into one long circular wall.

'Naso, you have always wanted my undivided attention,' Augustus said. 'Now you have it. Say what you have to say.'

'Fine,' Ovid said, standing his ground. 'You could have pardoned me before dying.'

'Death took even me by surprise. There are many unfinished things I left behind.'

'I know you are not really Augustus.' Ovid tried to sound defiant. 'You are just a statue. No more than the reflection of a reflection. My friends warned me—'

'You have no friends, Naso,' Augustus interrupted. 'Only acquaintances, who value you not for who you are but for what you can do for them.'

'Livia is my friend.' *That should do*, thought Ovid.

'Do not mention her in my presence!' Augustus scowled, precisely as Ovid had hoped he might. 'I never understood why she enjoyed your decadent writings. You will not know this, but she even appreciated the duplicity you displayed in the dreadful poems from Tomis. Only because of her are you still alive. You should be forever grateful to her.'

'I am grateful to anyone who has read my books.' Angering Augustus had made him bolder, and he took a step towards the statue. He had aged, Ovid could see it now in the lines on his face.

'I do not know how anyone can stand them. Your books, that is. All your poetry. It is so far removed from the truth, and based on such a lack of understanding, that I wonder how the muses even let you write it.'

'Do you refer to the *Tristia* or to the *Epistolae ex Ponto*? Perhaps I contradict myself from time to time, but who can blame an exile? Away from Rome, the distance between fact and fiction swells, as you may well have noticed from our encounter here.'

'A pathetic poet but a skilled exile, I see.'

'I needed to adapt my talent to the remote places I inhabited.'

'Adapt? Worsen, more like. In trying to continue to entertain your distant audience, you gave up even the last grain of your subtlety.'

'Oh. Perhaps I have misjudged you, Caesar. You can read literature. You can discern the difference between a poet and a lonely, ageing man far away from home. Perhaps you have even learned that feelings, if they are controlled and disciplined, can be released, like water from a dam, in a powerful, all-transforming stream. An ode.'

Augustus became alert. 'Naso, I sense that you are no longer planning an error, but a crime.'

'Whatever I am planning is of no concern to you. You are dead now.'

'I have been told that you have given up seeking immortality' – Augustus' voice was low, menacing – 'and have chosen a very wrong path.'

'And how did you react to such information?'

'With one thought – that the history of Rome is not a good subject for you.'

Ovid lifted his face upwards. It was a perfect occasion to check how much uproar his ode would produce in Rome. 'Just imagine, Augustus', he said. 'An ode, one which would show how Homer forged history, how he confused the world with half-truths about gods, heroes, humans, how he kept from us the most vital truth – that Romans are direct descendants of Hercules and the Hyperboreans. Can you imagine such an ode?'

Augustus dismissed the thought with the wave of a stone hand. 'This we know', he said. 'At least, some of us do. We do not need it made public. My advice is this. You should stick to your elegies. They may not have served you perfectly, but at least you are still alive.' It was the same tone with which he had banished Ovid all those years ago in the room with the laurel tree. 'Aeneas will forever remain as Rome's founder. Virgil constructed, under my close supervision, our past magnificently.'

'What about the truth?'

The Emperor turned green, ready to kill Ovid, even within his own dream. 'History is not about truth. It is about who we want to become.'

'I can imagine you', Ovid said softly, 'young, ambitious, yet with no chance of becoming Rome's first man. Here you are, finding your way to the Danube in the hope that the local tribes might support your ambitions in exchange for peace. Here, you choose Apollo the Hyperborean as your protector, and, following Hercules' example, you are ready to marry a local princess and work it out from there. And then – such fortune! – Caesar is killed. You grab your opportunity, marry the daughter of a patrician, become a triumvir, defeat Antonius, let go of your first wife, marry Livia, change your name from Octavian to Augustus, and then for the rest of your life balance the promises made in your youth with your position as Emperor.'

Augustus came closer. 'It seems you know it all', he growled. 'Is there anything else?'

'Yes', Ovid said, refusing to back down. 'Could it be that you hid Rome's oldest sanctuary, the cave where the wolf suckled Romulus and his brother, under your palace?'

'And so what if I did?'

'I imagine that such a cave could be the very place where, in fact, it was Hercules' Hyperborean who fed those twins. And you kept it hidden because this gave you power.'

The stone hand clenched into a stone fist. 'This', Augustus snarled, pulling it back behind his stone shoulder, 'you will have to find out for yourself.'

Before the lethal punch could land, Ovid awoke. And grinned.

The Fugitive

Ovid and Carp walked down to the banks of the Danube together. Here on this particular bend, upstream from the Iron Gates, it looked like a huge, glittering black serpent. The breeze carried a faint roar from the gorges: the water's reminder of its weight, its power. Like many others who had stood there before him, Ovid realised that he was gripped by a lethal attraction. He removed his boots and stepped into the river until he was ankle-deep. What if the boy could indeed become a Dacian king? And he his tutor? Ovid's misfortunes seemed removed to another state of being. The pebbles beneath his feet, agitated by the current, ripped at his soles as he hobbled across them.

'What are we going to do now?' Carp asked.

'If you really want to know,' Ovid said, 'I was thinking of crossing the river.'

'And give up on Rome?'

The sound of synchronised footsteps drifting over the water from the direction of the forest saved Ovid from answering. They followed the commotion with their heads to see, bursting from the treeline, legionaries. Running as one, they surrounded Carp and hauled Ovid from the water by his arms.

'Men,' he protested, 'what is going on here?'

'Quiet, poet,' a soldier shouted. Ovid recognised him as one of the three who had accompanied him to the cart, they who had witnessed the killing of their leader. 'You are under arrest.'

'Why?' Carp protested.

Ovid put his arm around the boy. 'Where will you take us?'

'To the garrison, of course', the legionary said.

'There is no garrison here. Only that half-abandoned fishing village set back from the pier.'

'Little do you know.'

Grabbed and pushed and poked, Ovid and Carp were frogmarched away from the river, through the forest. 'Wait', Ovid said. 'Under whose authority do you manhandle us?'

The soldiers looked at one another, unsure whether they should reveal what they knew and Ovid did not. Eventually one of them spoke up, perhaps deciding it could do no harm. 'General Vestalis.'

'But how does he come to be here?

'Be quiet now', the legionary said, though not without a semblance of kindness. 'All will become clear soon.'

As they passed the pier on their way to the village, Ovid felt Carp tap him on the leg. He looked down to see the boy gesturing towards the river.

Slowly and subtly, Ovid angled his head in the direction Carp indicated. There, out on the whirling waters of the Danube, a skiff was making its way towards the thin fog coming from the other side of the river. Scorillo, it seemed, had chosen flight.

Vestalis

'We were supposed to meet in Vindobona,' the Tribune said, trying to hide the fact that he was out of breath. The moment he had heard of the General's arrival, he had sprinted through the village to greet him.

General Vestalis picked up the jug of water that sat on the table before him and poured out a cup. 'No salute?'

The Tribune stepped forward and raised his hand. 'Ave Caesar.'

'Much better.' A slow sip of water. 'Now, to answer your question. Or whatever it was. Since Augustus' death, everything has changed.'

'Is that why I haven't heard from you since our meeting in Tomis?'

'I am on my way to Scythia. I am required there. But I have not forgotten your loyalty to me. You may join me, if you should like.'

'What about Ovid?'

'His existence is no longer of any interest to me. Or, should I say, his *continued* existence.'

'Interesting. I suppose you have a new plan.'

The General smiled. 'You speak plain. I like that about you. Others wouldn't, but I do. For this, you are fortunate.' More water, some missing the mouth and escaping down the chin. 'Our esteemed poet and I have unfinished business. He may not survive it.'

'That would contradict your original orders. And I have been here all along to ensure that they are maintained.'

'How obedient,' Vestalis said. 'When we first met, I wondered whether you were capable of such a quality. It seems I was proved wrong.'

'The offer you made me felt worthy of my obedience. Germanicus is Rome's most successful military commander. It would have been a great honour for me to serve him. However, I understand the situation has changed.'

'You may serve me instead.'

'A similarly great honour.'

'Honour.' Vestalis smiled. 'And for this honour, what would you be prepared to do?'

The Tribune did not answer. He knew better than to fall into such an open trap.

'For example, would you kill Ovid if I ordered it?'

'Not without a good reason. I do not kill innocent men. Not even for my life.'

'What about for your career?'

'My life is my career.'

At this, the General laughed. 'Do you know why Romans like us Celts so much?' he said, rising up from the table and walking around it to stand beside the Tribune. 'It is because we manage to keep traces of the moral values that they wish they had in the first place. We are regarded as men of integrity, and having us at their beck and call makes them feel better about themselves. If one cannot have integrity, one can at least have superiority.'

'I have always believed it is possible to have both.'

'The Romans would not agree with you. But you are young, perhaps you will prove them wrong one day.'

'You don't seem to like Romans.'

Vestalis turned away to look out of the window across the village. 'How is he?'

The Tribune thought about this for a moment. 'He is… transformed. One cannot sail along Okeanos without changing.'

'I heard there was a death. I thought perhaps it might have been Ovid's.'

'It was Plautus' centurion. The one they call the Squarehead.'

'Accident?'

'Murder. A man known as Scorillo.'

'I knew the Squarehead. Quite a man. Whoever outmatched him must have powers.' Vestalis stopped. 'Wait a moment. Why was the Squarehead here?'

'Commander Plautus sent him to watch over his boy and this man Scorillo.'

'Watch what?'

'That they travel together with Ovid.'

Vestalis seemed unwilling to understand. 'Travel where? Along the border of the civilised world? You have allowed a child to be brought here?'

'After the Squarehead's death, I knew not what else to do with him.'

'A *child*?' the General repeated. 'Maybe the perfect place for you is indeed Vindobona. There, nobody expects flawless execution.'

'Sir, I have done everything you have asked.' The Tribune held his head up as he spoke.

Vestalis left the window and came back to him, squeezing the Tribune's shoulder and adding a paternal smile. 'That is true,' he said, 'you have. And I am grateful for it. But the boy is an inconvenience. See that he and this Scorillo are returned to Tomis.'

'Scorillo fled over the Danube. And the boy will not want to be parted from Ovid.'

'Since when do we listen to the wants of boys? He will not have much choice in the matter.'

The Tribune eyed Vestalis warily. 'General, what will happen now with the poet?'

Vestalis kept his hand on the Tribune's shoulder. 'Do not worry about him.'

'I believed you to be his friend.'

'I was. But go now. See to the boy. I will deal with Ovid.'

Prisoners

Ovid and Carp were hustled through a damp courtyard and into a dark and windowless room, its wooden door heavy. 'This is no place for a young boy', Ovid shouted as the door slammed shut. There was no reply, only the unmistakable click of a lock.

A burning oil lamp, placed on top of a huge polished oak table, provided the only light in the room, revealing the walls to be devoid of the usual soot graffiti with which convicts liked to immortalise their incarceration. This was not a prison.

'I have something for you', Carp said, pushing his hand deep into his tunic and producing a folded piece of cloth, which unwrapped into a letter. 'It is from my mother. She is very fond of you. She always has been.'

Ovid reached out his hand to take the letter. 'Thank you', he said, holding the cloth up to the oil lamp to read.

Publius Ovidius, by the time you see these lines, you will be far from Tomis. I thank you for keeping my son safe. My brother believes Carp will be the future king of Dacia, but I have no wish for him to become a Dacian, even if a king. I have privately advised Carp not to follow my brother there, but to stay with you. Wherever you go, please take Carp with you and keep him safe. Dokia.

Ovid looked up from the letter at the boy, who sat huddled in a corner, his knees pulled up to his chest. He was brave, there was no doubt about that, but he was still just a child, and this imprisonment was surely terrifying for him. Ovid cursed himself for ever having led Carp down this path. The letter from his mother implored Ovid to take care of her son. He had, it seemed, achieved quite the opposite.

The door opened. Natural light and fresh air flowed in, followed by Spiros, pushed violently in the back. He fell to the floor and the door slammed shut once more.

Ovid rushed towards his former slave and helped him to his feet. 'What are you doing here?'

'Cursing the day I met you', Spiros said, brushing the dirt from his clothes. 'They arrested me shortly after Scorillo crossed the Danube. Without him to blame, they've been trying to pin the Squarehead's murder on me.'

'Maybe they're right', Carp shouted from the corner. 'If you hadn't hit me, the centurion would still be alive.'

'If I am to be accused of murder', Spiros said, advancing on the boy, 'then why should I refrain from doing it for real?'

'You're not capable of—'

The sound of the door opening silenced Carp and stopped Spiros in his tracks. The silhouettes of legionaries filled the entrance. Then they split to make way for General Vestalis, who moved between them and blocked the daylight.

The Way to Rome

The legionaries took a step back from the doorway. 'Be greeted, Publius Ovidius', Vestalis said, holding out his hand.

Ovid took it. It was unexpectedly cold. 'You here? I should have imagined that one day you would become my jailer.'

'Please. Join me.' Vestalis turned and left without waiting for a response.

This is not the tone of a jailer, thought Ovid, as he passed the legionaries and gestured back at Carp and Spiros. *It is the tone of an angry man. Maybe my executioner.* 'Can someone keep an eye on those two? They haven't been getting along too well lately.'

'I will watch them', one of the soldiers said. 'Or, if you prefer, I can domesticate them.'

'No', Ovid said. 'Don't hurt them.'

The legionary laughed, and those nearby chuckled along with him.

Vestalis walked out of the courtyard, through the narrow streets, and then down the grassy slope towards the bank of the Danube. Ovid tried to follow close behind.

'I hear you have had quite a journey along this river', Vestalis said.

'Did you really need to throw me in jail?' Ovid was panting. 'Or was it only meant to allow our chat to be a little... tyrannical?'

Vestalis stared back. 'You and I both know that we require more than just a chat. You broke your promise to me. For this I could do far worse than jail you. I could snap your neck right here and toss you into the water.'

'Then why don't you?'

The General appeared to consider it. 'Maybe I will. It depends upon you. Why have you not written the ode we agreed upon in Tomis?'

Even without the threat of strangulation, Ovid knew he had to choose his words carefully. He could not tell the General the truth, that he had been drunk when he had made that promise. And nor could he give the answer he wanted – *common sense.* He wished he had the honeyed tongue of the Celtic Hercules.

Vestalis grew impatient. 'No sane person, least of all an exiled poet, would have refused the offer I made to you.'

'Art can produce emotion, but it can only describe illusions of reality.' *Would this do? Or was it too subtle for a military man?* Ovid stared at Vestalis.

'What the fuck does that mean?' The General grabbed Ovid by the shoulders, looking for all the world like he might punch him.

Ovid sighed, resigning himself to whatever fate awaited at the hands of Vestalis. 'Did you really believe', he said, 'that one poem could have made the difference in the struggle for Augustus' succession?'

'Yes!' Vestalis cried. 'Yes! Of course I did! Why else would I have asked? You could have tipped the balance in Germanicus' favour.'

'You and I both know that only one thing can tip the balance in Rome, and that is the sword. It is not, and never will be, words.'

The General let his hands fall from Ovid's shoulders. 'Who made you a better offer?'

'No one.'

Vestalis sat down on the bank and looked back out over the river. 'Then why? This is what I need to understand, Naso. Why not just write the damn thing? Whether you believed in Germanicus or not? It would have been your way out of exile. Isn't that what you wanted?'

Ovid sat beside him and took a breath. Vestalis was right: he had made him an appealing offer. He deserved the truth. 'Let me rephrase the answer. I could not write the ode. Germanicus is a noble man and a fearless army commander, but there is nothing to write about him except boring verses. His character: flawless; the values he displays: perfect. Not even gossip can touch him. And all this makes him, for want of a better word, insipid.'

Vestalis plucked a blade of grass from the earth and twirled it between his fingers. 'Do you think he would have become a good emperor?' His voice was faraway, dreamy.

'That I cannot answer.'

'Try.'

'I am not a politician.'

'*Try*.'

'I think not.' There was a relief to honesty, Ovid realised, a cool and immersive relief, one that overrode even the threat of strangulation or the reality of further imprisonment. 'He never showed any willingness to change. The world around him is changing continuously, and yet he was and always will remain the same – a spoiled young adult. That is no quality for an emperor.'

Vestalis bit the head from the blade of grass and chewed thoughtfully. The two men sat in silence, gazing out at the river before them – the landing place, the crossing, the islands where smugglers used to hide, the boats that bobbed up and down in the swells, the thin fog that embraced it all.

Eventually, the General spoke up again. 'The Tribune says you have changed. I think he is right. Tell me, what more do you know now than when we last met?'

Ovid smiled. Not in a thousand years would this military man be able to comprehend all the ironies and contradictions that Ovid had learned on this journey along the border of the world. The truth would need to be diluted, or he would never understand it. 'I gained insight into how ignorant I am', he said. 'And that, for many years now, I have been someone's scapegoat. I believe that alone is reason enough not to have written the ode.'

'Publius Ovidius, Germanicus' generals counted on you.' Vestalis pressed his lips into a grimace. 'But Germanicus failed, and we have had to rethink. There is a new emperor, and it is to him that we have pledged our loyalty.'

'Then surely it is a good thing I never wrote your ode', Ovid said.

'It seems that may be the case.'

'Then why imprison me? Why am I here with you? What more could you want from me?'

'Our only concern now', Vestalis said, gazing out at the river, 'is your discretion.'

'Ah.' Ovid nodded. 'So you have been sent to kill me. There is no surer way to keep me quiet.'

'No, poet. Killing you would only raise suspicions. Instead, we are going to send you to Rome.'

'To Rome?' Ovid scratched his jaw. 'But that is all I've ever wanted.'

Vestalis turned from the river and clapped Ovid on the back. His smirk shone. 'This is no favour, Naso', he said. 'Do not mistake my intentions. The moment you set foot in Italy, you will become an outlaw. And Tiberius is known for treating outlaws as fair game. I doubt you will survive a week.' He stood up and rocked back on his heels. 'You see? There is no need for us to kill you. The good people of Rome shall do it for us soon enough.'

PART THREE

Home

Rome and Sulmo, December,
AD 14–Spring, AD 15

The Spymaster

They had not seen each other since Augustus' funeral. Livia stood by the window, in the space once occupied by her weaving chair, the symbol of her matriarchal virtue, which had been removed since the passing of her husband.

'I have given my chair to my granddaughter-in-law. A little practice might do her good.'

Opposite her was Augustus' spymaster, the senator, Ibis. Livia flexed her fingers, making no attempt to conceal the ageing that had wrought fine patterns across them. Ibis could not take his eyes off them: they were said to have woven some of Augustus' finest robes and cleverest plots, and while she might have given up on clothes she would never give up on strategies and schemes. Livia could, he knew, work as hard as any other woman in Rome. When she chose.

'Then I hope she makes some use of it', he said.

Livia grew impatient. 'What is the purpose of your visit, senator?'

'Your son, Tiberius, is in danger.'

'He knows how to handle that.' There was a slight upturn to her lips, as if the news pleased her. 'Who presents this danger?'

'The usual suspects.'

'Senator, do not try and be vague with me. There cannot be many enemies left. Name them.'

Ibis hesitated for a blink. 'Members of the Senate are

planning to persuade Tiberius to restore the laws of the old Republic.'

'This is old news.' Livia strode across the room to open a window. 'And, even if it were true, I am able to prevent my son from pursuing his republican convictions. Tell me the real threat.'

'The real threat to Augustus' Rome' – Ibis cleared his throat – 'is, and always has been, the generals.'

She burst into laughter. 'There you go again. These hackneyed statements might work amongst your colleagues, but they do not with me. Speak plainly. Who is the real threat?'

'I assure you, Germanicus' generals are plotting against your son—'

'Enough!' She cut him short. 'I have given you my time. And you have not used it well. I would be insulted if all you had said were not so stupid. But now you bring Germanicus into it. I warn you, senator, do not even think of trying to discredit a member of my family.'

Ibis squeezed the folds of his toga in his hands, lips pressed in a failing effort to keep his temper. 'Then let me warn you of another who wishes to destroy Rome', he whispered from his dry mouth. 'Publius Ovidius Naso.'

'Senator, you are raving. Our best poet is rotting in exile in that derelict port with an unspeakable name, because you managed to convince my late husband not to pardon him before he passed away.'

'Ovid is somewhere in the city, carrying highly subversive letters from…' Ibis paused. 'From *treacherous generals* stationed on the Danube.'

For a moment, Livia looked pleasantly surprised. But

then prudence restored itself. 'I see you are still intent on discrediting your personal enemy.'

'My lady, he has returned. Illegally. And he is no longer a petty corruptor of virtues. He is a high traitor now. And a law breaker.'

'Nonsense! Haven't you read his poems? Ovid has never been one to carry messages, not even from the gods. Though I wish he was. Do you know where he is?'

'In hiding. But as soon as he shows his face in public, we will apprehend him.'

Livia masked her relief. 'Your men could never unearth him. It says a lot for their abilities.'

'When the time comes, my men will do what they must. Rome cannot be preserved at a lesser price than that for which she was created. Harmony and peace must be maintained, and that takes inflexible morals. When they are required to do so, my men will act savagely, drastically and irrevocably.'

'Less of the speeches, senator. Unless I have got things wrong and you are applying for a job sooner than I expected?'

'Reason must govern Rome', Ibis continued. 'Ovid used poetry to enter the minds of Romans like an insidious worm. Now he has used his friend to enter Rome illegally.'

'I prefer the idea that emotions, not reason, are all that count. It makes the masses more manageable. You know as well as I do that individuals have two basic instincts: the will to survive and the desire to fornicate. Not even my late husband could abolish games and lust.'

'At least he tried. And exiling Ovid was a step in the right direction. Getting rid of a form of social evil.'

'He is an old man! Not a disease!'

'I shall destroy him.'

'Why don't you ask your wife Corinna to cast a charm on him?'

For the first time, Ibis' voice broke into a shout. 'He maddened my wife by killing our son!'

'Calm yourself, senator!' Livia snapped, and he breathed in twice slowly, composing himself. 'Ovid is incapable of killing a fly. And, of all people, he would never knowingly hurt your son Lucius. You should understand that perfectly well.'

Sweat broke out across his face as he struggled to keep his temper in check. 'Ovid must pay', he hissed, and then said no more.

Livia walked over to a table in the corner of the room, where she picked up and rang a bell. Two files of servants streamed in. 'Light the candles and assemble a fire', she instructed them. 'It's getting cold in here. The senator will leave shortly.' As the servants busied themselves with her orders, she approached Ibis. 'The news about Ovid's presence in Rome is a bad joke. Do not tell it me again. Now go home, and sober Corinna up. Tell her I shall pay her a visit soon. I have some questions for her that I would like answered.'

'The gods do not speak to her anymore', he replied sadly.

'Do what I said. One more thing.' Livia lowered her voice. 'If anything happens to Ovid, I shall ensure that the next person killed will be you. Do you understand?'

Ibis did not reply. Instead, he made the slightest of bows, and then turned and left the room.

'Bring me a scented hot bath and Urgulania', Livia said to one of the servants.

Both – the bath and Livia's most intimate friend – arrived

at the same time. The servants, in a well-rehearsed procedure, undressed Livia, tiara first. Arms stretched above her head, she was wrapped in a huge white sheet, which was released over the knee-high rosewood barrel as she stepped into it. Urgulania moved behind and began slowly to massage her forehead.

'That rat doesn't deserve your attention,' she said. 'He should be called Viper, not Ibis.'

'For good or for bad,' Livia replied, 'the senator is one of the few who have not changed in these past years. I salute his inflexibility. It brings comfort. Don't you think so?'

'He has always been a spy. For me, spies are utterly disturbing.'

Livia closed her eyes and let her arms float up in the water. 'Where do you think Ovid might be? Is it possible he could look for me?'

Urgulania shrugged. 'It is possible. Now that your husband is dead, he might see this as his chance to return unpunished.'

'Without Tiberius' permission to do so? Do you think he would really engage in a conspiracy against Rome?'

'Nobody can predict that.' Urgulania extended the massage from Livia's forehead down her cheeks and on to her neck.

'Do you think *I* might be sidelined by my own son?'

'Yes.' Urgulania did not mince her words. 'You might.'

Livia laughed at her friend's honesty. 'You know, I should like to see Ovid again. I have missed his oracular powers.'

'Oracular powers? What's wrong with mine? His never proved right. He is too obsessed with immortality to know anything about the future.'

'He knows everything about love.'

'We are too old for love.'

'You might be, but I am not.' Livia stood up in the bath. Free from the linen cover, her once marble-white body displayed its years of neglect.

Urgulania pushed out a lizard-like tongue, checked its firmness with her finger and then, in a series of regular movements, left wet slug-like traces across Livia's body. 'How did that feel?'

'Like nothing.'

'You see? Physical pleasures are no longer for us. But it is better to be disappointed by me than by him.'

Livia was not listening anymore. 'I need him. I need a good storyteller.'

'That, at least,' Urgulania said, 'he is capable of.'

Ovid, the Outlaw

The rain stopped at dawn. As the ceiling of clouds began to travel eastwards, the sellers in the square outside the triple-arched Porta Tiburtina prepared for another market day. In front of Janus' temple, four men wearing ritual veils over their wet clothes surrounded the altar and hummed an unintelligible hymn for the god. After sprinkling libations over the seven pieces of live coal, they watched as the skein of smoke – the aim of their civic duty – began to wend its way into the air. Some of the sellers clapped at the sight. Business had not been good of late, and in these times, when their market seemed forgotten by luck and customers alike, hope was all that was left.

From behind the semi-closed shutters of a window Ovid watched the morning progress. He had been staying at this inn – the only one on the square where food and women were not allowed upstairs – for the past ten days, watching from the same window with an ever-decreasing hope for much of that time. As soon as he had arrived, he had sent out word of his hiding place to friends of his in the city, but as of yet not one had arrived to fetch him.

In Tomis he had grown used to the thought that he was no longer wanted. But here, just outside Rome's walls, the desperation of it all brought him to a state of frantic perplexity, the kind he could imagine one experienced on the brink of death. After all, here, stuck in this inn, he had just as little hope for the future as a dying man. Once or twice he had tried to write – and then given up. The verses, pathetic expressions of stray emotions, had shown nothing except the pain of his dwindling expectations.

As if trying to demonstrate that he still had some free will left, he flung the shutters open, forcing the darkness from the room and exposing himself to this world, the only one available. He had always been frightened by Rome's suburbs, how they somehow grew and grew and grew while remaining unchanged, and he resolved that he would fear this particular one no longer. It was an ugly place, there was no doubting that, but it did not follow that he should be intimidated by it. What was it his father had said when they first left Sulmo? 'You'll get used to decay. And to Rome.' But he had not, to either.

Outside, the town crier made his way into the middle of the square, stepped up on the border of the water basin, and looked about, with apparently no intention of shouting in a hurry his messages to the agitated crowd around him. Ovid could see that he clearly enjoyed the privilege of knowing before others what had happened.

Noises from the staircase announced someone on their way up. The curtain-door was pulled to the side and the innkeeper – a heavy and exuberant woman who liked to accompany her words with theatrical gestures more suited to a pantomime than to real life – appeared in his room. 'You have to go', she said. 'I need your room.'

'Do not be ridiculous', Ovid replied. 'I have paid a full month's rent, and have stayed just ten days. Go bully someone else.'

'It will only be for the day. The new Emperor is entering Rome through our gate and I must watch him by myself.'

Ovid's senses heightened. 'Is he?' he said. 'Then I shall watch him with you.'

'You do not understand. I am a member of the Market Watch. It is my duty to observe the neighbourhood.'

'For passing emperors?'

She placed her hands on her sizeable hips. 'I look out for petty crimes. The kind that tend to increase when rich people are in the vicinity.'

'So use a different room.'

'This is the best to observe the market.' A silent discomfort flickered across the innkeeper's face, and then she began to cough repeatedly. Once she had quietened, voices could be heard from the stairway. It was Spiros and Carp, returning to check on Ovid. As usual they were in the middle of a quarrel.

'I want to see Rome', Spiros was saying. 'Not only some impoverished suburb.'

'Stop arguing and get in here!' Ovid shouted, and both entered, sheepish that they had clearly been overheard.

The innkeeper stared at the new entrants, and Ovid wondered how all three of them appeared to her eyes. An old, bearded gentleman, a young boy, and an effeminate Greek – probably the old man's pet or source of income or both.

'The innkeeper, this lovely lady, is trying to encourage us to leave the room', Ovid said.

'Does she want more money?' Carp piped up.

'Be quiet', Spiros snapped. 'You don't have any money to give her.'

'I can make some.'

‘How?’

‘I can dowse. It’s not so hard to predict the future.’

‘Will you two please learn to be friends?’ Ovid interrupted.

‘Why did nobody tell me that the boy can read the future?’ the innkeeper said.

Carp, puffed up with pride that someone was interested in his talents, took the pendulum from around his neck, rubbed it with his fingers, and then with a visible effort tried to hold his hand still. The crystal at the end of the string hung limp and unmoving.

‘What does it mean?’ the innkeeper said.

‘That the boy can’t dowse’, Spiros replied.

‘Listen!’ Ovid had given up on the trio inside his room and turned his attention back to the window. Outside, the town crier was bellowing for all around him to prepare for the imperial convoy. A hopeless chaos ensued as carts were moved out of the way and the paving slabs swept by anyone with a broom to hand.

‘It’s what we came to tell you’, Spiros said. ‘Members of the Praetorian Guard have arrived from the nearby garrison and are being posted along the road outside the ramparts.’

A sure sign, Ovid thought, *that a person of rank, probably Tiberius himself, is to pass by shortly.*

Sejanus

'Reinforcements are coming!'

The legionaries guarding the imperial litter relaxed at the news. They had grown increasingly nervous as they approached the Porta Tiburtina, and the announcement that fresh arrivals from Rome were coming to greet them was welcomed by all.

Sejanus, the young commander of the Praetorian Guard, conferred with his friend, Cotta Maximus, who was accompanying the imperial litter into Rome. 'Ride out to meet them', Cotta said. 'I shall ensure the convoy keeps moving in your absence.' Agreeing that this was the best course of action, Sejanus set out to encounter the approaching horsemen. Half a mile away, he came face to face with Ibis.

'I come with friends to protect the Emperor.'

'You came to help manage the crowd. Tiberius' protection is my job,' Sejanus replied, 'and nobody else's.'

Ibis raised his chin defiantly. 'My duty is to shield Augustus' legacy.'

No one in Rome could afford to disregard displaying their attachment to Augustus, even after his death. 'Hail Caesar', Sejanus said. 'We are grateful for your support, but it is unneeded. There is no danger for Tiberius.'

'I have word there is a plot against him.'

'A plot? Devised by whom? The few left in Rome who could

organise a plot are either too old or too clever for their own good.'

'A certain poet has returned. Ovid.'

'Who is Ovid?'

Ibis looked this young commander in the eye. His lack of recognition seemed genuine. 'You must communicate this information to the Emperor. Then he can assess the gravity of the threat.'

'Everything is under control.'

'Commander, I admire your boldness. Couple it with my experience and we could be unbeatable.'

Sejanus shifted uncomfortably under the steely gaze. 'I don't need more intelligence.'

'Power always needs insight.'

'I don't trust anyone who did not serve on the front', Sejanus said.

'I may not have done my time in that regard, but I am from the old school, and I have done far more than could ever have been reasonably expected to fulfil my duties. This experience has taught me one crucial thing which you would do well to learn – that unless our actions turn out right, we have done wrong. Do not do wrong, commander. Let me inform Tiberius. Or you do it.'

The hint of future failure, of potential disgrace, worked. 'You may talk with him', Sejanus said, turning his horse to face back towards the convoy. 'But I will be with you at all times.'

'I would not have it any other way', Ibis replied, his smile obsequious.

Sejanus led the way with Ibis easily keeping pace behind him, and his soldiers bringing up the rear. By the time they arrived at the imperial convoy, it had reached the marketplace. Members of the crowd jostled each other greedily, each hoping to get the best view of their new Emperor, and choking odours filled the square. The horsemen of the Praetorian Guard, standard in front, opened the way, raising dust to the sky. Trumpets sounded a merry tune. Then suddenly the convoy stopped. Tiberius himself stepped out of his litter, dismissed the ragged chorus of petitioners closest to him, and waved with characteristic unenthusiasm at the cheering crowd in the market.

The commander and the spymaster dismounted their horses, and Ibis began to stride towards the Emperor, when Sejanus stopped him with a hand on the chest. 'Tiberius', he said, 'loves to see to his people first.'

'His people', Ibis spat disparagingly, casting his eyes across the crowd. 'Worthless peasantry. I do not know why he wastes his time on them.' The sights and the smells of this filthy square made him feel sick. He wished he had been quicker, wished he had found the convoy earlier, so as to have avoided all this. Or, better yet, a private audience with the Emperor, in some cool chamber away from this heat and noise. Ibis scanned the crowd again, looking from head to ugly head, filling this square like cockroaches, pressed up against each other, all the way back to the buildings that lined the edges. His focus fell on one building in particular, an inn by the looks of it, and his gaze travelled up towards the window, its shutter open, where an enormous woman hung half in and half out, and where, next to her, sitting there as plain as day...

Ibis grabbed Sejanus' arm. 'There!' he hissed, pointing at the window with his free hand. 'Ovid! Seize him! Guards! Seize that man now!'

Condemned to Life

Livia paced up and down the living room of her villa, unable to dispel from her mind the meeting with Ibis. Was Ovid really back in Rome? Why had he not sent word to her? Did fear prevent him? There was only one thing for it. She needed to see his wife, Fabia. If anyone knew how to reach him, it would be her. The Empress sent for her without delay and, so as not to cause concern that the invitation might harbour any sinister inclinations, she requested that their mutual friends Marcia, widow of Fabius Maximus, and Lucius Pomponius Flaccus, the young general, join them.

Fabia and Marcia arrived simultaneously – two ladies in their forties, one sober in attire and deportment, the other wearing, as always, a dress that enhanced her stature. 'What a blow, my dear!' Marcia said as they made their way up the path to Livia's villa. 'Who would have imagined that Ovid would dare return from exile unpardoned? Such an imprudence.'

'You know?' Fabia asked, her voice barely a whisper.

'Of course. Everyone in Rome knows. It is all they can talk about. This city feasts on gossip. No secret is safe here.'

'I am hoping that Livia will help him to restore his position.'

Marcia laughed. 'It would be better for all of us if he stayed away for good.'

Fabia thought about this, and then, as matter-of-factly as she could, said: 'I've missed my husband.'

The very idea was dismissed with a wave of the hand. 'He was never right for you. You were just blinded by his glory. Now you have gained perspective. You are free to choose. And still young.'

'You hate him', Fabia said.

Marcia stopped walking and shut her eyes for a moment. 'No. I don't. Contrary to popular belief, my prating was not the real cause of Maximus' suicide, and I do miss my husband. Who in her right mind enjoys being old and by herself?'

'Livia', Fabia said, and both women laughed.

'Wait!' came a voice from behind them, and Fabia and Marcia turned to see Flaccus coming towards them, waving his hands with characteristic drama.

'You're here!' Marcia screamed, and ran to hug him.

Flaccus lifted her in his arms and then came forward to kiss Fabia on the cheek. 'Do you know why we needed to come all the way from Rome out here to Galina Alba?'

'Do you think she has hidden Ovid down there?' Marcia said.

'My husband does not need to hide', Fabia replied.

'So, you too know it', Flaccus said.

Together, the three of them approached the door to the villa. The servant guided them along past brightly coloured statues, raised the lamp over a flight of descending steps, and with a studied gesture invited the guests downstairs. Dressed in a blue-green robe, blending in with the colours of the wall painting, Livia sat on her leather throne. 'You are all late', she said. 'If I had attended to your frequent requests with the same speed over the years, none of you would have achieved a thing.'

'I recognise a bad start to the day when I am in it', Marcia said.

'Since you are late, let us waste no more time. Have any of you heard from Ovid?'

'He does not write to me', Marcia said, as if the very idea were absurd.

'My brother Graecinus got a letter from him', Flaccus said. 'But he is careful, and is awaiting Tiberius' permission before he replies.'

'So Tiberius is informed?' Livia said.

'Of course he is', Flaccus said.

'I have received two messages from him', Fabia said timidly. 'I have answered neither.' All eyes turned to her.

Seemingly satisfied that she was being told the truth, Livia clapped her hands and ordered more candles. 'Why is he hiding?' she said as they were brought out. 'Ovid has never disappointed me.' She looked away from her visitors, into the false distance of the painted landscape. 'Flaccus, *you* should talk to him.'

'And so I would, if I knew how to reach him', Flaccus protested.

'When you do, tell him to return to exile', Marcia said. 'I cannot imagine how upset my husband, his patron, would have been to know Ovid was in hiding like a rat.'

'Oh, stop it, Marcia', Fabia said. 'We are here to discuss finding *my husband*, not to hear you complain about how poorly life has treated you.'

'Stop calling him your husband. He makes me nervous', Marcia retorted. 'I have never understood why you loved him.'

Fabia turned to Livia. 'Marcia does not understand love altogether. She should have read Ovid's poems.'

'You should have followed him into exile!' Marcia said.

'Enough!' The tone of Livia's voice would have closed any subject, and silence fell around her. 'I want Ovid to feel at home in Rome again. All three of you, find a way to let him know that he is welcomed back.'

Flight

Ovid watched from the window as the guards broke away from the convoy and rushed towards the inn.

'It's you they are coming for, isn't it?' the innkeeper whispered, staring at Ovid in shock.

'It seems the Emperor has sent them to fetch me.'

Carp grabbed the innkeeper's dress. 'Please!' he wailed. 'You must help him! They will kill him!'

Bewildered, the innkeeper looked over at Spiros, who said nothing, but gave a single solemn nod.

'Come with me!' she ordered, spinning Ovid away from the window and forcing him down the narrow, steep stairs to an untidy room, where she opened a wardrobe door.

'I shall not hide—' he began, but was cut short when, her hot breath in his face, the innkeeper squeezed her bulk against him, pushing him into the wardrobe. He fell against its far wall, which toppled, opening a way into an unlit corridor.

'Go!' the innkeeper said.

'But the boy…'

'I shall see he comes to no harm.' And with that, she slammed the wardrobe door shut.

Ovid crept into the corridor, understanding that he was no longer in the inn but in its next door building, which, by the looks of it, was uninhabited. He could hear pounding coming from the inn: the guards had kicked their way through the door and were calling out his name. Ovid moved away from the noise, down the length of the corridor. At its end came a beam of light. He approached it with caution. A thick rectangle of cloth hung over a doorway. He pulled it aside to see his way out – on to a small alley that led off from the square. He poked his head outside. No one awaited him. He ran.

'There he is! That's him!'

Even as he fled, Ovid understood the futility of it. The slapping of sandals on the paving stones behind him were fast and powerful. He would never outrun them. Before he could turn around to confront his pursuers, two pairs of hands had grabbed him under the arms and lifted him up so that his feet swung helplessly beneath him.

'Got him!'

'This way! Quick!'

The guards did not carry him back to the square as he had expected, but away from it, further down the alley. He turned to look at his captors: by their dress, unmistakeably Praetorian Guards – in disguise. But where were they taking him? At the end of the alley a litter awaited him, not the same as Tiberius had been brought in, but run-down, with torn curtains and an all-pervading smell of grease. He was thrown inside on to the bare floorboards, the curtains were strapped down, and he could feel the litter lifted and spirited away.

The noise of the crowds abated, to be replaced only by the rhythmic pounding of feet. A sudden darkness engulfed the litter. He guessed they were passing through the pedestrian tunnel of a city gate, yet there were no usual exchanges of salutes or official checks of the occupant. The litter passed through without stopping. Had they carried him inside the nearby garrison of the Praetorian Guard?

Light returned, and then doubled as the litter was set down and the curtains pulled back. Ovid shielded his eyes and peered out. The square was one he did not recognise. With its clean marble façades, freshly painted statues, perfectly arranged paving stones, trimmed trees and shining door handles it looked less like a Roman square than a storyteller's description of one. Everything was there except the people.

A serious-looking guard stepped forward to greet him.

'Where are we?' Ovid asked.

'I have been instructed to bring you here', the guard replied, leading him out of the litter and across the square to stop beneath a colonnade. Slowly, Ovid began to get a sense of his whereabouts. To his left were hills he knew well, part of the Esquiline, where there were gardens belonging to some of the wealthiest families in Rome. It was they who used their power to keep the nearby city gate – the one he had surely just passed through – shut for all but their carriages. It was known colloquially as the Closed Gate. This was an area of influence, no doubt, but he could not fathom why anyone would bring him here.

'Who exactly are we waiting for?'

Rather than reply, the guard – to Ovid's immense surprise – walked away, leaving him alone under the colonnade. A whistled melody sounded from behind him, followed by the distinctive scent of expensive hair oil, thyme and lavender. Before turning around, Ovid already knew who it was.

Marcus Aurelius Cotta Maximus Messalinus – known as Cotta Maximus, Ovid's old friend, son of his patron Messalla and brother of Senator Paulus Fabius Maximus – advanced with wide-stretched arms.

'It is good to see you, my friend', Cotta said as they embraced.

'And you, Cotta, and you.' Ovid allowed himself a wide smile. 'Was this your doing?'

Cotta stood back to take in the sight of Ovid. 'I received your letter. Why else do you think the imperial convoy came that way? It was not part of the original itinerary. But when I read that you were staying in that inn, I decided to accompany Tiberius. It was on my advice that his route back to Rome was changed to pass through the Porta Tiburtina. I hoped that you might be able to make yourself seen by Tiberius, that he would stop the convoy and ask you to explain yourself. Unfortunately,' his face darkened, 'Senator Ibis spotted you from the square.'

'But how did you know my escape route through the adjacent building?'

Cotta laughed. 'I did not! I merely waited for Ibis to rush into the inn first, then I instructed some of the guards to try and get to you before he could. I had no idea it would actually work.'

'So that *was* Ibis', Ovid said, grinding his teeth as he said the name. 'I thought as such, but could not be sure. I wish I could kill him all over again.'

'What?'

'Nothing', Ovid said. He did not want to explain his Hyperborean hallucinations to Cotta. It would only make him sound mad. 'A Tomitan expression. I have been there too long.'

'That is the truth. But no more, my friend. And allow me to be the first to welcome you back to where you belong. Rome.' Cotta wrapped his arm around Ovid's shoulders and led him along the road that wound away from the colonnade and down the hilly plateau.

'Let us go to my house on the Palatine', Ovid said.

'Why? Nobody is there.'

'Not even Fabia?'

Cotta shook his head. 'She moved back with her family. Did you not know this?'

Ovid felt betrayed. Why had she not told him? They had always been more than lovers; they were friends. In her last letter, she assured him of her loyalty.

'I have somewhere more suitable for us. Come, let us quicken our pace. I believe it may start to rain soon.'

The two men began to hurry, through large alleys bordered with massive oak trees that led away from the affluent Esquiline Hill and then upwards towards another plateau, this one lower, muddy and littered, before descending to a dark and hostile valley with streets flanked by tall buildings that all Romans knew well: the urban canyons of the Suburra, the prostitute quarter. Ovid looked over at his friend as they darted from one narrow alley to another. Was Cotta about to suggest a visit to the whores as in the old days?

The answer, it seemed, was no. The Suburra was just a shortcut, and they were soon out the other side of it. 'Where are we going, Cotta?'

'To meet someone.'

'Who?'

'He would prefer to introduce himself.'

Ovid sighed. 'All this secrecy. One grows weary of it after a while.'

'I can imagine.'

'I feel compelled to ask you,' Ovid began, and then paused. There was a question he had long wanted answered regarding his friend, but to voice it could perhaps cause offence. He trusted his instincts, and proceeded. 'Did anyone here do anything about my pardon? Did anyone try and encourage Augustus to grant it?'

Cotta continued looking ahead. 'By anyone, I assume you mean me.'

'Well,' Ovid said, 'did you?'

'I did all that was in my power.'

'There was something you did not do.'

'What was that?'

'You did not come to visit me. Not once.'

'In Tomis?' Cotta seemed astonished at the very idea.

'It was not an impossibility. Our common friend Flaccus did it once – he came to see me on his way to fight the Scythians. I always thought you might too. But you never did.'

Cotta stopped walking. 'Naso, I owe you a great deal. That this now stands between us is a cause of immense regret. All I can offer are my apologies. And my hope that simply by being here with you now, my actions have gone some way towards rectifying any upset I may have caused.'

'Of course,' Ovid said, 'I do appreciate you coming to fetch me today.'

'Good.' Cotta smiled, and both men felt like some of the air between them had been cleared. 'But I am happy to talk with you about the time you have not been here, should you wish.'

'What is there to say? Little happened in Tomis. And probably in Rome too.'

'Not quite. These have been strange years, and I find them difficult to explain.'

'Go on.'

'We all wondered why Augustus never confiscated any of your properties, why Fabia kept hers as well, why your poems were not forbidden. In fact, they kept getting published, even the ones you sent from your exile. Did you know that people have put on pantomimes based on your work? Successful ones, too? And not to mention how well your play *Medea* was received when that was staged.'

'The Emperor offered me a choice', Ovid said. 'Was this information not spread?'

'What choice? My friends and I knew nothing.'

'Actually, there were three choices. The first option was that I could kill myself. The second that I could attend a public trial – one that Augustus assured me I would lose. The third was that I could be relegated to the Black Sea. I chose the latter. It was the only way I could keep my life and my work.'

Cotta nodded slowly. 'Two important things.'

'For me, the most important.'

'And do they remain as such?'

'Why do you ask?'

Cotta looked at his friend. 'You are different somehow, Ovid', he said. 'Not just in age. There is something else about you. Something I cannot quite put my finger on.'

'Do you want the truth?' Ovid said.

Cotta nodded.

'The truth is that right now I just don't want to meet anybody. I want to be left alone.'

'You may get that, my friend', Cotta said, a smile playing about his lips. 'You may well get precisely that.'

'From this person you are taking me to meet?'

'You asked if I wanted the truth. They were apt words. For that is precisely what this man wants from you. The truth.'

'About my exile?'

'About Rome. Your Rome.'

'It's Tiberius, isn't it?' Ovid felt a sharp pain down his side: the stab of betrayal. Was this how Caesar had felt when they had come for him?

'No', Cotta replied. 'It is not Tiberius.'

'Then who? For the sake of our friendship, Cotta, just tell me. Please.'

'I cannot. All I can say is that he was not best pleased with your last poems. You praised Livia too much for his taste.'

'Then it must be Germanicus', Ovid said. 'What about the many poems in which I paid homage to him?'

Cotta did not answer, but placed a protective hand on Ovid's shoulder. 'Now there is something I must ask you. There are rumours that you are carrying messages from generals to be given to senators here in Rome. If you have such letters upon you, then I cannot help you.'

'Isn't the morality of Rome built upon what a man can get away with?'

Cotta's face turned white at Ovid's answer. They walked on in silence through the now clean streets, passing women dressed for the season, insistent merchants and omnipresent pickpockets. Cotta kept his gaze fixed on the ground as they moved on by the succession of shining white arcades built into the slope of the Capitoline – the opportunistically named Portico Augustae – and then around and away from the Forum. Ovid stopped at the next crossroads. From here, he could climb up the Palatine and to his house. 'My friend', he said, and Cotta stopped beside him. 'I have no letters.'

'You...' Cotta hesitated, as if frightened to ask for confirmation. 'You speak the truth?'

'Yes. I do.'

With a yell of jubilation – or maybe relief – Cotta launched forward and embraced Ovid. 'Thank the gods!' he called out. 'I knew it! I knew I could trust you. But please, next time someone asks you if you have carried letters here, deny it immediately. Do not leave them wanting like you left me!'

'I shall do as you say, my friend.'

'Come, we should hurry, the boat will be waiting for us.'

The boat? Ovid rushed after Cotta, towards and then down the bank of the Tiber. There an enormous man waited beside a skiff, beckoning them to board, and for a brief moment Ovid remembered the Danubian Charon who had taken him across Okeanos. He considered telling Cotta everything that had happened to him during those surreal days, but doubted he would be believed.

They boarded, the huge man lifted the plank, and the boatman dipped his oars into the water.

'Where are we going?'

Cotta pointed to the island in the middle of the river, and Ovid understood instantly. They were to visit the Asklepia, a dubious hospital for only the most desperate of cases, a place no sane person would visit willingly.

The boat ride was short, and as the two men disembarked on the island they were welcomed by a man dressed in plain clothes and the sandals of the Praetorian Guard. Entering the Asklepia through the portcullis in the white wall that surrounded the hospital, they crossed a poorly lit oblong courtyard flanked by white windowless buildings with low entrance doors. The noise of their steps on the cobblestones produced a ghostly echo that brought to Ovid's mind the Herculaneum, where his hallucinations had revived Augustus.

Cotta moved directly to one particular door. It was clear he knew where he was going. He opened it and entered, and Ovid followed. There, in the centre of a grim, damp room, a man lay on a couch, his eyes closed, his feet covered by a white woollen blanket, his face turned towards the door. Around him, candlelight flickered and two harps harmonised in soft and lilting loops.

'Ovid', Cotta said, and the man opened his eyes at the name, 'may I introduce the commander of the Praetorian Guard, Lucius Aelius Sejanus.'

Ovid took two steps forward and nodded his head.

'And this', Cotta continued, 'is my friend Publius Ovidius Naso.'

Ovid froze. Had he been lured into a trap?

'That is the first time I have ever heard you refer to someone as a friend', Sejanus said. His voice was slurred and his eyes bloodshot, and Ovid wondered if he had fallen asleep on the couch after too much wine.

'Should I stay for this meeting?' Cotta asked. 'Or would you prefer me to leave?'

'Stay', Sejanus said. 'I am half-drugged and I need witnesses.'

Drugs, Ovid thought. *That explains it. But what sort?*

Sejanus had fixed his wandering gaze on the poet. 'The Republic needs sacrifices', he said.

Ovid did not reply.

'This he knows', Cotta said, filling the silence.

'I am glad you were able to flee that inn,' Sejanus said. 'Senator Ibis ran in there like a man possessed. I believe that had he found you he might have run you through there and then.'

'We have long been enemies,' Ovid said.

'Rumour has it you killed his son.'

'That is far too simple a statement for what is a long and convoluted story. One I do not have the energy to tell here.'

'Good,' Sejanus said. 'Because I do not have the time to hear it.' He rubbed his eyes. 'All that was found in your room were some notes about Hercules. So tell me, poet – where are the letters you carry from Germanicus' generals? Or have you delivered them already?'

'I am nobody's courier,' Ovid said.

'He has told me that there have never been any such letters,' Cotta said. 'And I trust he is telling the truth.'

'Trust…' Sejanus' head rocked from side to side as if too heavy for his neck. 'Yes… trust is important… we must trust him to do it…' All of a sudden, his eyes blinked wide open, and he yelled out: 'Doctor! Bring me some more!'

The door swung open. For a moment, Ovid wondered if he were hallucinating again: crossing the room towards Sejanus, jug of orange liquid in hand, was none other than Antipater, his doctor from Tomis.

Antipater did not look at Ovid, though it was clear his presence had been registered. Ovid kept quiet, betraying no recognition, as the doctor filled Sejanus' cup with the orange liquid.

'You should try this medicine. It works miracles,' Sejanus said. 'To the top, man! Fill it to the top!'

Antipater silently obeyed.

What are you doing here, Ovid wondered, *here with the commander of the Praetorian Guard? Are you trying to kill him as you once tried to kill me?*

Sejanus took a long draught of the liquid, and half closed his eyes with pleasure. Ovid recognised the reaction. A curious ache ignited within him, a longing he had not felt for some time, and one he did not miss.

'Most senators are useless at best and criminal at worst…' Sejanus said.

He's rambling, Ovid thought. *The medicine works quickly. I remember it well.*

'… but few of them are plain stupid. They want to govern, but they are no longer pleased to kiss arses and stay put at their estates. We need facts about these imbeciles…'

As he ranted, Cotta turned to Antipater. 'Doctor, please may I introduce you to my friend, Publius Ovidius Naso. Like you, he has travelled to the Black Sea. Perhaps you have crossed paths?'

'There are many ports and I have not been in all of them', Antipater replied, looking once at Ovid and then away again.

'Don't interrupt me!' Sejanus shouted. 'I was talking. So listen. Listen.' He sat up on the couch and pointed into the middle distance. 'To business. Ovid, you know who I am and how close to Tiberius I am. Cotta tells me above all else you wish for a pardon. I can get you that pardon.'

'I'm listening', Ovid replied, noticing Antipater observe him from the corner of his eye.

'If I suggest to Tiberius to approve your pardon, he will do it. Of this I am confident. But for such a favour, I would expect you to do something for me in return.'

'And what might that be?'

'I need to know what is going on here in Rome beyond… beyond *appearances*.'

The man's speech may have been slurred, but to Ovid his meaning was clear. 'You are asking me to spy for you', he said.

'You catch on fast!' Sejanus laughed. 'I like it! Yes, why not? Ovid the *delatore*. It has a certain ring to it, no?'

'I have never denounced even my enemies', Ovid said.

Sejanus ignored him. 'This needs to be celebrated!'

'I have not agreed to—'

'Celebrated, I say, celebrated!' Sejanus leaped up from the couch, his eyes like mussels in brine.

Ovid thought to try again, to protest once more, but saw the futility of it. Sejanus was dancing around the room, listening to no one but whatever strange music the orange liquid was putting into his head. It was likely that he would remember little the following day.

'Cotta!' Sejanus implored. 'You must welcome your friend back into high society. You must organise a party. A *party*! A party to celebrate his return. Yes! Yes! A *party*!' He began to sing a bawdy song, sweeping his toga back and forth like a young girl in her first dress. 'Yes! A party!'

Cotta took Ovid by the arm and guided him out of the room. Sejanus did not notice. On their way out a servant approached them, handing Ovid a small wineskin. 'This is for you', he said. 'From the doctor. Use it with care.'

Ovid opened it and sniffed the wine. It was not the scent of the familiar orange powder that assailed him, but something far more lethal. He recognised it in an instant. This was the poison that had been used to kill his Tomitan cook, Corrales.

It was, he guessed, Antipater's bribe for his silence. 'Have it delivered not to my house but to my villa outside Rome', he said, and then he and Cotta left the Asklepia.

Discovering Rome

'A poet, you say?' The old man shook his head.

'A poet. A love poet,' Carp said. 'Ovid. Publius Ovidius Naso. Surely you know of him. He told me he was famous.'

'Sorry, boy.' The old man turned and began to walk back into the tavern. 'I cannot help you.'

Carp joined Spiros, who waited for him out on the busy street. 'I don't think he had ever heard of him,' he said. 'Did Ovid lie to us?'

'I don't think so. The fact that these uncultivated inhabitants do not know him says nothing,' Spiros said. 'Come on. I have a friend in the city. Maybe he can help us.'

'Has your Greek lover made it to Rome as well?' Carp teased.

'Shut up! Antipater is a fine man. And he adores me.'

The pair trudged on. To their uninitiated eyes, Rome looked like a loaf of bread that had failed to rise evenly, with roads that curved around unclaimed marshes and pine-covered elevations. The jigsaw of narrow streets sunk between flimsy-looking buildings was disorienting, and it was not long before they realised they had begun to walk in circles.

'This is what happens when non-Greeks plan cities,' Spiros said. 'Chaos.'

They came to a busy thoroughfare, where a crowd had gathered around a small table. Four men were playing a game with three stones and a leather cup.

'What is this?' Carp asked a bystander.

'The Vulture', came the reply. 'You could have a go if you wanted. But you wouldn't win.'

The challenge excited Carp. 'Let's try', he said, tugging on Spiros' sleeve.

'Your money is limited. Don't waste it on this.'

'Please?' Carp persisted. 'Come on, let's have some fun. There has been so little lately.'

As much as Carp irritated him, Spiros had grown fond of the boy. It was difficult enough for him, a grown man, wandering out here in this enormous and intimidating city, and he could not begin to imagine how overwhelming and bewildering it must be for a child. 'Okay,' he said, 'but just for a few minutes. No more.'

With a whoop of joy, Carp skipped up to the table and asked to be allowed to play.

'You need money for this game', the guide said.

Carp reached into his tunic and produced a coin. 'Will this do?' he asked.

The guide smiled. 'Yes', he said. 'That will do.'

The crowd around them swelled as Carp won the first game, and then the second, and then the third. Spiros stood behind him and watched, remaining quiet as Carp grew more and more animated. At the close of the fourth game, that Carp won again, Spiros suggested they count their blessings and move on. But when the guide offered an all-or-nothing rematch, Carp was too swept up in the heady joy of gambling to listen to Spiros, and agreed to the guide's terms.

'Choose your number.'

Spiros glanced at the guide's fingers as he shook the dice.

'Seven', Carp said.

The guide released the dice. All of Rome seemed to come to a stop as the three cubes rolled across the table, settling on a two, a two and a three. A great roar of triumph erupted.

'I won!' Carp screamed, leaping up and down. 'I won I won I—'

The wind was knocked out of him as a man picked him up by the arms and slammed him down on to the ground. Spiros grabbed at the man from behind, then doubled over when a fist shot out from the crowd and punched him hard in the belly. The man on top of Carp pulled out a razor, slit the boy's tunic open, extracted the purse, and sprinted off into the crowd.

Carp began to cry – long, childish sobs that wracked his entire body. Groaning with pain, Spiros pulled himself to his knees and put his arms around the boy.

'Don't even think of following them', a bystander said.

'Consider yourself lucky they missed your belly', said another.

'Boys should not carry money anyway.'

'Think of it as your entry fee to Rome. Everyone has to pay it at some point.'

'Any provincial who has made something of himself here was once empty-handed.'

Carp wiped his eyes and gazed at Spiros. 'It was everything I possessed', he said.

'I know, I know. But we will survive. We have made it this far. What is one little robbery to us?' He helped the boy to his feet, and both dusted themselves down. 'Are you hurt?'

Carp shook his head.

'Good. That's the main thing.'

'Are you? I saw them hit you. It was hard.'

'I've had worse.' Spiros chuckled. 'Boy, have I had worse.'

By now the crowd had dispersed, off to find their entertainment elsewhere. Only one woman remained, blonde and provocatively dressed. She was staring at Carp with big eyes and a slowly spreading smile.

'Can we help you?' Spiros asked her.

'I know you', the woman said, not taking her eyes off Carp. 'I have seen you before. You are not from here, are you?'

'No', Carp said, feeling himself wilt under her gaze.

'You are from Tomis.'

'How do you know?'

The woman laughed. 'Your father was the best lover I had.'

Spiros moved towards her. 'Look, I think you're mistaken—'

With firm hands, the woman pushed him away from her. 'Commander Plautus', she said. 'Am I right?'

Carp gasped. 'You know him? You really know him?'

'Of course, my dear. I remember some of my clients – intimately. And I saw you too. You were playing with other boys on the pier. He pointed you out to me through the window. I remember thinking then how much you looked like him, like a miniature version carved by some great sculptor. The resemblance is even finer now.'

Carp blushed. He wanted to reply to this blonde woman, but something about her made him freeze with timidity.

'Was Plautus good to you?' Spiros said.

'Plautus? He was the best.'

'Then, please, help his son. And me, his guardian. We are new to Rome and lost. And now robbed too.'

'What can I do for you?'

'Perhaps offer a bed for the night. And maybe some food. And then directions. Tomorrow. To the Asklepia on the Tiber.'

The woman laughed out loud. 'A bed for the night? Normally I charge for that. And didn't you just say you were robbed?' She looked at Carp again, who could not tear his gaze from her, and perhaps pity melted her heart, for she said: 'Come on. Let us speak with my Madam. Maybe we can work out some arrangement.'

Carp and Spiros tottered behind the blonde as she led them through the rotting streets hemmed in by fragile three-storey tenement buildings, through the mud and around the stinking pools that dotted the pavements. Greedy eyes watched them through shutters of broken windows as they passed.

'Is this how the greatest city on earth looks?' Carp asked.

'It's even worse at night', the blonde answered without stopping.

The putrid labyrinth ended abruptly in a wide stone-paved square, in the middle of which a six-faced fountain was surrounded by people queuing for water.

'Be quick here', the blonde warned as they hurried through.

Two streets later, they arrived at the uninviting entrance to a yellow two-storey house.

'Both at once?' the caretaker said with undisguised admiration as he opened the door.

'Don't be disgusting.' The blonde pushed past him. Spiros and Carp followed her inside. 'Where is Madam?'

'Have you ever seen her before lunchtime?'

The blonde climbed the stairs, pushing open a door at the top. 'This room will be free for a while', she said to Spiros. 'You can stay here.'

'And me?' Carp asked.

'You can stay with me.'

Carp did not know whether to feel delight or terror.

Spiros disappeared into his room, claiming fatigue and the desperate need for some uninterrupted sleep, leaving Carp to follow the blonde to her cubicle: a mess of lipsticks, nail files, eyebrow charcoals and combs, all in much greater numbers than any one person could ever use in a lifetime. 'I should tidy this', she said, stepping over clothes, cups and scarves to open the shutters.

Carp fiddled with the nail files, arranging them like soldiers. 'Did you know my father well?' he asked.

She shrugged her shoulders. 'Not well. But I liked what I saw.'

'Did he not talk about my mother?'

'Of course not!' She smiled, and then tempered it when she saw the boy's dismay. 'But he talked about you. When he pointed you out that day, I could tell then how much he loved you.'

This helped to brighten Carp again. He picked up one of the handheld mirrors, realising that, if he angled it correctly, he could observe the blonde's décolleté unnoticed. It seemed to him nothing less than magnificent.

A shrill voice carried up the stairs.

'That is Madam', the blonde said. 'After I introduce you to her, tell her your full name. And, unless you want to be thrown out, show willingness for whatever she asks.'

Moments later, Madam – a merry-looking, sturdy woman – appeared in the cubicle, sipping from a cup of wine. Carp stood and did exactly as he had been instructed.

Madam looked him up and down once, and then said: 'You'd better have a good story.'

'He was robbed by the Vulture players. He has nowhere else

to go. I know his father.'

'We are not in the habit', Madam said, 'of offering family deals.' She had not taken her eyes off Carp. 'Where did you steal the money from in the first place?'

'I didn't steal it', Carp said. 'My mother gave it to me. Twenty silver coins. They were supposed to be for my education.'

Madam laughed, though there was no joy in her eyes. 'Twenty silver coins. If you are serious, you can perhaps make that back in a month of clever begging.'

'I don't want to beg! I just want my money back! It's mine!'

Madam appraised him like a mule in the marketplace, spying the amulet that hung from his throat. 'What's this?'

'A pendulum. My aunt gave it to me.'

With a sudden flick of her wrist, Madam had the amulet off Carp's neck and in her hand. She rolled the crystal back and forth between her fingers. 'Can you dowse with this?'

'Yes', Carp said, trying to keep the uncertainty out of his voice. 'What do you want to know?'

'Something I do not already.'

She placed the pendulum in Carp's palm. He drew a circle in the dust on the floor and, with a trembling hand, pinched the string between thumb and forefinger, letting the crystal hang low. The pendulum did not move.

'A waste of time!' Madam cried, throwing up her hands in exasperation.

'Do you have any other skills?' the blonde asked kindly.

'I can read Latin', Carp said, placing the amulet back on his neck.

'Here', Madam said, thrusting a heavily used scroll into his hands. 'Read this.'

Slowly, Carp worked his way through the words. His pronunciation faltered here and there, but never beyond comprehension, and he could feel the blonde beside him beaming with pride.

'Much better', Madam said. 'This I can use.'

Carp read to the end of the scroll, his eyes coming to rest on the name of the author. *Publius Ovidius Naso*.

'Ovid!' he cried out. 'I know this poet! He is my tutor!'

'Don't push your luck', Madam said. 'You read well enough. You do not need to try and add favour by lying to us.'

Carp stopped himself from protesting. It did not matter if Madam did not believe him, it only mattered that she allowed him to stay. 'Have you heard of Ovid?' he asked.

'Have I heard of Ovid? The boy asks if I have heard of Ovid! What kind of uncultured moron do you take me for? Of course I have heard of Ovid! Who in Rome has not?'

The knowledge that his tutor had not been lying to him all this time, that he really was well known in Rome, flowed through Carp on a wave of relief. 'Do you have any more of his poems?' he asked.

'I will find some for you. Your job will be to read them to my girls, at least two poems a day for each. Perhaps Ovid's words can teach them how to behave better with their customers.' Satisfied, Madam bustled out of the cubicle, leaving Carp alone with the blonde.

She came towards him and touched him lightly on the arm. 'You read very nicely.'

Carp shivered slightly at her proximity.

'Are you okay?'

'It's as if you carry small lightning in the tips of your fingers.'

'Oh', she said. 'You are not as young as I first believed, I think.'

'I'm not a boy!' Carp boasted. 'I will soon be a man.'

'Will you now?' The blonde reached out, took his left hand, and placed it on her right breast. 'Have you done this before?'

Stunned, Carp could only shake his head.

'And how about this?' She slid his trousers down and stroked his stomach and thighs. Before her hands could reach it, his penis exploded.

'I'm sorry', he said instinctively.

'Such a mess.'

'Your guess was right. I've never done that before.'

'So not quite a man yet.' She kissed him lightly on the cheek and then stepped away. 'Sleep if you need to. I must get changed. Work will start soon.'

Light-headed from the violence of his first orgasm, Carp crawled onto the bed and closed his eyes. He was just beginning to drift off when Madam reappeared.

'I have instructed you to read to my girls', she said, sniffing the air, 'not fuck them.'

'I didn't!' Carp protested.

'He is not lying', the blonde said, applying charcoal to her eyebrows. 'He got overexcited. Do not worry about him.'

'The Professor is here', Madam said.

'So? You know he does not favour me.'

'You are right. He prefers a more mature woman. But there is something else he likes.'

'What?'

'Fortune tellers.' Madam turned her gaze back on Carp. 'Soothsayers. I happened to mention we have a new dowser resident here. He is keen to meet you.'

'But…' Carp looked at the blonde in confusion. 'But you said I could not do it. I tried. It did not work.'

Madam smiled. 'The Professor does not know that. Just cause the pendulum to swing and make something up. He will pay for it.'

'But I thought I would pay my way by reading to your girls?'

'That is how you will pay for yourself. And this is how you will pay for your friend in the other room.'

'Spiros…' Carp said.

'Forgot to mention him, didn't you?'

'Madam, I am so sorry', the blonde said. 'I just wanted to ensure the boy's safety first. I was going to tell you later.'

Madam held up a hand. 'If this child can impress the Professor, then we need speak no more of it.' She turned and walked out.

'Go with her', the blonde said, gently pushing Carp after Madam. 'And make sure you are convincing. For the sake of your friend.'

Slowly, Carp descended the stairs. At the bottom, Madam stood beside a bearded gentleman with large hairy ears.

'Introduce yourself!' Madam snapped, and Carp did as he was told.

'An interesting accent', the Professor said. 'Where do you come from, boy?'

For some reason he could not explain, Carp thought it best not to specify. 'From outside the city', he said.

The answer seemed to satisfy. 'And Madam tells me you can work magic with your pendulum.'

Carp nodded.

'He fears he has an illness inside him', Madam said. 'He would like to know the root of it.'

'And the remedy,' the Professor said.

'Then please,' Carp said, summoning as much authority as he could muster, 'lie on this sofa. Face down.'

The Professor, obedient, did as he was told. Carp held the pendulum above him and, to his abject surprise, it began to swing of its own accord, describing wider and wider circles.

'You are soon to betray someone,' he said. He wondered who.

Home

Despite Cotta's offer to host him until the party, Ovid was determined to go to his house on the Palatine. His home.

The sturdy bronze knocker on the front door produced the penetrating low tone he remembered so well – one that was usefully loud on the inside, but that had a tendency to unnerve visitors. He hoped somebody might answer. Cotta had already delivered the depressing news that Fabia had long moved out, but a handful of servants would have been left behind to maintain the building's upkeep. One of them, at the very least, should have been home. He knocked again.

'Nobody is here!' The voice was loud and close, just on the other side of the door. He had heard no footsteps approaching it.

'Open the door. It is me. Publius Ovidius.'

A pause. 'How do I know?'

'Oh, for goodness' sake. If you do not recognise my voice you will recognise this. Look.' He thrust his ring with the family emblem up towards the peep window so that whoever was on the other side could see it.

The door opened. He knew the servant: one of Fabia's, who had reluctantly followed her mistress to his home after their marriage. She had never liked him, and he had never liked her. Their greeting proved that, in this regard, nothing had changed.

'A gracious welcome', he said, pushing her out of the way and marching inside.

He stopped and looked about him. Here he was. Home. The place he had dreamed of for all those years in Tomis. Had he ever even liked the place? It had been his late patron, Messalla, who had recommended that he should buy it. The proximity to Augustus' palace, he had said, was its prime feature. But what if he had never listened to Messalla? What if he had bought what he had actually wanted, that city dwelling on the other hill, the Capitoline? Not so close to Augustus and his cohorts. Would his life have turned out differently? Would all have been better?

He walked aimlessly about the various objects he had visualised so many times on the Black Sea. The objects now seemed unfamiliar to him, as if things could change just as people did. The water basin in the middle of the atrium was covered in a rotting moss. The obligatory bronze sculptures were unpolished and somehow even more ridiculous that way. The wall paintings featured new cracks that further divided gods from men. All in all, it was a depressing sight.

The servant hovered at his side. 'Should I go to buy dinner?'

Ovid shook his head. He was not hungry. 'Just ensure the lamps are lit. And the fire in the study.'

She scurried away.

Where was Fabia? Why had she left? Were she still here, the decay and the filth would not have mattered in the slightest. It was Fabia who had made this house a home, not these superficial possessions. He stumbled into the study. On his desk, a stack of unused wax tablets and his collection of styluses. He pulled the keys from their hiding place and opened the mahogany chest. It was empty. At least Fabia had done that for him – removed, and presumably hidden, his manuscripts.

He sat down and lowered his head into his hands.

'Sir.' The servant had appeared to light the fire.

'Ignore me.' Ovid looked up at her through tear-stained eyes. 'I miss my wife, that is all.'

'She was here recently, you know. She left something.'

'She did?'

The servant nodded, left the study, and then, a few moments later, reappeared with a scroll holder. She handed it to him.

Ovid unrolled the letter and began to read. It was for him. It was brief and unemotional – Fabia had, at least, not changed that about herself. She was spending the unsettled period of Saturnalia with Marcia outside Rome. She did not want to attend the mass for the Mother Goddess that Livia celebrated each year, which was happening in just two days' time in the temple of Isis and Serapis. The short letter ended with a command.

Do not meet anyone before seeing Tiro. Him you must see right away. F.

Ovid rolled the letter back into its holder, stood, and wandered from the study. He came to the house altar, which had gone unnoticed when he first arrived. On it sat three bright red apples. Fabia had always insisted that so long as the Lares, the house gods, had fresh fruit, their marriage would be safe.

He felt his mood begin to change – for the better.

Tiro, the Publisher

Ovid rose early the following morning, refreshed and ready to face the day. 'Fetch me the camel-hair coat!' he ordered, and the servant brought it to him with her customary scowl. Any friendliness she had exhibited the previous night had vanished once more.

The shortcuts he took through the maze of the Palatine were as familiar as his favourite poems, and he hurried along them. One noticeable thing, however, had changed – on gates, shiny copper medallions of the Medusa had replaced the old door protector, Jason. Had that god, with his two faces, ended up frightening the thieves inside the houses more than the ones who came to intrude?

Ovid walked faster, making his way to the square that marked the entrance to the dangerous district at the foot of the hills, the shortest route to his publisher on the other hill, the Capitoline. Light fell strangely on the white temple of Fortuna, and he considered slowing down his pace and spending a coin – perhaps the goddess's influence on his life was worth it. Exile had taught him that fortune favoured the virtuous: being in the wrong place at the wrong time was not just a case of bad luck, it was also a shortcoming.

In the poorer quarters at the foot of the Capitoline, where Tiro lived, he recognised the tenement buildings that still stood sentry, even though one or two appeared to have almost burned to the ground, waiting for the owner to build them up again. Walking to the house of his publisher resembled more than an act of courage – an ascent into another world. Smells wafted out from the ground-floor taverns, indicating that this place was one not just for vice but for good food too. At the far end of a long and filthy street, Ovid entered a corridor that spat him out in a dark and slippery inner yard that saw sunlight only when the buildings around it collapsed – not the most regular happening, but not the most infrequent either. Perhaps, Ovid estimated, three in the last ten years before his banishment.

He knocked at a half-open door.

'Come in, if you dare.' The voice was hoarse and croaky, and the words unmistakeably Tiro's. He had always had a penchant for the dramatic.

A head shorter than Ovid and almost double his weight, Tiro struggled against his own mass as he rose from his chair, throwing onto the floor a stained grey overcoat he had wrapped around himself, and opening his arms to welcome his friend. 'If you are found here, Ibis will tear down my shop', he said, and then embraced his old friend with joy.

'Have his men bothered you lately?'

'No. I became too unimportant for them when you left.' Tiro hugged Ovid once more and then pushed him away. 'Your books have helped me and my family to survive, though.'

'And now?'

'Well, people have their own worries', Tiro said.

'It surprises me that I am still in demand. I have been away for so long.'

'You *were* in demand. You had loquacious adversaries.

Whom you teased by staying alive. Their talk about you kept your name fresh in people's minds.'

'And now?'

'You bored Rome with some of your letters from the Pontus. You were too lenient with Augustus. Now that he is dead, he is useless to you anyhow. You neglected to make new enemies.'

Ovid nodded. Popularity in Rome rarely depended on friends; far better to have quality enemies to assure one's fame. 'Which books have been selling the best?'

'People still like to read your old subjects – love, sex, fashion. All Romans want is to feel good, and you still make an excellent guide for that.'

'I am working on a heroic ode. I wonder how that will fare.'

'I imagine it will not fare well. Your poems from exile didn't either, though you could maintain the same level of quality as we've seen in your *Metamorphoses*. I have enjoyed them greatly. Especially the ones that commend Augustus.'

Ovid's face broke into a smile. Praise from Tiro was a rare thing. Many years before, Tiro had flat-out refused to publish some of his earlier love poetry: he had not considered it cultured enough to be worthy. When Ovid had then written the controversial books of *Ars Amatoria*, Tiro had agreed to publish them, but he had never uttered a word of praise. He was a cynic at heart. To receive a single positive word from him was an achievement of great magnitude.

Tiro beckoned Ovid into the kitchen, where he poured a brew of Cypriot herbs into two cups and offered one to him. 'Good for the bowels,' he said, sipping from his cup, 'if not the mind.'

'When you find a drink that is,' Ovid rejoined, 'you must tell me.'

'You will be at the end of a long, long line. First I would ensure those brilliant men of the Senate drank some. Stupid people. I'll tell you this, even had they intentionally planned the mess Rome is in, they could not have done a better job.'

'The city is a shambles?'

'The food supply from Africa is short. Public entertainment has been cut to virtually nothing. Most of the magistrates are uncontrollable drunkards, and most of the generals are worse, concerned with nothing other than unprofitable wars. The truth is that nobody is seeking the answers to Rome's problems, but instead they are spending all their time trying to demonstrate either that there are no problems or, if there are, that there are no answers to them.'

'Words like that can get you banished', Ovid said.

'Quite right', Tiro replied, and then raised his voice, as if someone were listening. 'We have never had it so good', he shouted.

Ovid picked up a pamphlet from an otherwise empty rack. 'Greek', he said, leafing through the pages. 'Is nobody writing in Latin anymore?'

A bust of Virgil stood on the counter next to Tiro. He laid his hand upon its head. 'You have been too long away from Rome', he said.

'I could not agree more.'

'You should write a book about the art of being happy. It would not make us rich, but it might help us survive Tiberius' downfall', Tiro whispered.

'Happiness has never been a theme I have been drawn to exploring. The problem with happiness is that one cannot pursue it. It happens, or it doesn't.'

'Hmmm. It sounds like they have converted you to philosophy. Have you written anything of interest?'

'I have a plan, but even for you it might be too daring.'

Tiro dismissed the possibility with a smile. 'You have nothing to lose. You can afford to write anything. Even if you fail, the public will not blame you for it. They will blame it on censorship, on the emperors – dead or alive. They would even blame themselves for not getting your message.'

Tempted, Ovid prepared to disclose his plan when the ringing of the entrance bell interrupted Tiro, who hurried to the vestibule, while Ovid stepped behind a papyrus chest in an unlit part of the room. It was better that he stayed unseen.

'I came to fetch the books.' The voice was confident, and not unfamiliar.

'They are not ready', Tiro replied. 'Come back tomorrow.'

'I'll take whatever you have. Now.' There it was again. Ovid knew that voice, knew its owner, but he could not quite summon the image of a face.

'Wait here', Tiro said, before racing to the copy shop and bellowing at the scribes in at least three different languages, none of them Latin.

Ovid heard the visitor's footsteps. He was walking through the room, investigating the scrolls, reading a few words aloud from one, and then another. In a flash of insight, Ovid suddenly realised precisely who this man was. He stepped out from behind the chest and stood before him.

'Ovid', the man breathed, as if gazing upon a phantom.

'The Librarian of Tomis', Ovid said. 'Is this an illusion? Or have you followed me here?'

The Librarian placed his hand over his heart. 'I had no idea you had left Tomis.' He smiled warmly. 'I admit, it is good to see you.'

'And you', Ovid replied. 'This is a fitting place for our reunion.'

'Despite his despicable opinions about man and life', the Librarian said, 'Tiro is the only publisher whose books I am interested in.'

At that moment, the subject of their conversation appeared back in the room, gazing from one man to the other. 'You know each other?' Tiro said.

'Something I have never told you', the Librarian said, 'is that I come from Tomis.'

'I often forget that there are other parts to this world,' Tiro said, still amazed at what he saw before him, 'and that lives are lived there as vividly as my own.'

The Librarian, eager to resume his conversation with Ovid, turned back to the poet. 'When did you leave Tomis?' he said. 'And how did you come to be here?'

'That is a long story. Too long to tell now.' It suddenly struck Ovid that he had not thought of Carp since fleeing the inn at the Porta Tiburtina. *How had the boy slipped from his mind with such ease? Had he not changed for the better?*

Io Saturnalia!

Ovid knew well his way to the party. He had been to the house many times before. Cotta and Paulus Fabius, his brother, had chosen to celebrate Saturnalia in the house of their father, Ovid's late patron, Messalla. Ovid arrived before any of the other guests, a habit developed in his youth, when he had been inexperienced and provincial. Now it proved useful: his introduction needed to be carefully orchestrated if it were to appear spontaneous. And it had to appear spontaneous. At stake was nothing less than his future, as much as he might have left at his age.

In front of the entrance a small crowd of gapers had gathered. Some were excited at the prospect of spotting select citizens who were due to attend, others were there to applaud their patrons. Since none had as yet arrived, the crowd killed time by watching the musicians unload their instruments and tune them up. Ovid pushed them aside with faux confidence, relieved that no one recognised him, and entered through the gate asking for Cotta.

He was shown into Messalla's study, a room that had remained unchanged after his death. Cotta welcomed him with joviality, as if all those years of exile – and the recent meeting with Sejanus – had never taken place.

'Has Fabia accepted your invitation?' Ovid asked hopefully.

'Not yet', Cotta replied. 'But that does not mean she will not attend. I know that Marcia is coming.'

That name spelled hope for Ovid: in her letter to him, Fabia had remarked that she would be staying with Marcia outside the city. If the latter was coming, it was likely the former would too.

'Are you ready?' Cotta asked.

'I think so. It has been a while.'

'Just do what you have always done best – don't be boring. They will be so busy checking how much *they* have changed in comparison to you that they will easily fall in love with you – because you look unchanged.'

'What subjects are considered boring these days?'

'Politics', Cotta said. 'And stories from exile.'

'How do you know they are boring? I have not yet told you any.'

'And for that I am grateful. It seems that everyone has been exiled at some point. Don't forget I was exiled myself for two years. Now listen. Here is the plan. You will make your entrance from the private quarters. Then you will cross the atrium and stop close to the statue of Augustus. Talk with whoever you find gathered there.'

'Talk, but not about politics, and not about my exile. Perhaps I shall fall back on the old favourite of Roman society.'

'Which is?'

'Reconciling history with the present.'

Cotta laughed. 'It is like you never left. Keep talking to them until I toast you. When that happens, use the break in the conversation to move across to the low platform at the other end of the room. And it is there that I will ask you to recite your poems.'

'Will that not seem forced?'

'They will love it. Just like they used to. But remember to fit the verses to the mood of the guests.'

'I do not know if I can gauge such a thing anymore.'

'If you do not, I will discreetly interrupt by offering wine. White if you should change the subject, and red if you should just shut up altogether.'

Ovid did not want to admit to his friend that he had given up wine some time ago. A spasm of thirst for it ricocheted through his body, followed by a greater hunger – for the orange powder. How that would calm him, how it would help the evening pass with a smooth and delightful ease.

Music began to filter into the room. The singer was warming up her voice with a short, unpretentious melody of elongated vowels, which she abruptly changed for the difficult passage of a proper song. She tried twice to hit the highest note, replaced it with a tremor, and spoiled her first impression.

'Your safest bet', Cotta said, 'is still a poem from *Ars Amatoria*.'

'Isn't the time for love long extinct?'

A servant opened the door, and the music echoed louder. 'The guests have begun to arrive, sir', he said.

Cotta passed a hand through his hair, arranged his tunic, and said 'Wait for my return.' He left the room.

Ovid sat down in an armchair, alone. He felt an overwhelming impulse to spoil the whole plan and leave, but no one else in Rome would dare organise a party for him, an outlaw. What lay ahead would be tortuous, but it would also be necessary. Without Cotta's help, he might never be accepted back into Rome again, and that was a notion he could not bear to entertain.

A struggling candle attracted his attention to the bronze bust of Messalla on a side table, which stared back at him as if disapproving of his very presence. This was the man who, so solid in public and yet so fragile in private, had offered Ovid an alternative to the boring political path he had envisaged before him, and had helped him to outgrow his inherent provincialism. Some of his sayings Ovid had never forgotten.

'The Senate nowadays is good evidence of life after sex. Write about sex and they will pay attention.'

'You need more imagination than literary talent, and more luck than courage to mock Augustus, and to get away with it. If you find you have neither imagination nor luck, praise him. Nobody can praise Augustus enough.'

Those were good days, Ovid remembered, when his star had first begun to shine brightly with the considerable success of his play *Medea*. It was around that time that he had fallen in love with Corinna, then a courtesan, and she had taught him about the difficulties of relationships, irrespective of class, age, or even gender. Love became a strong theme of his poetry, and Messalla encouraged him to pursue it: as Rome struggled with Augustus' imposition of moral restrictions, it could not have been more timely, nor more topical. 'Address the women', Messalla had told him. 'They are attracted by any display of confidence, genuine or false. They know that the world is about appearances. Women think with their heads more than their genitals, which gives them a natural advantage over men. Just write well and you will get away with it.'

'But what about the politics of it all?' Ovid had asked.

'That you must not embrace. Not directly, at least.'

And so he had – not the real politics, but the politics of the Olympian gods. Messalla had defended him, even against Augustus. Ovid dared to use the gods as a vehicle to carry his messages about the unspeakable art of loving and the means to express it. Controversy and distaste had ensued, but Augustus had trusted Messalla – an old, pro-Empire friend – just as much as Ovid did.

The candles flickered rhythmically, one went out, and the shades that had been cast across the forbidding bronze mask lost their contours, as if the life were leaving Messalla yet again. Ovid took a candle and held it under the chin of the bronze head, hoping to coax the memories of his patron back to life.

'What are you doing to my father?' Cotta was back in the room.

'Seeking his help', Ovid said.

'Not even the Emperor could force that from him.'

Ovid turned and looked at his friend. 'It is time?'

Cotta nodded. 'It is time.'

A skeletal servant led the way. In the corridor, Ovid was struck by the sound of their footsteps – Cotta's purposeful; his nervous; the servant's all but nonexistent. They came to a heavily curtained door. A burst of high-pitched laughter sounded from the other side. The servant pulled the curtain aside a fraction so that Ovid could see the guests without them seeing him.

He recognised the blend of scents – fresh African lavender, heavy Asian rose oil – but almost none of the faces. All he could see was that there were a lot of them. The hall was filled. 'I did not expect there to be so many', he whispered.

'Almost ready', Cotta said. 'Now we just wait for the...'

With perfect timing, the musicians struck up the well-known song of Eurydice's return to the living. The singer's voice reached effortlessly high as Ovid was pushed through the doorway.

'Publius Ovidius Naso!' a bodyless voice announced, and all turned to witness the entrance of the guest of honour. He stood there, mute, paralysed, while Cotta raced to the stage, making a sign to the musicians to quieten their music so that he might be heard over them.

'Friends!' Cotta shouted, his easy confidence filling the room. 'It is depressing to think how many times we offered libations to the gods for our missed friend, and for all that spilled wine to have caused nothing but messy floors. Whether they would help, we never knew. But one thing is for sure: he is back. So, please, one and all, join with me to salute our friend Naso, the bravest of us all!'

'Hail Naso!' The response was so coordinated and enthusiastic that for a moment Ovid wondered if it had been rehearsed. A cup was pushed into his hand, and he glanced down at it. The wine was red. He remembered Cotta's code. *Stay quiet*, he thought, holding the cup up and smiling politely.

He could not see Fabia. There were matrons frigid in their immobility and courtesans who fanned their elongated eyelashes with uninhibited abandon, but his wife was nowhere to be seen. Through the crowd, Marcia – alone – moved towards him, her bun of thick false hair bobbing behind her as she walked. She wore a grey palla, *de rigueur* for an aristocratic widow, yet it did not conceal her ageless sexuality.

'We've missed you!' she said, her deep, rich voice resonating around the room as she slipped between his arms, the utmost sign of familiarity she could get away with in public. A powerful sensation flowed through him, and, for a brief moment, he considered giving her a hug. 'Please be prudent', she whispered.

Cotta gently unchained her from Ovid's arms. 'He is too old for that.'

'I would be surprised if he had changed that much!' she giggled.

A young woman with alert eyes joined their little group. 'My father sends his apologies for his absence', she said.

Cotta introduced her to Ovid. 'You might not recognise her, but doubtless you will remember. This is Pomponia, your friend Graecinus' daughter.'

Ovid nodded. 'And niece to Flaccus. The only one who visited me in Tomis. Of course, I remember.'-

The cup of red wine was taken from his hand and replaced with another filled with white wine. It was time for him to address his audience. He looked out across them. They were well dressed, well nourished, good-looking, and dull beyond belief. Marcia leaned close to his ear, her heavy perfume suffocating.

'Disappoint them', she whispered.

To do such was the safest option. He could tell them that old joke, the one about the father who wanted to rid his son of his optimism by offering him nicely packed horseshit for his birthday. 'What a wonderful gift', the boy replied. 'A pity that the horse left.' But even that might induce a flutter of polite laughter. No, far better to just be boring. He thanked his patron's house gods for bringing him back, thanked Cotta for organising the party, and thanked everyone for attending.

A young man stepped forward, grinning. 'Tell us about your years away from Rome.'

'What a want of delicacy', Marcia said, looking revolted.

'Not at all', the young man persisted. 'Many of us would love to know how Rome looks from exile.' He inched closer to Ovid with each word, a tremor of hostility bubbling beneath his grin.

Cotta stepped in. 'This is Cornelius', he said. 'The youngest son of Ibis.'

Son of Ibis, Ovid thought. *And of Corinna. So the brother of… Oh.*

'It is a pleasure to meet you, Cornelius.'

'Is it?' The young man maintained his grin, though now Ovid could see how false it truly was. 'You seem, for want of a better word, nervous.'

'Not at all.'

'I would not be so surprised if you were. Exile is the closest thing to death, and what makes a man more nervous than that?'

Is he threatening me? Or is he just showing off?

'I feel that such topics may be a little tender for our society', Marcia said.

Cornelius ignored her, never taking his eyes off Ovid, or that strange grin off his face. 'I believe you might be the first scapegoat I have ever seen return', he said. 'Is it wrong of me to want to find out more about life… out there?'

'What exactly do you want to know?' Ovid said.

'Where have you been? What was it like there? How was

the journey back?' He paused. 'And are you not afraid of being here, in Rome?'

Ovid laughed loudly, and in an instant the gathering tension broke as all in the hall laughed with him. Cornelius looked crestfallen. 'So many questions!' he said, still laughing. 'You are lucky you are young. If you were my age, you would not have time for all the answers.'

The assembled crowd continued to laugh and Cotta, seeing his opportunity, took Cornelius by the elbow and guided him away. Marcia leaned back in to whisper the same command into Ovid's ear.

'Disappoint them.'

Perhaps, he thought, he could tell them about Hercules. He knew the first dozen verses or so of the *Gigantomachia* by heart; the rest, if they wanted more, he could make up quite easily. Zeus, Juno, Hercules, the Titans, the vast world of the gods created for the benefit of man – he could speak about them all for hours, a sure disappointment for these people gathered before him, whose only aim was to have a good life free from responsibilities. Or perhaps it would be better, he decided, to focus on that, to elucidate to these people all the shocking senselessness of their lives in Rome. After all, he had not just travelled to the border of the civilised world, he had crossed it, and if anyone could afford to be free from conventions and restraint, it was him. He opened his mouth to speak, but before a word could escape his lips the musicians launched into the melody known to introduce dinner.

The crowd looked about themselves, confused. It was too early for food, and wasn't the esteemed poet about to give the inaugural recital of his return?

'Sorry, sorry!' Cotta said, waving his hands at the musicians. 'Bad timing. The food is not yet ready, I can assure you!' He pushed his way through the crowd to silence the music. Within seconds, Cornelius had appeared back by Ovid's side.

Ovid raised an eyebrow. 'More questions?'

'I have been thinking,' he said, 'if we consider what Rome has become, it is more logical that Hercules, and not Aeneas, the Trojan fugitive, was our forefather. Is this what you want to recite?'

Ovid stared at him in disbelief. 'My notes…' he said. 'The ones your father seized from the inn. About Hercules. You have read them?'

Cornelius leaned in close and lowered his voice. 'To suggest that we are all descendants of Hercules would have been inconceivable in Augustus' time. What makes you think you can get away with that kind of treason now?'

The music stopped. Ovid felt red-eyed, frothing and bloody. He stared down at the young man, who looked so like his mother, and yet acted so like his father.

'My mother told me that you are an exceptional man,' Cornelius said, loud enough for all to hear. 'So please. Recite to us. And prove it.'

The gauntlet was laid. Ovid felt as if a white fog had descended from the ceiling to encase him, to work its way into his lungs, his heart, his very soul. He understood that whatever he was going to tell them now would mark his future in Rome. *Disappoint them*, Marcia had told him. For safety's sake. *Disappoint them.* But no. He would do no such thing.

He straightened his spine. 'Dear friends, I should like to read to you from a new poem of mine. It is not in Latin but

Gaetic, the language spoken in Tomis, my place of exile, and it is a poem for our departed Augustus.'

He did not have the scroll with him, but he knew the words well enough to recite them with a clarity and authority that surprised even himself. As he spoke, he could see the poem working its way into those assembled before him, unsettling them. They may not have understood each individual word, but they understood the accumulation of them. And when he reached his end, they were smart enough to applaud.

'Are you now writing in Vulgar Latin?' Cornelius said.

'It is proto-Latin', Ovid said. 'It celebrates Augustus' entrance to the gods. Why?' He smiled broadly. 'Do you not approve?'

Cornelius knew better than to reply to that.

'This should be the poem for the coming Saturnalia!' a voice called out from the crowd. Ovid recognised the man, a consul he had once shared many a discussion with. 'Io Saturnalia!'

'Io Saturnalia!' someone else shouted. 'Naso should be the king of Saturnalia this year!'

The audience cheered.

'No, no', Ovid said. 'I do not like kings. I am a convinced republican.'

'You know best what misrule is!' the consul shouted. 'You will be the perfect ruler of our chaos!'

Again, the audience hollered their approval.

Cornelius placed his hand on Ovid's arm. 'I shall report your bravado to Tiberius' he said, and then, with a half-hearted salute in Cotta's direction, left the room.

Cotta grabbed two empty cups, made his way to the middle of the hall and banged them against each other, doing his best to control the uncontrollable. 'Dinner is ready!' he shouted. 'Please, make your way to the dining area!'

He was ignored. The crowd, too whipped up in their own excitement, went nowhere. Giving up on then, Cotta pushed his way back to Ovid.

'Congratulations, Naso', he said. 'It seems that, once more, you have taken on the role of scapegoat.'

The Pythagorean Temple

From the moment he left Tiro's shop, the Librarian had scoured the streets and alleyways of Rome in search of Carp. He asked everyone he knew and many people he did not if they had seen the boy, describing him as best he remembered from the last time he had seen him in Tomis. It was only when he bumped into a man he knew from the Pythagorean temple, a professor of music, that he finally received the answer he had been hoping for.

'I believe I know the boy you mean', the Professor said. 'I saw him at my usual brothel yesterday.'

'A *brothel*?' The Librarian was aghast. 'You did not…'

'What do you take me for? Of course I did not do *that* with him. No, no. Perish the thought. He is a dowser. He read my future for me.'

'Take me to him', the Librarian said.

'Would you like to know what he told me? About my future?'

'If you do not take me to him immediately your future will be very short indeed.'

'Are you happy to be seen in the brothel? I thought that was against your standards.'

The Librarian considered this for a moment. Ever since arriving in Rome, he had worked his hardest to cultivate a reputation: one of sobriety, culture and education. It was unlikely that he would be spotted entering the Professor's brothel, but if he was – if just one person saw him and spread the word – the reputation he had strived so arduously to build could be ruined in a matter of hours.

'Perhaps you are right', he said. 'If I can avoid the whorehouse, then I should. Do you think you might be able to get the boy away from it? Tell the Madam there that you would like to take him out for the day?'

'I think so, but she would doubtless smell an opportunity in that. It would cost.'

'I have money. Here. Take it.' The Librarian reached into his tunic and produced a handful of different-sized coins, which he pressed into the Professor's palms. 'Just get the boy out of there safely.'

'Where shall we meet?'

'The Pythagorean temple. I will go there now and wait for you.'

The Professor, thrilled by the intrigue of this little mission, set off through the streets. When he reached the brothel, Madam received him with a knowing smile.

'Back again so soon?'

'I was impressed by that boy's divinations yesterday.' The Professor had rehearsed what he would say while he walked. 'Friends of mine would like to test his abilities. At the Pythagorean temple. I promised I would bring him.'

Madam licked her lips. 'How many friends?'

'Several.'

'Each will need to pay.'

The Professor held out the coins. 'Will this serve?'

Madam counted through them, and then slipped them into her bag. 'Yes', she said. 'But tell your friends I have given them a good price. Next time it will cost more.' She turned around in the doorway. 'Carp!' she yelled, and the boy dutifully tottered up to her. 'The Professor here has a day out planned for you. Go with him. Do as he bids.'

Carp knew better than to disobey, and without a word allowed the Professor to lead him away through the streets. It was only after a few minutes that he cursed himself for not telling Spiros of his departure.

'We are going to a temple', the Professor said. 'Have you heard about the Pythagoreans?'

Carp shook his head.

'A marvellous place. You should be excited to see it. It is the only temple on the Capitoline that maintained its original shape during Augustus' reign. You see, renovating it would have meant acknowledging support for the fellowship of the Pythagoreans, and he would never had done that, for they challenged him more than anyone else.'

'Why didn't he just tear it down?' Carp asked.

'That would have been immensely unpopular, too much so to risk. So instead he had it renamed. The Temple of Orpheus the Thracian. And then he infused it with his spies and agents, who reported back to him everything untoward that they learned there. Do you understand why I am telling you all this, Carp?'

'No.' The boy shook his head.

'You will meet someone there. This man you can trust. But do not trust any others. If you are asked questions, keep your answers short and vague. I suspect that you might have secrets they would like to uncover.'

They reached the temple. A gong announced the fourth

hour of the ever shorter winter day. In the treeless inner yard, a young crowd had formed themselves into lines to enter the classrooms through low doorways. The Professor led Carp behind a line of six students into a dark room and then, beyond that, a damp yard. 'Wait here', he said, and left.

Carp watched through the open doorway as the six students sat themselves at the harps which had been arranged in a circle. A middle-aged woman began to talk to them about three fourths, about one half, about seven eighths, and as she spoke the students somehow translated her words into sounds, plucking a synchronised melody from their instruments. Carp could not understand how they knew what to play, or when to play it.

'Who are you?'

Carp spun around. A tall man towered over him, his dark eyes narrowed.

'A new student', Carp said, remembering the Professor's instructions should he be questioned. *Keep your answers short and vague.*

'Music?'

Carp nodded.

'Then I should have been told. This is my faculty.' He bent down and peered at the boy. 'You look familiar to me. Do I know you?'

Carp shook his head.

'You look like someone.' He leaned in so close that Carp could smell his fetid breath. 'Yes, you look very much like… someone.' He righted himself. 'Enjoy the lesson', he said, before walking away.

The yard somehow seemed colder, damper, in the wake

of his strange conversation with the strange man. Carp was grateful when, moments later, the Professor reappeared. A tall gentleman accompanied him, staring with disbelief. When Carp recognised the Librarian, he ran towards him and flung himself into his arms.

'Carp! I am so pleased to have found you.'

'You were looking for me?' Carp hugged him tighter.

'Of course. Once I learned you were in the city, I promised myself I would seek you out.'

'But how did you know I was here?'

'Ovid.' The Librarian said the name with barely concealed satisfaction.

'You've seen him? Where is he? *How* is he? He is the reason I came here, to Rome, but we were split up, and I lost him.'

'Dear boy, *he* lost *you*. And he should never have let that happen. Do not blame yourself for it.'

Carp smiled. 'I am just so happy to see you again.'

The Professor looked upon them both. 'And I am proud to have instigated this little reunion.'

In all the excitement of seeing the Librarian, Carp had almost forgotten that he had something to tell the Professor. 'Someone was here', he said. 'He asked me questions. But I did as you said. I kept my answers short and vague.'

'Who was it? Did he give you a name?'

'He said that this was his faculty.'

The Professor paled. 'Oh no', he said. 'The Dean.'

The Librarian looked at him. 'You know this man?'

'He is my superior. And a notorious spy.' His eyes flickered about the yard. 'What did he say to you, Carp? You must tell me exactly.'

'Not much. Only that he recognised me. That I looked like someone. Could he have been talking about my father? The woman at the brothel said I looked like him.'

'I fear it may be worse', the Librarian said. 'You do look like your father, but you also look like your uncle.'

'Who is his uncle?' the Professor asked.

'Scorillo the Dacian.'

Silence.

'You know my uncle?' Carp asked, unsure if he wanted to hear the answer.

'This is Rome', the Professor said. 'Everyone knows Scorillo. Or knows of him. He was a respected Pythagorean.' He bent down to tighten the straps on his sandals. 'Come on. We must go. Now. The Dean will have passed on this information. We do not want to find out who to. Follow me.'

Out they went, the Professor in front and the Librarian behind with Carp in the middle, racing down poorly lit corridors and through rooms where students battled mathematical equations and physics problems and philosophical paradoxes, arriving finally at an exit which was far from the site of their entrance.

'Professor! Stop!' The voice was loud and commanding, and Carp was horrified to see that the Professor obeyed it without question, freezing to the spot. Both Carp and the Librarian turned to face the voice. The Dean marched towards them, at his side a tall man in an impressive costume. Ibis.

'Ibis', the Librarian hissed, placing himself defensively in front of Carp. Ibis pushed him out of the way.

'Where is Ovid?' he said, jabbing his finger into the boy's chest.

‘I don’t know’, Carp said, trying to keep his tears at bay.

‘He killed my older son. Did you know that?’

Carp shook his head.

‘Liar. You are all a bunch of liars. But don’t you worry, I’ll squeeze out the truth from you.’

‘Leave him be, Senator’, the Librarian said. ‘He is just a child.’

‘You I do not know.’

‘I know you.’

‘What of it? Many do.’ Ibis pushed the Librarian aside once more. ‘You will lead me to Ovid’, he said, his finger back to work once more, prodding and poking.

Carp looked across at the Professor. Perhaps the man had done so unwittingly, but it was clear now whom he had betrayed.

The Triple Mother Goddess

Flaccus arrived to take Ovid to the traditional Good Mother's mass. Ovid was grateful for the excuse to leave the house. It had begun to feel dark and cloying there, and he was embarrassed to admit to himself that he had felt more spirited in his Tomitan home, as though his true self had not made the trip back to Rome and was waiting for him on the shores of the Black Sea. His poems from exile had meant to fill his absence here, but they hadn't. And his friends were not supposed to have changed, but they had. He had lost them, he had lost his wife, he had lost his position in society, but at least he had not lost his wits. And he intended to keep them about him at the mass.

Dusk fell across Rome as the two men walked together. Crows cawed from the right, a bad omen, and a thin rain fell in intervals against the last light of the day. They chose the back streets to avoid being spied on, where people of the lower classes drank and shouted. *Maybe they are rehearsing for Saturnalia*, thought Ovid.

'I always wondered how can they enjoy themselves in this biting cold', Flaccus said.

'My friend, you do not know what a real biting cold feels like', Ovid said.

Pickpockets were rife in this area, and Ovid checked his robe for the sachet of tormenting herbs that the driver had given him on the far side of the Danube. He was not entirely sure why he had brought it along for the mass, but something about the event made him suspect he might be able to make use of it.

Opposite the Campus Martius, Flaccus knocked at the door of a nondescript house. From behind a latticed window, a pitched voice discouraged them. 'Today there is no one here.'

'Mother has asked us to come', Flaccus said, enunciating each word with care.

The gates opened and they passed through. Inside, a box hung on the wall, and Ovid flung a coin into it: a gesture worth the monetary waste. The box sounded hollow. He wondered if anyone else had done the same.

The mazes of arched corridors were familiar in their danger. He recalled celebrating private masses here for the Good Goddess long ago. They had, he remembered, invariably turned into ceremonies for Isis, a cult that had been forbidden by Augustus – yet another of his interdictions that few had complied with. Least of all Livia.

Livia. She would be here. Ovid knew it. He looked forward to seeing her again. He had always admired her for her undisputed beauty and intelligence. By instinct or reason, they had long maintained a close relationship. To him, she embodied the uncontested matron, and to her he became a symbol of the free-spirited, post-civil-war youth – or so he believed.

The stairs leading to the temple's subterranean quarters crunched noisily. Down there, in contrast to the cave-like smell above, the air was fresh. Rumours that Livia had built underground connections between shrines of the Alma Mater must have been true. An attendant approached Ovid and Flaccus, asking them to put on grey tunics as they entered the main room – a large polygon with a concave ceiling where lit candles drew one's attention to the zodiacal signs on the ceiling. It was a typical setting for a mass for Juno Lucina, the Mother of Light, Livia's preferred incarnation of the Mother Goddess.

Ovid checked the altar, a massive granite block, for stains or any other signs of recent sacrifice, but it was polished and clean and held an Egyptian glass cylinder and a golden boat-shaped dish holding small charcoal pieces. Three side doors opened and worshippers, like a flock of oversized hares marching on their back feet, entered holding unlit candles. Ovid, succumbing to the absurdity of the scene, forgot to hide his face. Augustus would have banned the entire gathering if he were alive.

A voice called out: 'The fire!'

The fourth door opened and a figure, face half-covered with white flour, carried a lit torch to the granite block. It halted for a moment to allow the worshippers to collect themselves, and then held the flame over the oil lamp. The worshippers moved forward and raised their candles above their heads. Light filled the room. Then, one by one, the candles were placed around the walls and, quietly, the gathering, as though at random, arranged itself in the centre of the room.

A voice – one that sounded to Ovid distinctly like Urgulania's – recited: 'Juno Lucina. Goddess with many eyes. Immortal queen. Wife and elder sister of Jupiter, the Thunderer. Come among us!'

A frail and hooded creature sidled up to Ovid and whispered

to him. 'For the gods' sake, Naso,' it said, 'I hope the ravages of time are less visible with me than they are with you.'

'Livia,' Ovid said, turning to face the creature. 'The friend I have not seen for all these years.'

'You will celebrate the mass today.' She used her commanding tone: the one stripped of inflections, friendly or fiendish; the one she used when it mattered.

Refusal is possible, he thought, *but stupid*. And besides, he could not deny that he felt a certain warm glow at being the centre of attention in aristocratic society.

Cords, invisible until then, began pulling up towards the apex of the ceiling a series of white triangular sails. The painted night sky of the ceiling, belonging to Juno's celebration, was replaced with the interior of an Egyptian royal tent, friendlier in shape but far more menacing in potential. He fingered the sachet hidden in his tunic, hoping there would not be an unwelcome turn of events.

Livia placed her gloved claw on his shoulder and pressed it into his sweating flesh. 'I hope you always knew, Naso,' she said, 'that I never supported your exile.' And then she lowered her hand and slowly began to back away.

Her voice rang out across the room. 'The statues of the one Universal Mother.' It was the beginning of the ceremony. The crowd focused on her. 'Mistress of all elements. Primordial child of time. Queen of the immortals. Should the statues enter?'

If they expected a reply, it was not waited for. Three golden idols of Queen Isis were brought in, carried high on stretched hands so that all could see them, and so that they could see all. Ovid suddenly felt nervous. He should not have been here.

Unlike other places in the Empire, celebrating the mass of Isis was forbidden to men.

Urgulania – for it was she – removed her grey tunic in a flow of dramatic movements and, displaying a crocus-yellow dress with light blue borders hanging in fine folds from a knot on her left shoulder, she commanded with a wail: 'Ave Queen of Heaven!'

Gracefully, she took a torch from the wall and placed the flame over the boat-shaped gold dish on the altar, holding it there until smoke emerged, frail and slender and utterly insubstantial. The worshippers, skilled singers as they were, pushed across the room pulsating sounds.

Livia plucked the Egyptian glass cylinder from the altar and marched towards Ovid, holding it out ceremoniously. 'You who have been to the end of the world!' she cried. 'Prove it to us! Drink this!'

It was here, now. The time had come, it made him sick with anxiety. He fingered the sachet of herbs in his tunic once more. He only hoped that Isis – if indeed she existed and was a loving Mother Goddess – would understand why he had to change the mass, would understand that he would be nobody's scapegoat, not ever again.

He marched to the altar, tied the three statues of Isis together with the belt of his tunic, and placed in front of them the glass cylinder that Livia had handed him. Using the gestures of the Hyperborean priests from that smoke-filled shed, he raised one hand, turned his back to the audience, and began to pray. 'Peace up to Heaven, Heaven down to Earth.' He listed the three manifestations – maiden, mother, grandmother – and what they stood for. Then, with both hands, he raised the cylinder, and was relieved to see despite the dwindling light that it contained merely water and sand.

The crowd were silent, mesmerised, as Ovid spoke. 'Across this world, you are worshipped in many forms, with different rites, under different names. This mass is for you, Triple Mother Goddess of the Okeanos, whose son, the Hyperborean Apollo, was the patron of our Augustus, himself a Hyperborean, if not by birth then by conviction.' This was his ultimate revenge for the man who had banished him.

He could feel all eyes on him, entranced by this new twist to their traditional ceremony. He hoped they would remain so for what he had planned next. Putting the cylinder aside, he retrieved the sachet from his inner pocket, spread the contents over the embers of the boat-shaped dish, pursed his lips, and blew with care. Thin flames flickered and Ovid, with the delicacy of a snake charmer, poured some drops from the cylinder over the live coals.

Slowly, the smoke began to rise. He remembered the scent well from the shed on the far side of the Danube. The smoke was whiter, less smothering, but there was no mistaking that it was the same. He surreptitiously pulled his scarf over his mouth and nose, hoping no one would notice and do the same. They did not. Drawn by the strange new smells, the crowd surrounded the altar, allowing Ovid to slip away from it. He wondered what they might hallucinate. He did not envy them the experience.

A thin hand grabbed his arm and pulled him to the side of the room. Perhaps he had not entirely escaped the effects of the smoke, for Livia appeared to him no longer as the famed Empress, but merely as a ravaged elderly woman.

'Augustus the Hyperborean', she said, allowing a faint smile to play across her lips. 'I am glad you never called him that when he was alive.'

'Would he not have liked it?'

'Oh, I don't know. But you would have lost *me* as a friend. I did not like him being associated with the places of his youth.' She gazed at him, amused. 'You know, I used to be able to read your mind far more easily. You have changed, Publius Ovidius Naso.'

'As have we all.'

'I hope this was worth the effort. Later, when the mass is over, be sure to look for me in my rooms.' She gazed at the crowd, who had begun to melt into each other, formless and malleable under the potent power of the smoke.

'Let us pray your herb will teach me what I long to know.' Livia slipped into the crowd, vanishing amongst them.

Hovering nearby, Ovid saw Flaccus, also with a scarf over his mouth and nose.

'You should try it', Ovid said. 'Or you will miss the fumes of your life.'

'I trust no smoke.' As if to prove his point, Flaccus tightened the scarf. 'Is there more?'

Ovid shook his head. 'I think I have done enough.'

'Good. Then come with me.'

'Why?'

'Someone awaits you.'

The Call for the Augustiada

In a tiny cubicle on the ground floor, Fabia – shivering with cold – waited for him.

Ovid rushed towards her, but she stopped him with an upheld hand. 'They are watching us.'

It was the first time he had heard his wife speak in years. There were new melancholic tones to her voice, but the dignity he remembered still underpinned them.

'I am so grateful to the gods who brought you back,' she said, 'when all of us here in Rome failed.'

'I am back', he said, desperate to run to her, to hold her, but that raised hand warned him off. 'I am back and, this time, I shall not avoid trouble.'

She smiled. 'You have never been a coward.'

He laughed. 'Perhaps cowardice has not defined me, but I was no stranger to it.'

'I understand there are things you must do', she said. 'But this time you are not going anywhere without me.'

'Separation was the price we agreed upon to save *my* name and *your* possessions.'

'A price which, I came to learn, was too high.' She crossed the room, letting her hair flow down as she did so.

'Aren't they watching us?'

'They are. So let us embarrass them until they stop.' She began to undress slowly, the way he liked. Her breasts hung lower than he remembered and her motions were somewhat clumsier, but she was still the same Fabia whom he adored. Naked, she stood before him. 'Your turn', she said.

His head tumbled with images, a thousand pairs of eyes dotting the ceiling like stars, watching every movement of his, judging and commenting on each flap and fold. Nobody wanted to be caught making love, even to their wife, within the precinct of Isis' temple. 'I cannot', he said.

With the same slowness as before, Fabia dressed again. 'You just need more time.' She blew out the lamp, and he felt the darkness cloak him. It was a relief. 'You will do the right things. I know it.'

'Sometimes', he said, 'I am not sure I can.'

'You can. I am telling you. But you will need money. You must find yourself a patron. Speak with Flaccus. He knows some rich merchants who aspire to be admitted into society.'

'I should not lower myself to that. Tiro tells me my books are in every household.'

She touched him, a sign that he should listen carefully. 'Because of me. *I* gave them away among people of the lower classes. In the new Rome, it is they who decide who is or is not famous. I spent all our money publishing your books. When my family found out, they complained to Augustus. He allowed them to repossess what was left of my dowry.'

There was no power that could have stopped Ovid kissing his wife now. She returned the kiss with passion, the darkness hiding their act.

'Now that I have returned,' he said, 'will you come home?'

'Home? Where is home? Our old house on the Palatine? It has been filled with spies for years. There was only one servant

I trusted; the rest I could not bear to be around. If you want me to return there, we need to find trustworthy personnel. But first we must get through Saturnalia. And you should stay away from Rome until it is finished.'

'I still love you', he said, holding her close.

'Good. But put the practicalities first. It is the only way we can be together again.'

Livia's chief guard entered the room. By the time he had lit the candles, Fabia was out of Ovid's arms and leaning against the far wall. Livia marched in moments later. She fixed her gaze on Fabia. 'I must talk with your husband. Alone. Leave us.'

Head low and silenced, Fabia departed the room. Ovid watched her go, but she did not look back at him.

'Put this on', Livia said, holding out a red tunic. It was an odd colour to choose for a man – purposeful, he realised. In it, he would look ridiculous. He removed his old tunic and changed into the new one.

Livia did not bother to suppress her laughter. 'You look funnier than I had anticipated.'

'Power and beauty always go together', he said. 'You are living proof.'

He could tell how much she enjoyed that remark. Livia had never been impervious to flattery. She was the daughter of an unimportant nobleman and those base traits of hers had survived all the way through her journey from nobody to the first woman of Rome.

'How did you manage to get hold of that smoke?' she asked.

'The herbs were given to me. On the barbarian side of the Danube.'

'So they are the supplier of the Eleusinian Mysteries. Why

did you so malign those places out there in your poems? You sounded so miserable, and yet from all I hear it is a blessed part of the world.'

'My poems were meant to build up my case and restore my freedom, not promote barbaric lands.'

'Oh, that was abundantly clear. You repeated it incessantly, and we often wondered if you thought us stupid.' She crossed the room towards him, pushed two of her bony fingers into his mouth and then walked them over his lips. Her hand was cold, icy, in contrast to the red heat that flamed in her eyes. 'I want the name of the general who eased your passage to Rome', she said.

Ovid saw no reason to lie. 'Gaius Julius Vestalis, the commander of the Lower Danube.'

'He sounds fictional.'

'Ask Ibis. He knows the man.'

'I will.' Never taking her sea-blue eyes off him, she covered her claws in green velvet gloves and instructed the guard to bring her the glass cylinder filled with water and sand. 'Take it.'

'Do you want me to drink from it?' he asked.

'Just hold it. You have performed enough magic already. I learned great things from your smoke, things I have longed to know for some time.'

'Such as?'

'The next twelve Caesars will be my descendants. They will carry both my blood and my determination. And whether they will be monsters or wise men, whether they will inflict terror or guard peace, they will all believe themselves to be gods, and never question that I was one too.' She smiled. 'It was you, after all, who first called me in one of your poems the universal mother.'

Before he could stop her, Livia snatched the cylinder from his hands and drank the contents. 'Don't!' was all he had time to cry.

She wiped her lips. 'Do not worry. Whatever happens, I know you will save me. You are a magician. You will build a Rome for me with words that architects did for Augustus with marble. He believed that we depend on our buildings, that our surroundings transform us, that stones embody the ideas we respect, that they are a vision of our own ideals. But I believe in words. Nothing has such power. And you, Ovid, you can harness that power. The master of the *Metamorphoses* himself will write an epic about how I and Augustus together transformed Rome, and created an almighty Empire.' Her large eyes, like two wet alabaster stones, pierced his own. A curl from her bun found its way loose, and she pushed it back, with some difficulty.

'This is what you want me to write for you?'

'You can do it. You can do it like no one else can. A vast and beautiful epic. And we shall call it the *Augustiada*.'

Ovid smiled. 'I can do it', he agreed.

'You can and you will.'

He closed his eyes and nodded. With this commission, he would no longer need to worry about his immortality as a poet. His name would be forever linked with Augustus'. Livia coughed loudly to bring him back to reality.

'However', she said, lowering her voice, 'you must leave the gods out of this. They have no logic.'

Ovid bowed. 'You are the logic', he said.

Livia's hardened face relaxed into a smile.

The Plots

'The senator is waiting', the lieutenant announced.

'Send him in.' Sejanus sat back in his high chair and awaited the arrival of Ibis. When the senator stepped through the curtain-door, Sejanus rose to greet him with his right palm over that of Ibis – an unusual greeting for two men who had little in common.

Sejanus sent his lieutenant out of the room. 'I received the information you sent', he said, 'and checked it too. It was right, though incomplete. I wonder, which of the unfolding plots do you think Tiberius should fear most?'

'In his better days, he did not fear anything.'

'Careful, senator. Your words might be interpreted wrongly. My house is no different from others in Rome. It is populated with large ears and small brains.'

'I apologise.' Ibis' smile was thin.

'Exactly how many conspiracies are you aware of, senator?'

Ibis mimicked counting on his fingers. 'A number', he said.

Sejanus was beginning to lose his patience. 'Do you want the job of spymaster or not?'

'I *am* the spymaster. Tiberius has never officially dismissed me. The title remains until he – or someone else – does.'

'Then perhaps you should be more cooperative, for if one of the plots succeeds, a new emperor may well dismiss you.'

Ibis thought about this for a few moments. 'The least

dangerous', he eventually said, 'is the plot of the patricians.'

'Which of them?'

'The one organised by the former consul to ensure that none of Germanicus' retarded sons will ever rule Rome.'

'And what about the plot of the generals?' Sejanus asked.

'As long as they do not march to Rome like Caesar did, I do not think they will present a problem.'

'It seems, then, that there is nothing Tiberius needs to take seriously.'

'There is one, about which I do not have enough details.'

'Not enough details? I told you your information was incomplete. What kind of spy are you?'

'The best. Of that I can assure you.'

'So where might we find the information that you need?'

Ibis paused. 'From Tiberius himself.'

'Speak!'

'Rumours go that he and Germanicus are plotting against the patricians to restore the old Republic.'

Sejanus looked past Ibis. 'I have heard this before. Nobody believes that story.'

'Let us hope it remains a story. For if it evolves into truth, few of us will remain alive to tell it.'

'A civil war…'

'Precisely. The end of Rome.'

'What evidence do you have that the rumour might be true?'

'There is a general on his way to Rome. He carries messages.'

'Who is this general?'

'The commander in chief of the legions of the Lower Danube. A Celt. He does not fear death.'

'He must be stopped.'

'I believe it has been tried, but has proved... difficult.' Ibis raised his eyebrows to suggest it was beyond his control.

'These messages', Sejanus said, wrinkling his nose at the word, 'when will I know what they say?'

'He will not give them up to you willingly. The only way would be to force him to speak out in front of the Senate.'

'And why do I need you for that?'

'To orchestrate a trial. For high treason.' Ibis left a pause. 'But for this, I have a favour to ask in return.'

'Tell me.'

'Give up your protection of Ovid.'

'I do not know where he is. How can I protect a man whose whereabouts are unknown to me?'

Ibis grimaced. 'Then promise me this. When I find him, I shall expect no resistance or retribution from you.'

Sejanus flattened his hair with his hands and then, so slightly that it was almost imperceptible, nodded.

Satisfied, Ibis turned and left the room. Moments later, a hidden door opened and Cotta stepped out, breathing heavily and fanning the air before him. 'How can you trust anyone who uses that fragrance?' he panted.

'Did you hear everything?' Sejanus said, pouring out a cup of wine and handing it to Cotta.

'Yes.' He took a long gulp, draining half the cup in one. 'I need to get Ovid out of the city.'

'You are a good friend to him', Sejanus said. 'But is he a good friend to you? How do you know he hasn't talked about you?'

'Because', Cotta replied, 'I am still alive.'

Roman Fog

Livia's request for him to write the *Augustiada* changed everything. After years of exile, insulting injustice and an ostentatious lack of recognition, at last Ovid had the proof that Rome could not do without him. No other poet, with the exception of Virgil, had ever been commissioned to produce a historical ode of national importance. He had never been closer to eternal glory.

A thin smell of the city and the noise of screeching gulls came to him from the atrium. He walked through the house to investigate the cause, to be confronted by the only remaining servant.

'You should cover your head', she said. 'This is the fog of Saturnalia. It twists thoughts.'

Romans feared fog, that great symbol of the unknown, perhaps more than anything else. Creeping up the hills, coming from the Tiber, it was the one thing that the gods did not govern, and as such it was more unearthly than death. Ovid did the only sensible thing. He closed the door.

'No! The fog needs to get out first!' the servant said, rushing to reopen it. As she reached out to place her hand on the handle, a series of violent thumps on the door made her jump back in fright. 'They are coming to fetch us!' she screamed.

Ovid could not resist teasing her. 'Then let the demons in!' He pushed her aside and swung open the door, to leap back in a similar fashion when three sodden and muddy creatures slid into the house. *Nothing exists unless observed*, he thought.

Six pairs of eyes stared at him. Three mouths grinned. One of the creatures exclaimed: 'Master!'

Ovid opened his arms and rushed to greet each of them – Carp, the Librarian, Spiros – in turn, caring not that his tunic became as wet and mud-caked as theirs in the process.

'Carp! You are alive. To see you here now brings me unspeakable joy!'

Carp wrapped his arms around his tutor. 'I wasn't sure I would see you again!' he cried.

Ovid looked across at the Librarian. 'This is your doing, isn't it? I owe you a world of thanks.'

'Divert them towards this man,' the Librarian said. 'It was Spiros who saved us.'

'Spiros?' Ovid could not quite believe his former slave was capable of such chivalry.

'That man, that Ibis,' Carp tripped over his words as they spurted from his mouth, 'he had trapped me and the Librarian in the Pythagorean temple, but the Professor went to the brothel to tell Madam and the blonde woman, and Spiros was still there, he hadn't run away, he was waiting for me to come back, and when he heard I was imprisoned, he came for me, he sneaked into the temple while no one was looking and he found the Librarian and me and he got us out before Ibis came back to kill us—'

'The temple? The brothel? Madam and the Professor?' Ovid laughed. 'It is too much information for an old man such as myself.'

'But, but—'

'Easy, Carp. You can tell me the whole story later, at a slower pace so that I might enjoy it. For now, I am just glad you are safe.' Ovid looked up at Spiros. 'And I am eternally grateful to you. Giving you your freedom was one of the best decisions I ever made.'

Spiros did not answer, but coyly looked at the floor and flushed red.

The Librarian stepped forward. 'Ovid, listen to me. Senator Ibis is after you.'

'As happy as I am to see you, you did not need to come all the way here just to tell me that. I am perfectly aware.'

'But perhaps you are not quite aware of the magnitude with which he wants you. He means harm.'

Ovid stood up and brushed himself down. The Librarian would not be humoured with flippancy, and perhaps rightly so. The situation demanded a certain level of gravity. 'What course do you recommend I take?'

'Run!' Carp shouted. 'Run and we will run with you!'

'The boy speaks simply,' Spiros said, 'but he echoes my beliefs in the matter. You should flee. We will lend you the support you need.'

Ovid looked at the Librarian.

'I agree,' he said solemnly.

Ovid sighed. 'I need to travel to my villa outside Rome.' He would not tell them about the ode Livia had commissioned him to write.

The Librarian scoffed. 'This is not the run we mean. You must go out of Ibis' reach. For a man who has travelled the Lower Danube with Scorillo, you have learned little.'

'That is not true. I have changed. I am far freer', Ovid said.

'To truly be free you need to cast off any need for an audience. And you have not done that yet.'

A violent knocking on the door brought silence. The servant, who had been lurking in the shadows, went to answer it. Cotta Maximus stepped inside. He and Ovid greeted each other briskly.

'Who are these people?' Cotta asked, looking about the room.

'Friends', Ovid said. 'Friends from Tomis.'

'So the place must exist!' Cotta said, introducing himself to the Librarian, Spiros and then Carp. He turned back to Ovid. 'We must talk', he said. 'In private.'

Ovid led him through to the study and closed the door behind them.

'You need to leave Rome', Cotta said. 'This Saturnalia is the first since Augustus' death. Several open accounts will be closed. The scale could be larger than expected.'

'Rome should not be dragged through the pain of another civil war.'

'Do not concern yourself with politics. Concern yourself with yourself. Does this house have a back entrance?'

'Of course. Why?'

'The house is being watched. By more than one party.'

'But I have harmed no one.'

'You were commissioned by Livia to write Augustus' history. There are no secrets in Rome. The only mystery is Augustus' and Livia's story. Little is it known. It will be up to you to imagine, to fictionalise. Posterity will trust those elements as real. And since there will be many involved, there are plenty who do not want you to create their new history for them.'

Ovid nodded. 'It is for the same reasons that Augustus

opposed the *Gigantomachia*. It seems I must continue to travel in the same circles. Around and around.'

'Unless you break out of it. Now. Leave Rome. Forget your villa. Forget Surrentum and the coast. Campagna also. Take your companions with you. The boy seems spirited and the servant loyal. These qualities are difficult to find nowadays.'

'Where shall I go? I have travelled so far and so long to get back here. Plus it is wintertime. Nobody in his right mind travels in the winter.'

'The hardships you may suffer on the road will be as nothing compared to those you will face if you stay.'

Ovid fell into a despondent silence.

'We need you alive', Cotta said, trying to flatter his ego. 'And writing.'

It did not work. 'I feel like I am being used.'

'I am sorry', Cotta said. 'That was never my intention.'

'Don't apologise. It is the expected behaviour of every educated Roman.' Ovid could feel the palms of his hands sweating. As much as he hated to admit it, he knew his friend was right. He thought of Carp. To expose him to yet another tumultuous journey was a cruelty. He should be given the chance to stay here, to make the most of Rome while he was still innocent enough to enjoy it. 'If you agree to take the boy under your patronage and provide for him,' he said, 'then I will go.'

Cotta accepted immediately.

'I must give him the news', Ovid said, leaving the study with Cotta behind him.

Carp did not like it. 'Why are you giving up on me?' Carp wailed, fresh tears flowing down his dirty cheeks.

'Dear boy, I am not giving up on you', Ovid said, laying his hand on Carp's shoulder. 'This is best for you. Believe me. I need to leave Rome, but I am a selfish man incapable of caring for others. You deserve better than that. My friend Cotta here will look after you well.'

'But I don't want to stay with him. I want to go with you.'

Ovid looked at the Librarian for support. 'Tell him I do not lie.'

The Librarian nodded. 'Your tutor is right', he explained to Carp. 'Going with him will only put your life in danger. But Cotta Maximus will provide a fine life for you.'

Carp sniffed and cried some more, but his protests ended.

Ovid stood and embraced Cotta. 'Thank you for this', he said. 'Please look after him well.'

'I have promised you,' Cotta replied, 'and I shall honour it. Now. Let us make our plan. And let us be quick about it. Your time runs short.'

The back entrance had been boarded up during Ovid's absence, and so a trick was devised to misdirect anyone watching the front door. The Librarian dressed in Ovid's clothes and made a dash for it. A loud rustling from the nearby bushes made it clear that those who had been guarding the entrance had fallen for the ruse and chased after him. As soon as they were all out of sight, Ovid, Spiros, Cotta and Carp raced down the streets of the Palatine to the Porta Chiusa, the Closed Gate, where they had arranged to reunite with the Librarian. The moment he had removed Ovid's clothes, the men chasing him had realised the deceit and hurried back to the house, leaving him to proceed alone. A wagon took all of them through the gate.

Once they were beyond the city wall, Cotta stopped the wagon. 'I have paid the driver. He will take you all the way to Sulmo.' He squeezed Ovid's shoulder.

'Sulmo?'

'Isn't that your home? Where you come from?'

Ovid embraced his friend and then turned to Carp. They did not exchange a word, but hugged each other for a long time.

The Way Home

Travelling the passage that led eastwards away from the chaos of Rome was a purifying experience. There was beauty beyond words and peace beyond art in the plains of the Campagna, in the ravines and terraces of the Alban Hills. The forecast was good, and so long as the road across the Abruzzi Mountains did not become blocked by snow, they were predicted to reach Sulmo within three days.

Nights passed without incident and the alpine landscapes of their mountain passages revealed themselves teasingly through veils of haze. Freezing clouds rolled down from the hillsides, tearing the tops of the trees, filling the narrow valleys and transforming them into mysterious torrents. There was an ethereality to the spectacle, and had Ovid seen Augustus or even his own father riding down these waves he would not have been surprised.

Ovid felt fortunate that the views from the cart proved so wondrous, for his two travelling companions were a bore: Spiros slept for much of the journey and said not a thing, while the Librarian refused to shut up. It was as if his life depended on forcing his Pythagorean wisdom on to Ovid. In the canyon of Forca Caruso they passed under the Arch of Livia to enter the country of the Paeligni, and when Ovid revealed that Livia had not been present at her monument's unveiling, the Librarian treated him to an hours-long history of the Paeligni, replete with all their rebellious conformism and republican traditions, much of which Ovid already knew, and knew well.

Finally, on the third day of travel, the relentless monologue of the Librarian was interrupted by a singularly majestic view. Piercing the white winter sky, the mountain of Maiela, with its snowy peaks and steep grey cliffs, presided over the impenetrable forests below. Ovid pointed his walking stick at the bottom of the valley far in front of them. 'Sulmo', he said.

'Will we reach there by nightfall?' the Librarian asked.

'Yes', Ovid replied. It was refreshing to be asked a question rather than lectured to. 'I should think so.'

'It is the eve of the winter solstice. Will anyone host us tonight?'

'If it is still there, we will stay at my house.'

The Librarian looked from side to side, clearly choosing his words carefully. 'I do not know how you are perceived in Sulmo, but in Rome – and in Tomis too – your resentments seem to precede you.'

'Nonsense. I resent nobody.'

'What about Augustus?'

'Without his stupid laws, my wit would have been less appreciated.'

'Ibis?'

'He is a bastard, but a good enemy to have.'

'Virgil?'

Ovid looked sideways at him. 'There are many things one can say about Virgil, but at least one has never been bored by him. Maybe by his poetry.' He smiled. 'I wish I could say the same about you.'

The Librarian took the barb in the spirit with which it was intended – as a jest. 'I envy you', he said.

'Why on earth would anyone envy me?'

'A simple reason', the Librarian said. 'Because you are about to arrive home. One of life's greatest pleasures.'

They crossed the muddy valley of the two small rivers and rounded the outskirts of the city of Sulmo. The Librarian pointed uphill to a huge stone building in the middle of the forest.

'The temple of Hercules the Unifier', Ovid said, and then told him the story of Hercules Quirinus, his grandmother's Hercules, who, like Romulus, was said to have united the local tribes. It was good, for once, to be the monologist.

A rough road led into a forest. Spiros – jarred awake by the bouncing cart – stirred, stretching and yawning.

'He rises!' Ovid said.

'There are times', Spiros replied, 'when all there is to do is sleep. Such as when two old men talk for three days.'

Soon the wagon came to a stop before the gate of Ovid's estate. The paint was peeling, the chain rusty, and the lock unforgiving.

'Break it', Ovid ordered, and the driver set to it with lustre, smashing at it with a rock until it splintered into a thousand sharp fragments and they could pass through.

On foot, Ovid led the way, crossing the soaked white gravel of the path, leaping up the squeaking wooden steps, gingerly stepping over the slippery planks of the veranda, and then peering in through the window. There was a deathlike stillness to the house, one that seemed so at odds with the site of his childhood.

'No one is here', Ovid said. 'Life does not treat me fairly.'

'If it did, you would be dead by now', the Librarian said.

'What should I do? It is too dark to seek shelter elsewhere.'

The Librarian came alive. 'Face reality. Break into your own house, and then clean up the mess after.' It was not a polite suggestion, but a vociferous order.

Before smashing a window, Ovid tried the front door. It was unlocked. Opening it revealed an almost perfect darkness and the smell of old, cold damp: the new masters of this house. He returned to the cart and took from there a torch, ready to reconquer his property. His shadow crawled across the walls as he stepped inside. The enormous oil lamp that had once stood to the side of the door was no longer there, nor were the statues which had presided over it. Feeling like an animal in a den, he pushed onwards, through the caretaker's cubicle that reeked of stale urine, and into the atrium. The furniture had been chopped to pieces with an axe, and the mosaic in the corridor was stained with oil from smashed lamps. Beyond it, his father's study was empty save for a multitude of spiderwebs and two busts he had never liked – of Socrates and Caesar. And then, in his own room, nothing at all, not even his old bed.

From outside, someone called Ovid's name, and he picked his way back through the darkness to the front door.

'There is someone here to see you, master', Spiros said.

Ovid poked his head outside to see, leaning over the fence, his old schoolfriend Marcus. Blurred childhood memories, jockeying for attention, turned him speechless. One that recurred was of Marcus' refusal to accompany him to Rome, despite the insistence of his family. He had never been interested in leaving Sulmo, and had never explained why.

'Ovid! So it is you! You were seen passing the outskirts. I

did not believe it for a second. "Ovid?" I said. "That is a body we shall never see around these parts again!" And yet I was wrong. Here you are.'

'Marcus', Ovid said. 'Glad to see you. What has happened here? To my house? Where is everyone? Where is everything?'

'Your father never told you?' Marcus said.

'Told me what? He died many years ago.'

Marcus took a deep breath, clearly not relishing what he was about to say. 'This house and the estate belong to Hercules' temple now.'

'But how?' Ovid spluttered.

'I am the high priest', Marcus said. 'I negotiated the sale of your family estate myself. With your father. But don't worry, there is a buy-back clause.'

Ovid stamped down, crushing something brittle and unidentifiable below his foot. He knew it was not his father's skull, but for a moment he wished it was. If so, he would have kicked it hard, would have watched it sail off into the night sky with grim pleasure.

Saving the Julio-Claudian Dynasty

Nobody knew better than Livia that Rome was in danger. Having gathered a group in the basement of her villa at the Prima Porta – not to perform a mass, but to devise a plan – she paced along the enclosure of the painted garden, as if pondering whether to leap over the brushed fence and run free into the fake landscape. Her guests had left time and life behind when descending to her apartments, like sheep besieged by a lonely she-wolf. Both impatient and amused, she circled her prey, shifting her gaze from the trees and flowers over the fence to her prisoners, discerning on their faces the reflections of their souls.

'Sejanus,' she said, fixing her eyes upon him, 'how many traitors support the plot?'

'Many', he replied, keeping his own eyes low and respectful. 'Romans are always interested in downfall.'

'Some traitors are more harmless than others', Livia said, looking around at each of her guests once more, hoping some might take her loaded glances personally, 'depending on the occasions of betrayal. Some are our friends, few are our enemies.' She rested her eyes again on Sejanus. 'By tomorrow, you must find at least two turncoats – and execute them. But be aware, if you punish the wrong people, you will risk a mutiny.'

Sejanus nodded. Livia went on.

'Can it really be that my son Tiberius is conspiring with his close friends against his own position as the Emperor?' She directed the question to Flaccus, who did not respond. 'Surely not. You would have noticed. You still want to become next year's consul, I presume.'

He did not reply, and this seemed to satisfy her.

'Cotta,' she continued, crossing the floor towards him, 'it is up to you to ensure that we are not deserted by our friends.'

'And our enemies?' he asked.

'Don't worry about them, we know how to deal with each other.' She raised her thin eyebrows. 'Marcia and Fabia, have your clans formulated their demands to support the Julians?'

'Yes.' The reply was so soft it was impossible to tell which of the two matrons had uttered it, yet still it was enough for Livia.

'Good. Urgulania, command your son to take over my personal protection. And make sure that you do not stop casting spells over our adversaries, not until we have rid ourselves of them all.'

Livia took a few steps back so that she might see all her guests at once.

'Now. Tell me. Who shall deliver the speech to discredit Germanicus' generals in front of the Senate?'

'Does anyone dare discredit our generals?' Urgulania looked mortified at her own question as soon as she had uttered it.

'Not all our generals, of course,' Livia said. 'There will doubtless come a time when Rome is governed once more by a general. But that time shall not happen while I am alive.' She paused for a few moments, and then, as if the idea had just occurred to her, snapped: 'Bring Ovid back to Rome! He shall make the speech.'

'Ovid?' Fabia said. 'Why must he always be Rome's scapegoat?'

Livia whipped around to face her, furious. 'Isn't it embarrassing for a matron to display such vulgar love publicly?' she snarled. 'Watch your behaviour.'

'But', Cotta interjected, 'a knight, and Ovid is only a knight, is not allowed to speak in front of the Senate.'

'He will, if I wish it so.' Livia nodded, decided. 'Yes, Ovid shall represent me. Whatever he says will be in my name. Where is he now?' She looked at Sejanus, who shrugged. 'Someone ask Ibis. He always knows where his enemies are.'

'By now', Cotta said, 'Ovid must be in his native Sulmo.'

'Sejanus, get him back.' Livia clapped her hands, the sign that the meeting was over. A servant brought out a large silver plate filled with identical small vases. 'If any of you discloses our plan,' Livia warned, 'here is the sure antidote for treachery. Hemlock.'

Knowing More Than a Priest

The knock on the door ripped Ovid from his dreamless sleep. He looked about him in a daze. The oil lamp was still burning. He could remember only that he had been brought to the temple. He was too tired to remember the rest.

Marcus appeared in the vaulted room wearing a long white robe – much too white in the gloomy cold – and holding out a flickering candle in front of him, which produced a play of yellow shadows in his grey beard and deepened his owl-like eyes. It was a visit Ovid could have done without.

'Is it already morning?' Ovid said, rubbing his forehead.

'People from the valley are streaming up the slope of the Maiella. They saw the fire in your estate and have followed the call. They are coming for you. We must prepare the solstice dawn ceremony.'

'I didn't call anyone.'

'Your fire did.'

Ovid remembered now. Last night the Librarian had taken great delight in playing with the flames of the pyre, and had been delighted yet further when fires in the valley had appeared to answer his game. Ovid stood up ready to dress. He looked around and recognised pieces of furniture from his childhood. 'My father's furniture…' he said.

'Yes', Marcus said. 'Your father's. He lived here for the final years of his life after becoming head of the Paeligni assembly.'

Ovid had not known that his father had lost his mind and turned into a local politician in his last years. 'When was this?'

Marcus named the year. It was well before Ovid's banishment.

'And how was he in that role?'

Marcus smirked. 'Not the most popular. He wanted to turn the region into the confederation we were a hundred years ago.'

Ovid moved his palm over the polished surface of the oak desk, caressing it slowly. Then, with an oddly illicit thrill, he let himself down into the leather throne – he had never been able to use it while his father was alive. 'Why did he do it?'

Marcus walked into the adjacent room, the library, beckoning for Ovid to follow him through a labyrinth of corridors and spindle-shaped stairs, until they arrived at an iron-clad gate, which opened for them without a knock. Ovid realised they were in the highest part of the temple, in front of the shrine, which, according to his grandmother, contained not only the statue but also the secret of Hercules. The noblemen of the Paeligni, dressed in dark blue coats with silver borders, were waiting for them. Their greeting was unenthusiastic.

'Some did not like your father', Marcus explained.

'I don't blame them.'

They entered the forbidden shrine. The floor was decorated with river waves, dolphins, vine tendrils, rosettes and Pythagorean signs. The ceiling showed a distorted view of the Great Bear, similar to the one in the Herculaneum on the far side of the Danube. On the back wall, behind Hercules' statue, painted in oversized proportions, was Virtue, half-naked and staring with a hypnotising glare at Vice, who, shy and secretive, appeared the more chaste of the two. The Librarian stood before the painting, looking back and forth from Virtue to Vice as if wondering which was which.

'The famous choices of Hercules', the Librarian said. 'One meets them all over the place.'

'You, here?' Ovid asked.

'Marcus told me people would gather here, and I thought I might like to see the spectacle for myself', the Librarian said, turning around.

'They are here already', Marcus said. 'On the terrace below. I must go and see to them. Stay here and ready yourself.' He left the room.

'So it is true', the Librarian said.

'What?' Ovid replied.

'That you are to play the high priest.'

'It's nothing.'

The Librarian snorted. 'Not to me. I would sooner kill myself than mess with the gods. It is a certain way to doom oneself.'

'How else can I become immortal?'

'Oh, Ovid.' The Librarian sighed. 'Such a long journey to get here, and yet you have not even learned the basics.'

'Which are?'

'That nothing is forever. Health, intelligence, talent, even spirituality – they will all be lost one day. And sooner if you do not work for them. Not pray for them, not meditate for them, but work for them. Work hard.'

'I have worked hard. I have laboured and suffered for my art.'

'Suffered? Art? You have misguided the world with the

illusion of depth through witty verses and cleverly chosen subjects. Sex. Transformations. But in reality you do not give a damn about either. Your books have no deeper meaning. You lack any purpose in life. And this is why you perpetually seek immortality – because you are afraid of dying without such purpose.'

Ovid looked up at the sky, which was slowly morphing from black to violet. Below, the crowd chanted for light. 'I will take your words for an insult.'

Marcus reappeared with a white robe and unlit candle, both of which he held out to Ovid, who took them. 'It is time', Marcus said.

Ovid pulled the white robe over his winter tunic and walked to the balcony overlooking the main terrace. Silence filtered through the crowd at his appearance. Between some of the people he could swear he saw spears, their shining tips pointing up towards him. He remembered Cynthia's story about her husband, the Dacian hero, who had thrown himself on to his people's spears gladly. He could only imagine the quality of faith it must require to do the same.

A breeze sent its chill through his thin hair, and the landscape around him began to lose its depth until the mountains darkened and flattened, like mere paintings against the sky, which was now turning from violet to pink. Another memory came to mind. The viewpoint above the Iron Gates, where he had stood with the Celt Tribune and stared at Okeanos thundering into the gorge.

Six priests lined themselves up behind him. In the valley, cockerels began to crow. Ovid fired his candle and raised it above his head. 'Light!' he called. 'Come and get light!'

Above the Secinaro peak on the other side of the Peligna Valley the clouds had turned orange, and the courtyard of the temple looked like a lake of flickering flames – its walls, porticos and arches, so solid in the darkness, mere ruins in the light, their various stages of decrepitude visible. The crowd watched anxiously as the first ray of sun emerged from behind the mountain. Placing their candles upright on the ground, they started a chain dance to celebrate the sun reborn, the defeat of the Dark God, the end of the longest night of the year.

'Bless them', one of the priests whispered to Ovid. 'We will deal with the rest.'

Ovid complied.

A Visitor From Rome

Marcus granted Ovid an apartment – part of the temple – to move into while he wrote. It was cramped and hardly conducive to work, and as such it reminded him of his house on the Palatine. It was certainly unsuitable for a heroic ode, and he struggled with his composition. The scribe whom the priests had assigned to him – a tall, lean and always shaved man who possessed the ability impeccably to fit any item of furniture he perched upon – helped with the physical act of writing, but not at all when it came to the inspiration. Come spring, Ovid would get rid of him.

On the third day, instead of staring at Ovid and waiting for him to produce the next verse, the scribe produced a set of keys. 'There is a secret library down there', he said. 'On the lower terrace. Three arches along. I thought it might interest you.'

The place, once a warehouse, was filled with scrolls. The documents in the front room described, through two hundred years of history, Sulmo's efforts to please Rome. To Ovid's dismay, he learned that his own family were frequently mentioned for reasons that became unbearably humiliating. Together, the mentions explained why none of his family's properties had been confiscated during the tumultuous years of the Roman civil war, why his father and he had been so well received in Rome, and why politics had never been discussed in their house.

The scribe guided Ovid through the back rooms of the

library and towards a series of well-hidden books. These contained another story – the entire history of the Paeligni resistance to Rome. It was clear why they had been hidden. Had any Roman procurator chanced upon them, he would have been so infuriated by what they revealed that the temple would have been torn down, and perhaps all of Sulmo. The unknown authors, prudent enough not to mention their names, deplored the fact that, some two hundred years earlier, Hannibal, after having the idea to cross the Alps and attack Rome from the north, instead of unifying Rome's enemies plundered the Paeligni, who had greeted him as a liberator. Gold-bordered parchments contained the treaties, which everyone had believed destroyed, testifying to the founding of the Italic Republic with the capital in Corfinium in the year 663 from the foundation of Rome, wherein a Naso – all his ancestors had remarkable noses – was mentioned again as one of the five hundred rebel senators.

'Are there any books on Hercules?' he asked. It was easier to deal with legends than to deal with history.

'As far as I know, not in this temple', the scribe replied.

'Then where?'

The scribe shrugged. Though Ovid was grateful for access to this secret library, the confidences it contained were too depressing for further perusal, and he signalled to the scribe that it was time to return to the apartment and continue working. They ascended the stairs together and, to Ovid's surprise, were told on their arrival that he had a visitor from Rome.

'Would you like me to accompany you?' the scribe asked.

'No. Wait here. If I need you, I will call.'

Ovid entered the apartment alone. Despite the light breeze

that drifted through the open windows and the cold drizzle that had dampened his tunic, he could smell the unmistakeable scent of a repulsive rose-oil fragrance. Ibis.

In the private reception room, analysing the mosaic with the jumping dolphins, stood not Ibis but his son Cornelius.

'State your business,' Ovid said, looking about him for anything he could use as a weapon.

'Livia sent me,' Cornelius said, turning around.

'You have proof?' Everything about this encounter reminded Ovid of the same he had endured with this man's brother, Lucius. How could it be that this scene was almost identical to the one in Tomis? Had fate run out of imagination?

'A general you know, Gaius Julius Vestalis, is on his way to Rome.'

'I don't know any generals,' Ovid said, keeping close to the door.

Cornelius grinned. 'We shall see if there is any truth in that,' he said. 'The Empress wants you to appear as witness before the Senate.'

'You haven't shown me the proof. Besides, I have no intention of being dragged into politics.' Ovid checked the young man for malice, but saw only a face lined with fatigue from a long ride. 'Now I am writing. And I am not to be disturbed.'

Cornelius considered this for a moment. 'How disappointed do you think Livia will be when she learns that you have not yet started the *Augustiada*? That instead of this you have been playing Hercules' high priest?'

Fucking scribes, Ovid thought, *they're all spies!* 'I am not returning to Rome.'

Cornelius nodded, as if Ovid were entirely justified in his

obstinacy. 'Changing the subject. Who killed my brother?' he asked suddenly.

Ovid sighed. 'Not me.'

Cornelius seemed satisfied with the answer. 'Yes, my mother has assured me of that. Looking at you, I am inclined to believe her.'

Ovid felt a surge of relief mixed with anger.

'She is very fond of you, you know,' Cornelius continued. 'She claims that you are the finest person who has ever lived. You shall have plenty of time to convince me of it on the way to Rome.'

'I have told you. I will not go.'

'My mother thinks that you should return. She sends you this.'

Cornelius produced a small bronze lamp, which Ovid recognised in a flood of memories. When Corinna lit it behind half-closed shutters, it was the sign that he could come in. He wondered if Corinna had told her son the code. Or perhaps Cornelius had stolen the lamp to delude him. There was one way to find out. He knocked on the table as he used to at Corinna's door: four short taps, one long, three short. Cornelius smiled and, without taking his eyes off Ovid's, answered with two short taps, one long, five short: the correct sequence.

'Why does your mother want me back?' Was it another of Livia's traps?

'Not for herself.'

'She was always one for impenetrable secrets.'

'I do not care to know them,' Cornelius said. 'Nor do I care for how she regards you. All that matters is that I was sent here to perform a duty, and that duty is now performed. Tomorrow morning, I shall leave one hour before dawn. If you choose to rot here, so be it.'

Corinna

Leaving Sulmo had always come easily to Ovid, but not this time. The college of priests agreed to let him go before finding a new high priest, on the condition that he renounce the buy-back clause for his estate. The Librarian, enthralled by this city and keen to learn more about it, chose to stay on and try to save Ovid's estate. Spiros, on the other hand, was desperate to return to Rome, and eagerly agreed to accompany Ovid and Cornelius – though he admitted that he was not looking forward to the journey.

All the way from Sulmo to Rome, Ovid and Cornelius exchanged less than a hundred words. In the absence of the Librarian and his monologues, it was Spiros who prodded Ovid into conversation each morning, and his comments on the world they passed were as superficial as the Librarian's had been both profound and profoundly dull. Nevertheless, Ovid missed his Tomitan friend. They had often not seen eye to eye, but he could not deny that the Librarian's unapologetic commitments to Pythagoras' teachings and his constant determination to better himself and those around him were commendable qualities for any man. And how right he had been when he had exclaimed that mankind's principal enemies were greed, lust and resentment – all of them so utterly Roman feelings. It was no surprise that he had opted to remain in Sulmo, at least for the time being.

They arrived in Rome on a sunny day just before New Year's Eve. Ovid decided to visit Corinna before meeting Livia. The city felt empty. Spiros was dispatched to look for Carp, while Ovid and Cornelius walked down the west side of the Esquiline, before taking a shortcut to Corinna's house through a gloomy network of alleys between a confusion of imposing houses. Ovid hesitated in front of the entrance he knew so well, but Cornelius pushed it open and ushered him through with the kind of violence that he could only have inherited from his father. Once they crossed the threshold, the torment of the neighbourhood was left behind. Corinna's courtyard was the very antithesis to Livia's painted subterranean garden, with shrubs of all sorts planted in pots of all shapes and placed in a way that defied any sense of order, like an urban living forest. He remembered once asking her why she chose to keep it so. She had shrugged and replied: 'This is how it looks inside me.'

A window shutter cracked open. From the far side came the rustle of a dress. It was Corinna: a disembodied voice floated out from behind the shutter.

'Be welcome', she said.

'I think you are right.' Cornelius addressed his mother. 'It was not Ovid who killed my brother.'

'This I already told you. Your anger-blinded father was the real killer.'

Cornelius hesitated, as if unsure whether to take his mother's statement figuratively or as literal truth. 'Ovid took care of his funeral. Apparently it was the most sumptuous Tomis has ever witnessed.'

'How do you know this?'

'I asked one of Ovid's friends about it.'

'Please,' Corinna said, still hidden behind the shutters, 'leave me alone with him. He has bewitched you, I can see that. I must talk to him in private.'

'Of course.' Cornelius turned and whispered to Ovid: 'Don't ask her about the parrot. It died recently. I shall wait for you outside.' And with that he left.

Footsteps announced Corinna's approach. Ovid took from his pocket the ring that he had removed from the body of her son in the Aedile's house, displaying it so she would see. When she came out of the house, he drank her in. She had given up dyeing her hair, which was now pewter-coloured, parted loosely in the middle and tied back in a bun. Her lips, those that had given him the best kisses of his life, looked unusual without make-up. Her face, a network of new lines and wrinkles, harboured her inimitable smile. How could anyone age so gracefully?

She took the ring from his hand. 'I warned Lucius,' she said. 'I told him nobody stands a chance against your luck.' She twirled the ring in her fingers. 'Did he suffer?'

Ovid shook his head. 'No. He was only surprised that someone could stab quicker than him.'

'Did he have the chance to ask you who his real father was?'

'The only thing he wanted from me was my death.'

A noise came from the house. Not a parrot; perhaps a servant. Corinna seemed not to notice.

'Aren't we alone?' he asked.

'We are never alone. You are safe here.'

'I trust neither man nor god.'

'And how about me?'

Ovid said nothing. He did not want to offend her, the only woman he had ever loved.

'I do not need to spy on you,' she said. 'I already know everything about you.'

'Enlighten me.'

Her face turned into the white mask of the Pythia whom Ovid had met in his dream. 'To become free you must die. And you are finally ready for it.'

What a macabre prediction, he thought. Out of the corner of his eye he saw a finger pushing out through one of the shutters. It looked like some sort of claw, and could have belonged to a monkey. But that was impossible. Monkeys didn't agree with parrots. Corinna moved quickly in the direction of the shutters as a voice whispered something unintelligible from behind them.

Moments later, the house door opened and Livia sailed out. 'My dear,' she said to Corinna, 'love at your age is nothing short of pathetic.' She turned to Ovid. 'Listen, poet. I will be brief. Rome has to be saved from the generals. A certain Vestalis, whom I have learned you know from Tomis, arrived two days ago from the Upper Danube with a message for Tiberius. Fortunately we were able to convince Tiberius not to meet him. The general has gone into hiding, but tomorrow he will be interrogated by the Senate. I need you to testify before the Senate that Vestalis represents a conspiracy about which Germanicus is unaware.'

Ovid shook his head. 'Condemning someone for high treason does not require my presence. For this I interrupted the *Augustiada*?'

'Do not pretend with me. You haven't written a single line.'

'Does everyone know that?'

Livia sighed, exasperated. 'My poetic friend, the moment I begin not to know is the moment when I should give up leading Rome.' She fixed him with a hard stare.

'Did your spies tell you about my contribution to the solstice mass?'

Corinna intervened. 'They did. You were brilliant.'

'Shut up!' Livia snapped, whirling on Corinna. 'If you were able to read the signs for me, I wouldn't need to be asking Ovid any favours.'

'I am sorry', Corinna said, contrite. 'My mind gets muddied sometimes. You should know not to rely on me to foresee the future. If I had been able to foresee mine, I would have known to keep him.'

'You were much too infatuated with the power that men gave you, my dear', Livia said. 'As he was with immortality.'

'But we have changed. I am a recluse, and he no longer doubts the certainty of death.'

Livia turned her hawk-like stare upon Ovid. 'I can see no physical decline, no sign of insignificance. Everything in his life clearly continues to be its own reward.'

'Eros longs for immortality. A wise Greek said that.' Corinna's laugh was small and drained of any feeling. 'Denial only proves that he was right.'

'Sometimes', Livia said, her teeth clenched, 'I wonder who you think you are.'

'The second-brightest woman in Rome.' Some of Corinna's old defiance had returned to her voice.

Or perhaps, Ovid thought, *her defiance never left*. 'Let's not quarrel about something that all three of us agree on', he said, just stopping short of uttering the word 'love'.

Livia turned to face him. 'You know what I require of you. I hope the choice you make is the sensible one.' She walked back into the house.

'You are, it seems, attracting both good and evil', Corinna said. 'And you have the ability to transform both. That is why you are the perfect scapegoat – like my parrot, which she killed the other day.'

'Would you do what she asked', Ovid said, 'if you were me?'

'If I did, I would not mention Germanicus by name in my speech.'

Ovid nodded, though he did not understand why. 'Any other advice?'

'Yes. If in doubt, side with the generals.' Corinna took from her pocket a small mirror and cleaned it on her palla. Holding it in both hands, she de-spelled it, and then handed it to Ovid. 'And use this.'

A breeze jostled through the shrubs, pushing them up against each other in a dance that reminded Ovid of the forsythias in his Tomitan garden. He took the mirror, understanding it for what it was – a parting gift. He left.

Cornelius was waiting for him outside the house. 'You need to avoid my father', he said. 'Some fathers should be met only at a crossroads.' It was as if Oedipus himself were talking.

The Mirror

The Senate hearing was to take place outside the Curia, so that the public could witness the most powerful men of Rome defend the Republic. Trills of excitement rippled through the crowds. Would the senators be willing to reclaim the Republic's supremacy over the power-hungry generals and restore its ideals now that Augustus – their master, patron and guardian – was dead?

The priests hurriedly performed their duties, displaying the entrails of sacrificed sheep. The augurs searched the sky for the right kinds of birds, the ones announcing divine approval.

Ovid had always enjoyed waiting for the public, so he arrived early, only to be disappointed by the fact that not a single person acknowledged his presence. A cold wind streamed in along the Via Sacra, and he took shelter behind Augustus' statue. In his hand was a scroll, and he opened it, hoping for inspiration. But its blank yellow surface was the proof that all his efforts to draft a speech – any speech – had failed yet again, and that he would be forced, once more, to rely on his talent to improvise.

Why had Corinna asked him not to mention Germanicus? And why had she told him that, if in doubt, he should side with the generals? Didn't she know how much he despised them, those symbols of personal ambition, power and glamour? Didn't she know that these were the ingredients that led to anarchy, civil war and tyranny? After all, how else to explain Sulla, Caesar, and, finally, Augustus?

Around him the area began to fill with people of varying sorts. Many of them, clients of powerful patrons, had interrupted their winter holidays to be there – not because they wanted to, but because they did not wish to be suspected of disloyalty. The times were far too unstable for such a risk.

The low-voiced conversations and murmurs of unease muted as thin smoke rose from the altar. The senators stepped out of the Curia. Not one of them was comfortable taking the lead, so they walked in an awkward cluster. The discomfort of having a general addressing the Senate was almost palpable. Too much in the world had changed since Sulla dared the unthinkable and led his legions against the city, too much had changed since Caesar went a step further and crossed the Rubicon. The senators, like everybody else, wanted peace, Augustus' peace – as submissive as it had been.

A tap on the shoulder made Ovid hurriedly roll up the useless scroll and turn around. But nobody was there. The only thing present was the statue of Augustus, which, now that he looked closely at it, somehow seemed to be pretending to look away. Ovid shook his head. Another hallucination. They came so frequently these days that he almost trusted them.

The horn announced the start of the proceedings. General Gaius Julius Vestalis, escorted by soldiers of the Praetorian Guard, came out of the Curia. His countenance bore nothing of the defiance expected from a rebellious military commander, that arrogance of a victor worthy of his rank, which Rome had grown so used to. Instead, he stepped leisurely, ambivalently even.

The first speakers presented the case. Much was said, but the dominant theme seemed to be the notion that Rome's traditional ideals must prevail over personal ambitions.

The consul whom Ovid remembered from Cotta's party stepped up to the podium. After a few twisted words and ambiguous phrases, he admitted having supported some individuals, believing wrongly that they were in the right. He wanted to save his property and his life – and, if possible, both.

Ovid felt a burning glare stab him from behind repeatedly. On an impulse, he pulled out Corinna's mirror to look behind. Through the mirror, he could see only the statue of Augustus staring back at him. And then, to Ovid's addled bemusement, the statue winked.

Ovid whipped his head around, but the statue had returned to its earlier posture – gazing off into the distance, indifferent to all but itself. Feeling like he might finally be losing his mind, Ovid turned his back on it, held up the mirror once more, and looked into it.

The statue's golden laurel crown had turned phosphorescent. 'People do not change', Ovid heard the statue say, in a voice almost Augustus', but not quite. Something extra had been added to it: a stone-heavy density.

'But don't people deserve a change?' Ovid asked, hardly believing that he was engaging in conversation with the mirror image of the statue of a dead man. 'Doesn't Rome deserve a change?'

'My legacy must never be changed', the statue said.

This needed a firm reply. 'Your legacy was about the

moral greatness of Romans. But wouldn't a different history transform people – for the greater?' *Am I talking or just thinking? Does it even matter? Is one of greater madness than the other?*

It was then that the statue did something Ovid would never have anticipated. It blushed. This was a chance he could not miss, no matter how unreal. He hammered the words.

'Aren't you ashamed of having transformed your precious Romans from free men into disempowered, albeit disciplined, beings, displaying their obedience whenever occasion demands? I am not talking about the plebs, but about Rome's aristocracy – *the very same people you tried to protect from my writings*.'

'You are envious, poet', the statue said, the blush gone, replaced by a glint in the eye. 'You can't stand anyone having eternal glory. The people of Rome forced me to become Augustus. They were tired of wars and scared of politics. They craved a strong patron. They got what they wanted. And so did I.'

'They needed freedom.'

'They asked for bread and entertainment.'

'I shall include this dialogue in the ode Livia commissioned.'

'We don't need any ode. And certainly not one from you. You don't have Virgil's genius to equal the *Aeneid*, and you don't have Horace's ironies for subtle propaganda. We are too big for you. Now let us listen to this general, who, so far as I know, is an ignorant provincial. Rome is not what army people think she is. She is about sex and power. And he does not represent either. For us victors, sex and power are institutions, not tedious pleasures. They are the virile desire, a simulacrum of hunting, a game of will.'

Ovid let his focus switch from the statue to the mirror itself. The polish was gone and hundreds of small dots peppered the surface. Suddenly he heard the statue laughing, or thought he did. He gripped the mirror tighter and refocused on Augustus, immobile and immortally fit. He felt decidedly light-headed, but did not dare to turn. Some things were better left unchecked.

The forum's trumpeters blew. Ovid looked up to see the Speaker of the Senate ask Flaccus to hand over the questions that the people of Rome demanded General Vestalis answer. Flaccus did so, and in his bellowing voice the crier announced the beginning of Vestalis' speech. Ovid could hear the reed-thin voice of Vestalis, who, extreme in his confidence, reported in his abrupt but friendly manner that the only message he carried was for Tiberius, and that since the Emperor had shown no interest in receiving the message he had followed instructions and destroyed it, unread. As for the list of questions prepared by the Roman Senate, he would not answer any.

'That's it?' Ovid whispered. 'That is all he has to say?'

'It would seem so', the statue laughed. 'Now it is your turn. Go and defend my generals. These idiots.'

Ovid's name was called. The crowd parted for him. He put down the mirror, turned to look at the statue – which, without the conduit of the looking glass, was and always had been a statue and only a statue – and then walked down to the podium.

'Be brief', the Speaker commanded.

'Briefer than the General?' Ovid asked.

The Speaker did not reply.

Ovid looked at his audience. He had delivered numerous recitations in his life, but this was different. If he failed to say precisely what was needed, his reputation would be slain. And the very prospect was terrifying. He surprised himself with a brief and murmured prayer for help, addressed to no god in particular, and then began.

'While we here are safe, fed and entertained, the best of us are fighting at the frontiers, which are as far away from Rome as the gods from humans. I can understand that peace has taught us to despise the army and resent its generals. Only free people can afford to be thankful. Free in their ways of thinking, I mean. And I can understand that many a general sees citizens as a necessary evil, and believes that, instead of admitting there are powers greater than the army, it would be preferable to restage their victories to induce fear and obedience. Finally, I can understand why this man', he pointed at Vestalis, 'must be condemned. And why he should not.'

People in the square became nervous. Some edged forward, filling the vacant spaces in the front.

'We must acknowledge that Rome is no longer able to fix its shortcomings by itself. Nobody in this square – and I am no exception – can cleanse himself watching wild animals in combat, gladiators in murderous fights or mock battles ending in real death. Nobody. The times when violence alone purified the city are over. We need a scapegoat.' He lifted his hands into the air. 'Take me!'

A silence settled over the crowd. Ovid remembered Cicero, who had once written that it was this silence that Romans feared more than death.

The Speaker ordered the trumpeters to blow their horns

and for the senators to retreat. The public, angry that Ovid's speech had been cut short, began booing. Up on the podium, Cotta approached Ovid to lead him away.

'I preferred you wittier', Cotta said as they left the stage.

Flaccus came to join them. 'I can't believe you disobeyed Livia's orders. Why didn't you defend Germanicus?'

'I did.'

'You must be mad', Flaccus replied. 'This time, you've really fucked your future. You aren't even worthy of being a scapegoat anymore.'

Ovid wanted to ask him which of the many futures he was referring to, but felt no inclination to enter into such a discussion.

Sejanus approached, waving a scroll with a huge wax seal: all recognised it as being that of Tiberius. 'The Emperor will be pleased that you had the courage to defend his generals.' He raised the scroll he held in his hand. 'It is the exile order for whoever would have condemned Vestalis.' He paused. 'Do not go home, Naso. Ibis is waiting for you there. Allow me to deal with him myself. Until the turmoil passes, use Cotta's villa in the Campagna.'

Ovid looked up at the statue of Augustus that towered over them all. Its eyes seemed to overlap into a single one, as if they were gazing down the length of a bow before releasing an arrow. He heard the voice inside his head, as clearly as he had heard it before the speech. 'Don't be a coward again. Go to your house, go to where Ibis awaits you. Look for Death. Find out for yourself that Death it is not the ultimate metamorphosis. Become immortal. If you dare.'

You make more sense as a statue than you ever did in real

life, Ovid thought, before noticing something he had missed. There, in the statue's outstretched hand, was Corinna's mirror.

This time, Ovid had no doubt that he could hear the statue laughing.

The Art of Freedom

Pale winter sunlight softened the shapes and colours around him as Ovid flung open the gates of his villa, overlooking the Tiber River where the Cassia and Flaminia roads converged, and marched through. Beyond the heavy double doors the smell of Ibis' rosewood perfume, heavier than that which his son preferred, produced a brief indecision. Should he have not trusted Augustus?

Walking along the corridor began to feel like climbing a path up a cliff face. He was leaving the lower world behind and moving towards the edge, from where all one's problems could be solved with a simple jump. The final door was opened for him. They had heard his approaching footsteps.

'You never cease to surprise me, Naso,' Ibis said, his voice hoarse. 'This time by your courage.'

Four men peopled the room: Ibis on the couch, two guards who stood behind him, and Spiros, who had been tied to a chair and whimpered softly. Ovid sat in the armchair and made himself comfortable.

'May I ask what the purpose of your intrusion is?'

'You know full well,' Ibis growled.

'Yes.' Ovid nodded. 'Yes, I suppose I do. Another question, then. Why on earth have you tied up my slave?'

'We couldn't have him running to tell you we were here.'

'Quite right. But now that I *am* here, the ropes are redundant.

Let him go. You are here for me, not him.'

Ibis nodded at one of the guards, who untied the ropes. Spiros sprung up from the chair and rushed to a corner, where he hovered nervously. It was clear he would not leave the room while his master was still alive, and Ovid was grateful for his loyalty. Over their long and strange journey from Tomis together, he was pleased that they had formed some semblance of friendship.

'Let's get this over with', Ibis said.

One the guards retrieved an hourglass from a bag and shook it to loosen the sand, then placed it on the table before Ovid. The other guard produced a silver knife from the folds of his coat, checked its blade for sharpness, and then laid it down next to the hourglass.

'Your final hour, Naso', Ibis said.

'And at the end of it?'

Ibis closed his eyes. 'You may use your bathtub. To save the mess.'

'How kind you are.' The knife glinted in the soft light that streamed in through the broken shutters. 'Would you be so kind as to permit me one final glass of wine?'

'I heard you had given up drinking.'

'I had. To prolong my life. A reason which no longer bears any meaning.'

Ibis chuckled. 'I will permit it. To die with wine on one's lips is not such a bad thing.'

Ovid turned to his former slave. 'Spiros, bring us the wine I received at the Asklepia.'

Fire flashed in Spiros' eyes, and Ovid was relieved to see it. Spiros knew exactly which wine was referred to. He rushed out of the room to find it.

'If you really had any friends,' Ibis said, 'they would have warned you I was here.'

'They did.'

'They did?' Ibid repeated the words slowly, as if they did not make sense to him. 'Who dared to warn you?'

Ovid raised his eyebrows. 'The statue of Augustus.'

Ibis glared at him but did not press the matter. Soon, Spiros appeared in the doorway, looking scared and cautious. In his hands was a plate, on it four silver cups and the correct amphora.

'Gentlemen', Ovid said, smiling at Spiros and waving him in. 'I would be grateful if you would join me for this, my final drink. Please. The wine is good, I assure you.'

The winter sun shone low into the room as Spiros filled each cup and handed it out, first to Ibis, then to the two guards, and finally to Ovid. He stared at his master as he passed him the cup, as if waiting for confirmation, and looked at the floor in dismay when Ovid took it.

Ovid held his cup aloft and made a bold toast. 'To our enmity!' he said, and then drank from it in small sips, hoping the poison would not disperse too rapidly throughout his body.

Ibis took a long draught, as did his two men. They nodded their heads appreciatively. 'From which Asklepia is it?' he said. 'I have not tasted this one before. It is better than my Falernian.' He took the amphora from Spiros' hands, walked with it to the window and checked the stamp against the dim light.

I have to make him drink the full cup, Ovid thought. 'Your spies have been swapping it for information.'

This Ibis liked. 'I knew they were smart', he said, drinking the whole cup down and demanding another. 'To our enmity!' he said, plunging down on to the sofa.

'To you and me, the two young provincials who did not want to leave the city and fight for Rome!' Ovid called, forcing jollity.

'To Augustus!' Ibis shouted, drinking again. 'Do you know, I understood why he enjoyed your poems so. He had a great sense of humour.'

'I am not sure he enjoyed them', Ovid said.

'He had them checked and double-checked for hidden meanings. This I know.'

'Well, there were plenty of those.' Ovid toasted again. 'To the poet and the spy!'

'I have never liked the word spy', Ibis said, after a long gulp. 'I merely throw light at the darkness. Nothing more.'

'Would Augustus agree?'

'You can ask him yourself when you meet him by the end of this hour.' Ibis pointed at the glass on the table, through which the sand flowed freely.

I need to keep him drinking, Ovid thought. 'Until then, how about some entertainment?' Without waiting for an answer, he began to recite unwritten verses from the *Augustiada*, rambling away about how Hercules helped Augustus to find a Hyperborean princess, how a spy warned the Roman Senate of the alliance, and how they opposed it. *A pity I did not write a single verse*. He gestured for Spiros to circulate and refill.

'Livia Augusta is the only real friend you have ever had in Rome', Ibis said, holding his cup out for Spiros. 'I was never able to find out what really happened between you and her.' He tried to stand, but his legs gave way beneath him and he fell back on to the sofa. He looked at the cup in his hand, laughed merrily, and drank some more. 'This is indeed good wine!'

The light in the room began to change to dark orange. Ovid looked inside his own cup. He had yet to finish his second – while Ibis and his guards were on their fourth – but still he knew that what he had drunk would be enough to kill him. At least they would die too. With an odd feeling of calm, he realised how easy it was just to keep drinking.

'Do you remember when I killed you in my dream?' Ovid said.

Ibis' eyes glittered. He opened his mouth to speak, but no words came. Behind him, one of his guards had slumped against the wall, while the other stared at the ceiling with his mouth open and a string of saliva dangling from his lips. His own end could not be much farther away, thought Ovid, emptying the cup and asking for more: he would not be present at his own death.

'Augustus would never have allowed you to send his own son to the end of the world.'

'That was my son,' Ibis said, perplexed at his own statement, as if surprised he could speak such words without understanding what they meant. 'The boy was mine. Mine! Mine!' His rant morphed into a harsh and rattling cough. 'And you killed him.'

'Tell me,' Ovid said, 'why did you order my killing?'

Ibis coughed again and then wiped his mouth. 'The generals. It was Germanicus' generals.'

'Lies!'

A jet of wine and blood erupted from Ibis' mouth. He raised his hands to his lips, trying to hold them closed, trying to swallow the blood back down. But it did not matter. His body began to convulse and more red liquid flowed from him, filling his lap. Behind him, both guards had fallen to the floor, their bodies wracked with seizures. Ovid stood up from the armchair, his feet unsteady beneath him.

'Master!' Spiros shouted, rushing towards him, but Ovid waved him away. He would be down there soon too, on the floor, vomiting, convulsing, dying, but first he wanted to see this, to witness the death of his oldest enemy.

Ibis, flat on his back on the sofa, was drowning in his own vomit. His head lolled to the side and his eyes, bulging from their sockets, found Ovid. There was a dim rage in them, a rage that turned to helplessness, a helplessness that turned to hopelessness, and a hopelessness that turned to nothing at all. He was gone.

Ovid fell backwards. To his surprise he did not hit the floor, but passed right through it, tumbling down and down and over and over until he came to land gently on his feet. Before him was an enormous marble parapet, and he pushed his face eagerly over it, revelling in the fresh, enlivening breeze. Twenty feet below the parapet began the gentle downhill slope towards the river – a band of shining gold – that marked the boundary of Cotta's property at Tibur.

Behind him the party was lingering. Laughter from a joke he did not understand. Someone called his name. *I'd rather jump.*

'Naso, invent for us a transformation game! We want to be forever happy!'

The party cheered. Happiness, an entitlement. Discontent and dissatisfaction, unjust interruptions. Life lived to the full.

It was either them or him and it couldn't be them. He began

to talk. The Celtic Hercules tightened tongues like rope; he pulled them into the mountains. Experience the difficult existence. If he knew how to play the lyre he would lead them into the sea. Orpheus.

A transformation story that did not contain a real metamorphosis. Poor Icarus. He was just trusting his genial father, didn't listen carefully to the instructions, got too close to the sun. Plunged into the sea.

'We'll fly without wings.' His voice or theirs – but who was theirs? He fluttered his arms. Stupor. Would they accept his game? Unearned state of euphoria the main goal of life. 'The first to reach the river is the winner. The price is…'

'Forget the goal. If we get high it is all we need', somebody shouted.

How right the Pythagoreans – for undeveloped beings the illusion of activity was the illusion of achievement.

Docile alignment at the base of the terrace. Cotta, host, gave the signal. A battle of arms. They ran, down down down down the hill, down down down the hill. Carp running after the boys on the wasteland, trying to keep up. Abandonment, guilt. Sun, absolution. Everybody was present.

In the sun plate, a dark dot. He hit the ground. Chewing mud mixed with grass. The most forbidden taste ever. The taste of Mother Earth. Cheering friends.

He stood and jumped, suspended in the air.

'Watch out to your right!' Cotta. Panicked.

The black creature: unidentifiable. Outsized bird or overblown bat? It charged. Non-earthly. The sky darkened, he changed his direction, flying up. The blood-smelling something, its black beak clapping, missed. Inches. Scattered on the slope, his friends, petrified. They had witnessed many a gladiatorial combat, but in the air? In the air?

A wide turn. Beast, no-known bird, No-Known, attacked anew. But no fear and why no fear? He did not want to be anywhere else. Bird he was not and as long as he swam in the air he was. The sun had the answer; his reason the eternal enemy of hope refusing. The dark spot grew larger.

No-Known darted. Arms above head, he spiralled sideways, professional jumpers performing from the cliffs of Naples. No-Known darted again, missed, hit the ground at full speed. Pain sounds. Moaning ball of feathers. Ovid pushed his hands into its neck and twisted. Ibis or Augustus? His own father? Or only a shape-shifting heap of feathers, flesh and bone? Attach whichever identity you want. Even your own. What was it they said? Things only exist when observed.

All depended on thought, that was clear. Hovering over a dying bird. No courage to kill the shadow. What would bring it back to life? The magical operation: intensive thinking. Forcing through his writings the non-real entities into presence. Poems proving that fiction could become nature and nature could become fiction in readers' minds. Real message of *Metamorphoses*: demonstrate to Rome how a human could be god-like?

The dark spot almost covered the sun entirely. Again.

Three chariots, loud, rushing on the road. Leading to Tibur. At their windows, gesticulating hands. Farewells or warnings? Impossible to tell. Twilight.

Flutter of wings. He was not alone in the sky. The resurrected bird, No-Known, sped towards the chariots, grabbed a holder on the box top, waved back in triumph. 'I will win the race!'

Four horses at full speed, impossible to beat. No struggle between reason and emotion. Detachment won.

A blast. In the twilight, the aftermath of what had happened. The work of guesses. In its exuberance, the spectacle of its revival, No-Known did not see the low arch of the aqueduct under which the road passed. Its body a black stain on the grey wall – like a coat of arms fastened over an entrance. Its feathers a hanging, shape-shifting cloud.

'He is alive!'

Voice. Beside his ear. Familiar.

'He is alive!'

Panting. His own.

'It can't be.'

Reply, man – tell him!

'Feel! A pulse.'

A grating sound. His own voice, strangled inside his throat.

'Ibis…'

'Ibis and the rest all died some time ago.'

A blade pushed between his teeth forced Ovid's mouth open and a sweet, sticky liquid was poured in. It tasted like the hallucinogenic potion he had drunk on the far side of the Danube. The darkness around him became ash-grey. The edges of the plain seemed to be pulled up, as if heaved out of the ocean by an unseen fisherman. Things slowly began to make sense. They were trying to bring him back.

Is this what I want? To become mortal again? After all, what could possibly be on offer that was worth another journey into the shadow of death?

Something pulsed through his body: a fire, or the spark of one. He recalled the many unfinished poems of his

Metamorphoses, some baffling, others redeemable. And the missing introduction: the planned dedication to Pythagoras. Without it, what would people believe – that he had never understood that existence, although forever an unsolvable mystery, was so much more than a shape-shifting illusion?

Possessed by a wild impatience Ovid had not experienced since his youth, he spat out whatever they had been pouring in his mouth, and loudly asked for a cup of water.

Acknowledgements

Foremost, I am thankful to my mother, Cornelia, for her steadfast encouragement throughout the considerable duration of this project, for our long conversations on the subject, and especially for her invaluable comments on the often confusing drafts of the earlier stages. She proved to be my most critical and attentive, as well as most affectionate, reader. Unfortunately she will miss the publication of this book – as she did, by two months, her hundredth birthday.

My greatest debt is to Liliana. Without her help the new beginning of my journey would not have been possible.

To Mirela, for her care and her support during the pandemic, I owe the courage and the peace of mind to revisit Ovid's journey and rewrite it.

Patrice Chaplin was essential as I was writing. She helped me to stay focused, not to get lost in research, and to overcome my tendency to abandon drafts and start all over again.

Many books were useful to me while writing this novel, but there are some without which I could not have done it. On life in ancient Rome, Paul Veyne's contribution 'Roman Empire' in *A History of Private Life*, Vol. I, *From Pagan Rome to Byzantium* (Harvard University Press, 2003), was essential. Professor Patricia J. Johnson's article 'Ovid's Livia in Exile' (*The Classical World*, July–August 1997, pp. 403–20), which she kindly sent me some years ago, shed new light on one of the most fascinating women in history. I benefitted greatly from reading Nicolae Densuşianu's *Prehistoric Dacia* (first published in 1913), which inspired my imagination. The comparative study of mythology and religion, *The Golden Bough: A Study in Magic and Religion* by Sir James George Frazer (Wordsworth Editions, new edn, 1993), enhanced my understanding of the world of rituals, symbols and religious practices, but foremost of the institution of the scapegoat. Last but not least, my research would have been incomparably restricted were I not able to use the wealth of information available on the internet. To the many contributors I am indebted.

Of the numerous people I met in the course of my research I would like to thank in particular Dr Livia Buzoianu, the very enthusiastic research scientist from the Museum of National History and Archaeology, Constanta, who, based in 'archaeological realities', introduced me to the antique history of Tomis, and Ilio Di Jorio, the friendly former director of 'Ovid', the high school in Sulmona, who took time to share with me his views about Ovid and the local traditions – a thought-provoking experience.

The responsibility for the book, including any errors or misjudgements it may contain, is mine.